APPETITE

D1099068

APPETITE

ANITA CASSIDY

RedDoor

Published by RedDoor
www.reddoorpublishing.com

© 2018 Anita Cassidy

The right of Anita Cassidy to be identified as the author of this
Work has been asserted by her in accordance with sections 77
and 78 of the Copyright, Designs and Patents Act 1988

ISBN 978-1-910453-47-6

A CIP catalogue record for this book
is available from the British Library

Cover designer: Clare Connie Shepherd
www.clareconnieshepherd.com

Typesetting: WatchWord Editorial Services
www.watchwordeditorial.co.uk

Printed and bound by Nørhaven, Denmark

For Marc

Chapter One

David

Looking down, resting awkwardly against a lamp post, David kept out of sight of the school for a little longer. He always did this. And he always spent the time hoping, after each blink, that his eyes would open to find the buildings blown up or the pavement underneath him bathed in a strange, pale light before it fell away, his body being sucked up into a spaceship full of friendly, intelligent (female) aliens. But the bomb never fell, the UFO never came. With appalling consistency, it always got to 8.45, the bell always began to ring and he always had to walk over the road and through the gates.

Even while he had been enjoying the coloured lights and comforts of the recent Christmas holidays, this had been on the edge of his mind, causing the same lingering sense of unease as a receding nightmare. When he wasn't imagining the destruction of the school or the convenient abduction of himself, he was watching. Watching grey trousers and grey jackets against grey concrete. A parade of uniform and uniformity marching steadily towards black gates holding black bags. And there, with blazers stretched across their backs, bunching up under the armpits and pulled taut across

1

the hips, were the fat kids. Winter coats hung open loosely. They rarely fitted properly anyway, but after Christmas? Well, you could just forget about buttons then. They were, as always, bringing up the rear, looking only at the ground as they lumbered towards the looming metal gates, some of them quickly finishing chocolate bars and bags of crisps as they walked, the actual cause of and the imagined cure for their misery scrunched up and tossed on to the pavement before they entered the playground.

I hate fat kids, thought David. Everyone hates fat kids. Or pities them. Which is even worse.

Watching them as they went through the school gates was like watching a grinding-machine at work. Hard cogs relentlessly turning, breaking things down, chewing them up. Once he stepped inside he was trapped: as far from home and its comforts as he would ever be.

Today, he thought, should be a good day. Today, I am feeling unusually angry. These days, the days when he felt this rage, were the easy ones. It was the sad days he found the hardest to bear. Days when the sadness was there when he woke up in the morning and followed him until nightfall like a weary shadow. The sadness was viscous, a tar pool that pulled at him, wanting to drag him under.

But today he was angry, and the edge that gave him made what lay ahead seem more tolerable.

The bell rang.

Crossing the invisible line that traced across the tarmac, he felt his back go rigid.

'Hey, fat fuck!'

'Who ate all the mince pies? Pretty bloody obvious from here...'

'I didn't think it was possible for you to get fatter, but Jesus...'

And it wasn't just the older kids. The younger ones taunted him too. Taunted and laughed.

Automatically and unconsciously, David's shoulders hunched and his head went down. It was an attempt, no matter how futile, to minimise the space he filled. The rage, though it formed a hard carapace around his mind, was as ineffectual at protecting him from the verbal assault course he was enduring as the rounding of his shoulders was at disguising a simple fact. The simple fact that, of all the fat kids, he, David, was the fattest.

Three years ago, when David had started at the Rivenoak Academy, the existing group of fat kids had tried to welcome him into their ample arms. It hadn't taken long for their warmth to be frozen by his expansive cold shoulder. But it had taken David a while to figure out why they were so surprised that he hadn't wanted to join them. Surely, he had thought, on that first day, surely they understand how much I hate myself? How I can't bear to be around those who remind me of what I am?

But, after a few weeks, he had realised that they were even less self-aware than the other kids at this lower-end secondary school, and so he did a rare thing, and copied them by actively ignoring the fat ones.

Not that the other kids were worth giving the time of day to, either. Obsessed with themselves (and their selfies), the Diet Coke Crew were the same hard, shiny girls who had ignored him in the last year of prep school, and the Uncool remained as oblivious to their low status as they were aware of the latest tech developments. There were the BJ Boys, those already porn-addicted lads who hassled every girl within a three-mile radius for a blow job, and there were the Too Cool for School kids, those who were already tuned into the alleged appeal of adult life, just about hanging on until they could drop out.

There were various other sub-cliques, built around the standard riffs of emo and tech – and then there was David-and-James. The fattest and skinniest kids at the school, they had been at the same prep school, a small co-ed in a nearby village. The f-word formed the latter part of both of their secondary school monikers. As James had observed in that first term: 'The names don't demonstrate much in the way of imagination, but they are evidence of at least average observational skills.'

'And,' David had added, a rare smile on his face, 'unlike the interchangeable plastic girls and nerdy boys, at least we never get mistaken for one another!'

This first morning, with form time over, David hung back. This was something else he always did. As the other pupils left the science room that served as their form classroom this year, David glanced at his watch and, once everyone else had filed out, he went down the pale corridor and ducked into the nearby toilets. Stepping sideways into the cubicle like a crab, he unzipped the front pocket of his bag. Taking out the chocolate bar, he opened it: three big bites and it was gone. Perched awkwardly on the seat, he stared at the back of the toilet door, eyes glazed over as his mouth was filled with smooth chocolate and caramel. The toffee glued his tongue to the top of his mouth. Using the tip of it, he cleaned the thick sweet paste out of his teeth and gums. Then, he pulled a half-empty bottle of Coke out of his bag. Swigging back the lukewarm sugary liquid, he swirled it round his mouth like mouthwash, the acid and the bubbles helping to rinse away the chocolate. Then, with a sigh and lots of effort, he got up and manoeuvred awkwardly back out of the cubicle, leaving the toilets and going to join his first class of the day.

The history lesson was well under way.

'Nice of you to join us, Mr Wallace...!'

Sitting down, he pulled his books out and tried to tune in to what the teacher was saying, but he was really only focusing on one thing: break-time.

*

It was the in-between places that were dangerous. The corridors as well as the toilets between classes. This was one of the reasons why David always avoided them, even if it meant being late. These unsupervised spaces and times were when David felt most vulnerable. Here, he could be insulted, jostled, jeered at or even, sometimes, just plain ignored. But, given his size, ignoring him was a very conscious and strangely aggressive act. David had found it was mostly the girls who did that.

Like an elephant approaching a watering hole, on edge and anxious but driven by hunger and thirst, David walked along the corridor towards the dinner hall as quickly as he could: head down, eyes scanning from side to side, warily alert, shoulders hunched, trying not to be noticed.

And, just as an elephant must experience relief when it sees a giraffe drinking at the edge of the lake, long neck stretched out, knees bent – another animal also taking a risk, leaving itself vulnerable – so did David when he saw James waiting for him outside the double doors. Nodding at each other by way of a greeting, they walked side by side into the already noisy hall.

'I'm starving,' James said, glancing back at his friend before he turned to scrutinise the school dinner counter.

David nodded in reply. One of the unspoken rules of being fat was that you never expressed any enthusiasm for food or eating.

The brushed aluminium gleamed dully under the hotplate lights. They were among the first in the queue today, so the food still looked appealing, having not yet begun to congeal beneath the heat.

David pushed his tray along the counter, and then, using the little steel shovel, he filled half of his plate with fat yellow chips. Chips: the cornerstone of almost every pupil's meal. He smiled a little as James chattered away about the day's options. This running commentary was one of the things that David loved about his friend. There was also the small fact that, having known David since he was five, James was the only kid at the school who gave him the time of day.

'I see we have pizza on offer today, our tasty Monday staple, as well as the ever-popular pasta bake with tuna. Good for those who want a side helping of dead dolphin on their conscience along with their luncheon. I think the broccoli looks great today, but – oh, sorry, Mrs Bevan…' James glanced up and gave the freckled lunchtime assistant his broadest of broad grins '…I think someone really has overdone the carrots today!' Reaching over, he picked one up delicately between his thumb and forefinger and added, 'Look! This one's as limp as my friend's d—'

'All right, mate!' David interrupted, stifling a laugh. 'Get a move on, Taylor, you're holding up the line.'

They went through the payment till and then sat down opposite each other at the bank of tables closest to the wall at the back of the dining hall. The room was busy, the chatter and laughter of teens rising up to the greasy grey plastic tiles on the ceiling. The corner David and James had chosen was beneath a flickering fluorescent light, on the periphery of the lunch room as they were on the periphery of school life itself.

David hunkered over his plate, elbows resting on the table. The red plastic chair felt flimsy beneath him. Every day he had to try to eat without relaxing enough to let his full weight sink into the chair. Its base always sank with a comedy squeak as he sat down and, while James always ignored it, it was another reason for choosing a seat in the corner.

Alternating a forkful of the pasta bake (he always chose that as the portions were bigger – they made you go back for extra pizza and he hated having to do that) with a forkful of chips, David ate quickly, as he always did. The watery tomato sauce laced with flakes of tinny-tasting tuna had little flavour, but the processed food, assuaging something other than hunger, did not need to be savoured.

Between mouthfuls, he asked James, 'Ready for double science later?'

'Yeah,' James replied. 'Want to take a look at the work sheets?'

'Sure.' David shrugged, eyes averted, feeling both relieved and awkward. 'I can check that over for you…' Glancing up, he gave his friend a grateful smile and James grinned back.

They finished the rest of their meal in silence. The room was getting noisier now as other pupils came in to eat. Or, to not eat. For some of the girls (and more than a few of the boys), how long they could go without consuming anything other than Diet Coke was a competitive sport. James looked around idly and waited while David cleared his plate and then rapidly ate the first of two small pots of muddy brown chocolate mousse, each with a token swirl of bright white ersatz cream on top.

Another unspoken rule was that, to give him plenty of time, James always let David move first. He looked on neutrally as his friend used the table to steady himself and then swayed up to his full height.

Their goal at lunchtimes was always to get out of the dinner hall without incident: to leave the watering hole unscathed.

David walked towards the double doors, shoulders down and eyes on the floor as he went past the other tables. And, just as monkeys would quiet their chatter as an elephant lumbered by, so the buzz of conversation inevitably ceased as the boys passed. Those kids who didn't usually see David around school stared at him, their eyes wide.

The open doors were visible. The empty corridor stretched out ahead like a linoleum savannah. There was one more table to get past.

David felt something hit his back. Then something else. Cold, greasy chips began to shower against the back of his grey jumper, making a damp, soft thud as they hit the floor.

'Fucking fat fuck,' hissed one of the boys.

David turned to look. The boys themselves were averagely lean, averagely fit.

'You still hungry, you fat fucker?'

'Here! Have another chip!'

David could feel James pulling at his arm but something had rooted him to the spot. It wasn't fear but fascination: fascination with how angry he and his size made them.

'Leave us alone, eh, guys? Come *on*, David…' James spoke quietly, still tugging on his friend's arm.

There was a teacher nearby. With the pinched features of all women in their late forties who worked a little too hard to stay slim, she was looking on with an expression of sour amusement but also not looking or, at least, not seeing – a skill acquired from years of judging rather than asking. Her arms were tightly folded across her flat chest, hips jutting to the side in a trim, dove-grey A-line skirt as she stood propped against the wall. She didn't move and her face made her thoughts very clear: the fat boy deserves that.

The whole table were hurling chips at David now, laughing and cat-calling. One of the boys stood up. He stared hard at James, who was still trying to pull David away.

'Fuck off, skinny fuck. Let the fat fucker speak for himself.'

David was tall but this boy was taller. He poked David in the chest. Holding David's eyes, he glanced down and then, looking back up, he made a big show of grinding the chips into the floor with the dirty sole of his scuffed shoes.

Holding the boy's glare, David could see the hatred in his eyes. Behind the hatred was fear and anger. Fear of the fat, anger at David for being fat, for being there, for being there and for being fat. That fear was like a shy child that ran behind its mother's legs at the sight of a stranger. Peeping and cowering, it believed itself to be hidden but was completely visible.

David bent down awkwardly. Picking a handful of gritty squashed chips off the floor, he stood up and looked straight into the eyes of the boy opposite him. Opening his lips wide, he put the dirty, cold food in his mouth. Shock rippled over the boy's face, a wave of disgust and terror. The laughter stopped. David chewed, slowly and deliberately, all the while holding the other boy's gaze.

Then, as he turned and walked away, he thought, You might hate me but, believe me, I will always hate myself more.

Naomi

Looking up, one hand shielding her eyes from the low early-morning sun, Naomi pointed with her index finger and sketched an outline over the tree.

'I want it cut back and I want it cut back hard,' she said. 'The birds, the noise, the mess. I can't stand it. I know it will take a while and, with the work that's needed round the back, I'm expecting you to be here for at least a week, but *this…*' she gestured at the tree again, a dismissive and impatient flick of her fingers '…*this* is the priority.'

Naomi's tone was the same clipped, no-nonsense one that she used to get James, and Scott, up and out of the house every morning. The lack of eye contact was also deliberate. Eye contact meant connection and connection meant conversation. There was no time for such niceties in her morning routine, especially when that routine was already being interrupted by this appointment. There was also the small fact of her embarrassment: she didn't know this man's name. He had been recommended by someone at work and, busy, she had just saved him in her phone as Tree Man.

Lowering her hand, Naomi turned, looking properly at Tree Man for the first time.

He was not looking at her. Instead he was staring at the tree with an unusual degree of intensity.

What Naomi on the other hand was staring at was his thick forearms. His broad shoulders and tanned skin made it obvious that he worked outside for a living, and the morning light was catching the blond hairs on his arms. She noticed the way his wrists narrowed as they met long-fingered hands.

There was a cough and, vaguely aware of a voice saying, 'Mrs Taylor? Mrs Taylor?' Naomi snapped back to the present. And back to herself. Or, rather, back to the self that didn't stare at the muscular forearms of men ten (fifteen, her mind jeered) years younger than herself.

Making a big show of looking at her watch, Naomi squeezed her hands together, a frown deepening the lines that ran across her forehead.

'Well,' she said, 'I need to go. You said you can fit me in soon? Fine. Just make sure it's all done as I've outlined.'

Smiling at Naomi, Tree Man said, 'Have a good morning. In a few weeks' time, you'll barely recognise her.'

Then, looking back up at the tree, he reached out his hand, and placed it gently on the gnarled trunk. Naomi raised her eyebrows, surprised by the tenderness in the gesture. When was the last time someone had touched her like that? Dismissing the thought, and with one last glance at Tree Man (who, with his sandy hair, warm blue eyes and *those* arms would now be known in her mind as *Sexy* Tree Man), she climbed into her black Land Rover and pulled out of the gravel drive.

The 7.57. The seat by the window. The third carriage from the front. The same people in the same places wearing the same expressions. Monday mornings were always the quietest: a stunned silence seemed to be the only appropriate response to the fact that it was the start of the working week. This was further exacerbated by the fact that it was the first full week back after the Christmas break. The media proclaimed the most miserable day of the year to be in mid-January but, judging by the expressions around her, it might as well have been today.

Naomi had placed her laptop bag in the overhead rack and now sat, phone out, scrolling through her emails, getting prepared for the day ahead. Tapping open her planner, she saw the note about the Tree Man coming at 6.45am. A flush flared on her cheeks and there was a tingling between her legs as the image of his arms and hands filled her mind briefly and intensely. Crossing them, she thought how ridiculous she must have appeared, gazing at him like a schoolgirl.

Staring harder still at her diary, she tried to will the image away. It didn't work.

She knew what the day held without even seeing the details: meetings, more meetings and yet more meetings. Maybe one of them would be productive. A one-out-of-three strike-rate seemed to be the best she could hope for at VitSip. Early attempts to energise the lumbering decision-making process had proven fruitless. Ha! she thought sourly. A bit like our new drinks range...

Scanning over the details of the mid-morning production meeting, she saw the name J. Winters on the attendance list and her mouth tilted into a more optimistic curve: his was a name she had become aware of while at her previous company. Bold and demanding, Jonathan Winters, VitSip's managing director, had been responsible for VitSip's last drinks launch. That launch had seen her old company's market share plummet by an unprecedented five per cent and was also one of the reasons why she was now here and not there. Swiping the diary screen away, she went on to her favourite finance site and began to scan the headlines.

This is what one is meant to do on the way to the office, she told herself: absorb the latest stock market information. Not daydream about Sexy Tree Men...

As the journey progressed and people began to feel the benefits of their station-bought lattes, a few conversations began. Someone mentioned a TV programme that Naomi had also seen and really enjoyed. She half turned round to say something but, suddenly wary of interrupting, she went back to her silent phone. She never had been very good at making friends.

Staring at the headlines, Naomi was as oblivious as the train itself to the sparse beauty of the countryside as they progressed from the rural outskirts of Rivenoak to the industrial estates lining the flat, grey river which cut across this edge of the county. Travelling out to an anonymous building at the rougher end of East Kent had initially felt like a backward step for Naomi. She missed the bustle of the City, the sharp suits and even sharper elbows at the ticket gates, but even she had to admit that being under half an hour away from home rather than well over an hour was a bonus. What she found harder to admit, and what she was only just realising a few months in, was how much she missed the social side of her previous job. With no local bars or restaurants, with most people driving, there was no excuse for a quick drink after work or an impromptu night out.

Although she was at least fifteen years older than the average person who had attended those evenings, she had always felt that she could hold her own with the younger members of staff, prided herself on it in fact, but then there had been that time... Her mind resisted the memory. When the offer of a sideways move to another, expanding company in a less glamorous locale but much closer to home had come up, Naomi had been relieved to have the excuse to move on.

Standing and ready to disembark before the train had even pulled into the station, Naomi pressed the button impatiently as she always did and then walked quickly across the platform, her heels clicking smartly on the concrete. She loved that sound. Brisk, efficient, it set the tone for her whole day.

Crossing the road without looking, she walked through the glass double doors into VitSip HQ.

Waiting in the small staff kitchen for the kettle to boil, Naomi loaded her cup with a heaped teaspoon of coffee and, after a tentative sniff at the top of the carton, added a dash of skimmed milk. There was a coffee machine in her office but she liked to come in here. Any manager worth their salt knew that the best gossip always came out in the kitchen. It didn't do to seem too distanced from the more junior members, to seem too aloof. After nearly fifteen years as a manager, Naomi knew the value of being seen rinsing out your own coffee cup.

She also knew the value of getting in early enough to avoid most of them before they got in. The sales teams would be hungover and grumpy and some of the managers would be too. One too many glasses of red wine with Sunday lunch was as big a cause of the Monday blues as too many lagers or bottles of WKD on a Saturday night.

Back in her office, she attached the laptop to her monitor and keyboard and sipped her coffee while the machine started up. Leaning back on her chair, she stretched her legs out a little, widening her toes out against the hard, shiny leather of her shoes. Opening up the technical documents she needed to review before her first meeting, she got to work.

An hour or so passed before she got up to refill her mug. Animated chatter filled the corridor now as people were arriving and settling into the working week.

Settling in slowly, thought Naomi. Ever so slowly.

Hiding her impatience at the sight of a queue for the kettle, Naomi gave a cheery smile and stood, by the wall, waiting. After a few polite greetings, the few people there began chatting among themselves. Naomi did her best to not look as excluded as she felt.

Sitting back down at her desk with a sigh and glancing at her watch, she knew that she should make best use of the half-hour before her first meeting by preparing for the next one but, having done an hour's work already, she just didn't feel like it. From behind the glass windows of her office she watched people as they walked past in groups of twos and threes, chattering, sharing their experiences of the weekend.

Just as she was about to force herself to open up the files she needed, a light voice called her name from the doorway. 'Naomi! Hi. How was your weekend?' Naomi looked up. It was Carla, the marketing assistant who had also joined VitSip just before the end of the previous year.

'Hello there!'

'Can I come in?'

Naomi felt the guilt of knowing she should be working tug at her, but not as hard as the need for chatter and distraction. 'Sure! Come on in!' She moved over to the pair of small sofas that filled the far corner of her office, near the sideboard with the coffee machine. 'I'll turn this thing on,' she said, going over to the coffee machine and pulling a few of the metallic-topped capsules out of the tray. 'The trick,' she continued, as Carla took a seat on the pale blue sofa, 'is to always carry a file about with you. That way you always look as if you're on your way to something or to someone *about* something. Even a piece of paper is enough... You just need something in your hand!'

Carla laughed and sat back. 'Oh, God, this sofa is so comfy. How do you not just curl up on here and go to sleep?'

All of a sudden the younger woman yawned. Her brown eyes widened with embarrassment as she tried to cover her mouth with her hand.

'Tired?' said Naomi, bringing two coffees over.

'Yeah, a bit,' said Carla, as she yawned again.

Naomi looked at her. She looks a bit pale, her skin a bit dull, she thought. The girl's eyes sparkled as she chattered, though. Before you hit thirty, Naomi thought, hangovers can still be got away with. Just.

'Well, you know, it was meant to be just the one! The Bloody Marys at this bar near us are ace but then we had another and then we stayed for lunch and before we knew it we were at the late-opening pub and dancing till midnight. Seemed like a good idea at the time! We have this plan, you know, to avoid the January blues by pretending it's still

Christmas until at least March. You should have seen Mike this morning, though. He looks *so* much rougher than me.'

'I remember you both dancing at the New Year thing!' Naomi said, sitting down. 'And why not? You've got to make the most of it. Now everyone's married and had kids we never get to go dancing any more. Most of the fortieth parties we've been to over the last few years have been pretty sedate. Everyone organises daytime things to accommodate the kids, or they get so excited about being out that they're plastered by 8.30 and in bed by 10!'

Carla laughed again. That was the other thing that Naomi liked about the younger woman: she was always laughing. That's something else, she thought, that I seem to do much less now. When *was* the last time she had really laughed?

'Oh, and it was just so funny... One of our friends is planning her thirtieth. She wants to make cocktail ice lollies and Mike got a bit carried away with creating a marketing campaign for what he called "sticky boozy popsicles". He is hilarious sometimes.'

Carla ran her hand through her dark brown hair and finished her coffee. Putting the mug on to the low coffee table, she said, 'We're both looking forward to that pub lunch in a few weeks, too. Thanks so much for inviting us!'

'Oh, well, it won't be anywhere near as much fun as dancing till the early hours but it should still be good... We go every month. I love the food and, even more, I love not to cook!'

'We both enjoy a roast dinner. Open fires, red wine – sounds great to me!'

Carla's enthusiasm had been the thing that had come across most during the induction programme they had shared and it was that, as well as the younger woman's open nature, that had led Naomi to get to know her a little. Also, it was just so refreshing to talk to someone who didn't have a family yet. She and her husband Mike had only been married for a year or two and, while Carla had talked in the past about their plans to start a family, she was still very much more into the latest box-sets and music than pushchairs and school catchment areas.

The younger woman was still chattering on about her weekend, but Naomi glanced at her watch

'Sorry,' she said, standing up. 'I'm going to have to go to this meeting now.'

'Cool, OK. Maybe catch you later? We could have lunch or coffee...'

'Sure,' Naomi said, smiling at the girl's relaxed tone. 'I'd like that. Oh, and if you need the details about that pub lunch again let me know, otherwise we'll see you there. The table will be booked under my name.'

Matthew

Matthew knew he was in trouble the moment he walked into the staff room and saw all the zombies. His friends, Solange and Jim, were nowhere to be seen. Instead, everywhere he looked, there were the Undead.

'Is it really the first day back already?' said one, from deep within a faded armchair.

'I know...' groaned another.

'Uggghh,' came from across the room.

The silence in between the groans was resigned and resistant, the air thick with the collective sighs of people who had long ago lost their hunger for anything other than sweet tea and biscuits. Matthew had taken several deep breaths as he had approached the staff room and now he exhaled: determined to be cheerful, to set the right tone for the first day back, he called out, 'Morning!' with all the energy he could muster.

His cheeriness startled the zombies. Some of them turned to look at him, eyes hollow and angry, confused. What was all this noise for? Why was he so *happy*?

Matthew went to check the noticeboard. Picking his way over the outstretched legs and slumped chair-bound bodies, he asked one, 'How were the holidays for you? And your family?'

'Terrible...' the zombie muttered back. 'Spent the whole of Christmas on the M11 with the kids trying to kill each other in the back. Bloody kids. You think the ones here are hard work – try going home to them too. Bloody nightmare.'

'I thought Christmas was more fun with kids?' asked Matthew, undaunted.

'Ha!' the zombie exhaled sourly. 'Not a bit of it. They argue over what they got, or want something they didn't get. Ungrateful little shits, the pair of them. Rest of the family's no better, mind...'

The zombie stared back down into his tea-filled mug. Others nearby roused themselves to nod in agreement.

'Well, I went travelling in Brazil...' Matthew said. 'For a few weeks. The children there don't even really get presents at Christmas. It's just all about family and being together. I spent the whole of Christmas Day eating this incredible meal, everyone just talking and sharing. One of the best days of my life, actually.'

'Gggnnngggh,' said the zombie, staring up at Matthew with dead eyes.

'I went to Brazil once,' piped up an older, female zombie.

'Oh, where did you go? Did you get to visit any of the food markets? What did you think?' said Matthew, hoping to spark some conversation and going over to where she was propped up against the sideboard by the kettle, staring into the steam as if the mist contained a message about the meaning of this Monday morning.

'Hated it,' she intoned back, dully. 'Smelly, awful place. Got sick. Never went back.'

'Oh,' said Matthew, stepping back slightly, feeling his spirits finally drop. He glanced around with a sense of rising panic. Surely he wasn't being sucked back into the mire of teaching misery after a mere – he glanced at the clock – seven minutes? His heart sank, heavy as his bags full of books.

The bell went. The zombies groaned again, a low murmur of misery. They began to shift and shuffle towards the door.

Keeping well back, Matthew watched them and then, once they had left, he followed.

Walking across the playground, he shifted the bags on his shoulder and, seeing the groups of girls ahead of him, braced himself. Very early on in his career, Matthew had realised that the only thing more difficult than being a science teacher at a secondary school was being a science teacher at a secondary school who looked as though he might once have been in a boy band. With his thick, wavy dark hair and blue eyes, Matthew had the kind of clear-skinned, square-jawed and symmetrical face that seemed specially designed to appeal to teenage girls. Recently reaching and then passing thirty had only seemed to make it worse.

He ran the gamut of lisped and drawled 'Morning, sir's and full-vowelled 'How are you, sir?'s and 'How was your holiday, sir?'s with a carefully cultivated air of uninterest that he never pulled off quite as effortlessly as he hoped he would.

As the calls, laughter and chatter continued across the playground, Matthew, despite his good mood, braced himself. Even on bright-sunshine, blue-sky Monday mornings such as this one, there were dark journeys being undertaken by men and boys all over the world, and Matthew was just beginning his own.

At the end of the school day, Matthew sat clutching the edges of his desk, like a man thrown overboard clinging to a piece of driftwood in a dark sea. He had been buffeted all day. The deadening complaining of his colleagues and the post-Christmas hysteria of some of the kids, as well as the even more alarming sour sullenness of the rest, who, having got all they could possibly want, still wanted more, had taken its toll already. And this was just the first day back, he thought, trying not to give in to the panic.

His phone buzzed. A message from Solange. *Let's go!* Typical French use of the imperative, thought Matthew, smiling a little. Only the trainee teachers worked late on the first day back. For everyone else – well, for the holy trinity that was him, Sol and Jim – there was a very particular ritual for this particular day: the pub.

He felt a twinge of anxiety. He had always thought that he would enjoy talking about his Brazil trip when he returned, had imagined the conversations and the fascinated reactions as he told his family and friends about what he had experienced. But his mother had responded to the photos with a muted, 'Very nice, dear. Did I tell you that the week we always wanted at the timeshare in Greece has finally become free?' and, given the response he had received this morning in the staff room, maybe it was best kept to himself after all. Like a masterpiece stored in the vaults by a billionaire businessman, the memories seemed to be diminished through sharing, and were best enjoyed alone.

Opening his desk drawer, he carefully lifted something out: *Brazil*.

Coming in last week to drop off paperwork, he had brought the brochure with him, placing it gently on top of all the desk-drawer detritus.

Using the tips of his fingers, he looked through it for a few moments. Stuffed full with leaflets and cards from bars and shops as well as his own notes and scribblings, the brochure had served as the written journal of the trip. Now it was his touchstone. Sure, the photos had gone on to Facebook and Instagram, but this pack, the pack that he had carried around with him the whole time, was the most poignant physical reminder of the trip.

She had given it to him. It was what had sparked that first conversation, a simple conversation that had resulted in a truly life-changing trip. Life-changing even though she hadn't taken it with him. Matthew closed his eyes, the sour memory of the day he had just lived through now replaced with a memory of an even sourer one.

'You'll never do it.'

Lucy had said that. Standing in the hallway of his little flat, her arms folded and her eyes narrowed. 'Now I'm leaving, you'll *never* go. That's just you all over: all talk and no action.'

'I will, you'll see,' he had replied, arms folded too, trying to look determined even though his lower abdomen felt strangely watery, having just liquefied at the prospect of a solo backpacking trip around Brazil.

'I won't see,' she had spat out, turning to the door. 'I've changed my status already and I've unfriended you. I don't *want* to know anything else about your pointless little life. It's over.'

You'll never do it.

She had tossed the gauntlet down on the worn blue carpet of his hallway as she left, the door slamming angrily behind her. The same worn blue carpet where they had frequently enjoyed equally angry sex in the six months they had been dating. She had always seemed quite angry with him. Matthew had never understood why, but it did mean that the sex had been great. Her resentful passion for him had been matched only by her passion for change, for doing something different. He had heard from a friend that she was in Africa now, working hard to help educate girls there. She had thought his job teaching Kent kids was pointless.

But perhaps, he thought, something she said had had an impact after all. When she left, he had gone ahead, sorted out every aspect of the trip alone – alone except for the echo of those four words. Not that he had told anyone about that. The fear, the intense anxiety about taking the trip alone…he had hardly been able to admit that to himself, let alone anyone else.

Staring at the page open in front of him now, he looked at his neat, spidery notes all around the margins. He loved the internet, but there had been something satisfying about jotting things down in his own handwriting. Here, in the pages detailing local food specialities, he had written the Brazilian words for his favourite types of local beer and food. Bringing his nose to the page, he felt that if he inhaled hard enough he could still smell the *baião-de-dois*, the *tacacá*. Closing his eyes, he could almost taste the way in which every fresh ingredient, spice and herb worked in perfect harmony to create something that was so simple and yet so vibrant.

Having been able to take additional leave in the quieter month of December, as part of his credits for having done five years at the school, he had been able to stay in Brazil for nearly a month. It had almost been long enough. He suspected that if he had stayed longer he would never have come back. Not only was it beautiful, it was just so *alive*. Everything and everyone had seemed so vital and vivid there, unlike here with the grey skies and grey paths and grey faces. He had been inspired, had been shown how life could be traditional yet modern, relaxed yet productive, positive without being irritating.

He flicked over: the next page showed the lush green of the yet untamed forests that formed so much of that country. On here, among the wildness, he had written down the name and address of the girl he had met there.

Andrea. Andrea, who had taken him out on to the river. He didn't need to close his eyes to summon that image: the image of her, of that fateful afternoon, was for ever branded on his mind. She had shown him how big food companies were tainting the lives of the disadvantaged there. How the food and drink manufacturers took fizzy drinks and snack food on boats out to the poorest districts; how they paid people to peddle the specially designed small, cheaper portions of high-sugar, high-fat snacks in the most desperate parts of the cities and towns. He had helped her. He had leafleted, picketed, got involved…had felt fired up with passion and energy. But now, now that he was back, change began to seem less possible. The

21

mountain of preparatory coursework he'd been sure he would feel refreshed enough to tackle upon his return had nearly killed him in the few days since he had been back, and still wasn't finished. And now, on the first day, he could already see how easy it would be to get sucked back into that stultifying routine of long, deadening days followed by nights in the pub to numb it all.

How to say no, he wondered. How to say I've changed. How to say I want more than this. And, how to admit I have no idea how to go about it...

It sounded so absurd but that was what he hungered for: to feel as if he was *actually* making a difference. He had thought, long ago, that teaching might do it, but now, several years in, that idealism had faded.

'Matthew!' called a voice from the doorway. 'Come on!'

It was Solange. Slender arms folded, just as Lucy's had been when she had left, but with an oval face, framed with long dark hair, that was relaxed and smiling warmly. Hastily he put the brochure back in the drawer.

'What was that?' asked Solange.

'Oh, nothing,' said Matthew, still seated. 'Nothing...' After all the talking and shouting he had had to do throughout the day, he didn't feel like talking about anything right now, let alone the trip. Being here, where everything already felt hard, rather than there, where anything had seemed possible, just made him feel incredibly sad. 'Actually,' he said, glancing across at her from his desk and then looking back down, 'I really need to catch up. I'm so behind already. Do you mind if I leave it tonight?'

Solange uncrossed her arms and looked at him, brow creasing, and concern in her large, light brown eyes. 'Are you OK?'

'Yeah, honestly I am. I just, you know, I still feel a bit jet-lagged...'

His words tailed off. He had always been a bad liar.

'*Pas grave*,' she said, slipping into her native tongue. 'Friday?'

'Yes, definitely.'

'*D'accord. A bientôt!*'

He had never lied to Solange before, but he hoped she would understand.

She left, closing the door behind her, and as soon as it clicked shut he took the brochure back out of the drawer and went back to where he once had been.

Naomi

It was 6.30. That hissing sound could only be the kettle going on for a post-commute herbal tea.

6.31: a grunted, 'Hello,' from the kitchen table followed by the regulation two minutes of reluctant chat with James about his school day and the evening's homework.

'What is it today?' Naomi asked, beginning to take things out of the fridge for supper.

'French and maths.'

'Ah. Your favourites! *Très bien! Tu aimes...*' She hesitated.

'*Mes devoirs, maman.* Or *tes devoirs* if you're saying it to me...' James replied quietly.

As Naomi poked about in the fridge, she couldn't see James as he mouthed: *I really should dig out those French CDs your dad got me for the car...*

'I really should dig out those French CDs your dad got me for the car,' said Naomi as she closed the fridge door.

'Uh-huh.'

Naomi turned and smiled at James, who was now looking down at his books. She knew she was lucky that James just got on with his homework. And luckier still that he seemed to enjoy it. She gave herself credit, however, for the fact that she had never allowed him to watch television after school even when he was small, so he had never developed the habit that so many of his friends had of slumping in front of a screen for hours before then having to tackle the work. The routines she had always followed had helped him, she believed.

Naomi began to chop the onion and then diced the red pepper and tore the spinach. The chicken breast was next, on a special board for raw meat.

Ingredients prepared, Naomi looked in the cupboard and pulled out a jar of curry sauce and two pouches of pre-cooked rice. This mixture of convenience and fresh was her solution to the challenge of cooking every day. If someone were to tell her how much salt and sugar was in that jar she would have been appalled, but it was an expensive brand and had the words Low Fat emblazoned on it. She tended not to think about it much further than that.

6.45. Dinner was half ready so the next thing now was to go and get changed before, at 7, going back downstairs to finish her tea and then pour a glass of something a bit more exciting. First she needed to text Scott quickly to see exactly what time he would be back from work. His position as associate director at an architecture recruitment consultancy had always meant long hours, but usually they were flexible ones. Having settled down to a calmer routine for a while, his working hours had increased again in the last six months as business had begun to improve. More business meant more interviews and more clients, but also that more consultants were needed. Scott was having to get involved with the day-to-day task of interviewing on behalf of clients as well as co-ordinating a recruitment drive for the company itself. He had reassured her that it was only a temporary return to longer hours – a promise she hoped he would keep this time.

Text sent, Naomi went upstairs to get changed out of her clothes and into a pair of leggings and a comfortable jumper. It always felt good to get out of her work things. The fitted skirts and tailored blouses were necessary but restricting. And she liked the way her legs looked in leggings – being tall, she had always been happy to show them off. Frowning at her face in the mirror, she tried and failed to dismiss the next thought: *Especially with the way your face is going...*

Pulling her skin back, she tried to erase the lines from around her mouth and eyes. She raised her eyebrows to smooth out her forehead a little. Scott had got so angry, last year, when she had talked about Botox that she hadn't dared to mention it again, but at least once a week she stared at herself and fantasised about her face being plumped out, the lines and years smoothed away.

With a sigh, she moved away from the full-length mirror and walked along the cool corridor to her study. The computer was already on so she quickly opened up her emails. Nothing new. Clicking on her junk mail folder, she saw there were a few messages from the social network that she had joined a year or so ago. With a glance at the clock, she opened up a browser and logged in. It took three goes before she got her password right. How long had it been since she had looked at this?

Scrolling down the page, there were endless photos, links, videos. *God,* she thought, *who has time to look at all this stuff?*

Frowning at the unfamiliar screen, she clicked on the red flags in the corner. *You have two Connect requests*, the message said. One was from a woman at the school who she had got chatting to at Christmas, and one was from a Mike Burnham.

Burnham? she thought. *Mike Burnham? Who is that?*

Oh, she realised. *Mike. Carla's Mike. Of course.*

She clicked on *Accept* for both of them and then went back to scrolling through the feed, vaguely curious but also not at all surprised at how little she had missed, despite having not been on here for nearly six months.

There was a beep.

Slightly startled, Naomi looked around for her phone, but it wasn't that. A little box had popped up on the screen.

Hey Naomi, it read, *welcome to my friends list!*

It was Mike.

Smiling, she tapped back, *Hi there – thanks! How are you?*

Very well, thank you. You?

Yes, she replied, *very well. Busy as usual!*

Ah, the reply came back. *We're looking forward to seeing you on Sunday…*

Yes, she said. *Me too!*

Bye for now ☺

Smiling to herself but unsure of how to add a smiley face, she just typed *Bye!* and then logged off.

Back downstairs, she saw that she had had a text back from Scott. He'd be home in half an hour. Glancing up at the clock, she said, 'Dinner's at 7.45, James. Please make sure the table is clear by then.'

6.57. Three minutes ahead of schedule but close enough, she thought, and, pouring her glass of cold white wine, she went to watch the news.

After thirty minutes of twenty-year-old sex scandals, soaring house prices and the bad weather that was coming soon, she went back into the kitchen. She clicked the gas on underneath the wok, ready to cook Monday night's wok-fried curry and rice.

James was tapping away on his phone.

'If you're done, can you clear it all away now, please?' Naomi asked.

'Uh-huh.'

Still staring at his phone, James began to pile all the books up and push them over on to the far side of the pine table.

'Away, I said, not just piled up in the corner! You know how much I hate that … Come on …'

Naomi tried not to sound exasperated but she was hungry now and getting irritable. Picking up a piece of half-cooked red pepper, she popped it back in the pan and added the sauce. As it sputtered, she popped pouches of white rice into the microwave and set the table.

James lifted his elbows as she set the places around him.

Sighing again, Naomi put glasses and the water jug on to the table.

'Can I have Coke, Mum? Please…'

'Oh, OK. But just one glass before your dad gets back…'

James leapt up and poured himself a pint of Coke. Naomi went to say something about the size of his glass but bit her tongue.

The front door clicked as Scott came in and, doing a 'Drink up!' gesture to James, Naomi threw the spinach into the curry and stirred.

'Hello!' said Scott cheerfully as he came into the room. 'Something smells good!'

Naomi was tearing open scalding hot pouches of rice and, without looking up, said, 'It's ready! Sit down!'

She had always taken great pride in the fact that they shared their evening meal. Never missed the opportunity to mention it and always mentally added it to the *doing OK* column whenever she felt doubtful about her parenting skills. The articles she read online went on so much about the benefits of eating together as a family, and she had that box well and truly ticked.

James and Scott sat down in the same places they had sat for the thirteen and a half years since James had been weaned in his yellow plastic high chair. Naomi placed the warmed plates full of food on to the table and then sat down too.

James started to add salt.

Naomi said what she always said: 'James! Taste it first, please!'

Scott said what he always said: 'Looks great.'

Naomi asked what she always asked: 'Good day?'

Scott replied what he always replied: 'Not bad.'

Scott asked James what he always asked: 'How was school?'

James replied the way he always replied: 'Not bad.'

They all smiled at each other, as they always did at that.

Then they carried on eating.

As soon as the meal was over, James said, 'May I get down?'

'Yes, of course.'

Pushing his chair back, James grabbed his phone off the side and went upstairs. Homework done, meal eaten, that would be the last they saw of him until the morning.

Scott got up too. 'Sorry,' he said, 'I still have work to do.'

'Oh, OK...'

Naomi began to clear away the plates and glasses. With the kitchen tidy, but not wanting to go and sit on her own in the living room, she went back upstairs. Sitting there at the computer, sipping a honey-sweetened mint tea, she logged back in to the social site she had visited earlier. Such a curious thing, she thought, the way people announced so much of what they were doing; announced every passing thought in their heads. Very few of her own friends were on here and, even if they were, they weren't that active. She knew a lot of people with older kids went on the site to keep an eye on what they were up to; she also knew that the kids made sure whatever they were getting up to was happening elsewhere. Though they were probably not up to much. Despite all the media hysteria about teens and sexting and porn, the teen years didn't seem that different now from when she had been a girl. Boys talking about sex and not really having it and girls pretending to talk about something else and also not really having it. Even so, none of this stopped Naomi from being relieved that James, at fourteen, was still more interested in computer games than girls.

Opening up another browser, she read some news pieces and then sat staring into space. Why was she sitting here? She should go back downstairs, but with Scott working and James in his room she didn't really feel like it.

'I must find a new book to read,' she said out loud to herself, and, tapping into Amazon, she began to scroll through the list of the latest bestsellers, adding a few to the online shopping basket. Something caught her eye: the other tab was flashing. *Mike has messaged you.*

Smiling, she clicked on it and saw the message. *Hello again. What are you up to?*

Book shopping! she typed back, glad to be able to say that, rather than have to admit she had been reading celebrity gossip.

Interesting. What are you reading?

Well, I've just finished one, so nothing right now... I need to think about what I want to read next.

I wish I had the time to read.

Well, she teased, *spend less time online!*

Hey!

She suddenly felt anxious: maybe he hadn't realised she was joking? Hastily she typed back, *I was only joking!*

Ha! It's OK! I am easily distracted. YouTube is a strange and powerful force.

I never look at that! she replied.

Oh, it's great – I'll send you a couple of links. Lure you to the dark side ;)

Haha – you can try!

Sounds tempting...

There was a pause. She raised her eyebrows. Was he flirting with her or was she imagining it?

Right. The lovely Carla is calling, he typed.

Carla. Of course.

Bye for now xx

Night.

And, after a pause, she added a few 'x's. Logging off, she went downstairs.

Chapter Two

David

It was a chilly mid-January Thursday morning. David's room was still dark but warm and stuffy. The central heating had clunked on at 5.30am. Before he had moved out, Gary had always preferred the house to be the same temperature as his bed before he got out of it, and Kerri didn't know how to reset the boiler.

As usual, David's head ached. In fact, all of him ached. His head, his back, his legs, even his skin. Every day started with this all-over ache. Every day started with feeling tired, with this exhausting battle to leave the bed, leave the room. But if he left it too late he would have to catch the bus and that was a fate worse than death so, heaving himself up, he got out of bed and began to get dressed.

As he tied his black school tie in the smeared glass of the bathroom mirror, his eyes met his reflection for what would be the first and last time that day. There was a frown creasing his forehead, a visible sign of the ache behind his flat brown eyes, and this deepened further as he pulled his right cheek to reveal a fresh crop of spots around the corner of his mouth. Knocking the white heads from off their rounded tops, he pulled at his left cheek. He didn't need to shave yet but the skin around his jaw was beginning to darken as the hair follicles beneath the skin thickened. His body and face seemed alien to him. Changing all the time; he could not seem to get a fixed hold of himself. Running the thin black plastic comb through his hair, he went to brush his teeth, eyes now averted from the mirror.

Walking down the stairs, he tried to ignore not only the ache behind his eyes but also the nagging pains in his knees and lower back. At least, he thought, I know what old age feels like. Another reason to be pleased I'll probably never get there...

Jessica and Emily were dressed already and looked smart, as they always did, in their white shirts with neatly knotted red and grey striped ties and the grey pinafore and red cardigans of the spring term. They were watching TV and eating bowls of cereal. The TV was as loud as the bright cereal packaging and David watched as advertisements interrupted the stream of music videos that Jess was glued to. Fruit-based chew strips, Easter egg promotions and half-and-half bread all featured. Feeling vaguely nauseous, watching adverts was the closest David could get to food before he was at school. The queasiness and the headache would be gone once the second or third Coke had kicked in.

There was a muffled click from the kitchen as the kettle went on again. David looked down at the floor. Maybe he could leave before she came out? That was always preferable. He got up. 'See you later, Jess, Em, I'm going now.'

'Bye!' said Emily, brightly.

She smiled up at him, and, letting the innocence of her gaze rest on him, for a moment he felt light. He could see that she loved him despite his size – but how long would that last? Jess was already more physically wary, more reluctant to touch him or be near him. David dreaded the moment when that began to happen with Emily too.

Heaving his black school bag up on to his shoulder with effort, he left the house.

At complete odds with the damp grey of his mood, the morning that David stepped out into was crisp and bright. He could see his breath puffing out in pale clouds as he laboured down the road. At least the early start meant he could take his time. Even on better days – of which, he reminded himself, this was not one – he only had one speed and that was slow.

The other benefit of leaving early was that he could risk the corner shop. It was safe at this time of the day. By 8am, when others would be there, it would be too dangerous to risk a visit.

As he entered, there was a hollow ring from the bell above the door. David kept his eyes down and walked straight over to the double fridges at the back of the brightly lit store. Sliding back the plastic door, he pulled out two bottles of Coke (two was always a more cost-effective choice than one) and then walked down the aisle past the multicoloured tins and packets to the racks of confectionery on the right near the till.

The shop was empty and, gazing at the rows of sweets and chocolates, David felt a pleasant sense of anticipation. The colours and shapes were all so familiar and appealing, it was like greeting a room full of old friends. But what to choose? Smarties were for kids and anyway, the mini ones were crap: the ratio of chocolate to sugar-coating was all off. And what was with the colours? The natural ones looked so dull and faded; it was as if someone had licked them before they had gone in the tube. KitKats and Flakes could only be eaten sitting down. Wispas were, for him, an after-school treat. A Snickers bar was a popular option but only when his mum wasn't around: how many times did anyone need to hear that they used to be called something else? He took a Snickers duo and then scanned across and up and down the shelves. Starbursts were too fiddly; the individual wrappers made them only suitable for concentrated eating in bed or in front of the TV. Mars was too much like a Snickers but without the nuts: what was the point of that? Aero was a possibility but did he want mint, orange, chocolate or limited edition coconut? He grabbed the mint one. He could afford one more: which one? Which one?

The bell rang dully in the background and David felt a lurch in his stomach as he heard the chatter of boys coming into the shop.

'Only three of you in the shop at one time!' Standing at the counter, the tall, grey-haired man looked up from his newspaper and waved a hand towards the four lads. 'Two of you'll have to wait outside!'

One of the boys looked over to where David stood, still staring at the chocolate display. 'Maybe we should all get out?' he called out, his fair hair falling into his eyes. 'He takes up enough space for three of us!' They all laughed, the sound broken and choppy as their voices went from low to high register.

'Two of you out,' the man repeated, neutrally. He wasn't about to shame one of his best customers.

David quickly grabbed a large bag of peanut M&Ms and then shuffled over to pay. Keeping his eyes down, he handed over a ten-pound note and, taking his change, walked out. To his relief the boys passed him without further comment, though the last of them gave him a shove as he walked by. That, David could handle. Sticks and stones...bollocks, he thought to himself. He would rather be nudged, shoved, pushed and punched over verbally abused any day of the week. At least bruises faded and vanished.

Lifting the flap of his bag, he shoved the M&Ms in there for later and, as he walked to the bus stop, he unpeeled the shiny brown and cream wrapper of the Snickers. Holding one in one hand, he bit into the rippled chocolate coating of the other, closing his eyes briefly as the smooth caramel, savoury nuts and creamy nougat filled his mouth. He took another bite, faster this time, and then another until it was done. Then he ate the second one.

Balling up the wrapper, he put that in his pocket and then pulled the triangular points of the Aero wrapper apart and ate the bubbly bar in four quick bites.

Still walking, he opened the bottle of Coke, and took a few big, sweet swigs and sighed to himself. What was it about Coke, when it was ice-cold, that meant you could never just have one or two sips? He drank back the caramel-coloured liquid; it fizzed and bubbled in the curved bottle, the bright sun catching the plastic and the promise of his headache fading away feeling almost as good as if it were already gone. As the sugar and caffeine began to do their work, David finally felt able to lift his head and look around. Another twenty minutes and he would be in school, the routine and rituals of the day would take over, but for now, here in the cold sunshine, cold drink in hand, lips sticky with sweetness, his time was his own.

Now that it was Thursday, the week was almost over. Looking forward to Friday was something that always began on Wednesday, especially when this weekend he was going to be seeing Gary. It was two and a half years now since his dad had left, and the time that elapsed between visits had got longer and longer. David had not seen him since before Christmas now (Gary had said he wanted to spend Christmas Day with what he called his 'new' family, by which David knew he meant his 'not disappointing' family) and he felt as anxious as he was excited at the prospect of seeing him again.

That anxiety lurched in his stomach. Hoping to make it go away, he quickly finished the Coke he was holding, and then reached into his bag and pulled out the other bottle.

'Break-time is the best,' said James as he bit into the doughnut he had in his right hand whilst gesticulating at David with the Twix he held in the other. Sugar spraying out of his mouth, he continued, 'I love doughnuts more than life itself.'

David grinned back. They were sitting on a hard patch of ground towards the back of the sports field. It was cold but it was bright, and they were alone here; the other kids preferred to chase-fight in the playground or huddle in corners gossiping around piles of discarded school bags.

David stared out across the empty playing field. The washed-out winter grass brought back memories of the mud and discomfort of the weekly rugby and football lessons. Suddenly, there was a noise. It was a light and cheerful tinkling, like fairy bells or Christmas. It was the sound of girls.

And not just any girls, but girls they actually liked.

Both boys looked down at the ground.

'Hey,' said Christianne, looking at James and David through a sheet of long reddish-blonde hair.

'Hey,' echoed the other three girls. If the Three Graces of ancient myth had, instead of beauty, charm and creativity, represented acne, awkwardness and anxiety, then this was what they would have looked like. And yet, if they had just known it, they were all beautiful.

'Hey,' replied David and James in unison, still looking down. Acting together around girls was always easier than acting alone. David felt a nervous twist in his stomach and brushed at his mouth to get rid of any crumbs or smudges of chocolate.

'Didn't see you at swimming last week...' said Christianne to James.

'Nah, Mum was away and couldn't pick me up. I'll be there next week.'

'We can always pick you up, you know. We're right near you. Mum's cool with stuff like that. Not much else, but anything sporty, you know...anything that falls under the heading of *good for my only daughter*...'

The Graces giggled.

David sat up as stiffly as his soft body allowed. He thought about getting up, his legs were prickling with pins and needles, but, if he stood, his bulk would be even more evident. Self-conscious, he fidgeted, trying to pull himself in as much as he could while still appearing friendly. It wasn't really working. The girls continued to talk to James who, with his open face and easy manners, had always been approachable. He stood up now and, cursing him silently, David followed suit. While James had got up in one fluid motion, using his knees to rise effortlessly from the ground, David had to use his hands and arms as leverage. He heaved and swayed, the burning sensation from the pins and needles increasing as he placed his full weight on to his calves. It caused him to stagger slightly to the right as he finally pulled himself upright.

The Graces tried not to giggle again, and failed. Christianne was mature enough to look away, but not quite mature enough to not glance back after a beat.

'What are you doing for half-term? We're going skiing again,' she said, rolling her eyes as if this were the least funnest thing ever. 'It's like the least funnest thing ever. Mum gets pissed every night and then complains about having to get up at crazy o'clock. I'm always stuck in like some nerdy ski school with nerdy French kids who are all like six but can still ski better than me. It's *so* annoying.'

'Yeah, I hate skiing, too,' said James. 'We go every other year 'cos Mum can't stand it but my dad loves it – I love that they think they're doing you a favour taking *you* skiing when it's *their* hobby!'

'Yeah, right,' said Christianne.

'Yeah, right,' echoed the Three Graces.

David remained mute. There was nothing he could contribute to this conversation. Why couldn't James talk about films or books? Or lunch? He stared at the ground, kicking the damp mud with his shoe, occasionally glancing sideways at Christianne.

They continued to complain about their parents for a few more minutes and David continued to kick the ground.

Everyone knew his parents were divorced and, while he was hardly alone in that, he still felt the pain of it every day. Like the aches and sores in his body, the misery of their separation never really went away; and, like those aches and sores, he never talked about it.

Catching his eye, Christianne smiled and said, 'You all right, David? Your sisters are the same age as my little brother, aren't they? They doing the eleven-plus this year?'

'Next year,' he muttered at the ground. He tried to force his eyes up to meet hers.

'Yeah, Mum's already *soooo* stressed out at the idea of me doing my mocks and him doing his 11-plus stuff. She gets so wound up!'

The bell rang. Relieved now that he was already up and on his feet, David was also pleased when he noticed James hang back and keep pace with him rather than keep up with the trotting of Christianne and the Graces as they half-skipped, half-ran back to the main building. Trying to keep his voice casual, David said, 'I didn't know Christianne was in the swim club?'

'Yeah…' James shrugged.

David had never done communal swimming at school. His mum had addressed that well before he started. He had always been grateful to her for that intervention. As he watched the lithe, retreating figures of the girls, he felt an uncomfortable stiffening in his trousers as he thought about what those white shoulders and that red hair would look like coming up out of a limpid pool of blue-green water.

Trying to shake away the image, David involuntarily twitched his head from side to side, like trying to clear the screen of his childhood Etch-a-Sketch. He thought about how much he hated maths, the double period he had now, then he remembered that it would be lunch afterwards and it was hot dog day. He replaced the thought of quadratic equations with an image of hot dogs and mustard and onions and instantly felt better. Anything was tolerable if, afterwards, there was a frankfurter to be had.

The noise of the girls' squabbling and Kerri's shouting filled the hallway and rolled up the stairs, the aural equivalent of the fog that pursued him every afternoon and just as suffocating. Rolling over heavily, David stared at the screen and turned the volume on the TV up very loud. He didn't feel like going down just yet. Even barely a week into term, he was beginning to feel worn down, his mood lowered by the day-to-day grind of the bullying.

Sticks and stones may break my bones, he recalled. None of those sayings makes sense any more. Who needs the wisdom of old wives when we've got Wikipedia?

And it was rubbish anyway. Anyone who had seen the stats on teen suicides over the last few years could tell you that. Unlike bruises that could heal, and scars that would silver, the words stayed with you, ever ready to cut. They were never dulled by repetition; they only ever got sharper, more wounding. And his anger was like a whetstone: it honed the words that others used, honed them before he wielded them against himself. *Fat fuck. Worthless fat fuck. Fucking useless fat lazy fuck. Fucking useless lazy fucking waste of space fat fuck.* The voice in his head was no more creative than the kids at school, but he could never get away from it.

Shifting his bulky torso awkwardly, he reached his hand to the drawer again, pulling out one of the dozens of chocolate bars he kept in there. Without even bothering to look at what it was, he unwrapped the bar and ate it, feeling the tension in his neck release slightly as the sweetness masked the bitter taste of bile at the back of his throat.

Having flicked over to one of the many film channels, he was enjoying the start of some random nineties action film with Arnold Schwarzenegger in it. Random nineties action movies with Arnold Schwarzenegger in them were among his favourites.

'David!' Kerri's voice carried up the stairs. 'Dinner, David!'

He got up slowly and went downstairs.

The word *dinner* had always been used loosely, and this was especially the case since his dad had left. Walking into the living room, David smelt the meal before he saw it. The spicy aroma of fried chicken hung on the air, a calorific cloud. It smelt like Friday but it was still only Thursday. His mouth watered and he wondered why they were having this tonight. But, seeing the red and white boxes of crunchy chicken pieces, spiced burgers and onion rings, he suddenly didn't care. The chips were pale and limp as always but the onion rings and popcorn bites...well, they were worth fighting his sisters for.

Staring hard at Kerri's back as she walked into the kitchen, he felt the blackness from the day roil inside him. It was his favourite meal. Why had she bought his favourite? What was going on?

He sat down heavily on the sofa, waiting for her to come back in. The room was warm. It was dark outside but the curtains were still open.

'I'll shut these,' said Kerri, moving to the window. 'And then we can watch something... Shall we let David pick tonight, girls?'

'Sure thing!' said Emily brightly.

'Awwww,' moaned Jess.

Lying on the floor, mere inches away from the screen, she was watching it with wide eyes, little pointed chin perched on laced-together fingers. She passed David the remote and stuck her tongue out at him. He scowled back. He wasn't in the mood for her and her tween posturing tonight.

David continued to watch Kerri out of the corner of narrowed eyes. Having shut the curtains, she was now passing round drinks.

'So, David can choose and then we can eat! I thought you might enjoy this tonight. *And* I got your favourite for dessert. A Viennetta! I thought: let's go retro!'

David's scowl hardened. Kerri only chattered like this when she was nervous. He looked again at the table. All the extra food. His own choice of movie. His preferred pudding. Why would she be trying so hard to make him happy?

He felt a pulse of anxiety beat through him. Despite the heat in the room, his whole body went cold.

'He can't make it, can he?'

The beat of silence was audible even over the noise of the television.

'No,' Kerri replied, unable to meet his eyes. 'I'm so sorry, David. He texted this morning. Said he has to go away for work.'

There was another pause.

'I'm really sorry. I know how much you were looking forward to it.'

'That's the second time he's done that to David,' piped up Jess. 'Spanner!'

'Jess!' Kerri said sharply. 'You know I won't have you talk about your dad like that. Enough!'

David stared at the floor, face burning with a sharp mixture of shame, anxiety and disappointment, as well as that deep misery that only comes when someone confirms something that you suspected would happen all along. Not that suspecting it made it any easier to bear when it did eventually come to pass.

'So, I got your favourite things in. And I thought, over the weekend, we could have a movie marathon... Hot dogs, wedges, popcorn, treats! We can snuggle up, watch DVDs, play games...'

'Sure,' David muttered and, reaching out for a burger, he popped open the box and began to eat.

They watched and ate in silence. David chewed his way mechanically through three burgers. He ate the onion rings and the little deep-fried balls of crispy chicken. He drank his way right through the two-litre bottle of Coke that Kerri had placed by his side. As the film progressed, and after the girls had been sent up to bed, David glanced up and noticed that Kerri hadn't yet cleared the table of the things they had eaten. Despite feeling nauseous, he picked up the paper packet of chips and took a few out. They were stone-cold: granular and bland. The taste brought back what had happened the other lunchtime. He was used to the taunts but that had been something else. Feeling the knot of anger tighten beneath the sick feeling deep in the hard-soft folds of his belly, his fists and jaw involuntarily clenched. He sucked it up all day long at school and it was only at night or in the evenings, once the girls had gone to bed, that he could feel the anger heating up inside him, barely contained and waiting to explode like a chip pan about to catch alight.

Kerri came in with a mug of tea and a packet of biscuits. She sat down heavily in the armchair. David looked at the rolls of fat under her chin as she sat back and stared tiredly at the TV screen. Without even looking down, she peeled open the shiny dark-brown packet and took two chocolate digestives out of the top.

She's the one who never cooked, thought David. She's the one who was always busy, always working, always out doing something more important than preparing fresh food for us to eat. She's the one who brought takeaways home. She's the one who filled the fridge with fizzy drinks and sweets.

She's the one who let Dad leave.

'Do you want one?' Kerri asked casually, placing the pack on the table. 'I'll take them back into the kitchen in a minute; don't want to eat all of them…' She trailed off and looked up, a rare moment of eye contact with her firstborn.

And, with that, David's anger set alight.

'No, I bet you don't,' he hissed back, voice hot and spitting. 'Does it make you feel *better* to have someone even fatter than you to look at? Do you think I want to eat any more of the crap you buy? Do you think I want to look and feel like an enormous pile of shit every day? It's *your* fault I'm like this – it's your fault and I hate you. I hate you. I fucking *hate* you!'

'David!'

Trying to ignore the dampening effect that his lack of speed was having on the impact of what he had just said, he lumbered up and off the sofa. Kerri was staring at him now, eyes wide and mouth open, stunned. And this – the fact that she looked so shocked, so fucking *surprised* – just made him angrier still. How could she not know? How could she not know how much it hurt?

He turned his back on her and stomped up the stairs. The fact that his knees ached, his back hurt and he felt sick just made him feel angrier. By the time he got to his room he could no longer contain it. Punching the pillows, he hit them over and over again, the feathers yielding, his stomach wobbling, his breathing shallow with the effort. He lay down heavily on the bed.

I'm even too fat to be angry, he thought.

The tears came next. As they ran down his face, hot and salty, he could feel them leaving sludgy tracks over his swollen cheeks.

There was a tapping on the door. He saw Kerri's feet underneath it: patches of black against the strip of light coming through from the small hallway.

'GO AWAY,' he shouted.

The feet remained.

Minutes passed. There was another tap. 'David... Please...'

David turned the volume on the television up.

There was another tap.

He turned the volume up even higher.

The feet moved on.

Suddenly feeling even sadder, David pulled open the bedside drawer and grabbed a large, creamy-brown bag of

Revels. Handful by handful, he ate them all, and then he stared at the television until he fell asleep.

Lying in bed the following morning, David still felt angry, but there was also a sense of embarrassment, of anxiety about having to go downstairs and see Kerri. His emotions had been served up scalding hot, and now, cold and congealed, it all seemed less important. He wondered why he had yelled. Well, he knew exactly why – he had been angry – but he was often angry and he usually managed to hide it. It was just that sometimes pretending not to care was too much. Sometimes it had to be released, squeezed out like the pus from a spot; and now he felt lighter – not really better, but a little lighter. He hoped that what would happen now was what always happened: she would act as if nothing had been said, and he would do the same. That pattern of behaviour was fairly reliable. Which was more than could be said for his dad.

David sighed and then got up. If he left it too late he would have to catch the bus, and that would definitely not make him feel better.

Washed and dressed, he went downstairs. As he approached the bottom of the stairs, he stopped, wobbling slightly but hesitating. 'Jeez,' he muttered. Even with the inches of MDF in between him and the shouting, it was ear-achingly loud.

'It's mine! You CAN'T have it!' Emily was yelling.

'It is NOT yours! I got it out of my drawer! It's mine!'

Bracing himself, David went into the living room, wincing at the noise as he opened the door.

Kerri came in from the kitchen. She looked tired; her face was red and, with wet hair and her dressing gown still on, she was clearly also running late.

'Are you still fighting over that hair clip?' she cried out, exasperated. 'I asked you to sort it out between yourselves!'

'But it's mine!' said Emily.

43

'It is not! It's my one!'

'You both have one! Where is yours?' Kerri asked, looking at Jess.

'That one is mine,' the girl persisted, arms crossed, face scowling.

'If Jess said she found it in her drawer then it must be hers,' Kerri said to Emily.

'No, she TOOK it from me and hid it there!' Emily said, face pale and voice shaky.

'No, I didn't!' retorted Jess.

David knew that Jess was lying. David knew that Kerri knew that Jess was lying. He also knew that she would never confront her about it. The lying had started when Dad had left and so that had been left too.

'I thought you got a load of likes the last time you wore your hair in braids,' David commented mildly as he sat down on the sofa.

The reference to likes and braids stopped Jess in her tracks. 'What?' She was still scowling, but she had at least stopped yelling.

'Yeah,' he said, looking down at his phone and talking casually, as if he had not even noticed the noise. 'Yeah, the braids. You definitely got a load of likes when you braided your hair. Why not let Em help you do it?'

David knew Emily was always eager to help, and he also knew that Jess was equally eager to be given an out when she was lying.

'Emily?' Kerri prompted, quietly and kindly.

'OK...'

The girls sat down. Jess passed Emily the hairbrush.

'Jess?' prompted David.

She scowled again but then looked down and muttered, 'Sorry, Em...'

'S'OK!' the other girl said brightly. The brushing began and the absence of squabbling was, for that moment, glorious.

David glanced at Kerri. She was smiling at him. Her face was less red but she still looked tired. But, thought David, she always looked tired. They all did.

Silently she mouthed, *Thank you.*

Kerri went upstairs and, when she came back down fifteen minutes later, she looked visibly more relaxed. Jess was now helping Emily with her hair.

'Nearly time to go, girls,' Kerri said. She smiled at David again. He said goodbye as they left, and then turned the TV off. The silence was blissful. It had felt good to help. It had felt good to be out of himself for a moment, to be helping to make Kerri feel better.

Breathing in and out, he glanced at his phone: nearly time to go to school. And, with that, the good feeling was gone.

Naomi

It was now the end of what normally felt like the longest week of the year, but Naomi could hardly believe it was Friday already. Sitting in the living room, she was trying to look as if she was listening to what Scott was saying about his week.

'So, we still haven't found any decent consultants to interview. We're having to use the consultants of our own consultants to get candidates even worth seeing! And then there was this whole latest thing with Jeff – '

Oh, God, thought Naomi. Jeff. Hearing Scott talk about that guy drives me mad.

There was always one person in an office who did nothing, but whom no one could ever seem to get rid of, and, at Scott's work, that person was called Jeff. Naomi had been listening to tales of the man's ineptitude for what felt like a lifetime.

'Oh,' she said, cutting into the flow of conversation, 'do you want to order food? I'll go and tell James it won't be long.'

'Sure, OK,' said Scott. 'Indian?'

'Indian. Just get the usual.' she said. 'Or double-check with James. I'll get him to come down.'

Naomi went up the stairs. She tapped on James's door as she went by. 'James!'

'Uhghhhghh,' came a sound through the door. This was teenage for *yes, you may enter.*

Naomi opened and peered round the door. James was lying face-down on the bed holding his phone.

'Hey there, can you go down and tell Dad what you want from the Indian?'

'Can't I just text him?'

She raised an eyebrow. 'You know we don't do that,' she said, smiling. 'Go and speak to him. I'm just going to check my messages from work and I'll be down in a bit.'

'Sure,' said James, getting up.

'Thanks.'

Naomi went down the hallway to the study. Being up here was a convenient excuse to quickly check the computer. A quick glance at her emails so that she hadn't told a lie, and then she opened the web browser. She couldn't help but hope Mike was around. They had been chatting online all week but this was the first time she had started a conversation herself. She felt strangely nervous. And strangely excited.

Hi there. Happy Friday! she typed.

Hey you, came the reply.

She grinned at the screen. *How are you?* she typed.

It's Friday! I'm amazing!

Naomi laughed. *Of course! Me too :)*

She smiled at the screen again and wondered if he was doing the same.

What are you up to tonight? she asked.

I'm out, he said. *Need to get back to it really.*

Oh, she thought, strangely disappointed.

Chat next week though? I need you to recommend me some more books.

Oh, yes, of course. Have fun! she added.

And she went back downstairs, wishing she could go out too, the night in she had been looking forward to all week suddenly seeming very dull indeed.

Matthew

As he walked down the road towards the supermarket, the familiarity of the route, and the fact that he was spending part of his weekend doing something so mundane, made Matthew feel both relaxed – it was an easy chore and it was also more fun than marking – but also uneasy – it was the middle of January and he had still done nothing different since his return from Brazil.

Matthew had initially revelled in his return home. Appreciating afresh the ability to read road signs and understand the chatter around him, he had also enjoyed no longer having to be quite so paranoid about people brushing up against him to try to steal his wallet. He had loved the fact that the air was cool and fresh rather than humid and steamy, and he'd liked the way his phone behaved itself and picked up messages instantly. He had felt glad and very grateful for the clean, modern and efficient way that life here seemed to run, compared to Brazil with its inconsistencies, quirky timetables, and strangely over-effusive people. He liked being left alone, ignored and unimpeded as he went about his day-to-day business. He had felt all of this and felt it keenly. But now, mere weeks later, what had seemed comforting because of its familiarity was now stultifying. The air was clear and crisp today but he felt as though he was suffocating, the environment invisibly filled with something that made it hard to breathe.

He had decided that getting something practical done would give him some focus. And now, having slept slightly later than planned, he had got up and gone out. If he could just get these little jobs out of the way first, then he could get on with the important stuff that he wanted to do.

Walking into the huge store, it was the smell he noticed first. Or rather, the *absence* of smell. Pausing by the double doors, he stopped to sniff the air. People weaved around him, eyes narrowed with suspicion. Continuing to sniff around, like a trained dog doing its best to seek out a dangerous substance, he stepped forward.

The fruit and vegetables were in front of him. Piled high in their blue plastic crates, he could see red, yellow, green and orange peppers in two different varieties (romano and bell). He could see bananas that offered every degree of shade between unripe pale green to black-speckled yellow. He could see at least seven different varieties of apples, polished and spherical, piled high even though the British apple season had finished months ago. There were three types of pear, skins pale brown and speckle-free, as well as mounds of plastic bags full of green, white and black grapes. He could *see* them; he just couldn't *smell* them. It was like looking at a display in a wax museum: everything eerily perfect, but fake.

Walking around the aisles, he noticed there were tomatoes in every size, from swollen slicing varieties to vine-ripened, organic, miniature plums. They were all red, smooth and clear like the perfect skin on the flushed cheeks of a small child. He could see brown onions, red onions and uniformly dark green, straight and exactly-thirty-centimetres-long cucumbers, plucked from their hydropods of water and then vacuum-sealed in a tight sheath of plastic. They lay regimentally alongside avocados as hard as bullets. Avocados that had been pulled from glass-covered bushes in sterile soil and were now expected to ripen as beautifully at home in the chilled, sterile environment of a domestic fridge as they would in the natural sun and showers of their native earth. He could see starfruit, dragon fruit, sharon fruit. Fruit that the supermarket encouraged you to buy, he remembered Lucy telling him, for recipes that looked good in their magazines. And also because, he remembered reading, they helped make your fruit bowl look more exotic. So not actually for eating, then, he thought, his mind turning as sour as most of the fruits themselves.

Taking all this in, he picked one of the avocados up. Its knobbly skin looked flawless, a deep olive green, and its perfect regulation shape meant that it fitted neatly in the palm of Matthew's hand. He gave it a gentle squeeze but there was nothing, not even a hint of what should have been moist, creamy flesh within. Lifting it up to his nose, he breathed in and all he caught was the scent of whatever aggressive bleach had been used to clean either the fruit before it came to rest here in his hand, or was used to keep the vegetable aisle sanitary. Placing the fruit back to rest among its fellows in the plastic-lined crate, he looked around him again: the sheer abundance was overwhelming, but it aroused nothing. The air, the experience of it all, was antiseptic.

His mind went back to the market in Manaus.

There the smell had been intoxicating. Everything had lived and breathed. The flies had buzzed, excited and tantalised; the air had been rich with zest: an edible atmosphere. Not only that, there had been chatter, bustle, laughter and noise. Here it was silent: everyone had their heads down. Dead eyes scanning dead produce. They were selecting the cold, hard, dead fruits from crates and placing them into cold, hard wire baskets with less consideration and enthusiasm than they would use to select a pair of socks. Here children were trapped in metal trolleys, caged and then placated with salty or sugary snacks. There, they had tasted, explored and played.

Even the supermarkets he had seen in Brazil had offered the shopper ripe, fleshy, smelly, juicy and fresh fruit and vegetables, locally grown and picked. Here, food was a means to an end – eat and then get on with the important stuff of life: texting, tweeting, liking, pinning; shopping, buying, driving. There, food *was* life.

Taking a deep breath, Matthew consulted his list. A shopping list made him feel a little like a granny but he knew that it was the only way to navigate the store. Without a list he would end up wandering down aisles he should not wander down, aisles of distraction and convenience. Again, these were lessons learned from others. He could still hear Lucy's voice, the strident tone as she had harangued him about his fridge and cupboards full of dead food.

Smiling a little to himself, he bought the vegetables, fruit and then meat and fish he needed. He planned to make a big pot of the soup he had enjoyed so much in Brazil and then live on that for a few days. He ignored the little voice (it sounded like a strange mix of his dad and his mates, the men in his life) that was calling him a pussy for cooking. He knew real men cooked but he didn't know any actual men that cooked. The contradictory ideas settled uneasily in his mind, churning sourly, like his stomach after a bad night out when he had mixed beer and wine.

Concentrating on the list, he skirted the many aisles of distraction, bought some bagels and eggs. They were at the far end of the store for a reason, and he had a moment of pride in himself at knowing that he had navigated the middle of the store and remained focused. He then went down the freezer aisle, but only to avoid the alcohol. Frozen desserts were easier to not pick up than discounted January booze.

But, just as he neared the till, the pull of the aisle, the signage, the idea of a nice bottle of something became overwhelming. He backtracked and, intending to get just one, he saw it was cheaper to buy two.

At the checkout, he paid and then walked out, the bottles chinking against each other with every step.

Everything he did that afternoon needed doing. He needed to put the shopping away, he needed to check his emails, he needed to empty his spam folder, he needed to check his Instagram feed, he needed to tidy the living room a little and he needed to check in with his friends on Facebook, needed to fire off emojis and 'Hey, how you doing?'s and updates. And, now that was all done, he needed to do the things he had been promising he would get started on today: the big things.

But, sitting staring at the four patchily painted walls to avoid seeing the pile of marking still in front of him, Matthew felt too tired to do much else. It was 7pm on a Saturday night. There was that sense that everyone else was out having a good time, but, having been online, he was also very aware that that was not really the case: all his mates – the few that hadn't settled down and still went out – were too skint to do much in mid-January. His FOMO was an ever-present background buzz that he was accustomed to in the same way that he had become used to the noise of the busy road outside his Rivenoak town centre flat.

He stared at the screens in front of him, laptop open, TV on, phone by his side. He was connected. He could do anything. Anything. He poured another glass of wine and clicked *Play next episode*.

As the screen began to move, he was aware that he did feel different. That, having been on his trip, he *was* different. He was not, he told himself, just another person sitting in alone, watching Netflix on a loop. He was even seeing things differently, as he had at the supermarket today, but what to do with that feeling? Being here and not at the pub, for example, seemed like a good first step, even if all he had done so far this evening was not do the marking.

There was a sense of wanting to make changes, to be part of something, but he was still struggling to imagine what that something might look like. The idea was so large, the changes needed to make the world a better place so vast and insurmountable, that it was like standing naked at the bottom of Everest. He felt hopeless, helpless and ill prepared.

With another glance at the pile in front of him, and as the chatter on the screen began, he turned up the volume, poured another glass of wine, and said, 'Tomorrow! Tomorrow I will make a start!'

Naomi

Naomi had logged on over the weekend but had heard nothing from Mike. She knew he was busy and she had been too. The new year was already in full swing with James's schoolwork and all the usual housework and errands that needed running, but that didn't mean she didn't have time to think about him, about how much she liked talking to him. Now it was Tuesday night. She had told Scott she was working. She wasn't working. She had been chatting to Mike for well over an hour.

Oh, and then there's this guy at work who drives me nuts, he typed.

Ooooh, she said, *do tell… I want to hear all about it!*

Well, you know, he's one of those people who sends me very long waffly emails that use words like transformational and dovetail…

Haha, she typed. *What else?*

They tapped away, her asking lots of questions about work and his day and him telling her all about it.

Anyway, he typed, *I'm sure you have plenty of other things you could be doing rather than chatting to me about how annoying people at work are.*

I like to hear about it and it's good to have some company, she replied.

I like keeping you company ;)

Staring at the screen, she hesitated. There, she thought, what is that?

I like that you like that, she replied.

Cool.

She rolled her eyes at the screen.

Cool?

Cool is coming back; awesome is so 2014. It's time for our superlatives to move on...

What's going to be the next big one, then? she asked, smiling as she typed. *Maybe something a bit more English, like marvellous?*

No...I don't think so. Little bit old-fashioned.

Sorry! That's what happens when you ARE old, I suppose.

You are not old!

Yes, I am! Especially compared to you and Carla – there's over ten years between us!

No! You're kidding me.

No, I'm not!

Anyway. I think you're cool.

Cool? Really?

She smiled. At him, but also at the outrageous fishing for compliments that she was indulging in.

Yes. Very cool.

Well, she typed back, *if only you could tell my son that!*

She pressed *Return* to send the message and then instantly regretted mentioning James. It made her feel even older, and it also seemed to corrupt the idea of her family somehow. She decided instantly not to mention James or Scott again.

There was a pause.

What to say now? she wondered. The mention of family, the reminder of her commitments and her life away from this screen, seemed to have knocked the conversation out of its groove.

Fun plans for the week ahead? she typed, falling back on a conventional enquiry. *I bet you have an amazing one planned!*

Yes! Out for a birthday – showing support for the poor sods with January birthdays :)

Sounds fun!

It should be. How about you?

53

Oh, not much...though, she added, *you've inspired me and I think I might organise a night out!*

Great idea! he replied. *An even better idea would be to come out with us!*

Ha! she replied. Did he really mean that?

Another time?

Sure...

Staring at the screen, eyes tired and sore, she willed him to say something else. She really didn't want this conversation to end.

I'd better go. Goodnight! he typed.

Damn. She hadn't thought of a new hook fast enough. *Goodnight!* she replied.

Walking down the stairs, Naomi grinned away to herself as she recalled bits of their conversation, the words scrolling through her mind. In the kitchen she made some tea and then took her mug through to the living room. It was late, and James had gone to bed, but Scott was up, watching TV.

'What are you watching?' she asked, sitting on the sofa next to him.

'Documentary thing...it's fascinating.'

'Oh, OK. You all right? Have a good day?' Messaging made her feel chatty in the same way that snacking would stimulate your appetite.

'Yes, busy. Which I know I shouldn't complain about after the last few years but still...it would help if Jeff were less hopeless.'

Naomi felt her desire to listen suddenly vanish. It was like being hungry and then receiving a plateful of something you had eaten every week for the last month. Knowing that they were about to have the same chat about the same people that they had been having for the last six months (six years, her mind added) took her appetite for listening away.

Oblivious, Scott carried on, 'This week, he came in with yet another plan he has drawn up. It uses all sorts of buzz words but doesn't actually have any concrete ideas about how to make things easier for us...'

'Words like *transformational*? And *dovetail*?' asked Naomi, half laughing and feeling excited about making a private reference to the conversation she had been having with Mike.

'No...' said Scott, sounding a little confused.

Naomi stared into her mug as he carried on talking about work.

'Oh, and Dad called,' he said.

Naomi stared harder into her mug. Wiping from her face the flash of annoyance that any reference to Scott's parents caused her, she looked up.

'Oh, yes?' she said, forcing some lightness into her voice.

'Yes, he said that Mum's been given some stronger medication now...for the high blood pressure. I always thought because they were quite active and slim it wouldn't affect them, but it seems as though it's getting worse.'

'It's how they eat,' sighed Naomi, thinking, Here we go again. 'I can barely taste the food, the amount of salt she puts in everything – and all that baking! It's just the two of them. Why does she still bake so much?'

'It's her hobby,' he said.

'I know, but...' Naomi shrugged. She had lost count of the number of times they had talked about this. It might be her hobby but, she thought sourly, visualising in her mind all the jars clogging up the kitchen cupboards, no one in their right mind eats that much bloody jam.

'I said we would go and see them soon, maybe in the next week or so. Dad sounded a bit down. You know how they are.'

Oh, yes, she thought. I know EXACTLY how they are.

She wished she liked Scott's parents more but, in the absence of her own mother who had died many years ago and to whom she had never been close, she just found them annoying. They lived over three hours away. This meant that almost every trip involved staying over, and the constant food and cake, as well as the unhealthy dynamic of alternately bickering with and cosseting Leonard that Elaine indulged in, made Naomi uncomfortable. The older woman seemed to revel in making her husband feel small and then feeding him cake to make up for it. The idea of a visit, of being away from the computer, from Mike, made her heart sink in a way that surprised her.

'Want some more tea?' she asked Scott as she got up.

'No, thanks.'

Naomi stood in the kitchen waiting for the water to go off the boil. She was thinking about Mike. The similarities between his work gripes and Scott's had not escaped her – it was just that, well, Mike's were new, and that was enough to make them more interesting. She remembered how she had felt, waking up on New Year's Day, thinking that nothing could happen this year that would surprise or interest her. Lying there, she had felt numbed by the routine of family life; and yet, as she considered this surprising new friendship, she thought, maybe this year will be different after all...

Chapter Three

Wednesday 16th to Wednesday 30th January

Naomi

Naomi scrolled through the news feed. So many references to films and programmes she wasn't watching, music she hadn't heard, books she hadn't read. She knew it was how James and his friends spent a lot of their time and that was to be expected but these were all acquaintances of hers: adults.

Ignoring the nagging thought that she should be doing something else, that the week and the month were passing by and she had barely got started with things she needed to do at work and at home, she looked at Mike's feed and saw he had posted some references to books he was reading, too.

Was that aimed at her?

There was a beep. She smiled immediately and felt her stomach do a little flip of excitement in response.

Hey there, he had typed. *Working late again?*

Putting her tea down, she typed back, *Afraid so! How are you?*

It's been a long day but I'm OK. You?

Same, really. Busy but OK.

There was a pause. God. Since when had she become so boring? Did she have nothing to talk about except being busy?

No, she decided, she didn't. She felt the need to fill the gap so she continued: *January's a busy time for us. What are you working on?*

My tolerance to alcohol :P

Naomi raised her eyebrows. More drinking? Normally this would annoy her, but there was something appealing about his attitude, something she couldn't quite put her finger on. She had a sense of wanting to approve of him so that he would give her something back. Feeling unsure as to what that meant, aware of wanting something but not knowing what, she was keen to keep him talking to her. Smiling, she typed back, *Fair enough. Sounds like fun! Carla said you had a good time at the pub the other Sunday – dancing till all hours!*

Yes, we did. School nights are a temptation. Being too sensible isn't good for you, I don't think. Need to ration it.

I suppose!

Naomi leaned back in her seat and sipped her tea. She couldn't remember the last time she had gone out midweek, let alone on a Sunday. Since leaving London, she wasn't even having her Friday night drinks any more. After-work drinks were just not a thing at VitSip.

And I bought another book, he continued.

Oh! Really? What did you buy?

You inspired me to pick up a new copy of some classics. I had forgotten how much I missed reading.

Oh, great … I'm enjoying re-reading Bleak House.

That's a big book.

You think so? she wrote. *I like to take my time reading things, immerse myself in them. I have a bit more time now that my commute is shorter …*

Good. And I tend to agree that some of the best things take time.

They do indeed.

There was a pause. What was it about this messaging where she felt the urge to turn everything into a *double-entendre*?

Suppose I'd better go and read it, then... she continued. Praying that he would carry on talking to her.

There was another pause. There was something about these pauses: they seemed stuffed full of potential. She stared at the screen. The urge to *do* something was overwhelming. She went to type *Bye* and then saw the words *Mike is typing* and waited...

Talking of fun nights out, I often think about you at that New Year party. The party was dreadful but I loved your dancing.

Naomi cringed a little at the memory, and typed back, *You definitely need to increase your tolerance to alcohol if you think my dancing is good!*

I thought you looked great.

Another pause...while the phrase *Mike is typing* filled the message box. Naomi stared at what he had just written. Great? He thought she'd looked great. When was the last time she had heard that? And what would he say next?

I can promise you I wasn't drunk. If I had been, I might have had the courage to join you.

Naomi laughed and then frowned and smiled at the same time: a puzzled expression that twisted round on itself in the exact same way as her stomach was doing. God, she thought, is he actually flirting with me?

She sat up and then found herself typing back, *That would have been fun.*

She sat back and stared at the last few rows of text. Whether he was flirting with her or not, she was definitely flirting with him. Or trying to. Frowning again, she tried to remember the New Year party. She had had quite a lot to drink that night – after the Christmas they had had with Scott's parents, no one could have blamed her – and she remembered being introduced to Mike, but mostly she had spent her time chatting to Carla as well as trying to ignore the fact that Scott was sitting in the corner on his own, looking bored.

Though, she added, keen for the flirting to continue, *I am a bit of a demon on the dance floor.*

I'm fairly sure I could handle you.

You think so, do you?

There was a pause. Her stomach knotted a little tighter: what was she doing?

Oh, yes. Very much so. I think I know *exactly* what you need.

Oh…

She exhaled. What did *that* mean? Her skin tingled. Her body knew, even if she was pretending her mind didn't.

And she wanted to know. Wanted to know what he meant. Wanted him to tell her what she needed. Because, if he told her, then that would save her having to figure it out for herself. Because, sitting here, typing, having a conversation without moving her mouth, a conversation that seemed to be the more intense for being mute, she had begun to wonder what it was she was hungry for. She had also begun to feel a little scared.

And then he was gone.

Reading over the exchange again, she scolded herself for the flirting. It was all very U-rated, nothing that would upset the censors, but it was still there. Sitting back, she sipped her almost cold tea and continued to scroll through. Feeling slightly embarrassed at the ease with which she had begun to be suggestive, she wondered if it wasn't partly the medium that was to blame. There was something about the instantaneous nature of the messages, the way that you typed as you thought but also the fact that you couldn't see the other person. It induced a level of intimacy that would take longer to establish in real life. The lack of eye-contact, the removal of facial expressions, meant she worried a lot more about being misunderstood, but also that she went further, much further than she ever would in person.

It's just words, she insisted to herself. But, deep down, she knew it wasn't. As someone who worked in marketing, she was very aware of the immense power of words: that there really was no such a thing as *just* words.

And, given the numerous lectures she'd delivered to James, she told herself, lectures conducted at the kitchen table, and operating under the heading of THE MULTIPLE PERILS OF THE INTERNET, lectures at which he always rolled his eyes, she should know to be careful with what she put down in black and white on a website…

She read through the messages again. More carefully this time. Nothing to be too concerned about, she decided, passing judgement firmly in her own favour.

But, as she logged off, she told herself: I have to be more careful.

Mere days later, the warnings she had given herself had been forgotten. When she wasn't thinking about the messages, she was thinking about the fact that she was going to be seeing Mike at the pub lunch this weekend.

He had given her his mobile number. *Just in case you need it for the weekend*, he had said. She'd saved him in her phone under Carla's name. She wasn't completely sure why she had felt the need to do that, but that was what she had done. He had said how much he was looking forward to seeing her on Sunday at the pub, and she was finding it hard to admit to herself how much she was looking forward to it too.

Ordinarily they all watched TV together until late on a Saturday night, but Naomi had made an excuse about being tired and gone to bed early. Now, she was lying in bed staring at the ceiling. Was she really seeing him tomorrow? She could hardly bear the waiting. Various scenarios played over in her mind, each slightly crazier than the last. She had his photos on the website, photos she had stared at till her eyes had gone blurry, but she could barely remember what he looked like in person. All that filled her mind were the fun exchanges they had been having. The way he had made her laugh, the way he had made her take things less seriously for a few hours at a time.

Her stomach rumbled. She had not managed to eat much today, or the day before. She felt hungry but also queasy. Her stomach seemed to be the locus for all her emotions: fizzing and burning, it felt empty and yet strangely satisfied. Hands clenched again, she shut her eyes, willing sleep to come and bring the next day quicker. She couldn't wait to see him, to remind herself of the reality of him. Part of her hoped that she would see him and not want him, see him and think, Oh, no, what was that about? And then it could be forgotten.

It needed to be forgotten.

The door opened, soft light from the hallway filtering into the room. Naomi rolled over and sighed.

'You still awake?' Scott asked softly as he undressed.

'Gnnff,' she said. It was a sound which meant both yes and no at the same time: *Yes, I am awake. No, I don't want to have sex.*

After Scott had settled into bed, Naomi turned on to her back again and continued to think about the following day. It was all she thought about until she fell asleep and it was the first thing she thought about when she woke up. She was still thinking about it when the phone rang at about 10.30am. Still in her dressing gown, she was looking forward to a long, hot shower and to taking lots of time getting ready. She answered the phone, her voice light.

'Hello!'

'Nomes! Hi, it's Carla.'

'Oh, hi.' Naomi's stomach rolled over. There could only be one reason for the call. 'Um, how are you?'

'I'm so sorry but we can't make it today. Mike is really poorly! One of those viral things! Been ill since Friday night. I hate people that flake out by text so I wanted to call. I'm so sorry!'

'Oh, never mind,' said Naomi as brightly as she could. She hesitated and added, 'Say hi to him from me. Hope he gets better soon.'

'Will do. Sorry again. He's really gutted we can't make it...'

'Sure, OK. See you tomorrow!'

Holding the now silent phone in her hand, Naomi thought how much more satisfying it would be to have an old-fashioned phone that she could slam down.

It was Friday again and Naomi was working from home. Having said goodbye to both Scott and James, she had set herself up in her study. The heating was on full blast and had been since 6am, so the room was finally beginning to warm up.

It was a small spare room but, being upstairs and in the corner of the house, it had two external walls and so always felt cold. There was a knitted patchwork throw on the sofabed in the corner and Naomi often had to wrap that round her legs and feet to keep herself warm in here.

Having spent all week feeling alternately angry at Mike for cancelling and at herself for having got so carried away about it all, today she was just tired and had work to do.

By lunchtime she felt slightly better, but restless. She was waiting for some feedback from the technical team now and, having got a lot done in the course of the morning, she felt drawn back to the social network site.

Logging in, she scrolled through the almost unchanged feed, pretending not to notice or care that the little dot next to his name indicated that he was online. She then found herself reading his messages again.

It really was all in my head, she thought.

After ten minutes, she got up and went to make some lunch. On returning, she saw the red flag of a new message and, setting her sandwich aside, stomach burning with anticipation, she clicked on it and smiled. It was him.

Hey.

Hey, she replied. *Feeling better?*

Yep! Sorry about the other day. I was really sorry to miss it.

Never mind, she typed back, hoping that the typed phrase conveyed all the nonchalance that she was feigning.

Another time?

Maybe, if you're lucky, she teased.

I am pretty lucky :P

She paused. What else was there to say?

What are you up to? he continued.

Working. You?

The same. Or at least pretending to. The office is pretty quiet today.

Right. Well, I'm working from home so trying not to get too distracted.

Should I leave you alone, then?

No. Stay.

OK. If you like…

Naomi rolled her eyes at the screen. God, he was infuriating sometimes. He would reach out and then pull away. Such a boy. But it also made her feel like such a girl. And she quite liked it. She felt as uncertain as a foal; trying to come to grips with this new communication was like trying to walk on a pair of stilt-like, skittish, skinny legs. She was worried she was in for a fall.

They chatted on and off for twenty minutes. Or rather, she let him chatter away. It was all quite one-sided but she didn't mind. She didn't want to talk about herself. She liked the way he made her laugh, sharing silly stories about what he and his friends got up to. It reminded her of her teenage years. Not all the memories were good ones but he made her think of the times she had enjoyed, and checking out the songs and clips he sent made her feel younger.

I've got to go, he said, eventually.

OK.

Can I talk to you later? he asked. *I'm in tonight.*

I should be about…

Naomi took one bite of the slightly stale sandwich and then, taking the plate downstairs, she threw the rest in the bin.

She worked away through the afternoon. At around 4pm her phone rang. It was Scott.

'Hi,' he said.

'Hi, how are you?'

'I'm good. I had a call from Mum, though, and she seems to have completely forgotten that we're coming to see them. I know I told her but she got really angry and started complaining about Dad, saying that he must have not told her about it. She was calling him all sorts of names down the phone. It was awful! I think it's best if I go on my own tomorrow and see how they are.'

Naomi tried not to smile. Then she remembered Scott couldn't see her and she grinned. Forcibly turning the corners of her mouth down to subdue her voice, she replied, 'Oh, OK, well, as long as you're sure, hon.'

'Yes, I'm sure. I don't want this to disrupt James's weekend sport and things. I'll head up there tonight…'

The idea of having an evening free, no Scott, no dinner to cook, a whole evening to chat online, was very appealing.

'That's a GREAT idea,' Naomi agreed quickly. 'I'm sure your dad will appreciate it if he's having a tough time with your mum. You could treat them to dinner out at that local pub they like.'

'Good idea. You're so thoughtful. I'll come back to grab a bag and then head off…'

'Perfect. See you later…'

'Bye!'

Naomi smiled: this day was just getting better and better.

On hearing James come in from school, she went downstairs. 'How was your day?' she asked.

'All right...' he mumbled from his seat at the kitchen table.

Naomi put the kettle on then turned it off, deciding she would have a gin and tonic instead. It was Friday, after all. Looking back at James staring at his phone, she smiled. The one thing her own recent addiction to messaging had given her was an appreciation as to why James's phone was so important to him.

'Dad is away tonight so you can go and see David if you like. If he's free. I can give you some money for McDonald's...'

'Oh! Really? Cheers, Mum, you're the best!' he replied, rewarding her with a grin.

She smiled back. Being nice was easy when she was also getting what she wanted: an evening free to chat to her... What was he? A friend? Yes. A friend. Just a friend.

'I've got a bit more work to do,' she lied. 'I'll be down again soon. Help yourself to some money from my purse and I'll see you later!'

'Sure.'

Giving him a hug, Naomi went back upstairs.

I'm all yours tonight... she typed. *Let me know when you're free...*

An hour or so later, there was the red flag of a message. She grinned at the screen, her stomach and head feeling suddenly very light.

Hey.

She loved that *hey*. Scott never said *hey*. *Hey* was sexy in a way that *hello* never could be, not even if it tried really hard. Ordinarily she hated the way everyday English had become Americanised, but there was something about *hey*. It seemed so much more intimate than a stiff English *hello* or a studiedly casual *hi*.

Having been taught about mirroring in her management training, she replied, *Hey.*

How are you?

She smiled and, sipping her post-gin glass of water, she sent back, *Good. Pleased it's Friday! You?*

Yes, me too ☺

Have you got much planned for the weekend? she asked, curious as ever about what he was up to.

Just the usual stuff – shops, lunch, cinema.

Sounds nice – lucky you. Naomi smiled again. His was such an easy life, she thought. Not that she would wish to go through the whole baby thing again, but she hadn't had the leisurely thirties that so many people she worked with seemed to be enjoying – this extension of their twenties while they put off starting a family. It looked like fun – but she couldn't help thinking that it would only make the transition to life as a parent even harder.

Can I ask you something? he typed.

Sure.

What are you wearing?

Naomi sat up straight. Her stomach did a tight roll. Oh, God, what was this?

Simultaneously a small voice inside her scoffed, Ha! Like you haven't been *dying* for him to say something like that.

She had no idea what to type. Did you say what you were really wearing, or make something up? She felt her stomach churn again, panic and doubt gripping and kneading her insides. It felt like some sort of test, a test that she had to pass to progress to the next level of the game.

Her hands hovered anxiously over the black keyboard, then fluttered up to her face, and then, trying not to think about it too much, she just began to type.

I wear work clothes even at home...fitted navy skirt, cream jumper, tights...

It was only after pressing the return key that she read the word *tights*. Aargh, no! she thought. Tights aren't sexy! Why did I type *tights*?

She waited anxiously for a response.

Mmmh. Is it a short skirt?

That was an easy one. *Yes.*

What colour underwear do you have on?

Easier still.

Black.

Which was true.

She added, *Lacy and tiny.*

Which was not.

There was a pause. The seconds seemed to stretch out. Was that the wrong thing to say? Was lace not 'in' any more? She felt as though she had perhaps made some sort of fashion blunder.

I would love to see you in those.

Really?

Really. If I close my eyes I can still see you dancing at New Year. You looked so good. So alive.

Naomi felt her face flush. All she could remember about that night was how good it had felt to be dancing: drinking and dancing on her own after the long Christmas holidays with the demands of Scott's parents as well as having James sulking round the house for two weeks eating too much rubbish and getting grumpy because he missed his friends.

But I bet you look even better without anything on. I want you to show me.

The door opened.

Startled, Naomi jumped and quickly minimised the screen. Turning round, she was startled to see Scott. She had completely forgotten that he had said he was coming home first to pack a bag.

'I'm nearly ready to go! Are you still working?' She saw his eyes glance at the screen.

'Yes! Just thought, you know, that I'd get on top of it if you weren't here. Help keep tomorrow clear...' Her voice trailed off as her lie ran out of steam.

'Good idea. But don't work too late or I'll feel bad for you!'

He came over and kissed her on the cheek. As he walked away, she found herself unconsciously wiping the dampness off her skin.

She looked at the clock. It was 8pm.

Shit, she thought, shit, shit. Where had the time gone? And where had *he* gone?

Mike's little button had gone off.

'Ugh,' she groaned with frustration.

She waited for Scott to leave and then logged back on; he still wasn't there.

She typed, *I'll make sure I'm wearing something more interesting next time...*

And then she logged off and went downstairs, an unfamiliar numbness in her crotch as she walked into the kitchen, grabbed the wine and a glass and went in to the living room.

The 7.57. The usual grim Monday morning silence. Except, behind the neutral façade, Naomi felt anything but grim. She was more excited than she had been in years.

Shifting in her seat, she ignored the sideways glares of the older man next to her. It was impossible to sit still: her mind was racing so fast that her body was keen to get in on the action. Forcing herself to maintain the illusion of calm, she stared out of the window, hands knotted together in her lap. Every thought revolved around the same question: what was going on? What was going on? What had started out as a bit of banter and chat had turned, as of Friday's messages, into something else, but she wasn't sure what exactly. All she knew was that it was thrilling, and that she could think of little else.

Taking her phone out of her bag, she immediately put it away again. The urge to look at the messages once more was overwhelming but she couldn't. Not here. Not on the train.

Anyone might see. She laced her fingers together and placed her hands back on her lap. On her navy skirt. The line she had written came back: what had he thought when she had said that? Had he imagined her in it? Should she have asked what he was wearing too, or did you not do that? She had no idea.

Again she went to take her phone out of her bag and again she didn't. Instead, she knotted her hands together tighter, willing the train to go faster.

In the office, she turned the computer on and then went and made some coffee. Back at her desk, she logged in and read through the messages three times over. He had said she looked good when she was dancing; he had said he wanted to see her underwear. He had said those things. There it was in black and white. She smiled to herself.

Half an hour later, Carla walked by her door.

'Morning!' she called in, clinging on to the door frame as she always did, smiling as she always did.

'Hey,' Naomi replied. 'How are you?'

Carla swung into the room, saying, 'Yeah, good – we went out for the day yesterday which was fun.' Then she rolled her eyes, pulled an exasperated face and continued, 'But Saturday was a total write-off… Mike was drinking all afternoon on Friday, some client thing. He got *so* pissed and then spent all day on Saturday feeling sorry for himself and not wanting to do anything!'

Drunk. He had been drunk. Oh, God, Naomi thought. I am such a fool. Such an old fool.

She laughed politely, unable to reply. Luckily for her, Carla wiggled the purple plastic file she was carrying and said, 'It's not a macguffin this time – gotta go to HR! See you later!'

'See you!' Naomi choked out.

As soon as Carla was gone, Naomi sat back in her chair and said, 'Bastard,' in a hushed voice.

What had she been thinking? She got up and then sat down again and then, with an angry huff, she got back up and paced about the office. He had been drunk. He had only asked her those things, said those things, because he was *drunk*!

Pacing about, hands clenched into her fists at her side, she couldn't remember the last time she had felt this angry.

But, maybe, said a voice in her head, *maybe he was only able to say those things BECAUSE he was drunk*.

With a slightly different emphasis, the idea of his being drunk suddenly became her ally rather than her enemy.

Maybe, she thought, sitting back down at her desk, allowing the thought to get comfortable. Maybe. Oh, but even so, she had to be more wary. She had no idea what he was doing or who he was with when he messaged her. He might even be doing it to make his friends laugh. The memory of that night at her old job came back, as unwelcome as ever. The smirks that were almost hidden behind hands but not quite. The younger guys in the office, lips curled in a sneer as they looked over at her in the pub. The message in their hard eyes had been very clear: *What are you doing here, you old cow? Go home and leave us to it…*

The memory always made her feel a little queasy and, shaking her head, she tried to be rid of it. Alcohol loosened the inhibitions, that was all. The idea that being drunk had meant he'd felt able to say what he wanted to was a reassuring one, one that she was happy to cling on to for now. Yes, she said to herself, yes, OK, so he was drunk but even so…I need to leave it. Leave it for a few days. Wait and see what he says next.

Back at her desk, she opened up the project file and set to work.

So much of the next two days were spent wanting to message him and not doing so that, by the time she got home on Tuesday night, all her willpower had drained away.

After supper, she found herself staring at the screen, mentally composing the perfect message. In her mind it was the perfect balance of cool, calm nonchalance with just a hint of sexiness. *Hey, how are you?*

She then pretended to be interested in the other people on her news feed and in her emails, not staring at the photos on his profile page.

Seeing that he was now online, she tried to ignore the tension in her stomach as the minutes went by.

Then, there was the beep.

Hey there. I'm good. How are you, beautiful?

Great, thanks!

She had decided not to question him about Friday, to just wait and see what he said next. This decision – the decision not to query what he was doing or why – was a barely conscious one. If she had been able to be honest with herself, she would have said that she was scared: scared that if she shone too bright a light on whatever was happening it might vanish in a puff of smoke like a faerie or other imaginary, beautiful thing that was too impossibly perfect to survive in the real world.

Glad January is nearly over… he continued.

Yes! January can be rough but February is always worse! Got plans?

Not really. This and that but yeah, winter is dull, real dull. Needs livening up a bit, I think.

Oh, you think so, do you? she replied, hoping her teasing tone came across.

I do think so…

There was a pause. What was that meant to mean? He was so cryptic sometimes. It was frustrating.

How are you going to liven it up? she typed back, wincing slightly at her own forwardness but needing him to be clearer. She could feel her shoulders tense as she waited for the reply. With no facial expressions or eye-contact to go on, she felt as if she was operating blind, with no idea what type of response she might get next.

I can think of a few ways.

Can you now?

Oh, yes.

She paused. This is it, she thought: just say it, just say it...

Do they involve more questions about the colour of my underwear?

They might :P

Tease, she fired back, smiling.

Teasing is fun but being teased is even better.

I can do that.

Can you now?

She smiled at the mirroring. He probably wasn't even aware he was doing it but she recognised it.

What colour are they today? he asked.

Her face flushed again. Even when she was expecting it, hoping for it, it made her feel embarrassed.

White today but still tiny. Again, only half true.

Thong?

Might be? Is that what you like?

Yes. I like to bite through the tiny thin string at the side with my teeth.

She flushed even more and crossed her legs.

What are you wearing? she asked.

I want to know what else you have on.

White T-shirt, tight jeans...bare feet, red-painted toenails.

Nice – I like painted nails... I want to see those nails up by my ears.

Naomi sat back and gasped a little. She squirmed on the hard wooden chair.

Really? was all she could manage to write.

Really.

Oh.

Is that OK?

I don't know.

Well, if you don't want to play...

I don't know what I want.

73

There was a pause. It lasted a long time. These pauses had changed. They were stuffed full now: stuffed full of possibility, of potential. They were also almost unbearably sexy, the typed equivalent of a long, slow striptease. The sexual tension was pulsating down the phone lines or wherever it was the internet signal came and went from (God, how did she still have no idea how that worked?) and it seemed to flow in between her and the black letter keys. Her fingers dancing across the letters, like fingers tracing on skin. An image of his hands flashed into her mind and she dug her fingers into her palm, uncertain of what to say or do next.

Are you still there? he asked.

Yes. She hoped he understood that she was whispering.

I can stop.

Can you? she thought. I'm not sure I can.

No. Don't stop.

OK… If you need some more time, that's fine. I'm a very patient man.

Yes. OK. Thank you.

Staring at the screen, she reread what he had written. Something about him saying he would wait, could wait, made her feel as though *she* absolutely couldn't. Without thinking, not able to allow herself to do what she was doing consciously, she replied, *I'm on my own for a little bit of time tomorrow night.*

She then hurriedly logged off. Sitting back, she had to put her hand over her mouth to stifle a cry. She was trembling, her heart racing, her breathing fast and a little ragged. She had been typing so fast, she had barely even registered what she had said. She read over the messages a dozen times. They remained unchanged. Standing up, and running out of the room, she slammed the door shut behind her.

It was the next night. Scott was still at work and would be till late. James was out at football practice. Naomi was online.

74

She hadn't dared ask if he had been drinking. Instead, she had started herself as soon as she had got in. They had been chatting for an hour. She wanted him to make the first move. Wanted him to take action. In that way, she was absolved of the responsibility. Doing what you were told was an excuse that people had been using to justify much worse behaviour than she was hoping to indulge in. But she remained nervous, unsure. The tension, the holding back, was almost unbearable.

So, you're on your own tonight, he typed.

Yes.

Ah.

Ah?

Yes, ah…

Is this where you ask me what I'm wearing again?

This is where I tell you to strip.

Her face flushed and she shifted in her seat. Oh God, she thought, what am I about to do?

Do it.

Yes.

Naomi stood up, pulled the thick navy jumper up off over her head and wriggled out of her jeans. She felt terrified and yet exhilarated.

Tell me what you're doing.

I'm sitting on the chair, she typed, *in a black lace bra and panties.*

Put your hand inside your bra and stroke your nipple.

Easing her fingers uncertainly under the lace cup, Naomi felt the skin on her breast prickle under her fingertips.

Feels good. Where are your hands? she typed back slowly with one hand.

I want you to squeeze your nipple hard between your fingers then rest your hand on the outside of those panties.

Oh, that feels good.

I know it does. Slip your hand under the lace and then rest it there and press your palm against your clit.

She pressed her palm against herself.

It's so warm, she typed.

Massage it, rub it, and then slide a finger inside, hard and high, I want to feel inside you.

Oh, God, she thought, staring at the screen.

She could feel the heat under her fingers. She knew how long it had been since she had touched herself here. Knew it and yet none of that seemed important now. He was telling her to, and the telling changed everything. It helped her to forget about then and to focus only on now. It gave her permission.

I am already so wet, so hot and wet, she typed.

And she was saying it out loud now. Having waited and thought of little else for days, she could feel the anticipation herself: she was ready. The muscles in her thighs were tensing as she squirmed in the chair. Her face was flushed from the wine, her breathing beginning to quicken. On the hard chair, she felt the blood fill her pussy, felt the heat as every part of it began to swell and moisten.

Oh, God, she typed again. *I need to lie down.*

No. *Stay there. I want you to slide two fingers up there now – I want you to think about my hard cock sliding up into you.*

Oh, God.

I am sliding in and out of you – so hard and so deep – fucking you hard – I want to hear you come – what sound do you make when you come?

A loud one.

Make it then, come hard around my dick.

And Naomi slid to the floor. Pressing the heel of her hand to the soft swell of herself, she began to press there gently. Men wanted to think that you needed them inside you to make you come, but when she used to do this she usually stayed on the outside, teasing her clitoris and then building the pressure up until she came and came hard. With a gasp, she slid her fingers inside and cupped herself. She was so hot, wet and soft. Crying out, she could feel the inside of her vagina rippling as the waves of orgasm travelled up. Trying to slow her breathing, she wished she could take the noise back. The sound of her coming seemed to echo round the room. She wanted to take it back – take it back inside, contain it. But it was too late. And, more than wanting it back, she wanted to hear it again. Pressing gently, she slid her fingers in higher, rhythmically fucking herself.

After coming hard again, she sat up, face hot, breath ragged. Back on the chair, she looked at the glowing screen, staring at the last line he had written. Her hands were still shaking. They hovered over the keyboard. What had she done?

Hey. How are you? Are you OK?

Yes, she typed.

No, she thought.

That felt great, she added.

Yes, it did.

But, she thought, I feel kind of shitty now. Tell me that's normal. Please.

There was a long pause.

Are you sure you're OK?

Honestly? I don't know.

I haven't felt that turned on in ages, he replied. *You make me so hard.*

Really?

Yes. I want you.

She slumped in her seat, feeling happy but also completely overwhelmed.

Shit…I've got to go, he typed. *Can we talk after the weekend? I need to talk to you.*

Sure xx

Xx

And then he was gone.

The room seemed to get colder and expand out so that she was left, small and shrunken, in the centre of it. This, she

77

imagined, was what it must feel like after watching porn: cold, mechanical, sated but also empty and very much in need of a hug, some warmth and tenderness. Shivering, she picked her clothes up off the floor and, hands trembling, she slowly put them back on.

When Scott came home an hour later with a midweek takeaway treat and a bottle of wine, Naomi was curled up on the sofa already cradling a wine glass and staring at the television screen. She had no idea what she was watching.

'Hello, here's dinner!' said Scott as he put the bag down on the coffee table. 'You OK?' he asked as he went to get plates and cutlery and a wine glass for himself.

'Yes. Yes, I'm fine,' said Naomi, snapping to attention when Scott came back into the room. It was as if she was seeing him, her husband, for the first time. She saw his grey-flecked hair and soft hazel eyes; she saw his warm smile, the tired smudges under his eyes as well as the lines around his mouth and on his forehead. He was still striking on a good day, tall and broad, slim and smiling, but he looked tired. He would be fifty-one at the end of this year and sometimes, on a not so good day, that seven-year age gap looked and seemed more like seventeen.

'Went for the usual. James still out?'

'Great, and yes. Yes, he is. He texted earlier. He'll be back by 9.30. He's popping to David's after football.'

Scott served up the curry and passed Naomi a plate. 'What are you watching?' he asked as he took a sip of red wine.

'No idea!' Naomi laughed, suddenly feeling light-headed. Looking at the food, she suddenly felt very hungry. In fact she was absolutely starving. Eating quickly, forking the spiced chicken and rice into her mouth, she was amazed at how she could be sitting here, eating and talking, watching TV, sitting next to her husband so causally when only an hour ago she had been masturbating for another man. The contrast struck her as so stark as to be unreal. It was as if she had split in two and it was one Naomi who had done those things and a different one who was here now eating, talking, feeling warm in the cosy, firelit living room, sitting on the soft sofa in clean white underwear.

They talked and, as she listened to Scott, she marvelled at how much she loved him, how that feeling, the feeling of love for him remained unchanged by what had happened. For this she felt grateful, relieved and happy. Very happy. An hour later, James came in; he helped himself to the leftover curry and they talked about their respective days and the plans for the weekend. The strangeness of what she had done heightened the normality and naturalness of this moment even more: enhanced it, made it better.

Later, as Naomi brushed her teeth, she looked at herself in the mirror and thought, I got away with it. I really did.

And her next thought: I want to do it again.

Chapter Four

Matthew

It was only the end of the third week back and all that had changed was that Matthew felt constantly uneasy and unhappy with how little anything had actually changed. He had also run out of excuses for not going to the pub.

I'll be there in ten minutes, he texted Jim.

Get a shift on! I'll be ready for another by the time you get here! Jim messaged back.

Matthew rolled his eyes. Jim had managed one week of dry January and then, having come down with a cold, had declared that he functioned better with booze in his system, that it was some sort of antibiotic which he evidently needed to be fully himself, and had promptly returned to his post-school pub routine.

He glanced at the clock: it was 5pm. The science classroom was blissfully quiet and he had managed to get a fair amount of work done since the end of the school day. Now he was just staring into the middle distance, biting the nail of his index finger, a distraction habit from his own teenage years, and trying to gather the momentum required to leave. What was it about Friday? He had longed for it all week and yet, now he

80

was here, now he was here he felt a strange inertia. His phone buzzed again: Jim. Pushing his chair back, Matthew picked up the remaining exercise books and his laptop and put them in his bag.

The dark of early evening seemed darker still after a day spent under the harsh fluorescent strip-lights of the science lab. As he left the school grounds, he noticed some pupils hanging around outside.

'Evening, sir...' came a chorus of voices, the suggestive tone very much belying the age of the girls.

He recognised them, of course. It was some of the girls from Year 10, those teenagers on the brink of adulthood, some of whom already seemed more worldly than Matthew remembered being at twenty-five, let alone fifteen. He was grateful for the dark as his face flushed. He had never got used to the attention his appearance attracted. They were only children, but some of the things he had had whispered to him in busy corridors made his ears burn.

The high street was busy. People heading home or heading out – even in the winter there was a special warmth to the start of a Friday night. Matthew caught the eye of a young woman as he walked. They looked at each other and, in the moment that they passed, a small smile was exchanged. It was always incredible to him that in that millisecond of eye contact you could take in so much of someone's appearance. But then she was gone. Pulling the bag full of school work back up as it slipped again from his shoulder, he smiled rather than sighed this time. That brief moment of eye contact, of being checked out, of being seen and smiled at, made him feel good. Then, that moment of doubt: maybe she was only looking at me because I look bad? Or tired? Or fat? He glanced quickly in the shop windows as he walked past, it was an instinctive check: something about having once been overweight meant that you never felt quite sure that it hadn't all just come back again.

The interior of the pub was almost as dark as the night he walked in from. The landlord, Frank, kept a fire lit in the winter months because it attracted customers who wanted to pretend they were in a cosy hunting lodge. The same thinking lay behind the dark wood, the soft oversized sofas and the flickering candles. Frank was, and always had been, an unsentimental landlord. If it shifted units he would do it; if it might shift more units he would try it. He also knew the value behind knowing his regulars and, seeing Matthew, he gave him a welcoming nod. Matthew shifted the heavy bag again, his fingers feeling numb and his cold face tingling from the heat of the room. He looked round, unable, at first, to see Jim or Solange.

Then he spotted them. Jim was sitting in the corner by the windows. He looked grumpy and Matthew immediately understood why. In their usual spot, away from the double doors, on the big comfortable sofas near the open fire, there were two young women and a young guy, all sipping pint glasses of water, all still wearing their coats and all talking very animatedly.

'At last!' cried Jim. 'What kept you? Leave me and Sol alone for too long and who knows what might happen? Eh? Eh?'

Ignoring Jim's remark, Matthew put his bags down and kissed the French teacher on both cheeks. Jim's incessant teasing was standard, but Matthew really wasn't in the mood for it tonight. He looked over again at the group by the fire. One of the girls had pretty plaits in her hair, her pale face flushed as she gestured animatedly to her friends, both of whom were nodding as she spoke.

Catching the girl's eye as she talked, he suddenly felt more optimistic about the evening. 'I'll get us some drinks,' he said. 'Usual, Sol? Jim, ready for another?'

They were too busy talking again to reply. Matthew headed to the bar, glancing back as he did so at the group by the fire. The girl was looking right back at him. He looked down and then straight back but she had looked away.

Standing at the bar, he waited for Frank to serve him. Not daring to look round again, he wondered how he might be able to walk by the group without it looking odd. The toilets were on the opposite side of the bar so there really was no reason to be going anywhere near where they were sitting.

'All right? Usual?' asked Frank, already pulling Jim's IPA.

'Yes – yes, please,' said Matthew distractedly, still looking over at the girl while trying to look as if he wasn't looking at the girl.

'Looking at the girl, eh?' said Frank, putting the IPA in front of him and beginning to pour Matthew's pint of lager.

Matthew flushed and, handing over a twenty, picked the trio of drinks up awkwardly in his hands and began to carry them back over.

'Change!' Frank called after him.

Matthew started. That really was an unnecessarily loud voice.

Feeling the girl's eyes on him, he hesitated, wondering whether to go back and get his change but knowing that he had no hands free to do so. The damp glasses were sliding precariously between his fingers; the exact tension required to hold them while not dropping or crushing them was so precise that he could not bear the weight of the stares at the same time. Feeling the glasses slipping further, he flushed again and then hastily tiptoed towards his friends, like a nervous dancer in an ill-rehearsed ballet.

'Whoa there!' said Jim, standing up and rescuing his pint as the pale brown ale slopped all over the floor. He took the glass, bearing it tenderly towards the table, sipping the overflow as he did so.

'Matthew! *Attends*!' cried Solange, slipping into her native tongue, as the wine glass slipped too and spilt some drink on her skirt.

Now everyone was staring at him, and not in a good way. Frank was approaching with a mop, a cloth, and Matthew's change. Matthew felt his face burning. Sitting down, he waited for the hard wooden floor to creak open and swallow him up. It failed to oblige.

His pint now safe on the table, Jim picked up where he had left off. 'Sol was just saying, Barraclough's on a mission this term. SATS-attack again.'

Matthew shut his eyes. Barraclough was the head. The new year always meant renewed pressure on the staff about exam results. Am I really going to have to endure another year of this? he thought, darkly. The work was hard enough but, three weeks in, what was worse was the repetition: nothing ever seemed to change. Every day was timetabled to buggery and he knew what he'd be eating for lunch every day for the next twelve weeks. It made his heart sink.

Sol gestured to Jim to quiet down and smiled at Matthew over her glass.

'Are you ever going to tell us about your trip?'

Matthew looked down at his drink. He knew she meant well but, having done so little since he had got back, he felt increasingly awkward about the idea of discussing the details of the trip.

'Nah,' he said, 'I'll bore you with the photos and stuff another time…'

'Oh, come on,' said Solange. 'I'd love to hear about it! You haven't said a thing about it since you got back.'

Matthew shook his head and took another sip of his pint. 'Honestly,' he said. 'It's really dull!'

She was about to protest further, but all of a sudden Jim was on his feet.

'Look!' he said. 'They're off! Let's grab the sofa!'

The group had all stood up. The girls were picking up a few multicoloured string bags that lay on the floor by the brown leather sofa and the one guy, his thick dirty blond hair swept up in a quiff, was standing, eyelids lowered and mouth set hard as he caught Matthew's eye. The girl with the plaits continued to search in one of the bags as her friends began to walk to the door. Jim hovered nearby at that awkward distance which suggests *Don't hurry* at the same time as *Get a move on* and with that uniquely passive aggressive expression adopted by pub regulars when you have had the audacity to be seated in what they believe to be *their* place.

'Polly!' said the guy, as he held the door open.

Clearly ignoring the call, the girl gave Jim a dark look and then she was walking towards him: to where he, Matthew, was sitting. String bags slung over her arm, she was holding a sheaf of black and white printed leaflets in her hand. He sat up straighter as she approached, trying to look nonchalant.

A leaflet appeared under his nose. 'Tomorrow. If you're interested...'

Looking up, he saw that her eyes were fixed intently on his. They were pale brown, almost translucent, with short lashes; make-up-free and pretty. Standing up and taking the leaflet, he held her gaze as he said, 'Yes, sure.'

'You haven't even looked at it,' she said. 'Or maybe you knew about the demonstration already?'

He smiled back but, just as he was about to introduce himself properly, a loud voice called out again.

'Polly! We have to catch the bus!'

'All right, Lee!' she snapped back, not looking round. 'I have to go,' she said, looking at Matthew. 'See you tomorrow?'

Standing at the door, Lee scowled, pulling at the bronze stud in his ear.

'Yes, definitely!' Matthew said, clutching the bit of paper in his hand. Then she was gone.

Joining Jim and Solange over on the sofa, he felt the momentary glow of triumph that always came after a successful skirmish in the world of interpersonal relationships. He sipped his pint.

'Well?' asked Solange.

'Well what?' he said, trying to suppress a grin.

'Ah, you've cheered up now!' said Jim, laughing, 'Your round again, then, I think!'

Having spent all of Saturday morning marking coursework and project sheets, Matthew was now sitting on the sofa staring at the little black and white leaflet that Polly had given him. It was already a little softened from handling. He placed it on the small glass coffee table in front of him and then tapped the web address on it into his phone again. Having looked at it multiple times already last night when he got home, he just wanted one more look before he left. Glancing at the clock on the wall, he also hoped it would help kill some time. There was no way he wanted to turn up early; even he knew that appearing interested was the last thing that an interested person should do at this stage.

Now, as he scrolled through the basic, lurid and insistently exclamatory site for Snap Out Of It, he found himself mentally rewriting the code and redesigning the pages. Learning code had been his way of amusing himself in his teens and early twenties before he had discovered girls, or rather, until the weight had come off and girls had discovered him.

He carried on reading, chewing absentmindedly at the nail on his index finger. Pulling at the skin on the side of his nail, tugging at it with his teeth, he pulled too hard and tore a strip of skin off the side of his fingernail. He winced. Biting his nails, and the skin on his fingers, was a consequence of losing weight, or rather, it was a consequence of stopping the smoking he had taken up to help lose the weight. Both habits, he reflected, that had been a lot less useful than learning code.

Reading, he could see that the site made some interesting points, but so much of the impact was lost through poor navigation and the use of some truly terrible Photoshopping.

Clicking around, he found some broken links, and then he found a more up-to-date section on the deforestation and pollution caused by sugar-processing and manufacturing. Thinking about it now, he did recall something about that from his trip to Brazil. Andrea had talked a little about the impact that sugar-cane production was having on local farmers as well as the deltas and rivers. Her main focus, however, had been on trying to stop global food companies from peddling their fizzy drinks and snacks to the poor of the region. The very direct connections being drawn here by Snap Out Of It, between food manufacturing, the aggressive plans for growth of the big food corporations and the planet's limited and increasingly poisoned resources, were not issues he had ever really considered. That recent article had been posted on all the usual platforms and had generated a fair bit of buzz. Someone certainly had all the social connections in place, and he could see from the comments and shares that the group was growing in local support. It was just the site's layout and construction that let them down.

After reading some more, he glanced again at the clock. It was now half an hour since the demo had started and it was about a twenty-minute walk away.

'Perfect,' he said out loud.

Pulling on his leather jacket, he tapped his pockets. Phone, wallet, keys: the holy trinity. And the leaflet. Ready to go.

There was sleet in the air and the sky was stony grey but Matthew didn't notice either of these things. Smiling, he walked briskly (but not too briskly), along the path, towards the larger of the two big local supermarkets where the demo was taking place.

He heard them before he saw them. It was the drums that dominated. Or, rather, the out-of-time drums. The group's chanting was as loud and insistent as the font of their website. 'Big Food Out! Big Food Out!'

Behind them, the supermarket filled the low horizon like a squatting beast. It was a sprawling glass and white brick megastore which sold everything from TVs to TV dinners. When Matthew had been a kid around here, growing up on the nearby estates, this land had been playing fields, but now it was dedicated to plasma screens and party food. Given that the car park sign read FULL at three on a Saturday afternoon, it seemed that no one apart from Matthew minded much about that.

The drummer was the blond-quiffed and intense young man who had been calling to Polly from the door of the pub. Lee, Matthew recalled. He was also the one responsible for the out-of-time drumming, and, standing back to watch him for a few moments, Matthew could see why. If the lad put even half the attention he was giving Polly into his playing he might have sounded OK. On seeing him, Lee also clearly recognised Matthew. The younger boy's eyes instantly glanced over at Polly and then back to Matthew, whom he then continued to stare suspiciously at from beneath lowered lids.

Taking the folded leaflet out of his pocket and holding it in his hand as if it were some sort of permission slip, Matthew hovered near the demonstration. He could see that Polly had seen him but she was busy, trying to give leaflets to passers by, trying to talk to them. He didn't want to interrupt. Nearby there was a flimsy card table with a stack of leaflets held down by a battered plastic orangutan, and against the table there were propped a few laminated posters. *Stop deforestation! Orangutans killed and children enslaved to make your sweets!* read one. *End sugar plantation slavery!* read another.

Statements of such intensity didn't really need exclamation marks, but if you had a point to make these days you made it loudly or not at all. That was one of the things he had liked about Andrea and how she worked in the favelas. Her manner had been so gentle: she encouraged and coaxed rather than bullied and harangued. Maybe this was more effective here, though? he thought. How was he to know what worked and what didn't? He was hoping to learn more about that today. As well as to learn a little more about Polly: like her phone number.

Hovering by the table, he looked again at the already very familiar leaflet while simultaneously trying to look engaged, ignore Lee's glares and catch Polly's eye.

The drums continued to beat out of time. The sleet continued to fall from the grey sky. The shoppers continued to walk on by.

'You look a bit lost!' said a girl, coming over to him. She was a redhead wearing smudged, thick-framed black glasses. 'Did you want to sign our petition and get on our mailing list?'

'Sure,' said Matthew, grateful for the opportunity to do something rather than just stand there looking awkward. He looked for a pen and paper. The girl laughed and pointed her phone at him.

'I'll get your details via Bluetooth and we can automatically add you to the mailing list. You on Twitter? Instagram? Tumblr? Facebook? We can sign you up right now...'

The chanting had faded a little and, after the girl had taken his details, Matthew saw Polly standing alone. Taking a quick intake of breath, he walked over.

'Hey,' he said, hoping he sounded calmer than he felt.

This was the was easy bit. He had *Hey* mastered. It was what to say next that he was worried about. At thirty-one, this stuff was no easier than it had been in his twenties. Being approached was one thing, but going up to someone else was another, and it was even harder now because the game had been played before; rounds had been won as well as lost. There was the added pressure that, now he was in his early thirties, he had begun to hope that he might finally be saying *Hey* to the right, the forever girl.

'Hey,' she said back, brown eyes looking straight at him.

Her face was paler than he remembered, but her eyes were still pretty and her skin shone beneath the film of mist that came from the rain-filled air. She looked young, but her chin was tilted up confidently and he noticed she had those pretty plaits in her dark hair again. They made her look a little more feminine, a hint of the girl hidden inside the dark, shapeless clothes.

He looked back, holding her gaze. She flushed a little and then he felt a bit bad. It wasn't often that he took advantage of his appearance – he had spent too many years not having much of an appearance to be proud of – but even he couldn't deny that it felt good: felt good to see her pupils widen, her cheeks flush. Especially when he felt the same.

Looking down and then glancing back up, their eyes met again. Smiling shyly at each other, they looked away and at the shoppers rushing by, pushing trolleys, heads down against the sleet and the possibility of seeing one of the pictures of decimated forests, polluted rivers or, worse still, the disfiguring and debilitating injuries caused to sugar workers, some of whom were only children, as well as trying to avoid catching the eye of an intense young person with a piercing.

'How's it going here today?' Matthew asked.

She smiled, the expression doing much to lighten her serious face. 'Great!' she said, her enthusiasm clearly unaffected by the very low number of people paying any obvious attention. 'I just love being out here. I think even our presence helps. It makes people think, you know – think about what they're doing when they endorse Big Food, when they buy soft drinks and sweets. Did you know that sugar production is one of the biggest environmental threats of our time? That the insatiable appetite for sugar in food and drink production – food and drink we don't really need! – is affecting not just Africa and Brazil but the Great Barrier Reef as well as the UK... Soil erosion, polluted water, polluted air...it's all affected by sugar.'

She stopped to catch her breath. She had been talking very fast, her voice high and hurried. Matthew's mind was moving fast too. He was imagining him and Polly campaigning, crusading together. He saw himself cradling wildlife – something small and fluffy without sharp claws – which he had saved from the maw of crushing diggers, or perhaps receiving gifts from grateful local children whom he had rescued from inhuman working conditions… And then, kissing. Lots of kissing…

'I said: did you sign up? Did you like our page, start following us?'

She was looking at him, her arms crossed, frowning a little.

Looking up, he was slightly surprised to have his reverie about Polly halted by the actual Polly talking to him.

'Yeah, um, yes.' He coughed. 'I did. Of course! I…' He hesitated.

She stared at him, waiting for him to finish. Suddenly there was a loud bang on the drums. They both looked over and Matthew saw Lee glaring at him, scowl unconcealed, his hand making a very visible fist.

Following Matthew's eye line, Polly laughed.

'Ignore him! He's like my brother!' Her eyes still fixed on Lee for a moment, she put her hand on Matthew's shoulder and then, looking directly back at him, she said, 'Are you really interested in this? Really? Because if you aren't then it's probably best if you go. This is, like, my whole life, you know – it's *all* I do. It's all I *want* to do.'

It was the heat in her voice that did it. That was what he wanted: to feel like that about something. To know so clearly what he wanted and needed to do. After weeks of stumbling about on his own, unsure of how or even where to start, this was what he hungered for. He felt his stomach go watery again but this time it wasn't fear or desire, but envy. He envied her her passion. This is it, he thought. Perhaps this is where mine lies too? With her? Doing this?

He glanced back at the posters and then back at the shoppers, oblivious and hunched over and pushing their grey metal trolleys. He remembered the favelas and the trip to the river. He remembered seeing kids who had grown up knowing only natural food being lured on to a boat where they were giving away handful after handful of candy, bottles of pop, shiny silver packets of biscuits. He remembered the grim, scentless trip to the supermarket upon his return.

A small family of three walked by. Trolley stacked high with boxes of soft drinks, crisps and biscuits. The mother looked away but, as they passed, the father scowled and, glancing at the can of energy drink in his hand, he crushed it and then threw it at the table. 'If you want to make a difference, recycle this!' he yelled, laughing at his own joke.

Polly winced and then looked up at Matthew. *This is what we're up against*, her eyes said. *People like that*.

'Yes,' he said, looking at her, his own pupils dilated, his nostrils flared with desire: the desire to make a difference. 'I want to help. I want to get involved.'

'With me? Or with this?' she asked, eyes serious, mouth slightly turned up in a teasing smile.

'Both,' he returned, his voice deep with need.

'Good,' she said, moving back, her eyes flicking away from Matthew's face for a moment and back towards Lee. 'Great! See you back at the Bedford later then? About eight? We can talk some more then...'

And, with that, the drums began again, in time now and harder, more insistent.

Like a conductor, Polly waved her arms and the chanting began anew.

Matthew watched her for a moment and then, stepping to the beat, he walked home.

Later, the sleet had stopped and the sky had cleared. It was even colder but the air was crisp. Looking up, Matthew saw the night sky dotted with stars. It was good to be going out and he had been relieved when the friends he had been planning to meet tonight had agreed to change their plans and meet him at the Bedford. Checking his phone again, he saw a message from his mum and made a mental note to call her that week. He knew he should go home and visit his parents soon but he also knew he couldn't face another long weekend of watching his dad drink and his mum cluck round pretending not to notice his dad drink. He had got through a twelve-pack of cider on the Sunday that Matthew was there in late November and it had not been pretty watching the old man go from cheery to sour in the space of six hours. Resolving to just have a couple of pints tonight, Matthew patted his pocket to make sure his wallet was there and then checked his phone again. Looked like both the guys were coming along now. Maybe three pints, then, he said to himself as he walked down the long road, past the parade of pizza places and convenience stores and into the pub.

Iain and Paul were already there when Matthew arrived. He walked in and, giving them a wave, went to the bar and ordered a pint. As he stood there, waiting, he decided not to tell his friends about Polly, not to admit to how excited he felt. He couldn't quite face the interrogation – was worried that, if he talked about it, the feeling would evaporate.

Sitting down, Matthew sipped his pint and then sat back.

'Hey,' said Iain, after he had downed his own half. 'You need to catch up! I never get to come out: I'm going to get another… Want one?'

Matthew sipped again and shook his head.

'Ha! As if you're going to get away with that!'

And, with a wink, Iain went to the bar.

'How's it going?' asked Paul, leaning back into the leather armchair.

'Good…just getting back into it after the break. Nothing much has changed. You?'

'Yeah, pretty good. Planning the wedding is keeping Ellie busy. And I'm working even longer hours to pay for it as well as to avoid looking at sodding Pinterest boards…' Paul grinned. 'You're probably off again soon, aren't you? Half-term next, isn't it?'

What was it, thought Matthew, about those in the private sector and school holidays? They never seemed to hear or remember about the long days, the constant marking and assessments.

'Yeah, it's only a week, though, and I have work to do the whole time. Exams this term, and next, so it's busy. Lots of long days.'

'Mmm,' replied Paul, looking over for Iain who was coming back with the beers.

Without the holiday or Polly to talk about, Matthew wasn't sure what to say next. He fiddled with the slightly soggy beer mat as Iain began to talk about the cycling competition he had been at last weekend. Putting down the beer mat, and glancing at his phone again, he tried to tune in to what Iain was saying.

'I was in the faster group and I got a new PB.'

'You beat your PB again?' asked Paul.

'Yeah. Still celebrating now!' he laughed, tilting his pint glass.

'That's great,' replied Paul. 'Wish I could join you! Sounds great.'

'Well, it's the tri next. You should do it with me!'

'Ah, Ellie'd never let me get out to train! I'm only allowed out on Saturdays 'cos she wants to see the girls. I'm under the thumb already!'

'Yeah, but we know you love it! Anyway, I fit the training in at work. And Lauren is fine with it … Mostly!'

'There is no way Ellie'd let me cycle!'

Matthew couldn't help but recall all the other Saturday nights he had been sat here, in the same seats, listening to the same conversation. Paul and Ellie. Iain and his cycling. Did nothing change? Did no one else do anything?

Weddings. Sport. Weekends spent making plans to commit. Weekends spent avoiding family commitments. As Iain chatted on about spending all day away from the family he had recently started and Paul moaned on about wedding plans, Matthew wondered why they complained so much about choices they had so willingly made. He remembered Iain's face the night before he proposed to Lauren. He could not have been more nervous. Or more excited. And Paul was the same: both had got what they'd said they wanted, and yet all they seemed to do now was complain.

Matthew felt conflicted because part of him wanted what they had too. He didn't think that he wanted to get married, remained unsure of that as an idea for many reasons, but he did very much want to have a special person in his life to share his experiences and passions with.

One of the reasons he was reluctant to talk about Brazil was that, so many times during that trip, before he had met Andrea, he had just felt lonely. He had wished that there were someone with him to share the experience with. Retelling it afterwards just wasn't the same as sharing the moment. He was kind of hoping that Polly might become that person.

He fidgeted a little on the dark wooden chair, feeling restless. Where was she?

A gust of cold air blew into the bar as the double doors swung open and, as the clamour of excited voices came in along with the chill, Matthew turned round to look. It wasn't them. He glanced at his phone. Again. 8.30. He finished his pint and began to drink the one that Iain had bought him.

Another hour passed. Every time the door opened, he glanced round.

'What's up with you tonight?' Iain demanded, eyes narrowing as he looked at Matthew. 'Expecting someone?'

'No, no…' Matthew lied.

Making an effort to ignore the door, he concentrated on talking to his friends.

The door opened again and this time he knew it was them. He could tell from the clamour and energy as they fell through the door and into the pub, laughing and chatting: alive. Shifting in his chair, he felt nervous but also, awkwardly, a little too excited. Trying to hide the fact that he could feel himself stiffening up, he looked away from the door, taking a sip from his lager. The speed at which he did this led him to swallow the yellow, fizzy liquid too hard and began to choke a little.

Coughing, he put his hand over his mouth and tried not to look up as Iain and Paul laughed. His face burned red. But at least he wasn't getting hard any more!

He knew she was looking at him, could sense it even over the noise that Iain was making, laughing and snorting at his friend's discomfort. It was as if Iain had never seen anything funnier than this in his life before and, scowling at him, Matthew pushed the last of the pint away and said, 'I'm going to the bar.'

Wiping his mouth again to make sure he wasn't still covered in beer, Matthew got up off his chair. Even though they had spoken earlier, he still felt a fizz of nervousness as he walked up and over to the bar. Running his hand through his hair, he smiled as he saw the plaited hair from the back and he glanced down to take her in now that she was out of the shapeless black overcoat that she had been wearing outside the store. Her clothes were still dark and loose but he could see her slim frame beneath them. His imagination filled in the other details. She turned and gave him a small smile before turning back to the bar. His dick stirred again and he tried to dismiss the shifting images in his mind. He did an almost convincing job of looking interested in the bar menu while he waited for the sensation to pass.

As he did so, he felt another set of eyes on him. Lee. His face was crumpled with a scowl, his eyes narrow and watching as Matthew approached the bar. As he got closer, the lad shifted himself closer to Polly, his body angled defensively towards her.

Matthew stood at the bar, pretending to focus on the ales on offer as he listened to the conversation going on next to him. Despite the pub being pretty empty, the group were all animatedly chatting by the bar, clearly too excited to sit down.

'So, what's next, Polly? What's next?' Lee was staring at Polly.

'A drink!' she replied, smiling; turning to the bar, she failed to look at Matthew, who was standing only a few feet away and looked straight at the landlord.

'What can I get for you?' Frank said, eyes shining as they scanned over the crowd, doing a mental average spend-per-head calculation.

'A glass of tap water please.'

With the mere action of pressing the button for water on the nozzle, Frank managed to convey his utter contempt for this particular request. Matthew heard someone else order a soft drink and smiled to himself. The group were filling the bar but not exactly filling the till.

He swallowed, took a quick breath and, knowing that he could no longer convincingly act as if he was not standing there expressly to see her, he turned to look at Polly and said, 'Hey. It's good to see you again. Can I buy you a drink?'

'If you can tell me what was on the leaflet you can buy me a drink. I meant what I said,' she continued, 'about you needing to be serious.'

Matthew had prepared for this.

'*If you only knew,*' he quoted, '*that for every swig you take out of one of those tempting ice-cold plastic bottles, and for every bite you take out of yet another chocolate bar, rivers have been polluted, children enslaved and forests destroyed.*

'*If you only knew that men, women and children lose their lives just to make those treats. Treats you know you don't need. Treats that are slowly killing you as well as the planet, through overstuffed landfill and a raped environment… If you only knew…then maybe you too would SNAP OUT OF IT!*'

Her eyes widened a little in surprise but then she smiled. Matthew smiled back. Then she looked at Frank and said, 'Do you have any organic wine?'

Frank looked at her with the same expression of weariness that he had been wearing since this lot had come in and started ordering tap water. Then, he too surprised Matthew by saying, 'Yes, as a matter of fact, I do. Red or white?'

'A large glass of the red, please.' She glanced a little defiantly back at Matthew.

'Sure, make it two. I'll try some too.'

'Whatever you say, big shot.' Frank smiled and rang the cost into the till. Matthew hoped that the sum meant both glasses together, but the wine really was £7 a glass. As Frank lined up the glasses, he tossed a bag of peanuts Matthew's way. 'On the house, son,' he said, not even bothering to hide the smirk that had cracked on his face.

The group were excitedly bunched together around Polly. She was clearly one of the leaders of the group. Matthew felt oddly proud.

Tilting her glass to him she said, 'Thank you for this. Come over and join in.'

Matthew took the glass and glanced over at his friends. Iain was looking over at him, his eyebrows raised, Matthew raised the glass in salute and Iain returned the gesture. His eyes flicked across to Polly and, with a smile, he turned back to Paul.

Matthew listened to the group talking. Just being here, standing with them, made him feel good.

'That was so great, Polly! And the way you stood up to that security guard,' sighed Lee, staring at her. 'Wow.'

She took a sip of her wine and shrugged.

'What happened?' Matthew asked, curious.

'Well, just after you left we got asked to move along. But obviously we didn't want to, so I said no and then it all kicked off.'

'You were amazing!' Lee repeated.

'Just doing what's necessary,' she said, shrugging again. 'No one ever said it was going to be easy. Can't wait to do it all again tomorrow!'

Matthew felt his dick stir again. God, he thought, what was it about the idea of action? About doing something? He sipped some more wine. It was sour enough to distract him.

As they all talked, Matthew learned that the demonstrations were the beginning of a more active strategy for the group. He made a mental note of where they were going to be tomorrow and continued to listen. And yet the details of the things they were discussing were terrifying: he had never thought about it before, but he was hearing about the massive environmental impact of sugar production and was astounded.

They were all very enthusiastic and optimistic, though. They seemed to see it as a challenge but a very achievable one. That was refreshing. Which was more, he thought, as he took another tentative sip, than could be said for the organic wine.

'I'll be there again tomorrow,' he said.

'Really?' she asked, sounding pleased.

'Really?' echoed Lee, sounding annoyed.

'I'd like to help…' He hesitated. 'If I had your number…'

Polly's face flushed a little and Matthew's stomach squeezed into a knot, his own face going a little red. That was what he wanted: that reaction. The automatic reaction that said yes even before the word had been spoken.

Unlocking the screen and opening up Contacts, he passed her his phone.

She flushed again and, trying to hide a grin and not quite managing it, she tapped in her number. Passing him the phone back, she glanced up at him, brown eyes shining with the smile that was only half revealed on her lips, and said, 'See you tomorrow, then?'

'Yes,' he said. 'Yes, you will. And maybe,' he added, 'I can take you out for dinner afterwards?'

She looked down, head nodding. Matthew could feel Lee's eyes boring into him. He was fairly sure that if the younger boy's wishes would come true he, Matthew, would have exploded on the spot.

'Great! I'd better go back...' he said, nodding towards Iain and Paul. And, walking away, he felt both excited and nervous.

'Been making friends over there?' asked Paul, over his pint glass.

Matthew shrugged. 'I saw them earlier,' he said, putting the wine glass down. 'At a demo. It was interesting actually...all about sugar and Big Food...'

'Yeah,' said Iain, pulling a face. 'Green is the new black, eh?'

'They're making a difference,' Matthew said, frowning a little.

'They're making the place look untidy,' said Iain. 'And what *is* that smell?' he added, wrinkling his nose.

'Damp hessian!' Paul grinned back.

Matthew smiled involuntarily. There *was* a peculiar sour smell. Maybe it's the wine? he wondered, taking another tentative sip.

Not that it mattered any more. Sitting here listening to Paul and Iain, he felt immune. He had her number; he was seeing her again tomorrow. He would, he had decided, spend the morning doing some research. Finally, he felt, it was all about to start.

Naomi

It had been a long week but a good one. Every time work or home felt overwhelming, Naomi just thought about Mike and how he had told her how much he wanted her. When she felt good, those words served to enhance her mood, like the cherry on a cake, and when she felt bad they were a sweetness she could add to her day. His messages were like a treat: a reward for her hard work and good behaviour in her day-to-day life. Though that life was increasingly fading into the background, something she did on auto-pilot while her mind was elsewhere.

With the wire basket over her arm, Naomi walked round the convenience store. The choices were limited here but she hadn't made it to the supermarket, she had run out of apples and milk and, feeling even less like cooking than she felt like running errands, she was looking to get something quick to eat as well as some sweets for James. Scott had mentioned he had had tests at school. She hadn't remembered, this morning, and the sweets were her way of apologising.

Selecting a bag of apples, she then walked round to the fridges and grabbed some skimmed milk and then went to choose some ready meals. There was nothing nicer than an evening ahead which involved no cooking, just the piercing of film lids.

Standing, shifting the basket on her arm, she scanned over the sweet selection, trying to decide what to buy for James. She glanced at the long queue that was building up at the checkout. With a sigh, she looked away. Why was it always so busy in here? Why was there only ever one person on the tills?

A voice interrupted her stream of thoughts.

'Naomi?'

There was a woman standing nearby – or at least it *used* to be a woman. All Naomi could see was fat. There was a softness and shininess to the person before her that made it seem as if a human shape had been cut from a slab of marshmallow and then propped up in the store like some grotesque 3-D advertisement.

'Naomi? It's Kerri. Kerri Wallace…'

Naomi's eyes remained opaque with confusion.

'David's mum,' the marshmallow added.

A synapse sparked. Less than a fraction of a second later, the social instincts kicked in and a smile appeared on Naomi's lips. Her eyes cleared, but the fractional delay before they echoed the smile on her mouth made the insincerity all too clear.

'Yes! Yes. Of course. Kerri. How lovely to see you!'

Naomi swung the basket up on to her arm, all of a sudden very aware of her own body, aware of how she must look to the other woman. The other's fatness was a powerful visual counterpoint to her own slim frame.

'And you.'

Kerri's smile was genuine but she continued to keep her distance.

Naomi looked at her: saw the hunched shoulders, the buttons of the cardigan straining over enormous breasts. It was the face that filled her attention though. Bloated and shiny, like an overfilled balloon, it looked as if it would pop at any moment.

'I hear about David all the time, of course, but you're OK? And the girls?'

'Good, thanks. Fine.'

'Good.'

There was a pause. Both women looked at each other. The physical distance between them echoed the emotional one. It had been years since she and Kerri had been close. Years, and yet, before the divorce, before Gary had left, they had been almost as inseparable as the boys were now.

Naomi had seen how much Kerri had struggled after having the twins and had helped as much as she was able to, but with James older, and secretly, painfully envious of the baby girls she had increasingly kept away. When the news broke that Gary was leaving Kerri, that they were getting divorced, Naomi, like most people, had assumed that the other woman had let things slide, had let her marriage go much as she had let herself go. There had been hushed conversations at the school gate. Not ones that Naomi was proud of participating in but the kind that were had day in, day out as people picked over the bloody remains of the misfortune in other people's lives as it lay squashed in the middle of the road.

'Well, of course,' she remembered saying, 'he's not blameless, but she never did pull herself together after the twins. There really is no excuse, is there?'

And behind the bitching, behind the sharp tones, there had been the mental promises to have sex that week or give the husband that long promised blow job because deep down they all feared it: feared that the same thing would happen to them. But, it was much easier to be cruel to others than honest with themselves.

That had been around the time that James was doing his eleven plus, and Naomi had had the push for promotion at her previous job. It had been a busy time. Even busier than usual. Naomi felt ashamed of how she had behaved, but it had been so long ago, and surely Kerri had had other friends, other people to rely on?

Naomi shifted the basket again, the thin metal digging into her arm. Glancing down, she looked in the other woman's basket. In that one glance, she took it all in: white bread, chips, crisps, cakes, packets of casserole and pre-prepared mashed potatoes. 'I suppose I'd better get in the queue!' she said, making an apologetic face.

'Yes, yes, of course! Nice to see you!' said Kerri.

'And you! We really must try and do coffee some time.'

'I'd like that. Next week?'

'I'll get in touch!'

'Oh, OK, sure…'

There was a pause.

'OK, then. Bye!' said Naomi, and, as she moved away, getting in line, the relief she felt was instant. Seeing the hunger in the other woman's face had made her uncomfortable. And, beginning to unload the groceries, she smiled as she thought again how much more time she would have this evening. I might, she thought, treat myself to a read-through of all the messages. Right from the very start. The idea of such an indulgence made her tingly with delight. She could hardly wait.

Later, after unloading the bags and pouring a glass of wine, Naomi put the ready meals in the oven. Talking to James, who was seated in his usual place at the kitchen table surrounded by towers of exercise books, she said, 'And I really just didn't recognise her. She was just so…big…well, you know they say you don't notice when you see people all the time but, honestly, I felt so embarrassed for her. She just looked HUGE. Really enormous…'

'Mum!' James protested, an edge of anguish in his voice.

'Well, sorry, but it's the truth…how do people let that happen? I have never understood it. How? They must just buy some bigger clothes and then, what, they just keep buying bigger and bigger clothes and don't question it? Don't they think: *maybe I should eat less*? I'm surprised you never said anything…'

James rolled his eyes and put his head down.

'And, really, how hard is it to cut back? How hard is it to change habits? Bad habits?'

Naomi went over to the table and picked up the fruit bowl. Taking out the uneaten grapes and the softening pears and apples, she put them in the bin, and then tipped the fresh bag of apples into the bowl. James didn't even look up. Naomi carried on in the kitchen, getting plates out to put the processed meals on to. And then, an hour later, sitting at the computer, she began to read the messages, feasting her eyes on Mike's words.

David

It was early Friday evening. Coming back down the stairs after half an hour in the bathroom, David felt lighter. The journey home had been flushed away with the shit. The shitty comments, the shitty feelings. He had pressed the handle over and over until every trace of them was gone.

So hot and sweaty afterwards that he had needed to strip off and wash his torso and face, David now walked down the stairs in a fresh black T-shirt, his face still tingling from both the effort and the cold of the water against his hot, swollen pores. He sat down on the sofa, the softness enveloping him like a hug. He resisted the urge to hug it back. No one could hold him like this sofa could. It seemed to absorb all the insults, all the misery of the week, soak them up and turn their sourness into softness. He turned the television on. The girls were upstairs playing. Kerri came in. She walked to the kitchen with the heavy bags of shopping and David heard the thud as they were dumped on the floor. Then, without a word, she came back in and, one by one, drew all the curtains. The room was blissfully dim now, crepuscular and warm, a burrow.

'Hey,' she said. 'How was school?'

'Terrible.'

'Oh?' Her face creased with concern. 'Really?'

'Yes, really. How was work?'

'Terrible…' she said, smiling weakly. 'But it's Friday now. And I'm not going to give anyone another thought until Monday morning. I stocked us up and I think we should just stay warm, stay comfy and stay here…'

They shared a smile. David sank deep down into the sofa's embrace and Kerri did the same.

Naomi

She had bought and prepared all that convenience food but, inconveniently, she hadn't been hungry. Well, not for food. Everyone's eyes had been on the television, so how little she ate had gone unnoticed. And, after clearing away, she had struggled to stay in the living room and away from the computer. Sitting in the bathroom now, the text of their recent exchanges was scrolling before her eyes. Perched on the toilet, she was staring up at the ceiling. She could feel her body humming, pulsing with blood and heat and need. Every nerve-ending felt separate and alive. It burned. She touched herself. It felt so hot. Hot with need.

Even during the day she could feel the heat, and sometimes, when her mind wandered back to their exchanges, she would panic, fearful that she was literally lit up down below like a beacon. The heat felt inextinguishable: deep and endless. She imagined his lips, hot and hard. She imagined him tilting her head and pressing his stubbly chin into hers. She imagined his hand on the back of her neck, hard and callused, massaging the sweet, soft spots around the curve of her throat.

But she struggled to imagine someone else actually seeing her naked. She shuddered when she thought about someone else touching her breasts or stomach. Looking at her stomach now, she could see the scars of carrying and delivering James, scars and ripples that Scott understood the narrative of but which another man would surely only see as imperfections, as ugly reminders of her status as a mother: as an old, used woman. A wave of anxiety passed through her, and she pulled her top back down over her torso.

All she felt was need: need for his mouth, his dick. It seemed to flood her mind: to be the only thing that would fill the emptiness inside her. The force of her desire for him was even stronger than her fear and anxiety about her ageing body. This was incredible to her.

And every night was like this now. She dreaded going to bed. Dreaded the beginning of the thoughts. She knew she should stop but they filled her mind; the words were all she could see. In these hours she veered wildly between wishing she could just do something and have it done, to thinking that there was no way in hell she could risk her marriage for that.

Mostly it was Carla's face that stopped her cold. Imagining the look of hurt on that poor girl's face if she ever saw the messages, if she ever knew what Naomi had written, suggested, thought about. Because, reading over and over the messages, as she was doing now, there was no escaping what was being said. There was no room to deny that they had both said things that they really shouldn't have.

The words that they had shared as they tapped their way through this strange cyber-affair scrolled through her mind.

Crushing.

Pressing.

Hard.

Lips.

Tongue.

Occasionally she panicked that she was no good at it – that Mike's desire for her to be dirty, to be rude, was not matched by her PG-rated comments and phrases. *What am I doing now?* he would ask. And she would freeze, not knowing what to say. Did you start by talking about his penis? Did you even use the word *penis*? Cock, was it? Or dick? She had no idea.

Tell me.

He would be insistent and then she would feel angry at him for making her do this, for turning what they had into some sort of porn. She preferred it, she thought sometimes, when the flirting was more subtle, when there were hints and suggestions, oblique comments and sly winks rather than this directness…but they couldn't go back to that now, or it felt as though they couldn't. It seemed that now it had started it was impossible to stop it, to take it back to how it had been before. She knew now why it must be so hard for teenagers; it was so easy to get carried away. The medium lent itself to a boldness that just wasn't possible in real life. It speeded things up, fast-forwarded you from a *Hey* to *My dick is so hard* within moments. Though, in reality, as she realised from

107

scrolling back, it was amazing it had taken this long. They had been messaging privately for weeks now.

Lying there, later that night, listening to Scott breathing, she knew she had to stop. Had to stop. Must stop. She screwed her eyes tight against the constant scrolling of the messages that began whenever she closed her eyes. Damn those words. Every one of them was etched into her mind as if it had been carved in stone. So much for the ephemeral nature of the internet, she thought. So much for a picture speaks a thousand words. No. It was the words. The combination of simple black letters on the screen had created this. They felt good but they also hurt, hurt more than anything.

Unthinkingly, she had got so swept up in the words, in his wanting, that she had said and done things that already she could not even begin to justify to the jury in her mind.

So far, she thought, desperately, so far it *could* be explained away. The string of words could be deleted, erased. Yes, she decided, as she lay there, hands pinned to her sides, I will do that. I will delete them. Tomorrow. Tomorrow I will delete them and tomorrow it stops. Tomorrow I'll be good.

And she could manage it for a day or two at a time, could drag her focus back to where she was, could stop reading and thinking, could ignore the gnawing sensation in her belly; but then, after a few days of being restrained, she would be back: back and indulging herself. Stuffing herself full of him: his words and his wanting.

So much of her life was controlled. It had to be, otherwise it just didn't work. The routine of work and home life had been a comfort for a long time but now it felt restrictive, suffocating. The routine of suppertime, of stir-fry Tuesdays and weekend takeaways. The 9.30pm decaffeinated tea. There was the exercise for forty minutes three times a week; there was the regulation six pages of the book club book every night – God, when was the next book club meeting? She had totally forgotten about that…

When James had been small she had had to control the love she gave him. It had been a defence mechanism then, for she had feared that the overwhelming love she had for her little boy, her only child, would subsume her. So, he had gone to nursery three times a week, ostensibly so that she could go to the gym or run errands but in reality because it was what everyone else was doing and she had felt weird, like the odd one out, for wanting to keep him at home, for wanting to be with him. Feeling as if she was meant to, she had apportioned the time she gave him, trying so hard to avoid him becoming a spoilt only child (as Scott had been when they met). Containing her love in time-managed slots, she had allowed herself to fuss him in between, parcelling up the affection and doling it out the way, she now realised, that her parents had sombrely spread out her birthday and Christmas gifts over seemingly endless weeks.

But, now, she almost felt ready to let go. To let herself be swept along. Just for once. Just this one time to do something for her, just for her. To have something that would be hers and hers alone.

Another night, another hour spent staring at the ceiling, willing sleep to take the thinking away.

Lying very still, she listened, to be completely sure that Scott was asleep before she got up. Once she was certain, she crept out of bed and went into the study. Once the PC was up and running, she logged on and read the messages again.

It was midnight and she was amazed at how many other people were still online. What were they all doing? She had no idea.

Since the other night she had thought about Googling it, Googling *online affair*, *messaging sex* or whatever it was that they had done, but she couldn't. If she looked at it too closely, questioned it or examined it, it might vanish.

She was pretending to not notice he was there.

Should she message him? Surely he should message her, after what had been said? Surely that was only polite?

Then she stifled a laugh. As if the rules of etiquette her mother had taught her were remotely applicable here.

She clicked on the dialog box and began to type.

Hey.

Hey there. You're up late...

I can't sleep.

Me neither.

She paused. Did she dare ask why? No. Did she dare mention the other day? Yes.

Thinking about the other night is keeping me awake.

Yes, that was fun.

Fun? she thought, slightly annoyed. Fun?

Yes, she typed, *yes it was.*

I guess now is not a good time.

No.

Just thinking about you makes me hard.

Oh, God, she thought.

Really?

Yes, really. I think about you dancing, swaying those hips and singing and how all I wanted to do when I was watching you was fuck you.

Staring at the screen, she crossed her legs and typed back, *I have no idea what I am doing here.*

Probably best not to overthink it.

I think you're probably right...

Remembering the other day is making me hard again. Want to make me come?

She hesitated. An image of Scott walking in filled her mind. She was so scared of being caught. But she was even more scared of not giving Mike what he wanted.

Skin tingling, she had no idea what to say. She just had to go for it, she supposed. She began to type, cringing slightly.

Yes. How do I start… I can't believe I have never really done this before…

Tell me what you're doing to me with your mouth. I want to come in your mouth.

It was the word *want* that did it. His wanting her seemed to shift something inside her, seemed to tap into something she hadn't been aware of for a long time. A hunger for something new. It was the directness of it. She couldn't remember the last time someone had spoken to her so forcefully of their needs, their desires. When was the last time she had acknowledged her own? As her fingers moved, her conscious brain tuned out; she wasn't even aware of what she was typing. The words flowed straight from her primal brain through her fingers and on to the screen.

I'm kneeling in front of you and putting your hard dick in my mouth.

That feels good.

My mouth is so wet. I'm running my tongue around the tip of your dick.

Reading back over what she had written, she shuddered. It was a mistake to do that, to think about what she was doing: it made her feel too self-conscious. She carried on.

I'm taking you deep into my warm, wet mouth.

God, that's good – put your hand round my balls.

I'm cupping your balls and squeezing them while I suck you, my tongue running up and down your dick.

Oh, fuck.

I can feel you getting harder.

Where is your other hand? Put it round my dick.

Yes, I'm massaging your dick with my hand, sucking, squeezing…

She could feel her breath quickening. It was just words but it felt so good. She felt so turned on, sexy. Wanted.

I'm going to cum in your mouth.

Yes, come in my mouth, I want to swallow you down.

This was something she never did. She never let Scott do that and yet here she was. The words allowed her. Here she was free to do anything.

Oh, fuck.

Yes, she typed, *come, come in my mouth, I want to taste you – you taste so good.*

There was a pause. She sat at the computer, breathless and flushed, staring wide-eyed at the screen as she tried to imagine where he was, what he looked like.

Wow. That was great.

Thank you.

No. Thank YOU.

She felt strangely bereft. Sitting alone in this cold room, having just done that, she felt a sudden need for a hug, a kiss, a reassuring word. *I want to kiss you,* she typed.

I want to kiss you as well.

There was a seemingly endless pause.

I want to see you, he said.

She froze. God. No.

I don't know...

Well, we'll see...

Yes. I better go.

OK. Goodbye.

xxx

xxx

Reading over the messages again and again, her eyes began to blur and her bare feet went numb with the cold. Logging off, she crept back into bed. Her skin cold, her heart hot and racing, she lay, listening to Scott's breathing, trying not to cry.

David

For something to do, David checked the weather. It had been a glorious winter weekend, apparently, all sunshine and blue skies and cool crispness. David looked up from the screen and around the room: it was dark, warm and stuffy. Kerri had come in Friday night and shut the curtains. They had not been opened since.

There had been an almost constant stream of food in the last twenty-four hours. He hadn't questioned it, just enjoyed it. Any weekend where she fed them like this meant that he wasn't taking from his own stash, and that was a good thing.

If Friday night was defined by takeaway, Saturday was defined by snacks. Kerri always said she deserved a night off cooking and so Saturday dinner was always snacks: crisps, peanuts... oven chips in white bread was about as close as she got to preparing hot food. Kerri had been quiet and subdued and David had felt the same. Adjusting to being back at school, adjusting to the fact that it was a new year but with the same old shit to deal with (SSDD – same shit, different day, as he and James often said) just felt exhausting.

Sitting felt good, though. Eating felt good. Sitting and eating felt doubly so. And it seemed that Kerri felt the same. The world needed to be shut out. With the curtains closed, the TV on and the kitchen full of food, they could choose to interact with the rest of the world or they could choose not to and, given how that world had treated them this week, it seemed that what they were doing was the only sane thing.

Cocooned, fed and warm, David felt safe – safe, and, for the first time in a few weeks, happy.

Chapter Five

Matthew

With only fifteen minutes until the staff meeting, all the teaching staff were beginning to gather in the main staff room. As usual, there was a clear divide between the younger and older members. The walls of the stale-smelling room were a faded beige, kept plain under orders from Barraclough despite the fact that he never came in here himself. There was a fire door to the left, and one large window which looked out on to the playing field at the back of the school. It was a common joke to sit there eating biscuits and cake (it was always someone's birthday) and talk about getting enough exercise just watching the kids run around.

The other thing that marked out the staff over thirty-five was that most of them were carrying the extra ten or twenty pounds that were almost inevitable after fifteen years of sedentary work and staff-room biscuits.

Matthew and Jim – who taught geography, a subject as under-appreciated at the Rivenoak Academy as science and languages – pushed through the door and walked into the room. Most of the staff were there already, and there was a low hum as everyone talked about what the morning's meeting was likely to cover. 'We need to make sure we commandeer the biscuits,' Jim whispered to Matthew as they walked in. He passed Matthew his mug of coffee and then, after a few strides and a feint to the left, Jim grabbed the box of chocolate fingers.

Matthew smiled at Solange. She was sitting in one of the brown leather chairs by the large window, her slim legs neatly curled up beneath her and her back straight as she tapped the soft packet of cigarettes on her knee. Refusing to smoke the cigarettes they sold here, she always stocked up on her soft packs of Davidoffs when she went home to see her family in Normandy.

'Sol!' Jim smiled, waggling the box of biscuits at her. He sat on the arm of the chair and ripped the end of the box before tugging out the plastic tray. Rattling it and smiling, he said, 'Think we'll need these to get through the next hour.'

He pulled out a few biscuits before passing the box to Matthew in return for his coffee mug.

'I love that there's a serving size on these boxes,' Matthew said, turning the box over to look at the back. 'Who even looks at stuff like this on here?'

'I thought the *tray* was a portion!' said Jim, reaching over to grab another couple.

'Polly says there's something in these that makes them addictive,' said Matthew, frowning at the ingredients list on the purple box.

Solange and Jim exchanged glances.

'Polly says...' Jim mimicked, smirking.

Sol smiled coolly and continued to tap her cigarette packet on her knee. 'I'm going outside for one more moment before we start...'

Both men watched as she walked away. Every male and almost every female head turned to watch her as she left the room.

'Aw, man, she is so hot,' whispered Jim. He looked at Matthew with a wicked gleam in his eye. 'And you really haven't?' he asked, voice lower now. 'Seriously? She's well into you, you know.'

Matthew flushed and quickly glanced around to make sure no one had heard. 'Ssh!' he hissed. 'She's my friend! Anyway, I'm seeing Polly, aren't I? It's getting pretty serious, actually…we've been texting every day since last weekend and we even chatted on the phone last night. For over an hour.'

Two of the teaching assistants came over and Matthew excused himself. He wanted to go to the loo and check his messages before the meeting.

Staring at his phone in the toilets, he frowned. Still no reply from Polly about meeting up later.

Coming out, he saw that Solange was still outside. Putting his phone in his pocket, he went to join her.

'Hey. How are you?' she asked. 'I miss you now that you are not smoking.'

'Yeah,' said Matthew, trying to pretend that he didn't want a cigarette.

'I imagine that your trip to Brazil feels like a lifetime ago by now.'

'Yes,' he said, sighing, and wishing she wouldn't keep mentioning it. 'It was amazing, it really was, but it just seems so long ago. It has kind of stopped seeming real, which is odd considering how intense it was, but…' He hesitated.

'But?' she prompted, blowing out blue-grey smoke in a thin wisp.

'Oh, I don't know. It feels strange, but it's just left me with…this itch. This urge to change things. And being here seems to be wrong right now. I feel as though I'm never going to make a difference while I'm here, and that's frustrating. Really frustrating. Polly has so many great ideas and I just want to be doing that. Having to spend time helping kids learn how to use a Bunsen burner – well, it's not as though I ever thought I would change the world, but I thought I might help change *something*…'

'Things change,' Solange said, looking at him closely. 'People change. Maybe it is time to do something else, or maybe you are just in the stage before a change. A – how do you say – plateau? Only you can know that...'

'I suppose I'm just fed up with how hard this is. It's just the same thing, month in, month out.'

'We have to believe it makes a difference, otherwise we could never do it,' she countered.

'I just don't know any more. I feel as though I've been playing on the losing side for far too long.' He hesitated, kicking at the tarmac with the toe of his shoe. 'At least Polly is *doing* something. It seems so much more real, more necessary. Whereas this – well...' He gestured hopelessly around the chilly grey courtyard.

'I still believe...' said Solange, dropping the cigarette to the floor and crushing its glowing ember with the sole of her shoe. 'I still believe it is worth doing. If you have stopped believing that – well, that is something you have to decide for yourself. Faith in this is such a personal thing.'

Matthew looked down. He felt slightly better. Maybe she was right. Maybe it was time for a change? And maybe meeting Polly was the start of that change? He felt a twist of excitement at the base of his stomach.

'I think you're right...'

Solange gave him a soft kiss on both cheeks and then, together, they walked back to the main school building and the staff meeting.

Matthew looked down and arranged his papers, pen and coffee mug in front of him. These morning meetings were always short but they were almost always very intense. Barraclough usually took advantage of the time pressures by delivering some bad news right at the end and then scarpering back to his office. The door to that was scrupulously guarded by a woman with a face and manner as inscrutable as Barraclough's management-speak-littered emails.

Solange had sat down to his left and Jim was across the long row of tables to the right, next to the youngest and prettiest of last year's PGCE intake. The new teachers were all looking tired now. That first year of full-time teaching was so intense. Matthew had not forgotten, would never forget, how hard it was. At least two had not made it: the ones who remained looked shell-shocked but were alive, just, and all of them, especially Rachel, had enough nous to be able to deal effectively with Jim.

Matthew looked down, avoiding smiling at Rachel as he had seen her looking at him in the past and then, turning to Solange, he noticed again the stale smell of her French cigarettes. For once, he realised he didn't want one. There had been times in the past where he had wanted to bury his face in Solange's hair, the urge for a cigarette had been that bad, but, since meeting Polly, he had been too preoccupied to worry about nicotine. So infectious was her enthusiasm for what she did that he rarely thought of anything else.

He glanced out of the window, chewing on his index finger, staring at the sky. Whereas before he would have seen the chemical trails lacing across the clear winter blue and thought of his next trip, now all he saw was pollution. The beauty of the tessellated white streak was deceptive given the hundreds of toxic chemicals he now knew that cloud contained.

Writing a note to remind himself to check how to further neutralise his carbon footprint, Matthew then heard the door bang open and shut: Barraclough.

'Morning!' the head boomed, taking his seat at the top of the table. The volume at which he operated, like the chem trail's beauty, masked his ineffectual management of the teaching staff. Because of the results, he was popular with parents, and the board, but what neither of those groups of people realised was the degree to which those results were being achieved by pushing the already thinly stretched teaching staff to its absolute limits.

Barraclough sat down, putting his paper cup containing mocha-laced milky coffee in front of him. The takeaway coffee was the beverage equivalent of an egg timer. Once Barraclough took his first sip the meeting started, and as soon as it was all gone it would be over. It was always a venti at the start of term and then, towards the end, when he had become really fed up with them all, he would bring in a tiny paper cup with a shot of espresso.

They all watched as he took his first sip.

'Right,' he began. 'The main item for this morning's *very* quick meeting is this: coursework. I just want to emphasise again, even though I am *sure* I don't need to, that the school is judged on its English and maths scores. And, so, this is where we need the focus to be in terms of the time our students spend on coursework and projects outside of school. While I know *all* of your subjects are important, I also know that *all of you* understand *me*.'

It was rarely as explicitly stated as this, but Barraclough prided himself on being utterly clear as to where his focus was. He wanted the parents to be happy, and for the parents to be happy the numbers needed to stay high. For the numbers to stay high, the focus had to be on the core subjects.

Solange didn't even bother to disguise her sigh. Her subject was even more marginalised than Matthew's, and he knew how frustrating she found it.

For now, though, at this moment, he was too preoccupied to get upset or angry like he usually did. Hearing that speech from Barraclough, he felt as though the decision he had been agonising over had just been made for him.

Barraclough continued on in the same vein, ignoring questions or merely answering them with another question, a technique, Matthew thought, that they must teach people before they became school heads.

Finally draining the last of his drink, Barraclough tossed the paper cup into the nearby waste paper bin, nodded at them all, then walked out of the room. It was 8.15. Time to go to the classroom. Simultaneously, all the teachers under thirty-five took out and checked their phones.

Polly was coming over later. Matthew grinned at the device in his hand. He loved his phone so much sometimes.

David

Having overslept, David had endured the bus, which had drained the energy he had gained from getting an extra hour in bed. Walking into the science classroom, he was grateful for the chance to get the heavy bag off his shoulder as he approached his seat. He had had a Reebok-branded bag when he had first come to the new school. He had loved the wide straps and the purple colour, but the shit he'd got for having a sports-branded bag meant that he had ended up telling Kerri that he'd lost it, asking her to replace it with an unbranded one. If he shut his eyes, he could still see it sticking out of the bin in which he had angrily stuffed it after a particularly aggressive round of taunting.

David sat down at his seat, grateful to be sitting down, grateful for the fact that, in form time and lessons at least, he was mostly safe from the bullying. The lab was big and bright and at the edge of the class he had more leg room so he could at least try and balance, though in truth he was still uncomfortable. He was always uncomfortable.

Shifting on the small plastic seat, he listened for his name as Mr Holmes called out the register. The silence in classrooms was always false, a repression of noise rather then the true absence of it. The air seemed to fizz and bubble with all the things not being said. Chairs squeaked, tables were tapped with pens, paper and books shuffled about.

'Right, then,' said Mr Holmes, perching, as he always did, on the end of the main lab table at the front of the science classroom. This was David's form group class too. He had been so pleased, when he had started school, to be in the science lab for form time. It was so much more fun than a normal classroom, with its Bunsen burners, stained glass jars and mysterious locked cupboards. The sunlight-faded poster of the Periodic Table as well as the model of the skull with all of its removable pieces, the tongue that slotted out, the ear that came off in your hand, the eye that could be broken down into its component parts – David found all of these hypnotising. Or rather, he used to. As he had got bigger and bigger these past two or three years, he had found it increasingly difficult to concentrate on anything.

Mr Holmes was talking. David was thinking about the chocolate and crisps in his bag, thinking about when he would be able to eat something next. His head throbbed slightly and, trying to swallow, he found that his mouth was dry. The breakfast Coke or two were always his favourite drinks of the day but his mouth was now parched, his system dehydrated. He closed his eyes, trying to concentrate.

'So, we talked last week about marketing. About how companies use advertising to sell you stuff that you don't really need. Who can remember what things are not allowed to be advertised to children and young adults?'

'Fags, sir.'

'Booze, sir.'

'Yes,' said Mr Holmes, neutrally. 'That's right: cigarettes, alcohol. These things are restricted in terms of advertising. What things *can* be marketed at young people?'

'Food and drink, sir?' said Laura, a brunette who had, from the day he walked in and introduced himself as their form teacher, been crazy in love with Mr H. She didn't even bother to hide it any more, writing his name on her notebooks and scratching his initials on to her pencil case. The affliction was such a common one in this year group that no one bothered to mention it.

'Thank you, Laura. Yes, food and drink,' Matthew continued, and, clicking on the laptop, he brought up the slides.

£2.1 BILLION spent by Coke on global advertising in 2013

£2 BILLION spent by Nestle/Cadburys on advertising

£3 BILLION on fast food advertising in the US as against £76 MILLION spent on healthy eating advertising

'To make that more meaningful,' said Matthew, 'three billion looks like this…' He wrote on the screen:

3,000,000,000

'And 76 million like this…'

76,000,000

'A billion is a thousand million. I know both numbers look big but the fast food spend is bigger than the healthy spend by almost four thousand per cent – so nearly forty times more…'

There were a few appreciative whistles. The numbers were so disproportionate that even a reception-age child would have got some sense of what they were up against.

'And who owns these businesses? Anyone care to tell me who used to own the people that make Philadelphia cheese and those bright orange plastic slices you get on your cheeseburgers?'

There were groans and mutters. No one looked at him; they were all still staring at the numbers on the screen.

'Anyone heard of Philip Morris? The people that brought you the Marlboro Man as well as emphysema and lung cancer?'

Nods and stares.

'Well, that's who *used* to own Kraft – the company that makes cheese that can't actually be called cheese and a pasta dish that contains carcinogens. I say *used to* because Philip Morris sold its stake and it is now owned by parent company Heinz. Basically, you could infer that processed food manufacturing is so toxic that even a *cigarette* company doesn't want to be involved with it.'

David stared at the screen. The information was interesting, but all this talk of cheeseburgers was making him hungry.

Glancing up at the clock, Mr Holmes cleared his throat and concluded, 'Hopefully that has given you some food for thought...'

A wave of groans at the bad pun rippled through the class. David smiled a little. Why did teachers always make such bad jokes?

The bell rang indicating the end of form time, and the room echoed with clatters and screeches as chairs were shifted back clumsily, scraping against the hard floor.

Over the noise, the teacher carried on, 'We will be covering this in more detail after half-term and in your science coursework! That's something to look forward to, isn't it?'

No one replied. Filing out, David glanced back at the screen and then, completely unconsciously, he patted the front pocket of his bag to make sure his snacks were still there.

Matthew

It was lunchtime and, if he could have done it without anyone noticing, Matthew would have put his hand over his nose and mouth. Even the worst parts of the favelas hadn't smelt as bad as the dining hall did today with its mixture of cheap meat, dank vegetables and sweaty, post-PE Year 8s. The smell was that of deep-fried hormones.

Taking a brown tray from the stack by the door, he walked down the short side of the large rectangular hall to the food service area.

'Settle down, girls,' he said to a couple of bickering Year 10s. Hair pulled back in high ponytails, their faces flushed when they saw him.

Looking down at the ground, one of them muttered, 'Yes, sir; sorry, sir.'

But the other girl looked directly at him, her blue-grey eyes flashing with a knowledge well beyond her years. 'Sorry, sir.' She seemed to eat the last word, swallowing it whole with her full, non-regulation-rouged lips. Matthew nodded, and looked as sternly as he could into the middle distance.

Aware of the girl staring at his profile, he looked around, hoping to spot something that could take him away from this part of the queue. Some of the more confident girls (or boys) would sometimes follow him after they had chosen their food and ask him vaguely science-related questions as a way of flirting with him. He tried to avoid these occasions whenever he could but it wasn't always possible: teenagers in a hormonal flush could be very persistent.

The girls continued to stare at him as he made his selection from what was on offer. It was rice and curry day but there was the usual bank of overdone jacket potatoes and limp-looking salad vegetables and he made as health-conscious a selection as he could from there. No butter, lots of greens and a dribble of the dressing. Placing the sticky ladle back into the industrial-sized vat of salad cream, he nodded at the girls and walked over to the far side of the hall. He had to eat and then stand at the back and supervise the rest of the lunch session.

He ate quickly. The food, free as part of his covering the lunch room today, was hardly worth savouring, and, sitting at the empty table, he felt, for the first time since he had got back, how alien it was to eat alone. Although he himself had been travelling alone, he had noticed that every meal in Brazil was taken with others, with either friends or family. There the food was sliced, chopped and prepared by some members of the group or family and then eaten, shared and enjoyed in a communal and generally lively environment. Every mouthful of even the simplest meal, sharpened as it was with lime, chilli and spice, and bursting with flavour and texture, could be savoured. The bland fried pap of the increasing numbers of Western fast food places there had held little allure to him when this sort of food was on offer but, to a lot of the younger kids, the brands themselves held more allure than the food. It was becoming something of a status symbol to eat the crap but expensive food.

He frowned as he saw that his plate was empty – had he even noticed any of the mouthfuls he had just taken? Must eat more slowly, he told himself, he held his hand over his mouth to hide and try to wave away the onion-scented burp that followed his wolfing down of the salad. And I must bring my own lunch in tomorrow.

Getting up and placing his tray on to the racks at the side of the room, he assumed his position on the far wall and, looking across the hall, gave Clive a nod. The aged history teacher was propped up against the other side of the room. He looked as if he might fall asleep at any moment.

Matthew tucked his hands behind his back and scanned across the room. He caught the girls from before still staring at him and then he noticed some of the boys from his form class coming to sit at the back of the hall. Two of them were heading for the far set of seats, away from the rest. It was David and James: the odd couple, as the staff called them.

Watching the bigger boy sit down, Matthew thought, God, he's got bigger again since the holidays. He was used to seeing some of the kids coming back from their summer or Christmas break half a foot taller than before, and the odd extra chin was usually to be seen around the staff room at Christmas as too many people brought in large boxes of chocolates and sweets to share, but David seemed to have got incredibly big since the autumn term.

Sadness rolled over Matthew like a sudden winter mist: cold, diffuse yet all-consuming. Seeing the boy trying to manoeuvre around the tables, seeing the fat move as he walked, made him shudder. He himself had never been that big but he had been big enough as a boy, and the discomfort of it was not forgotten, nor would it ever be. There was something about being constantly made aware of what your body could not do that made you feel helpless, and he could see that in David's face from here: the lack of control he was experiencing. His eyes downcast and guarded, he looked lost and lonely.

Matthew knew from the head of pastoral care that David's father had left home a few years ago. The boy had been quite overweight when he joined the school but they had all noticed that since then he had got much bigger. It was hard to know what to do. The school, like all of them these days, had a paper policy on obesity, but judging by the way the student body was growing (in literal terms) it was as ineffectual as any of these strategies. He thought about bringing it up at the next staff meeting but then, imagining Barraclough's face when the idea of making less money from school dinners was mooted, he gave the idea up. That was yet another battle he had lost too many times before.

Suddenly aware that he was biting his nail again, Matthew put his hand down. The finger-biting and cigarettes. He had found his own ways to lose weight in his teens, but it still had not been easy.

Looking round the hall, Matthew felt as though he was there for the first time. The noise, the chatter, the harsh, strip lights were invasive – like having wasps crawling under your skin. Pulling at his shirt collar, he suddenly felt hot, sweat prickling out of his pores and forming a film over his skin. Going over to the water table, his hand shaking slightly, he poured himself a tumbler of lukewarm water. Feeling instant relief as the water washed away the foul taste and cleared his mouth, he put the tumbler down and, with a glance up at the huge clock on the wall, went back to where he had been standing.

As he stood there, he watched the children, those he had spoken to mere hours ago about the damage caused by bad diet, by too many chocolates and sweets and crisps. Children who had copied notes down about the degree to which these things interfered with the body and the brain. Children who had asked questions and discussed the extent to which they were at the mercy of massive marketing machines and had to make conscious choices about their diet. He watched and saw them eating sweets and chocolate, watched them washing it all down with enormous bottles of fizzy drinks, and he felt utterly hopeless. Despairing, he stared down at the floor. He could not bear to look any longer.

The last period of the day was the worst, and not just for the pupils. Matthew felt tired too, and the fidgeting of the girls as well as the increased agitation amongst the boys was beginning to irritate him.

He bit his lip. The urge to snap, to let out his frustration, was overwhelming. He took a deep breath and instantly regretted it. The smell of Lynx was so pungent that he could almost feel it in the back of his throat. He sipped some water and, as the students came to the end of copying down what he had put on the board, he began to talk.

'The next stage is to try the experiment for ourselves...'

There was the usual ripple of excitement. He usually felt it himself, but not now. Whereas before his frustration had motivated him, had given him the edge and the drive to do more, to come up with better solutions, more interesting projects, to write and create his own material for the PSHE sessions which he thought were vastly underrated parts of the curriculum, now he just felt tired and fed up: burnt out. He wasn't sure if he could bear it any longer.

Moving round the class, he helped various students with the equipment, corrected basic mistakes and held his breath as he stood by one of them. The boy was sweating curry. It made Matthew's stomach churn.

Going back to the front of the classroom he brought up the summary of the experiment and then began to run through it.

'So, what we are seeing here is the evidence,' he began, 'the evidence of what we are trying to prove. Without the evidence there is no proof. And yet all evidence is questionable. We have to ask neutral questions of the evidence to ensure that it is telling us the facts and not just what we think we want to know.'

There was a lot of seat-shuffling: the awkward sound of thirty kids not quite getting it. And, whereas before Matthew would have persisted, would have carried on until that shuffling had changed in tone to the sound of thirty pennies dropping, today he just stopped.

'Write that up and then we can clear up. We can go over this another time.'

There was a clatter as the chairs shifted and the noise levels increased as they all began to clear away the equipment.

The bell rang.

As the students filed out, Matthew watched them, looking for some sign of enjoyment. But he hadn't enjoyed it, so why should they?

He felt a wave of remorse: the guilt a teacher felt when he hadn't given his all. It tasted even worse in his throat than the sour onions from the canteen.

I must focus, he thought. I must.

As soon as the last pupil had filed out, the realisation that the day was over hit him hard. His stomach rolled over. *Now* he felt excited.

David

If the in-between times were dangerous at school, so it was with in-between-meal times. The walk home from school was less than two miles and on his way David passed three corner shops, a petrol station as well as a parade made up of two pizza takeaways (where there was one there would always be another one), a Chinese takeaway and a fried chicken shop. A still-empty Blockbusters. Today he had stopped at the petrol station and, as he passed the parade, it was only the lack of cash that was preventing him from buying something else to eat.

Indoors, he slung his bag down in the narrow hallway and then, kicking off his shoes, he took the thin plastic bag up the stairs to his room.

Afterwards, lying back on his double-bed, arms flung out, brown eyes heavy-lidded with fatigue, he could barely remember what he had eaten. The room was dim; the flatscreen television on his wall was on but with the sound turned down low. Legs were stretched straight out in front of him, his belly spread out and heavy, gravity pulling it back and down so that it seemed to flow over his mid-section like lava. He had slipped into an uneasy sleep, his mouth slightly open, a thin trickle of chocolate-coloured spit dribbling out of the corner of his slack lips.

All around him there were torn and split wrappers: the comforting purple of a double Wispa, the reassuring deep brown of a Snickers, the warm yellow of a grab-bag of peanut M&Ms as well as half a dozen packets of crisps, all empty, their silvery insides slick with saliva: his tongue had searched out every last crumb.

His breathing was laboured. After every few breaths there was a hitch, a hiccupy pause that caused his body to jerk and his throat to constrict. His eyes twitched from side to side under the thin lids. The television hummed and flickered, images passing over the screen in rapid succession. There were special offers on frozen pizzas, special offers on frozen chips. It was Great Tastes of the States week at McDonald's and they were advertising that day's special of a pork patty coated in a barbecue sauce served on top of crisp lettuce in soft, semolina-dusted bun...

After forty minutes of restless sleep, David's eyes fluttered open and rested upon the television screen. Still half asleep, he stared blankly at the screen, barely aware of what he was seeing. Inside his brain, the associations were already made: the connections between certain foods and happiness were well-worn neural pathways.

Downstairs there was a click as the front door opened. David sat upright. That sound triggered a Pavlovian reaction. He began to put all the wrappers and packets back into the thin carrier bag. Stuffing the carrier bag to the bottom of his waste bin, he pressed a couple of sheets of rough paper from his homework on top. He would empty the bin later but this would do for now. Kerri would never dare come in his room but he didn't want Jess or Emily to see the mess.

He could hear the giggles and chatter as the girls came into the house. He liked to listen to them when they were happy. It was one of the best parts of his day: lying unseen, listening to the life and laughter from downstairs. Even Kerri sounded happy today. He didn't know how he felt about that. He didn't know how he felt full stop, and tended to avoid thinking about it too much. The food helped. The food always helped. That was what people didn't understand: that, for those few minutes when he was eating, he felt incredible. There was no better feeling in the whole world than that warm, liquid love as it filled not just his stomach but his heart.

And now, in the afterglow, before the shame kicked in, it all seemed tolerable. All of it. Gently rolling off the bed, he went downstairs, looking forward to joining in the laughter himself.

Matthew

Sitting on the battered, mustard-coloured sofa in his flat, their knees almost touching, Matthew and Polly drank wine and talked.

Polly was cradling her wine glass in both hands and taking tiny sips, like a child drinking from a beaker. Matthew had noticed that she always did this with drinks and he thought it was adorable. Her frame was petite and the gesture seemed to make her seem even smaller and prettier.

The sips were small but the talk was big. There was always something very big to talk about with Polly. It was one of the things he really liked about her, especially after a day of dealing with petty issues such as the correct font to use in a cross-school bulletin. He wished he could un-see that email from Barraclough but, no, he had wasted three minutes of his life reading it.

Three minutes and the last seven years, thought Matthew darkly.

But here, now, sitting on this faded sofa in this tiny flat in this, the arse-end of a crappy town in Kent, while Polly told tales and painted pictures of jungles and corporations, he felt part of something bigger. Here they could discuss global stories of pain and fighting and the punishment that needed to be visited upon those who did not care deeply enough for the planet or the living creatures and plants that allowed us to share it. Being here and listening to her, this room, and the day he had had, seemed to fall away and he felt transported to these locations, transported to the places she talked of with such energy. Today she had been organising an aggressive online campaign against the pollution caused by chemical run-off in the water around El Salvador, one of the subjects of the leaflet that she had handed him all those weeks ago.

'I think it's great,' he said, as she finished telling him all about the hours she had spent working on a database of contacts to send the mailings out to. 'I spent an hour cleaning the lab today because Kim was off ill again and then I spent another hour trying to prepare the Year 11s for their GCSEs, only to discover that they remember literally nothing from the last six months. I dread to think what they will be like when they get back from half-term. And then there's the Easter break, which is never really a break anyway, what with all the marking and revision prep...'

He sighed and stared into his wine glass. Polly squeezed his leg. Matthew looked at her and smiled apologetically. He felt a twinge of panic as he saw the frown on her face. He had managed to avoid complaining about school so far. Only a few weeks into their relationship, he had not been quite willing to open up fully, to let himself be completely honest about how hard school was, how draining and demoralising. It had been so much fun talking about other things: sometimes he felt as though all he did was think about school, talk about school. It had been a relief to be focusing on something else. Like when they were going to have sex for the first time.

'It's OK!' she said, squeezing his leg again. 'I don't know how you deal with teenagers all day! I know I couldn't. Teaching at a school seems like such a waste of time. You should be doing something else! You're so much better than that. Why did you even start?' she added. 'I'm sure you could have done anything!'

He looked down. The six-million-dollar question. Why had he gone into teaching? There was what you were meant to say: *It was my passion. To educate was my passion and I never wanted to do anything else.* And then there was the reality. Which, for him, was that his parents had both been teachers and, with an average science degree and a very average sense of self, it had just been easier to go back to college and do a PGCE than it had been to face the challenge of having to grow up.

Surely I should have known, he thought to himself, surely I should have known the limits of the impact I could make?

He had witnessed his parents going through it but, like people who had kids and then spent the whole time complaining about how hard it was, he felt embarrassed by, and yet also nostalgic for, his original optimism about the whole idea.

'You'd think you would realise how pointless it was,' Polly said, echoing his darkest thoughts. 'Surely you could see for yourself what a nightmare schools are?'

'I guess I thought it would be different somehow…'

'Nah,' she said dismissively. 'That's crazy! Of course it's awful. People are awful. You know, we used to have pictures and details about the dreadful injuries and illnesses that sugar cane workers suffer from, the lung problems caused by the burning of the cane, the kidney infections that are killing thousands in Central America, the injuries caused by the hacking…and no one cared. Not really. We had to change it to monkeys and starfish, to information about the hacked-down rainforest and the Barrier Reef being poisoned, to even *begin* to get people's attention. They care more about animals than other people, they care more about themselves than the planet. They want it all to change without them actually having to do anything differently. And kids are like unfinished people so they are even more awful. Especially teenagers, who think they are finished but really aren't. No one ever learnt anything useful at school. No one.'

She smiled at him then and he smiled back, even though it really wasn't that funny.

'It's not too late, though,' she said, looking at him. 'There is still time to make a difference.'

'Well, you're making a difference to me already,' he said, a little shyly.

It was the first time he had said anything like that to her. Moving closer, he kissed her and she responded keenly enough as she always did. He put his hand on her thigh and began to run his hand up her back. Kissing her harder, he tried to get

133

closer still and then she was pulling away, looking up at him and smiling.

She squeezed his leg again and then, after a quick and what seemed very final kiss on the lips, said, 'Maybe you could get more involved? You said something about the website...'

'Yes!' Matthew replied, sitting up and shifting uncomfortably. 'I learnt some coding in my teens and I'd love to use it. Maybe I could have a look at it and fix some things? After, you know, we could...maybe...' He shifted closer to her on the sofa.

'That would be great!' she said. 'Can we take a look now? What could you do?'

Disappointed that they weren't going to be going to bed but delighted that she seemed so keen to see his skills, he said, 'Yes, of course!'

He picked up his tablet and they began to work.

David

It was late in the evening now, the girls had gone to bed, and David had decided to stay downstairs tonight. It had been a good evening. Nothing much to do, just being together, sitting, watching TV. Being a family.

'I meant to say thanks, you know,' Kerri began, as they sat together in front of the TV. 'Thank you for helping out with the girls the other morning. I really appreciated it...'

He blushed a little. Being put on the spot made him feel self-conscious.

'S'all right...' He shrugged and picked up his phone again, glancing at the unchanged, blank screen – anything rather than look at her.

'You're great with them both,' she continued. 'You're a much better brother than I am a mother sometimes... Work takes up so much of my time; I worry we don't talk enough. I know you don't like to, but you can talk to me, you know…about school, about anything that's bothering you. Girl stuff, even…'

Her big watery eyes looked at him. Looking back at her briefly, he could see the concern in them, just a flash, then, just at that moment, just as he was about to open his mouth, she glanced at the TV.

Nah, he thought. She's gone.

And, sadly, she was.

He went back to texting James. The thought that he could share what she had just done crossed his mind, but he didn't. He could barely acknowledge his anger to himself most of the time, let alone share it with his only friend. How would James feel if he knew the sour stew of thoughts that filled David's head? The self-loathing that caused him to think about killing himself some days; the hatred for everyone else that filled his grey and brown dreams with scenes of mayhem and apocalypse. And then there was the fact that the feelings would come and go so fast: was that normal? Was it like that for everyone? He had no idea.

The unease that he had managed to keep at bay all evening with food and TV was beginning to gather, rolling towards him like a distant fog. He got up. If he went to bed now he could get away with not eating anything else and hopefully avoid feeling any worse. He had to be quick, though. And he had to resist the drawer. The drawer was the thing.

'Night,' he said, quickly.

'Oh, OK, goodnight, love,' said Kerri, still not looking at him.

As he lay awake an hour later, David's mind was tired but his anxiety was active, scurrying round his mind. Feeling his thoughts spinning, he remembered the hamsters that Gary had bought for Jess and Emily when they were small. The girls had been obsessed with the idea of the pets but then there had been the reality of them: the small, scratchy boniness and the fact that they woke up when it was time for the girls to sleep, as well as the damp smell of the wee-soaked straw. David remembered being able to hear the background noise of the hamsters whirring in their exercise wheels as his parents argued downstairs.

That memory was enough to force him out of bed and downstairs. A drink and a snack always helped. Or, rather, having a drink and a snack was better than lying there not sleeping.

Downstairs, he poured a glass of lemonade and put some toast in the toaster. Thickly buttering it, he carried it through to the living room and sat in the dim, cooling living room, listening to the radiator tick as the metal contracted. When he was eating, his mind went blank.

Licking the crumbs off his fingers, he put the plate down and then saw them. The magazines.

It always started with the magazines. Just one or two to begin with, every year after Christmas. Then, inevitably, they multiplied in the magazine rack and all of a sudden, by early February, there would be half a dozen of them in the house. David couldn't help but think that the recent bumping into James's mum had also contributed. Kerri had been really down after that. Diet Day was on the horizon.

If anyone had had any doubt as to the time of year, a cursory look at the cover of these magazines would have eradicated it instantly. *Fabulous February! Be the best you EVER! I lost five stone on juice diet. Lose weight my way: a new DVD by...* David rolled his eyes but still opened the magazine.

A few pages in, he found himself settling back and settling in. The colours, the simple text, the drastic before-and-after images. It was an assault on his eyes and mind, a barrage of exclamatory capitalisation, but the narratives were utterly absorbing. The battle of the bulge, the war on sugar, the fight against the flab. Strategies were outlined, failures mourned and victories celebrated. Page after page of this magazine was filled with stories: tales of young women and old. Age was not a factor in the war against excess weight. The only constant was the desire: the desire to be other than what they were. And the only other constant was the degree to which they were never honest about the real reason they wanted to lose the weight. David knew. And he suspected that Kerri knew too. He knew how much he hated himself and he knew, deep down, that these women – for it was always women – did too.

Why *was* it all women? Men didn't read these magazines. Or rather, they never bought them. Men had different ways of punishing themselves for how they looked. It was called *Men's Health*.

The solutions proposed were as numerous as they were unreliable. They were seductive too. Every technique promised maximum results for minimum effort.

He left the room and went upstairs. It was late but James was still online.

I found some magazines at the house today so I reckon I have about five days…five days till she goes nuts again…

Eh? James texted back.

Oh, she always does this: the mags then the pre-diet binge then the crazy diet and then the diet-breaking binge.

Oh. I see.

Yeah, it's like a seasonal thing. Like Hallowe'en but worse :P

Ha!

*Yeah, right, 'cept it's more frightful than funny. *sighs**

Maybe she won't this time.

Nah, she will. The binges either side are quite fun…it's the bit in the middle that sucks.

Ah, fair.

You gaming?

Yeah. I had to hide upstairs. Mum was trying to engage with me :P

Hate when they do that. OK see ya.

See ya

:)

Getting quickly into bed, David lay there, hands pinned under the rolls of fat around his hips, willing himself to sleep.

Naomi

Up until now, Naomi had succeeded in keeping what was happening purely at home. It hadn't even occurred to her to check online or chat to Mike during the day. She was busy and he was too. But, sitting there, at her desk, with nothing urgent to do and only a meeting with the technical team to fill her afternoon, she found herself logging on and scrolling over the messages.

Her quiet, private office actually felt even safer than being at home. She read and read, reliving those evening chats and smiling to herself. She wondered what she had done with her spare time before this began to occupy it. The extent to which she enjoyed his online company both exhilarated and terrified her.

Glancing at the clock, she decided to go and get a coffee. It was mid-morning now; in the little kitchen, she put the kettle on and then stared blankly at the noticeboard as she waited for the water to boil.

'Hi there!' came a friendly voice. 'How are you? I feel like I haven't seen you in ages!'

It was Carla.

Naomi started, feeling guilty. This kind young woman had just interrupted her daydreaming about her husband! Naomi felt a wave of guilt roll through her. A little voice instantly justified her thoughts: What is not happening at home, though…? Something is clearly not working if he's talking to you…and you've only been married a little while…

'Hey!' she replied, relieved there was no one else in the kitchen to notice her awkwardness.

She took a step away from Carla as the younger woman moved closer to get a mug out of the cupboard. Her thoughts – what she had been thinking about doing – made her want to keep her distance.

'I haven't seen you around much,' Carla continued, as she made herself some tea. 'We must do lunch soon! I so miss chatting to you…'

'Yes, we must,' Naomi agreed quietly, taking her mug.

'Mike's been so busy with work recently, sitting up on his computer all the time, and we missed that pub lunch. Yes, we must catch up. That would be fun…'

Naomi looked at the other woman and wondered if she knew what she sounded like: like a woman whose husband was up to no good…

'I'd better get back to work,' said Naomi, glancing pointedly at her watch.

Back in her office, she tried to concentrate. Part of her was delighted about what Carla had said (*he's up in that room messaging me!*) and part of her felt awful (*that is the pretty, sweet girl whose husband I'm having an online affair with!*) and then, below those feelings, was a memory of shared coffees and chats and the sense that there was a friendship she could no longer continue, a friendship she had lost in her pursuit of something else. The feeling was an uncomfortable one.

Well, she *must* be doing something wrong if he's chatting to me, she told herself; other people never even crossed my mind in those first years of marriage… It's not my fault…

And, satisfied with that, she got back to work.

After lunch, on her way to her afternoon meeting, Naomi glanced at the agenda again. It was a management meeting today and she was hoping for an opportunity to discuss the details of the launch more carefully. It had been frustrating coming into the business at this stage, as she had found that much of the upper management, Jonathan Winters and Grahame Cox in particular, were so used to working together that they seemed to resent her asking questions or pressing her points.

In the room, she took a seat next to Simon, the marketing manager, and poured a glass of water from the jug. 'How are you?' she asked him.

'Good… And you?'

'Yes, just wondering what this is about… I can't help thinking that Grahame organises these things just to justify his existence…'

'They're both guilty of that.'

'You'd think, with all the articles about meetings and management time, we would have learnt something…'

'Ah, no one wants to change these things. My favourite bit is when a meeting starts with someone saying we should be wary of spending too much time in meetings and then goes on to talk for two hours. Anyway, the biscuits are good…why complain? I work hard; I just see them as a break…'

Simon grabbed two cookies and passed one to Naomi. They smiled at each other. 'Did you get a chance to look at that local activist site? The link I sent to you?' he asked her through a mouthful of biscuit.

'The one with the terrible font and appalling Photo-shopping?' Naomi sneered, as she sipped her coffee. 'Yes, nothing to worry about there.'

The door swung open and Jonathan walked in, holding the door open for Grahame.

'Hello, hello,' said the older man, smiling expansively as he took his seat.

Jonathan sat next to him, his usual place, on the other man's right. Naomi looked at him with a smile. And then looked down as the man who was her immediate superior completely ignored her. Her shoulders tensed. Well, if that's how you want to play it…

'Right, I know we're all busy,' Jonathan began, as Grahame poured himself a coffee and began picking out his favourite biscuits from the plate in front of him. 'I read something recently about meeting time, and so we will keep this to the point…'

Simon kicked her leg under the table and, with a sideways smirk at each other like naughty kids at the back of the class, they set their faces to *interested* and listened…

Chapter Six

Saturday 9th to Sunday 10th February

David

As he had predicted, David got up on Saturday morning to find Kerri in the kitchen, emptying the fridge.

'Clearout time!' she announced, as if it wasn't patently obvious what she was doing.

David grunted at her. It was late, he had slept badly and he was tired.

'I thought we could all go to the shops together!'

He stared at her. Why did mums always think that going with them to the supermarket was a treat?

'I'm going to James's today.'

'Oh. Oh, OK. I'll just take the girls, then…'

'You should do it online,' he said, as he picked up the half-empty bottle of lemonade that she had put on the side. Opening it, he heard the feeble hiss as the gas was released, and poured the almost flat sugary drink into a pint glass.

'I like to pick things for myself,' Kerri said, not really listening as she pulled half-pack after half-pack of cheese, ham and salami off the shelves and stacked them on the kitchen table.

Swigging back the lemonade, David took the salami and cheese and one of the three half-full jars of mayonnaise and made himself two sandwiches, slathering the mayo thickly on to the floppy white bread. Then, eating as he walked, he took the sandwiches into the living room and sat next to Emily on the sofa. The girls were watching the television. An utterly interchangeable selection of screechy American high school kids crossed the screen. David groaned and, a sandwich in each hand, he balanced the phone on his lap, scrolling through with a free finger.

Going back upstairs afterwards, David took what was left of his pocket money and put it in his coat. If Kerri was having a clearout, he would have to up the contents of his own stash. With a loud, 'Bye,' he walked out the door and went to catch the bus to James's house.

'Come straight up to my room,' said James, as he opened the door. 'She's being weird again today. Like, all happy. And odd.'

'Haha,' said David. 'Sure.'

He stepped into the wide hallway and they went straight up the wooden staircase to the middle floor. James had lived in this large townhouse in the centre of Rivenoak since David was a baby and the house was as familiar to him as his own. It was always so cool and bright. The large sash windows let in a lot of natural light and the original pale tiles enhanced the sense of calm. David had never been abroad, but sometimes coming here felt like going to a foreign country. He could imagine that this was what it would be like entering an empty church in a quiet city square in a foreign city on a hot day.

As they walked along the wide upstairs hallway, a door opened down the hallway to the left and James's mum popped her head out.

'David! Hello! How are you?'

David mumbled, 'Fine,' into the carpet.

'It's nice to see you! How is your mum? And the twins? Its been too long!' Naomi trilled.

David saw James staring at her, eyes wide with incredulity. They both knew that Naomi had seen his mum just two weeks ago; David remembered the amount Kerri had eaten that weekend. He continued to stare at the floor.

'Are you enjoying school? James is coming along so well. We are *so* pleased. What about you, how are you getting on? Have you got any plans for Easter…? I know James pretends not to want to but I think we're going to do the Easter egg hunt up at Ivy House. You used to love it up there when you were small, didn't you, James? I can still see you now, tumbling about all over the grass in your little rabbit outfit. Too cute really…'

She smiled at them both, her breath slightly short. She had been talking very fast.

'Mu-ummm…' groaned James, and he pulled David's arm.

'I'll bring you a snack,' she called after them.

'Don't worry…' said James.

'No, I will, it's no trouble…'

David stepped into James's room and the other boy slammed the door shut behind them. 'God, she's so annoying…'

Shrugging, David picked up the better of the two game controllers. 'Ready?'

'Hey,' said James, smiling, 'you always do that!'

'I do. And it's always tough,' said David, grinning and waggling the console. 'And now you're just stalling. Let's get on with it…'

Side by side, they played. What was it about sitting not talking that felt so good? David had so many memories of being in this room and, as they grew older, he had come to appreciate the time here even more. James might have followed him to the state comprehensive school very much against Naomi's wishes, but the other boy had quickly been streamed into different classes from David and so, apart from the few break times when James wasn't doing some sport or extra class, they rarely saw each other. It made their time together even more important.

As the game got harder, James began to complain about the advantage David had. 'I've had enough now…I can never beat you like this!'

He rolled back on to the bed, his long, thin limbs moving with ease. David took the slightly sticky hand-held console and shrugged, carrying on playing. 'I'll just whoop your ass without you, then…'

'Whatever,' said James, rolling on to his front and staring out of the large sash window to the right of his double bed. The room was large and square. The window had a view of the well-maintained garden. 'It's just so good to be indoors,' he said, sighing. 'Why does it feel so good to be indoors when the weather is nice?'

'Because outdoors is totally overrated!'

'Totally,' agreed James.

'In fact, I reckon, if I could, I would just stay indoors for ever. Indoors. TV. Games. Food. What else do you need?'

'Haha,' said James. 'Yeah, me too. As long as there's wi-fi and power points, why go anywhere? This is what Mum doesn't get. I'm out at school all week. The last thing I want to do at the weekend is leave the house: I just want to be inside. In bed or in here. And, like, on my own. Or, you know,' he shrugged, 'with you.'

'Gay.'

'Gayer,' James replied, not as quickly as he might have.

'Gayest,' David fired back.

James flipped his finger at David and sat up.

'Ha,' said David, putting the console down. 'Every time, you're reduced to pointless gestures…'

'And every time and always and for ever, you are a dick.'

'No. You're a dick.'

'No, you're a…'

There was a tap at the door.

'Hello, boys!' said Naomi. 'Can I come in?' she asked, coming in.

'No!' said James, scowling at her from the bed as she walked in.

'I bought you some pop and some treats. Just don't tell your father I gave you these before lunch…' she added, winking conspiratorially.

James and David shared a look and then David looked down at the ground and tried not to laugh. Pop? Why did mums always call it that? It was so lame.

'Whatever…' muttered James, grabbing the bottles and the packets from off the tray.

'Can you stay for lunch?' Naomi asked David.

'We're going out, Mum!' interrupted James.

'Are we?' said David, surprised.

'Yeah, yeah, we need to go out,' hissed James, his eyes telling David to stay quiet.

David nodded and stared at the ground before mumbling, 'Thanks anyway, Mrs Taylor…'

'Naomi! You *must* call me Naomi, David! Goodness, I've known you since you were a baby!'

That was the other thing, thought David: people seemed to think knowing you for a long period of time was the same as *knowing* you. Which it clearly wasn't. He continued to nod and stare at the floor. And, with that, she left.

'Out?' David asked once the door had closed.

'Oh, God, yes – the last thing I want to do is eat with them today. Nightmare…the pair of them barely talk to each other and then try and talk to me as if that made it any better. So lame. Can't stand it.'

'Fair.'

'I've got money,' said James. 'We'll head out soon. I'm starving.'

'Yeah, me too…'

'What's that over there?' James pointed to the window. David, distracted, looked over, and James grabbed his console. 'Sucker!'

'Aaargh,' said David, laughing.

And they continued to play.

'Cheers,' said David, pushing the tray away and leaning back in the plastic-coated booth that he was wedged into.

The fluorescent lights made the day outside look even brighter. The booth was deep mauve. The interior colour palette had changed quite recently. Clearly, this was a shift towards what was seen to be a more sophisticated Pantone range – a shift away from the primary colours that had always been associated with fast food. But everything could be wiped clean, like in a nursery.

'S'all right,' said James, who had paid for lunch with his generous weekly allowance. He found the straw with his mouth and slurped up the last of his large drink.

It was busy in the restaurant and noisy, the tinny pop music providing a bland backdrop to the lively Saturday afternoon crowd. People of all ages and backgrounds ate here. The allure of quick hot food served with no hassle and at low cost was a powerful one for people who saw lunch as an inconvenient pause in a day dedicated to distraction and entertainment. For David and James, the appeal lay in the anonymity, the fact that you could order and no one cared what you ate. The fact that it was cheap and fast, but also that it was a private space where you could just be and no one noticed you. The interior was like an inner-city street: busy, anonymous and with no one minding their manners. Unlike at home.

'Whatcha doing later?' asked James. 'I've got to go to football later *and* tomorrow and Mum probably has something lame planned that she will try and sell to me as being fun. She's always dragging me out to places...'

'Mine too...'

Except David knew that they wouldn't be doing anything. Eating. Sitting about. Watching TV. 'Chilling out', Kerri called it. Necessary, she said, but, even with the words 'Must see – new season' it was still doing nothing. Even David knew that. But he didn't ever feel like doing anything else.

He yawned. The caffeine in the drink wouldn't kick in for half an hour and he had to get home before he needed the toilet.

'Better go,' he said, yawning again, his mouth stretching and his eyes watering a little.

'Yeah, OK, me too,' said James.

They got up and left.

David made it on to the bus without any comments and, putting his headphones in, he kept his head down, hoping that he could get all the way home without hearing anything. He wouldn't and he couldn't, deep down he knew this, but on a good day – and a day spent with James was always a good day – he at least had the hope of it. And, as the hard stares began from people boarding at the next stop, David lowered his eyes and willed himself to be home.

Naomi

Naomi was up early on Sunday morning, tired and preparing breakfast, thinking only about Mike. As soon as her mind was conscious it was thinking about him. Thinking about sex. She laughed now when she considered how little she had thought about it before this. She would remember all the anxious and earnest articles she had read after James had been born, about trying to get back into sex, about how to think about sex and make it a priority. The candles. The dinner. The chat.

Her mouth curled up at the corners. No, she thought, as she boiled the kettle and started putting cereal boxes out on to the table, that was not the answer. It was hunger that was the answer. It was wanting. And, to want it, you needed to be thinking about it.

It occurred to her that this must be what it was like to be a teenage boy. To feel haunted by sex. To have sex interrupt every thought, to feel constantly in need of sex.

Catching herself looking at James as he worked away at his homework or as he sat, long legs askew, on the sofa watching TV, she found herself wishing that he were able to appreciate these precious few years before the full awakening of the sex drive. He was nearly fourteen but he was still just a boy. But she knew it was coming. She remembered her own early experiences all too vividly.

Of course, she thought, the things I used to do then. Things I used to do after Daddy...

Her nostrils flared. There was the intake of breath, the bracing, then the physical flinch as her body mimicked her mind's attempt to avoid the memory. There was the pause, always, even now, this dark space before the word could be allowed. After Daddy *died*.

So much of what had happened then had faded away, time dimming the memories, muting them, but that moment...well, that one had remained in Technicolor. Painfully clear.

There he was, right now: face pale, hair still jet-black despite him being in his early fifties, his beige garden trousers soaked brown as he came half-walking, half-falling into the kitchen.

Sitting at the kitchen table, doing her schoolwork, an essay on plate tectonics, she had thought the brown was mud.

'Daddy!' she had cried out, alarmed, already tense, anticipating her mother's reaction to the mess. 'The mud! Don't bring the mud in here! What will Mummy say!'

Then she had looked at his feet, looked at his sun-browned, hairless feet in grey sandals, and seen the trail. Blood, she had realised later, that had run from inside. He had pissed himself: pissed blood.

His illness had been short in the end. A mere three months after that day he was gone. The backache that now, in these more cautious yet also more aware times, would have been X-rayed and identified for the slow yet lethal cancer that had, over the preceding year, been brushed off by numerous doctors.

Then, on that bright, hot Saturday in July, he had come in from the garden, bleeding, and it was already too late. He had always spent summer in the garden. He had loved it, loved it more than anything, more even than Lynne. The only thing he had loved more was his little girl. Naomi, his only child.

Lynne had nursed him over those few months. Afterwards, they had walked away from the funeral, Naomi's face wet with tears, her eyes raw, mouth stiff from trying to hold in the screams. They were screams for a pain so intense that she thought it would destroy the world if she let it out.

To this young girl, aged only fourteen, her mother had said, 'Now, Naomi, no moping. We just need to get on.'

And so, her mother worked. She cared for the house and worked ever longer hours at her job. The garden that her dad had so lovingly tended was turfed over. 'I've no time for all that,' she had said, paying someone to pull the flowers out, to strip the raised beds away. The once living space had been covered in flat, dead yet alive fake grass. There was no time for flowers and tending when you had to 'get on'.

And there had been no time for a flowering teenager either. No time at all. That was why Naomi had always tried to make time for James. Always. She never wanted him to feel as unwanted as she had then.

As with so much about being a teenager in the 1980s, Naomi's life had, at fourteen, been both colourful and confusing. Left very much to her own devices, she had spent that year after her dad's death pretending to be OK, and pretending, like her mother, not to notice that her body was changing.

But, really, it was all she noticed. Late at night, she would stare at the leaflet she had been given at school about sex and periods. Hers had started about six months ago and her breasts had developed at the same time. Having always been tall and thin, she had now, according to the argot of the time, become 'fit'.

Still wary of the boys at school, she had taken to experimenting on her own in bed. Lynne still insisted on a 7.30pm bedtime and, lying there in the light summer evenings, wide awake, Naomi could still vividly remember the first times she had touched herself.

Looking at herself with a mirror on several occasions, she had been curious, though her wariness meant that she had never looked for long. The layers, and the pale, slippery pinkness of it all, so wet and new, had seemed a little appalling, frightening even. What went where and how? Initially, she had not dared to put her fingers inside herself, had not dared to explore any further, always putting the mirror away hastily, fearful of being caught and told off. She could still recall her hands being slapped whenever she had touched herself as a child, the sharp anger in her mother's voice.

And she could still remember the first time, the first time she had found it: the special place. It had started as the usual quick itch, a scratch at the growing hair, but as she had rubbed gently at herself she'd felt a tingle, deep within. Lying there, propped up on her Duran Duran cushion, she had been surprised at first. Then, she had begun to stroke herself more, rubbing on the soft mound of her crotch, the nascent fuzz soft under her fingertips.

The pleasurable sensation had been enough to encourage her to go further than she had before. Extending her index and forefingers, she had begun to feel inside. Wary of catching herself with her nails, she'd gone slowly, exploring carefully, not wanting to hurt herself, scared of doing some damage that could not be undone, that would be visible somehow.

Gently she had probed within and found the opening. More confident now that she had gone this far without hurting herself, she had pushed first her index and then both her index and forefinger inside. With what seemed like an instinctive need to push them up, she'd pressed them up against the soft wall at the front. The pressure had caused a jolt of sensation, a dart of pleasure that had rippled out from there and into her lower torso. Gasping, she had done it again, rubbing and pushing, her lower body beginning to move a little, working along with the rhythm of her fingers.

She'd let out a soft moan. Feeling her chest rising as the sensation built up, it was mounting within her, heat beginning to radiate, the pleasure building slowly as she moved her fingers within herself. Her other hand was still cupping her crotch and, softly palpating, she had moved both hands together, a dance of pressure, one working from the outside, the other within. She'd begun to feel her breath getting out of control and she had whimpered slightly, her voice beginning to rise as the rhythm quickened and the pleasure built to a crescendo within her.

It had been magical. A wonderful thing but also a thing she hadn't understood. What was this sensation? Who could she talk to about it?

She had carried on exploring. Happy to be sent to bed early now.

And then, one night, as she had cried out, trying to stifle the sound but unable to contain it any longer, her bedroom door had swung open.

'Naomi!' Her mother's voice had been sharp with anger. 'What are you doing?'

Naomi had tried to cover herself up, the thin pink summer duvet bunched up beneath her.

'Sorry, Mummy, sorry...' she'd gasped, her breath still shallow, face flushed.

'Disgusting girl!' her mother had snapped and, walking up to the bed, she had slapped Naomi across the face.

Naomi had screamed. 'Mummy, sorry, no...'

Lynne had gripped Naomi's wrist and pulled her out of the bed. 'Get up! Get up! How could you? What would your father have thought if he had heard such noises!'

This was the ultimate threat. Lynne knew that the worst thing she could do was to remind Naomi of how much everything she did would have let her father down. Naomi, the guilt following the pleasure in thick, hot, nauseating waves, had cried out, 'Sorry, Mummy, sorry... I won't do it again, I promise. Sorry...'

She had begun to cry. Her mother had released her and she'd slumped on to the floor, still crying, thin arms wrapped around herself.

'Put your nightclothes on and get back into bed,' Lynne had hissed, voice low and angry. 'If you ever do that again, you are out of this house. Disgusting, dirty girl.'

And, with that, she'd left the room, slamming the door behind her. Naomi had got back into her cotton pyjamas and crawled back into bed.

The shame she'd felt then had meant that she hadn't done it again. Instead, she had given in to the boys, with their awkward, scratching, clawing fingers; and, making sure it only happened when her mother was at work, she'd never got caught again.

And now, having taken the risk she had the other night, having got up in the middle of the night and risked being heard, she knew she had to be more careful. She would not get found out or punished this time.

Chapter Seven

Monday 11th to Friday 15th February

David

Monday. Mondays had a habit of being grim. Opening the fridge door as part of his post-school snack ritual, David suspected that this Monday, which hours ago had begun badly, then continued badly and now looked as if it was about to end badly, was no exception. The fridge had been cleared out. Kerri had been to the shops twice over the weekend and now, inside the wiped-clean whiteness, the food landscape had changed. Everything was white or green or red: the colours of health.

There was usually a comforting scene awaiting him when he opened the white door: yellows, browns, purples and oranges. Packaging that not only protected the food, but made the promise of protecting you. Now, there were low-fat yoghurts, bags of bitter leaves, a stack of low-fat cheese slices, jars of light mayonnaise. David knew from experience that what Kerri had bought would probably not help, but he didn't know why. He was resigned to watching Kerri go through this cycle of excess followed by miserable abstention and then the return to a gluttonous norm – he was expecting it; he just didn't understand it.

Moving the low-fat yoghurts and reduced-calorie dressings to one side, David saw the boxes of skinny pizzas, reduced-calorie lasagnes and pasta bakes. There were some apples rattling around at the bottom of the fridge and, taking one, he bit into it. He immediately spat it out into his hand. 'Ugh,' he said, tossing the remains in the bin. The apple had looked good, burnished red and green, a perfect replication of the treat handed to Snow White by the old woman; but, like that famous fruit, this had been nasty. He took a swig out of the already-open bottle of Diet Coke on the side and then, closing the fridge, he began to look in the cupboards for something else to eat. Surely there were still some crisps about?

Of course there were. Popping open the packet, David took a handful, closed his eyes and smiled. Mmmmh. You never opened a bag of crisps and found them to be mushy or off. Or, if you did, you got to email the manufacturers and then you got money back. He remembered the time Gary had encouraged him to complain about some slightly burnt crisps. He had been sent a £10 voucher. Getting free money that *had* to spent on snacks had made that one of David's best days ever.

He ate another packet and then ate an entire pack of six single-serving reduced-calorie cookies that Kerri had bought. Pouring the last of the Diet Coke into a glass, he went upstairs to do his homework.

When the door opened downstairs, he could tell from Kerri's voice that she was hungry. 'Oh, for God's sake!' she shouted. 'David! Why is your bag *always* in the middle of the floor?'

He pulled a face. She could yell all she wanted – like he cared. With a sigh, he turned his music up. She was always like this until she ate: as sour as the apple he had just tossed away.

There was a knock at his door. He knew from the timbre of the knock that it was Emily. Anyway, it was only ever Emily who wanted to come in here.

'You may enter... Hey, sis,' he said, not turning round.

She sat down on the edge of his bed. 'Hey,' she said, swinging her feet as she looked round.

'You OK?'

'Mmmhhhh.'

'Mum being stroppy in the car?'

'Yeah, kind of.'

'Thought so. It'll pass soon enough,' he said. 'Listen to this! It's a great new song...' And he put the track on repeat and turned round in his chair to watch her reaction.

After the song had finished, David said, 'I can help you with your homework if you like?'

'Can you?'

'Yeah, course.'

Emily jumped off the bed and left the room, returning with her maths folder.

Helping Emily with her homework was a relief compared to doing his own. He found the maths he had been given difficult, really difficult, and yet he also knew that it wasn't even close to the level he should be at. They sat side by side on the bed and began to go through her folder, Emily writing the answers into the boxes with her pencil. 'And this one?' she asked. David read the question.

If $A = 4$, $B = 6$, $C = 24$, $D = 0$, $E = 12$
What is $A \times B + (E \times D)$?

They both stared at the sum. David began to doodle on the bit of blank paper on his lap. There was silence.

'I think it's C...' she said.

'Yeah, that's just what I was about to say...'

Emily didn't look up, just wrote the answer on the sheet. Even at her age, kids knew who the kids were who just didn't get it.

As they went downstairs, the sound of Kerri 'preparing' dinner was evident. There were bangs, crashes, cupboard doors being slammed, hushed curses. The degree to which she was hungry was always reflected in the amount of huffing and puffing and slamming that went on in the kitchen.

David had seen her pack her lunch that morning: a packet of low fat soup, one of the mushy apples and a bag of low-fat crisps. And all she had had in the morning was tea. He couldn't remember what hungry felt like but it sounded pretty awful.

'Oh, for God's sake… Damn…'

David sat on the sofa. Jess turned the volume of the TV up. The microwave continued to whirr.

'Oh, Jesus…'

The microwave binged.

'Right,' said Kerri, puffing and sighing into the room. 'Here we go…'

She slapped plates on their laps. Loose mince spilled out from underneath chewy-looking pasta that was curled up and dark yellow on the edges like an old toenail. The cheese sauce, made mainly of water, low-fat cheese and salt, was pooling around the brown meat like pus. David sneered at it.

'If I see you look like that again…' Kerri warned.

The handful of leaves on the side of the plate were wilting and sour-looking.

David took another long draught of his Diet Coke. They all ate in silence. Kerri cleared the plates away, also in silence, and then, returning with a mug of tea, she sank into her chair and stared at her tablet.

The evening progressed and, without food to eat, Kerri fidgeted, making endless cups of tea. The girls went to bed. As the clock hit 10pm, David and Kerri exchanged a glance. 10pm was biscuit o'clock. David was not cruel enough to sit down here eating; he knew that he had stuff upstairs if he needed it. And, after the meal they had eaten, he really did need it.

The silent room was loud with Kerri's misery. David felt for her but mostly he felt for himself. He had eaten a normal lunch and even he still felt as though he could eat more. But he had to try not to. He wanted this to work as much as she did. Unfortunately, wanting that didn't make the effort of it any easier. The necessary effort to sit still and not eat was so colossal that neither of them had any energy left with which to talk. Maybe I should try and distract her, he thought, but his stomach rumbled and, shifting his bulk on the soft chair, he hesitated. They needed to do this and yet why was it so hard? Why, only one day in, did it seem so very hard?

'We can do it,' he said, quietly.

'Yes!' she said, her face smiling but wan. 'We can, I'm sure. This time we will stick with it, eh? Stick together?'

He smiled back.

'Sure, I'm hungry,' she added. 'But that's kind of the point, isn't it? To be hungry?'

'I guess so,' he replied, hesitantly. He had no idea, but surely eating less was always going to make you hungry?

'I think you just get used to eating a lot less,' she continued. 'You know… Like your stomach shrinks or something. That's what I read, anyway. You get used to eating less and so it gets easier to do.'

'Oh, right.'

'And, I looked at my calorie counter and I've managed to only eat 1,500 calories today.'

'That's great!' David said, genuinely impressed.

'Yeah, so I just need to keep it up, that's all.'

'You can do it!' he said.

'Yes, yes, it really is going to be different this time,' she replied.

And, happily, in that moment they both believed it.

Naomi

The outside of Naomi functioned as everyone expected it to, but inside all she thought about was what they had done and what they might do again. Speaking on the phone? She was thinking about fucking Mike. Having a shower? Thinking about fucking Mike. Sitting in a meeting? Thinking about fucking Mike. Loading the dishwasher? Thinking about fucking Mike.

At night, she ran the conversations over in her mind, the text scrolling behind her closed eyelids much as it did on and off throughout the day as she used her mouse to scroll down the messages again and again. The words she repeated endlessly to herself were like a canticle, a song of need and desire. It was a desire that filled the whole horizon, that made her pussy ripple and tighten; reading in her mind, thinking, she would feel herself coming, silently, as she lay under the covers, arms by her side, her whole body consumed with wanting.

She had never been more relieved to have successfully negotiated a private corner office. Spending countless minutes (hours?) scrolling through old messages, she also found herself, in meetings and when she was on the phone, doodling his initials on to her notepad or on to pieces of scrap paper. MB. MB. Sometimes she looped it round with flowers. Sometimes she made it angular. Sometimes she melded the letters together so that they looked almost like the kind of logo an overpaid consultancy might come up with for a rebranding exercise.

Knowing the behaviour was absurd didn't mean that she was capable of stopping it. Some days she felt almost giddy with it: the lightheadedness reminding her of the time she had tried a sniff of an aerosol can at the bus stop. What had that boy's name been, the boy she had been trying to impress that time? R-something… It didn't come back to her, but the feeling was the same.

There was also the overwhelming urge to mention the person's name in all situations and conversations (she had lost track of the amount of times she had started to talk about Carla just so she could mention Mike too). And she seemed to see his name everywhere. In television listings, on billboards, her eyes focused only on those four letters of the alphabet. She daydreamed and doodled her way through hours at a time, with no idea how she was managing to complete routine tasks. Coming to, she would find herself preparing dinner, or doing the online food shop, and wonder how she had ended up here; her head had had her firmly placed on the floor in the hallway with Mike between her thighs.

She had taken to cutting her nails really short but, as she was now masturbating at least once a day (either at her desk in the spare room or in bed or even in the shower), it was still becoming a little painful. Having started, it felt impossible to stop.

I'm so sore, she had admitted to Mike one night last week, late, after they had both resumed the civilised talk after a frantic masturbation which had resulted in her sitting there with damp pants, the feeling far from unpleasant.

Really? Not used to it?

No.

Were you not doing it before? I always used to masturbate in the shower before everyone else got up.

Really?

She loved the fact that he was always so blunt; there was no politeness here, no skirting around anything, it was all there in black and white.

No, she continued, hesitating, *I'm not sure I ever did it much...* The memory of that evening in her room at home flashed up in her mind. She was wary of revealing too much.

Ah, he replied, *well, for me it was always my reward for getting up at 5.30. And of course the morning glory kind of helps too.*

She laughed to herself as she typed **laughing** on to the screen.

These conversations would go on for an hour or two at a time and, while they tried to keep it to the times when they were both on their own, increasingly she found herself messaging him on her phone, from wherever she happened to be.

He put a stop to that, though.

Can you not text me any more?

Oh? Why?

Feeling like putting a *pouts* on the end of that, she decided against it. Still on her best behaviour, she found she was making a huge effort not to appear too needy or demanding.

Carla uses my phone sometimes, for photos and things. Also, he typed, *I read somewhere that it's best to keep this sort of communication private and in one place.*

Did you now? she thought, drumming her fingers on the edge of her desk.

Oh, OK, she replied. *No problem.*

Cheers!

And then he would be gone and she would read over the conversations. She edited everything. She never moaned about work or the house or stuff at home. He was getting an artfully arranged and presented version of her: a meal plated up for a magazine shoot, too pretty for actual consumption. Looking back, she remembered it being like this in her old dating days, the days when, before she had settled down with Scott, she had made huge efforts to appear appealing, appetising, so desperate had she been to be chosen off the menu. The early years with Scott had been a blessed release from that – had been a comfort, a retreat – but now she was back in the game and she was surprised at how effortful it was.

The last few years had passed by in a haze of work and the eleven-plus, but they had at least been set against a steady, neutral landscape. Now, she was experiencing such highs and lows that she felt giddy. It was like managing on a diet of rice and vegetables for years and then suddenly being given access to a banquet. She had been happy with the plain rice, but now she had had a taste of the rich stuff she wanted more.

Naomi had justified staying at home until lunchtime by the sheer amount of work she had to do but, having spent the half-hour since Scott and James had left at 7.30am sitting in her robe at the computer, reading over old messages yet again, she now just felt even more distracted and fidgety than usual. As she read the late-night exchanges, her hand found itself resting on the outside of her underwear. Could she? Glancing at the clock, she decided yes and began to apply some gentle pressure to herself through the thin white cotton.

Slowly, she let the pressure build up. God, it felt good. Why had she stopped doing this? She knew why, and the memory flooded her with shame and fear, feeling exactly as hot and sour now as it had been then. After that night, she had never done it again. Ever. Not until his telling her to had given her permission.

Pressing more firmly, she lay down on the floor so that her palm could apply a fluttering of pressure to her clitoris. The lightest touch seemed to work and she felt herself starting to come.

And once you pop, you just can't stop, she thought, laughing a little and then making herself come again and again.

The doorbell rang. 'Fuck...' she cried out. Irritated, she pulled her robe together hastily. Who could it be at this hour? Didn't they know she had work to do? The fact that she hadn't actually been working was something she was unwilling to acknowledge for now. Half walking, half staggering, she went downstairs.

Pulling the door open, she frowned. Her head was so full of scrolling text and her body still tremulous from coming that she swayed in the doorway, barely registering the man who was standing in front of her.

'Good morning, Mrs Taylor.'

'Morning,' she said, automatically. She looked around the drive, unsure of where she was. Running a hand through her messed-up hair, trying to flatten the frizz at the back from where she had been writhing on the floor upstairs, she looked again. This time she actually saw him. Tree Man. Sexy Tree Man.

'Sorry. Yes. Of course.'

'Oh, I'm sorry, weren't you expecting me? I did call and leave a message to confirm I was coming today,' said the man, meeting her eyes.

Seeing him look at her, Naomi felt her face flush and pulled the belt of her disarranged robe tighter.

'I was going to make a start at the back,' he continued, looking away from her as she rearranged herself a little. 'So if you're OK to open the side gate, then I can begin? I thought I would do the pollarding later in the month.'

Naomi frowned, confused. 'The what?'

'The work on this beautiful tree out here,' said Tree Man. He looked at her again. 'Are you all right?' he added.

'Yes, yes,' Naomi said, snapping back to where she was.

'Tree. Gate. Yes,' she continued, unaware that she was failing to speak in full sentences.

'Thank you.' He nodded and then walked away, smiling a little.

Putting the kettle on, Naomi quickly went upstairs to get dressed. Making two strong cups of black coffee, she took one out to the garden and called out, 'Coffee!' in her firmest, briskest voice before darting quickly back indoors.

There's nothing like being caught out to refocus you, she thought. Could she have looked worse? Could she have looked more like she had just been doing exactly what she had just been doing? What if it had been Scott or, worse still, James coming back? She really did have to be more careful. Lock the doors if she was going to do that again. But then, it wasn't as if she had planned it. Wasn't as if she had planned any of it.

It had just, well, *happened*. Shaking her head, she went back upstairs with her coffee and, with a feeling of reluctance, closed the site and his messages down and got back to work.

Feeling better after a few productive hours, she went back downstairs, ready to head in to the office for her late-afternoon meeting.

After what Tree Man had said, she checked her voicemail before she left, listening to and then deleting the message from him – aha, his name was Sean! – and also writing down two other messages that she had missed from last week. One was from the school, about a permission slip for a summer school trip for James that had yet to be returned, and one was from her dentist about a missed appointment.

Shit, she thought, I really have to keep on top of all of this stuff.

Glancing at her now straightened-out reflection in the hallway mirror, she thought back to how she must have looked this morning and, with a grimace, she said to the Naomi staring back at her from the glass, 'You're not allowed to do this unless you can keep all the other plates spinning too. Keep them spinning or you really are fucked.'

And, tucking a strand of loose hair back into her now neatly tied bun, she left the house, shutting the door firmly behind her.

Sometimes there would be no word from him all day and she would sit and stare at the screen, wondering where he was, what he was doing and who he was doing it with. She would obsess over him meeting other people, seeing people he might want more than he wanted her. The idea of that haunted her. It seemed so amazing to be experiencing this at all that she couldn't quite believe it wouldn't be over as fast as it had begun. If he had been so quick to want her, perhaps that was how he was with everyone: who were these other girls who clicked Like? The ones who left silly comments? Always with typos. She would stare and obsess and then she would get cross with herself. 'For fuck's sake,' she said to herself back at home that evening, 'you can spend the next few hours staring and waiting like a crazy person or you can get some work done!'

Given how behind she was, this was the only real option. She didn't close down the site but she did minimise it, and she made a commitment to herself.

'Right,' she said, mentally rolling up her sleeves as she opened up the file on her desktop marked Kale Kooler. 'Every forty minutes you can check and see if he's there.'

Double-clicking, she felt her mind come into focus and, taking a scalding sip from her fresh mug of green tea, she set to work.

There was so much to do on this new kale drink project that it would be easy to feel overwhelmed, but she had been brought on board specifically because of her experience with projects of this kind. She just needed to remember that and get to work.

Reading through the most recent report from the technicians, it was clear that they had eliminated all of the issues regarding the flavouring of the product, but there were huge red flags all over the final mix. Salt and sugar levels were sky-high, higher than even their most recent product launched, but she was confident that the marketing could overcome that. Doing a quick search, she was delighted to see that both kale extracts and chia seeds had been getting a huge amount of lifestyle media buzz of late. Bogus health claims for strange food products always sold more copies of magazines and papers. She felt bad for being so cynical, but she was also confident that she would be able to cover the sugar tracks of the new product.

Making a note of some questions, she then emailed Diane, the kale project's administrative assistant, telling her to arrange a meeting before the end of the week with the lab team. The lesson had been hard learned, but she knew now that there was little point sending an email to the techies: they would just reply back with the same sentence without the question mark. That was if they bothered to respond at all. It was much easier to deal with them in person. Then, unable to hide behind their screens and their jargon, they were defenceless and pliable.

That email done, she set the technical report aside and reviewed the marketing plan, taking into account the latest noises about kale and sending some links to Carla for her to look into further.

It was Carla's name and email address that sent her creeping back online. She opened up the site and there he was.

There was no way she was getting in touch with him now. She stuck her tongue out at the computer screen and, with a feeling of virtuous triumph, logged off.

Lying in bed that night, she felt good: clean and light. She had done it. She had managed to avoid the temptation today and it felt good. Really good.

Two more days passed and she maintained her resolve, not getting in touch, allowing herself to scan over the messages but trying to keep busy. He was there, of course. He was always there. Updating his status, posting silly links and videos, providing updates on some game he was playing. She resisted the urge to say hello, resisted the urge to click Like or to leave a comment. She had no idea what the politics of these things was: could she or should she Like things or leave public comments now that they were doing what they were doing, or should she keep her distance? If she posted something and he didn't Like it, she felt strangely bereft and ignored, as if it was some silent criticism. So few of her own friends used the site with any regularity that when she did post something he Liked he would often be the only one, and then she would panic, thinking that perhaps it was obvious something was happening or wondering what Carla would think.

Sitting there, working, or at least trying to, she thought, No, I'm not messaging him today, I'm not doing it today. I managed it the other day and I will not be the one to start it up again.

But then he would post a joke, or a reference to something that she was familiar with, and the thinking would start: was that aimed at her? Was he trying to get her attention?

And so she'd cave in, collapse under the pressure of her own need for him. Elaborate guidelines and promises would be made. Like someone taking just three biscuits from a freshly opened packet and returning it to the cupboard, she promised herself that she would be good. But, inevitably, the craving for more became too much and, like that person creeping back into the kitchen and taking that packet back out of the cupboard, her resolve crumbled like the proverbial cookie. The politeness of her words disintegrated. Talk of work and books quickly shifted to talk of beds, bodies, wetness, hardness and touching. And before she knew it, she was on the floor again, flushed and breathless…giving in to her appetite only making her hungry for more.

Matthew

It was the third morning in a row that Matthew had had to get up early to do the marking before he went in. Showering at 5am in a vain bid to wake himself up, he let the hot water run over him and began to wash his hair. The astringent, almost antiseptic smell of the foam, the steam…it all felt as if it should be making him more awake. But, having stayed up till well after one in the morning, he knew that what he really needed was sleep, not just a differently scented shower gel. Every time he shut his eyes he could see the computer, could see the code and the images, his head lit up from inside by the constant pale glow of the always-on screen.

Closing his eyes against the hot water, he suddenly had an idea and, quickly rinsing his hair, he leapt out of the tiny plastic cubicle and rubbed himself down with the soft blue towel. Wrapping it round his waist, he went to the laptop and began to make some more changes to the code, altering one set of links and setting up another.

Changing and updating the website for Polly had taken up all his spare time in the past few days. As a result, the schoolwork had built up. He had meetings to prepare for, coursework to assess, exam work to be getting ready, but all of it had been put aside to work for Polly.

As he stared at the site now and saw for himself the results of all the effort that had gone into it, he felt pleased and happy. This is what it was all about: about effort being realised; about making a tangible difference right now.

'It will,' he said, out loud to himself. 'Wait till she sees this… It *will* make a difference. We are making a difference. *I* am making a difference.'

And, getting dressed and making a cup of coffee, he got to work on the marking.

Walking to school, he realised he also felt excited for another reason: it was Valentine's Day. Polly had said she didn't do cards or flowers or chocolates, not even fairtrade ones, and so he hadn't bought cards or flowers or chocolates. It had felt wrong, though. It seemed like every young man's dream not to bother with Valentine's but he wanted to bother and so, instead, he planned to cook her a meal based on the delicious Indonesian-inspired broth he had eaten so often in Brazil. And he had gone up a price bracket on the wine. He felt optimistic about the evening ahead.

But he had the ten or so hours of day in between to deal with first. These were hours he felt much less optimistic about. A school on Valentine's Day was like a toddler at a birthday party: excited, and yet so unsure what to do about those feelings that it would eventually sit, slumped in a corner, red-faced and crying for no reason. All week there had been signs of the inevitable build-up. It didn't help that it was almost half-term: the kids (and staff) were overtired as well as overexcited. Always a dangerous combination.

Going through the gates, Matthew knew that he should have been here earlier if he had wanted to avoid the fuss, and so he accepted the first calls of 'Happy Valentine's Day!' with a cheery wave. I've done this before, he thought. I can do it again.

As he passed a group of the younger girls, one of them went a dark shade of pink as one of her friends called out, 'Sarah wants to say Happy Valentine's Day, sir!' The blushing deepened as he passed and he felt a surge of compassion for the girl. He could say nothing of course, but his heart went out to the quieter ones: the ones with deep and devastating crushes. He remembered what that was like: to want something without even really knowing why. It wasn't rational, but that didn't make it any easier to deal with.

There were three cards stuffed under the science room door. Opening them, he smiled at the neat handwriting and the tidy question marks at the bottom, then put them out for all to see on his desk. He was a little in awe of the courage these girls demonstrated. He knew himself how hard it was to say you cared: it was easier to pretend not to be interested. He had done that for much of his life. It was only now that he was realising how uncool it was to be cool about everything.

And its being Valentine's was a welcome distraction for the day. Ever since he had met Polly almost three weeks ago, Matthew had been doing more and more to help her, and was focused less and less on what was happening at school. Not that anyone seemed to have noticed. He was still there and he was still delivering his lessons but he felt increasingly tuned out, increasingly detached from the day-to-day happenings.

Coasting on autopilot, he also had twinges of guilt as he saw Jim and Solange going out after school, making plans and discussing school stuff. They had stopped asking him to come along, didn't want to hear about what he was working on with Polly. He didn't mind: the increased closeness between him and Polly was more than enough for him. Ever since he had said he could design her a new website, she had been increasingly affectionate and, while it still wasn't quite what he hoped (she still hadn't stayed the night), he was still confident that things were moving on. And he hoped that tonight would be part of that process.

The bell went, and his stomach clenched and his jaw tightened. Seven hours to go.

When he got home, Matthew noticed he had some post. Opening the envelopes in the hallway, he was delighted and surprised to pull a red, heart-covered card from one of them. He looked at the envelope again. The address had been printed on to a label and, inside, there was just a question mark. A strong stroke with a big bold dot at the bottom. He felt his face flush. Polly? he thought, but it seemed unlikely. Very unlikely.

He turned the card over: there wasn't even an FSC stamp on the back of it. It was definitely *not* from Polly. He smiled a little at that, and then the smile faded: she would be here soon. What to do with a card that was so obviously not from her? He felt a wave of panic wash over him, but at the same time a sense of intrigue. Who was this one from? He looked at it again, and then put it deep at the back of the bottom drawer in his room.

A little later, as he sat and waited, the TV was on but he wasn't watching it. Trying to avoid topping up his glass, he paced about the tiny space nervously. It was already gone 8pm. He checked his phone. She was often late, the demands of deforested Central America being constant and always urgent, but she usually let him know if she was running late.

Sitting down, he picked up his tablet and began to surf while half-listening to the TV. Maybe he could find out some more about the sugar cane industry while she was on her way. He knew this was her next big thing. Deforestation for sugar. 'It,' she would say, 'is going to be the next big thing. We need to do the research, we need to get the information and then we can go in hard. Everyone is all over the palm oil thing, as they should be, but sugar is mine. All mine!' She had clutched her hands to her boyish (and, Matthew thought, beautiful) chest. 'And I really want to make a difference with this!'

It was the reason he hadn't bought her any chocolates. Tempted as he had been by the piles of pretty boxes, bags of heart-shaped jellies, marshmallows and kiss-shaped foil-wrapped treats, he had resisted. It had been really hard, but remembering what she had told him about child slavery on cocoa farms, about the personal and environmental carnage caused by sugar production, had helped him to resist. It was incredible how much of a hold the habit of buying had over him. There was the constant presence and marketing of chocolate too, especially at certain times of the year, like Valentine's Day; and, well, he had realised, all the holidays seemed to be an opportunity to sell sweets and chocolate. Even knowing what he knew now, he still found it terribly hard not to just buy it.

Reading, he skipped from site to site, taking in the headline information, checking sources and references before digging deeper. He squinted a little, assailed by the sheer volume of data.

Checking the time again, he saw that it was nearly nine o'clock. It wasn't even as if he had to cook: the soup had taken days to prepare and was all ready to reheat and serve when she arrived. He stared hard at his phone. The urge to text her was only marginally weaker than his urge to appear self-contained and not needy, another half-hour and the balance might shift, but, putting the phone down, he carried on surfing.

Then he heard it: the sound of her rustling bags in the corridor outside. Jumping up, he was about to dash to the door to meet her and then stopped himself. Taking a few deep breaths, he sat back down.

The doorbell rang. He got up as slowly as he could manage and went to open it. 'Hey!' His voice was high, the need travelling up his throat from his stomach and making itself evident in his pitch.

'Hi,' she said, tumbling into the hallway, laden with bags.

Coming into the living room, she was clutching four paper folders, her multicoloured string bag full of more papers and pens and notebooks as well as her tiny netbook. He had never seen her without a stack of paper. It was as if it was part of her body, an essential part of her frame: physical evidence of her efforts. She smiled wanly, her face pale and eyes smudged grey.

'Hey,' he said again. 'How are you?'

'Tired. It's been a long day.'

'It's good to see you. Are you hungry? I've cooked...' He gestured towards the kitchen.

'That would be lovely!' she said, walking past him to the living room. Flopping on to the sofa, she began to spread the paperwork about her. Matthew handed her a glass of wine, which she took without looking up and, after one sip, absentmindedly placed down on the small glass coffee table. 'Look at this,' she said. 'I've been looking into some of the local businesses. Looks like our lovely friends at VitSip are about to have a big launch. That's a great opportunity for us to highlight the impact that making these sugary drinks has on the environment as well as on the health of local people. We can pull together the local and global strands. It's an amazing opportunity!'

Matthew sat next to her, pressing his thigh against hers and sitting close, leaning over the papers and brushing her thigh with his forearm as he did so. She moved to pick up another sheet. 'Read this!' she said, thrusting the paper at him. And then, turning the TV down, she added, glancing at her watch, 'Oh, and I really need to have an early night. That OK?'

Matthew's heart sank a little. He sat back and drank some more wine, scanning over the sheet.

'What do you think?' she said.

He frowned. 'It is tenuous but maybe, with a little more evidence, you will have something to go at them with…'

'Can you help?' she asked, suddenly squeezing his thigh. His penis twitched, ever-hopeful. Leaning in, Matthew could smell her: the sweet smell of her skin and hair. He breathed her in and then, getting closer, he moved in to kiss her. She kissed him back hard. And then her phone beeped. She looked at it. 'Oh! Look, we've just hit ten thousand followers!'

Matthew looked at her, her pale face lit up, and grinned. The heat in her voice, her passion for what she was doing… He took a look at the screen.

'That's great!' he said.

'The website improvements have really helped,' she said, kissing him on the cheek. 'Thank you!'

The kiss was followed by another, and then a hug. Pulling him closer, she whispered in his ear, 'There's something else I want to do…' And, taking the laptop away, she manoeuvred herself into its place on his lap. Feeling her weight on his legs, feeling her hips pressing into him, he felt a tingle of anticipation run all over his body. He had never wanted anyone so much.

'You've been so amazing… Working so hard, tapping away… I wonder what else those fingers are good at…'

Kissing, they slid off the sofa and on to the floor, the needs of the planet fully displaced in that moment by their need for each other.

He knew that most parents felt otherwise, but Matthew saw the half-term break as a vital and necessary pause.

Like a cessation in the shelling before the final push, he thought, battle-weary after six long weeks in the trenches of teaching. The evenings and weekends were beacons of light, and the long days in between had to be trudged through, the hours sucking him down like mud.

It was the final day of the first half of term now. Knowing that he was about to enjoy a week of full days that would involve no kids and no teaching, days that would be clear to do the important work for Snap Out Of It as well as now, finally, to kiss, touch and have glorious sex with the wonderful Polly was enough to get him up and into school early.

Checking through his lesson plans, he saw that today was the day he was handing out the Year 9 project. Picking up that folder, he scanned over the notes, the handouts and his own planning notes. He smiled a little and felt the knot of anxiety in his stomach relax. He was very grateful to his former self for the effort he had put into this project last year, before things broke down with Lucy, before the Brazil trip, before Polly. 'Thank you, former me,' he said.

'*Pardon?*' said a voice from the doorway. 'You are talking to yourself?'

'Hahaha, something like that,' he laughed. 'Morning, Sol, how are you?'

'I am well, of course; it is half-term.'

'Yes! I'm glad it's not just me.'

'It is never just you,' she said, smiling back. 'I am going outside, would you like to come?'

'I can't, sorry,' he said. 'I just need to get this ready for Year 9.'

'Ah, Year 9…'

'Oh, yes.'

'*Bonne chance.* I will perhaps see you later?'

'Sure,' he said.

And, as she closed the door, the urge for a cigarette, as well as the urge for the company and conversation that he had shared with Solange for so much of last year as they had smoked together in the courtyard, hit Matthew hard.

'No,' he said to himself. 'No, keep at it.'

He began to gnaw on the edge of his thumb as he went through the rest of his lesson plans.

'So, we're covering photosynthesis today but I also need to go through the forthcoming end-of-year project with you. Unlike some of the projects I have given you in the past, this one asks you to draw on subjects that you have covered in other subjects. *All* the other subjects. I want to see something that demonstrates to me the value and importance of science in the everyday, in relation to you and how you live. Because this, for me, is what science is all about – about explaining the miracle of the everyday because you, your bodies, this leaf…' he gestured to the plant beside him, the lush green peace lily that lived on the corner of his desk '…so much of what we take for granted is an undeniable miracle, and that is what I want you to get a grasp of. That sense of the miraculous in you all.'

Matthew was reading out words that had once meant something to him to a room full of students whose ability to be inspired he had also once believed in. He wished very much that he could get that feeling back, but he had begun to think that perhaps he never would.

'Take one and pass it on. Soft copies coming to you over the school system as always but I want you to read this and ask any questions you might have…'

As the sheets were handed out across the tables, Matthew walked back to his desk. Passing a bench, he caught part of a hushed conversation.

'There's no way I'm gonna have time to even think about this with the other coursework we've got.'

'Yeah, well, it's only science…and it looks kind of lame…'

That dismissive sigh and shrug filled Matthew's mind and body. His skin prickled and his stomach knotted: it felt as though he had just been struck. The months of work and study that had gone into planning that project, and the teaching that it drew upon, had been written off in one word, the ultimate teen put-down: *lame*.

Feeling instantly and finally disconnected from this class, his very own form class, kids he had seen day-in, day-out for nearly three years, Matthew taught mechanically until 3pm and then, when the bell rang, he picked up his bags, walking out of the door before the first of them was even off their stools.

Chapter Eight

Sunday 24th February to Friday 1st March

Naomi

Having not eaten properly in the last few weeks, Naomi had lost not just the usual Christmas weight but also those magical five to seven pounds that even slim women wanted to get rid of. As she pulled on her dark skinny jeans, feeling the slight looseness in the high waist as she zipped them up, she turned sideways to admire the curve of her thigh, the lean stretch of leg up to her buttocks. What was it about being wanted that made her feel so sexy?

What had, at the start of the year, been a simple idea about how nice it would be to get the new girl from work to come along to the monthly pub lunch was now a potential minefield. Would it be obvious that she and Mike knew each other better than people imagined? Would Carla notice? And Scott? Would Mike do anything, say anything? Perhaps he would ignore her for the sake of keeping their relationship undetected? That latter idea made her skin prickle with fear.

But, most importantly, what would he think of her? They hadn't seen each other since the New Year party. Extremely worried that he would not find her attractive, she was also worried that the reverse might happen. What if he looked terrible, what if it really had all been in her head? And, even worse than that, how was she meant to look him in the eye after all the things they had been saying to each other? After the last-minute cancellation in January and being desperate to keep things as they were, she had not dared to discuss any of this with him.

Her pussy throbbed and, with a sigh, Naomi pulled the tight denim slightly away from her crotch as she felt the blood in her lower half flood to her labia. God, but she felt horny. She glanced at the clock. There really isn't any time for that, she said to herself, though in her mind she could already feel how delicious that short, sharp orgasm would have been. There was something about coming fully dressed, about rubbing yourself through denim, that reminded her of being a teenager, of the countless ache-inducing dry humps she had experienced in her bedroom while her mum had been at work.

Pulling on a slim-fitting vest, she then slid a cream cashmere jumper over the top. Boots tugged on, the soft black leather fitting snugly against her calves, she snapped a chunky bracelet round her wrist and put a pair of gold earrings into her earlobes before taking one last look in the mirror.

Assuming an expression that was slightly moody but also very effective at smoothing out her wrinkles, she felt more confident now she was dressed. He really has no chance, she thought, as she stood in front of the mirror. It's almost cruel.

Arriving at the pub, Naomi let Scott and James lead the way. She wanted to make her entrance slowly and without a husband or son as a backdrop.

'You're here!' cried a warm, booming voice. 'Finally! Now you can go to the bar – first round's all done in...'

Peter. Well on the way, as usual. Buying a place round the corner from The Woodsman was the first foot Peter had set on the slow journey to alcohol-related liver disease. It was still several years away but it was coming, one large glass of overpriced merlot at a time.

'James! Come and sit next to Sassy and her friend!'

There were the light honey tones of Susan, Peter's wife. She was a friend of Naomi's only by extension of Peter and Scott's friendship, not through any mutual interests. Unless you included the mutual desire to be rid of said husbands for one Saturday a month while they went off to play golf. Naomi had always felt that it was impossible to be friends with someone who could call their only daughter Sassy.

The introductions began and, as Naomi walked in, Mike was already standing, shaking Scott's hand. Both men turned to look at her. She smiled, aware that she was flushing and prepared to blame it on the open fire that was blazing away in the corner of the snug if anyone commented. No one did.

'Wow, Nomes! You look great!' Carla whistled, as she came over and embraced her friend.

Hugging the younger woman tight whilst saying a mental *Sorry*, Naomi looked directly at Mike. He was staring at her, the hand he had been shaking Scott's with now dropped to his side. He was a little shorter than she remembered but broader; his shoulders looked muscular, especially now as he stood there, looking a little tense. His brown hair was starting to grey at the temples but was thick, swept back, and he sported a neatly trimmed beard that softened his jaw. His dark blue eyes held hers. The fact that they were slightly too small for his face didn't take anything away from the intensity of the look he was giving her. He looked like a caged animal that had just noticed the door had been left open.

Naomi released Carla from the embrace and then stepped back slightly, away from the table and away from Mike, completely unconsciously, afraid of what her body might do if she stayed too close for too long.

'What have you been doing?' Carla continued. 'Gosh...'

If you only knew, Naomi thought as she saw Carla sit down heavily, her pudgy face sinking in on itself a little. The younger woman had not lost her Christmas weight and, after what was clearly a few weeks of cut-price chocolates and midweek drinking, now looked heavier than she had been at New Year. Smiling sweetly, Naomi gave a self-deprecating shrug and sat down at the opposite end of the long wooden table. Carla poked about at the bottom of the empty crisp packet in front of her. Mike stared down into his pint. James glanced round at the adults, rolled his eyes, and took out his phone. The other teens were already doing the same.

Susan began to pour the wine and waved a menu at Mike. 'Would you like to look at this?' she asked. 'Or do you know what you want?'

Naomi looked up from the glass of red wine that Scott had put in front of her and straight at Mike. How was he going to play this?

'I already know exactly what I want,' he said, gaze fixed on Susan in a very deliberate fashion.

The rest of the lunch passed by in a blur of roast beef, Yorkshire puddings, red wine and chatter. Following that remark to Susan, Mike continued to behave scrupulously, being attentive to Carla, even spending time talking to James and the girls. Naomi followed his lead and was on best behaviour too, though she couldn't help wishing he would be a little more flirtatious. Much of this week had been spent fantasising about a possible encounter in the pub corridor, and now, realising that it was unlikely to happen, Naomi felt a little deflated.

Draining her glass, she topped it up and then waggled the empty bottle at Scott with a smile. He raised his eyebrows but, without a word, got up and went back to the bar to order some more.

James and Sassy were huddled over their phones.

'What are you looking at?' Naomi asked.

'Shoes!' Sassy said, her tone revealing the overconfidence that her mother's ill-advised choice of name had endowed her with. 'James has helped me find the most awesome wedges!'

Smiling, Naomi glanced at Mike. He smiled back. She took another sip of wine. It would be odd, she supposed, not to talk to him at all. That in itself, surely, would look suspicious.

Susan and Carla were having an animated conversation about the puddings they had ordered. The choices here were the usual custard- and cream-sodden winter favourites: apple pie with a buttery crust, sticky treacle tart. Naomi looked at Mike again and smiled.

'How's work?' he asked her, down the table.

OK, she thought, safe start.

'Busy,' she replied. 'We're about to start exporting Juice Shots into the States and I've also got a new kale drink that I'm finishing the formula for this month. Oh, and a rather distracting side project which seems to be taking up a bit of my time...'

She had not been able to resist adding that. God, being naughty was fun.

Face impressively neutral, Mike said, 'I've seen the advert for those Shot things. The one with all the animals and celebrities pretending to be kids so they can have one?'

'Yes! It's been very successful. The agency are pretty solid. We've used them for a while. Could just do with a bit less negative press about juice drinks. I seem to spend my whole time firefighting hysterical press articles about kids getting diabetes from drinking cartons of juice...'

'They're right, though, aren't they?' Mike continued, a hint of challenge in his voice. 'I thought there was a fair bit of evidence about juice being bad for kids.'

Naomi straightened her back and arched an eyebrow at him. Moving her wine glass slightly to one side, she replied, smoothly and deliberately, 'We only use natural fruit extracts and natural preservatives in the Shots. Kids dehydrating is a more crucial issue in some cases. I've seen reports that show without at least 500ml of liquid a day kids' brain function can decrease by about forty per cent.'

'And where was that report from?' Mike said, the challenge in his voice firmer now. 'Commissioned by VitSip by any chance?'

'We have a team…a team of scientists doing this research for us – they're perfectly impartial,' she said, her voice getting slightly louder. 'It's hardly the responsibility of our business to ration our products. If people are stupid enough to think six bottles of Juice Shots a day is appropriate then that's their problem. It's impossible to legislate for the uneducated. No one would ever make anything.'

'But I've seen the ad!' Mike protested. 'Even I wanted one of those things after I saw it! And if kids see it when they're watching whatever it is they watch these days then they harass their parents for it at the supermarket.'

Naomi glanced at her nails. She noticed that the red lacquer on her middle finger was chipped.

'There are plenty of alternatives to commercial children's programming, Mike.' She snipped his name out in individual letters. 'And have you not heard of Ocado?'

There was a murmur of laughter round the table followed by silence.

Mike shrugged and drained the last of his glass. 'It's nearly time to go, Carla.'

The younger woman looked up, an unfortunate dribble of cream running down her chin as she spooned the last of the pudding into her mouth.

Naomi chose that moment to stand up. Stretching out slightly, she elongated her lean body, making sure her legs and backside were in full view as she made to go the bathroom.

'So good to see you both,' she purred and, smiling, she walked away. She felt both triumphant and very, very angry. God, he was so annoying! she raged to herself in the bathroom. VitSip was one of the best-performing companies operating in the UK at the moment but, as they continued to expand and look for growth in emerging markets such as the Americas and

Asia, all they seemed to get was grief. *Sugar Peddlers Look East for Growth* was one headline she remembered recently. It made her job difficult, and it also painted the company as some sort of demonic entity force-feeding the innocents of Britain toxic sugar. Everyone knew that the government were just looking for the next revenue stream, and with tobacco already taking its hit, and having lost their battle to hit the boozers, they were targeting Big Food instead. People like Mike would never see it like that, though.

As she weaved her way back to the group, through the closely packed wooden tables, she felt relieved that he had already gone and pleased with how she had coped with today. There was a doubt, though, nibbling away at her mind: what if, after the argument, he no longer wanted her?

As she sat there, her confidence seemed to drain away.

Everyone that was left was talking about going home. Naomi went through the motions, barely aware of what was happening now that Mike had gone. All she wanted to do was get home and get back online.

That was an interesting afternoon.

I suppose that's one way to describe it.

I have to see you. On your own.

I need more time.

I can't wait. I want you. I have to have you.

There was the longest of long pauses. All she did was stare at those three words: *I want you.*

His desire for her seemed to drive everything. It was all she could think about. What had happened at the pub had made her doubt it – made her doubt whether, having seen her again, he still wanted her. And now there it was in black and white and it made her skin tingle, her crotch numb. Her body always responded to his words like this, in a way that continued to surprise her. The whole thing was such a surprise really. As she stared at the lines of text, she wondered how she had ended up here, how what had seemed like such an innocent thing, a hello across cyberspace – did they even call it that these days? – had mutated, transformed itself, via mere words, into a hunger more fierce than any she had ever known.

And now he wanted to see her. Now, like Pinocchio, the words wanted to be real, to experience and feel for themselves. What they had done through the screen was no longer enough. Real touch and real contact, skin on skin, was being demanded. She was being asked to play the game for real.

And she had known this was coming. The *I need more time* line had been an attempt, and a half-hearted one at that, if she would only admit that to herself. It was part of the mental defence case she had been building for herself so that she could say, hand on heart, that she had said no, that she had tried to wriggle free. It made her feel calmer, knowing that she could point to her attempts to get away.

But she was already caught, trapped like a fly in a web. There was something both delicious and terrifying about facing something that felt a little like death.

Yes, she typed.

Yes?

Yes.

Really?

Yes.

Oh, God, she thought, oh, God, oh, God, oh, God. It's really starting now.

OK. I'll sort something out. A hotel. That be OK?

Yes, I suppose so.

When can you get away this week?

This week? She felt appalled.

He seemed to sense her shock. *I told you. I have to have you now. I can't wait.*

Any night is fine.

OK. I'll message you when it's sorted.

OK.

Cool. Talk to you later.

And then he was gone. She cried out in frustration. This medium was not a tender one. She had acquiesced and she wanted softness and warmth, but all she got were blunt, black words. *Sorting it out.* It was a logistical enterprise now, a task to be managed. Calls had to be made, emails sent and received. Hugging herself, she felt suddenly cold and vulnerable, just as she had after that first time, the first time he had told her to touch herself.

Scrolling back over what had been said, it all seemed so bald, so bare. She felt sick. What was she doing? She laughed at herself. Who was she trying to fool? The mental jury? They weren't fooled. As she stared at the words again, her crotch throbbed; all the blood seemed to run to it like a river rushing to join the sea, inevitable and hungry. Seeing his mouth in her mind, imagining him kissing her, she touched herself and gasped as she felt how warm she was. She had never wanted anyone the way she wanted him right now.

It might only be a few more days but right now, as she got up, legs unsteady, breathing ragged, she wondered how she could possibly bear it.

The following morning, she was online before she had even put the kettle on.

Then came the message beep. It was him. In an almost Pavlovian fashion, her stomach fizzed with excitement; the blood in her body began to redirect itself to her pussy.

Hey.

Hey there.

How are you?

Very well. You?

Better for having a room sorted: do you know The Bell?

Yes.

Well, there. Any time from 3 but I imagine you'll be at work so, say, from 7?

What day?

Wednesday.

I'll have to check what time Scott is going to be home. I'll get back to you later.

K.

OK.

Later, then.

Yes, speak to you later xx

Back in the kitchen, the usual morning dance of toast, teacups, bag checks and routine discussions. Orders and commands for the day and week were waiting to be issued and Naomi included this in her list of demands:

'And can you be home before 7pm on Wednesday? I've got a school thing to go to. You know just a mums' thing…'

Scott didn't even look at her, he was packing some fruit into his briefcase: the daily banana, the daily apple.

'Yes, of course, no problem.'

And with that it was done. No queries, no fuss just: yes, no problem. Naomi skipped back upstairs and, having left the screen up, messaged Mike right back:

Done. I'll be there by 7.15.

And if anyone had seen her then they would have sworn she had grown wings. Flying down the stairs and out of the house, she felt as if she was floating, floating on a wave of pure anticipation.

David

It had taken so much work. So much effort.

That's probably why I'm crying, David thought, as he looked at himself in the full-length mirror.

He was slim.

The weight was gone and, like a stormy sea whose retreating waves sweep a beach clean, its departure had left him purified. His skin was clear, his hair thick and glossy. He appeared sharper, as if until now he had always seen himself out of focus. His jaw was a clean arc defining the bottom half of his face; angular cheekbones were strong buttresses around eyes that were no longer clouded with fear and misery but instead shone with confidence and ease. Reaching up to gently touch his face, David stared at the lean forearm that stretched to his upper arm and shoulder.

Looking down, he was no longer faced with a soft, shifting mound of belly; instead he could see his feet. He wriggled his toes and grinned.

I feel like saying, Hello, toes! he thought.

Grinning at the thought, he cried out, 'Hello, toes!'

And then he laughed out loud.

Running his hands down his sides, he felt the bones of his ribcage and the smooth, lean lines of his torso and hips. His grin widened as he looked at his dick and marvelled at how much bigger it seemed now it wasn't hidden under rolls of excess fat. It twitched involuntarily and he laughed again.

God, he had never felt this good.

Is this how slim people feel all the time? he wondered. No wonder they don't need to eat.

He was suffused with it: filled up all the way from his tingling scalp to his wriggling toes with complete and utter joy.

And then he woke up.

Closing his eyes, he tensed his whole body, desperately trying to keep hold of the feeling that the dream images had given him. The feeling of happiness, the sensation of lightness: he was still infused with it and perhaps, he thought, if he lay really still it would stay; but as his brain shifted up through the gears of consciousness the sensation began to fade. And, as he tensed more, clenching his eyes shut, the shimmering colours and vivid sensations began to dissolve, to vaporise like a fading rainbow. All of a sudden his mind was fully conscious and the hot bright glare of his misery burned the last of the dream happiness away.

Not only that, it was the first day back at school after the all-too-short week of the half-term holiday.

Curling up, he tried to force himself back into the dream, but it was like pushing at a locked door. Straining, he brought all of his mind to bear on the spot in his brain where the joy had resided, but it was no good: it had gone.

As his mind awoke fully, he became aware of his headache, his clammy skin, the sensation of not feeling remotely rested despite having been in bed for eight hours. The rhythm of his sleeping had been intermittently disturbed by what, another stone from now, would be sleep apnoea; and there was the smell. Who talked about the smell? No one. The sour, stale smell of sweat caught and squeezed between the fat rolls that covered his body. His bed reeked of it, even though Kerri changed the sheets, without comment, two or three times a week, something for which he was ever and always silently gratefully.

Getting out of bed slowly, he went to the shower. Taking his time, he let the hot water pour over him and began to wash under the rolls around his belly as well as those on his arms and at the top of his legs where the fat rested on his thighs. The inner parts of these were always raw and chafed. He was always quick in the water because it took so long to dry himself properly afterwards. He had to be thorough and he had to be careful. Wincing, he felt the full, painful force of the shame he had experienced when, at thirteen, Kerri had had to rub thick Oilatum cream all over the raw, peeling blisters, which were the result of his having left the skin under his fat wet.

He sighed again. The sadness settled over him. A grey darkness and leaden chill replaced the light Technicolor dream. There was a fresh bleakness to everything as if he were a trapped resident of a twilight world who had been given one momentary glimpse of a place full of sunlight. And now, returned to the gloom, the only relief his dispirited mind could conjure up was the contents of the drawer in his room.

Angry at himself, he resisted. Getting dressed quickly, he went to the kitchen and took a slightly soft apple from the bowl with resentful force.

Kerri was singing along with the radio and that annoyed him. How could she feel happy? That was the worst thing about the overweight kids at school: the fact that they pretended to be happy. For David knew. He knew the truth and he knew that the happiness, the empty smiles, were a front: a pitiful façade that would only eventually crumble under the sheer weight of misery that being very overweight caused.

She was singing and packing her sachets. This week was powdered diet lunch week and, watching her, he hated her. Hated her because he knew that the sachets had never worked before and that they would not work this time either. Hated her for the way she was fooling herself that this time it would be different when he knew it wouldn't be. Then he felt guilt, shame and most of all anger at himself, for he knew that he couldn't do it either; that he was the one filling his bedroom drawer up, that he was the one spending all his spare money on fried chicken.

It wasn't as though there weren't sometimes better days, he thought. If he tried hard, he could remember them. Like thinking back over a holiday or special occasion: there were days that stood out, days where he had felt good in spite of his size, days where he had felt light and shiny, pleased, even, about how he looked. But today was not going to be one of those days.

Later on, as he walked along the corridor, James chattering at his side, the thinner boy unconsciously shortening his naturally long and bounding stride to match his friend's slower

189

pace, David almost felt better. He felt full, which was always a good way to feel. Tongue still tingling from the bright yellow mustard, he was relishing the glorious aftertaste of salty frankfurters and glistening translucent onions. David recalled their savoury tang as he had pressed loaded finger roll after loaded finger roll into his mouth.

Having eaten and also managed to exit the lunch room with no abuse had already begun to improve David's day, and his mood continued to lift as they walked out into the noisy playground to find that what had been a dull, grey morning was now transformed into a luminous winter afternoon. The air was cold but the lemon sun was just warm enough. David could see Christianne and the Three Graces on the far side of the playground leaning against the black-painted railings, heads all together, their fashionably long hair touching. A keratin curtain behind which to hide their gossiping and glancing.

David liked to watch girls. Girls moved differently. When they walked, their hips and legs seemed to be moving to some magical internal tune: mere action made melodic by the rhythm. It had really only been since Christmas that he had begun to notice girls more but, now, as with opening a bag of sweets, he couldn't stop. It seemed to him that all girls were beautiful, even the plain ones with glasses and mousy hair. There was a sheen to them, a glow that he wanted for himself; it seemed to him that if he could just taste one of those cheeks, could just rest his lips on that smooth, pale pinkness then he too would glow, would feel the lightness enter his body and suffuse him.

'Mate? Mate?' James was nudging him gently. 'Mum says she'll pay for us to go and see that film you sent me the link for, like, next week?'

'Really?'

'Yeah,' James said.

'Sick.'

'Yeah, should be.'

'Why's she doing that, then?' David asked, glancing sideways at his friend.

James shrugged. 'No idea.'

They chatted some more about the film. The bell rang. The afternoon had begun.

Exactly two hours and forty-five minutes later, that Monday did something that days never did for David: it completely surprised him.

He was standing, waiting at the gate for James. The other boy always walked home with him on Mondays as it was one of the few days he wasn't engaged in after-school sports or activities, but today he was holding him up; he had forgotten his French textbooks. David hunched in on himself and stared at the concrete. Any type of hanging about was dangerous. He could not afford to linger anywhere, and here in particular, on the periphery of the school, away from the unreliable protection of teachers, anything could happen to him.

Scuffing the ground with his school shoes, alternating from foot to foot to amuse himself as well as to help against the cold, he pulled his coat round himself and tucked his chins into the scarf round his neck. He muttered to himself: why was James taking so long?

'Hi, David.'

David looked up. It was Christianne. 'Hey,' he said.

Suddenly feeling very hot, he tugged the black woollen scarf away from his neck. Christianne looked at the ground too. His size did that to most people, even the nice ones. There was so much of him, people seemed to find it hard to look straight at him.

David looked around. It was odd to see her unaccompanied by the Three Graces.

'They're all at hockey,' she said lightly, noticing his look. 'I can't play today. Need to get home.'

'Oh,' David said, instantly wishing he had said literally anything else.

'My dad's back from Afghanistan so we're all meant to be going out for dinner.'

'Oh,' David said again. Then, angry at himself for having said nothing else, he continued, 'That must be good.'

Christianne continued to stare at the ground and scuffed it with her non-regulation, heeled black patent shoes. 'Yeah, suppose so...' She hesitated, then continued, 'They tend to argue lots when he gets back and then make up just before he goes away again. Kind of annoying really.'

'Ah,' David said, frowning. He hadn't known her dad was posted abroad. 'Must be hard on all of you.' He paused. 'I miss my dad too.'

Christianne stopped scuffing and, for the first time, looked directly at David. 'Do you? Really? I miss mine all the time. Yours are divorced, right? Sorry if...' She hesitated, eyes clouding, unsure of what was the right thing to say.

David smiled. 'S'OK. At least I get to see him. Well, sometimes, anyway. Must be hard yours being away for, what, like, six months at a time?'

'Yeah, yeah, it is. He does bring some cool stuff back, though. That's pretty awesome.'

They shared a grin.

'Guilt gifts?'

'Yes!'

Their shared grins widened.

'Dad got me a tablet last year. He missed a few weekends in a row and, well, you know...' David's eyes gleamed wickedly.

'Yeah, I got a new 3-D TV last time and he's promised me an iPhone this time. It's not even my birthday till summer and, you know, he'll be away for that, which means presents before and on the day *and* after.'

'Cool!'

'It is kinda cool.'

'Yeah, it is. I love stuff. Sod love and attention – give me stuff! Lots and lots of stuff!'

They both laughed. Their eyes met again, faces lit up with shared understanding. There was a moment, a single tiny moment, when David saw that she was seeing beyond the fat, beyond it to David himself.

'Guys!'

It was James. 'Guess who was in the French room when I got there? Only Holmesy!'

'Really?' said Christianne, eyes now on the other boy.

David began to scuff the floor again. If only, he thought, James had taken a little longer.

And then what? his mind scoffed. If you'd had an extra five minutes she'd have declared her undying love for you? Get real!

David scuffed the ground again, harder this time, dislodging some of the crumbling tarmac and sending it scattering. He began to walk towards the gates. 'All right, mate! Ready to go?'

James waved at Christianne and she smiled.

'Bye, David!' she called out.

David didn't dare look back. He lifted his arm by way of farewell.

Only when they had got thirty metres away did he regret it and he turned to look at her, her braids swinging slightly as she walked away.

And, then, she glanced back round.

Elated, he gave her a big wave, smiling widely in the hope that she could see. She waved back. He floated home.

Naomi

Thursday afternoon. Not yet even a full day after 'it' had happened. Having made an excuse about a doctor's appointment, Naomi had left work early and, pulling into the drive, desperate to get indoors and to be on her own, she was surprised and annoyed to see Tree Man standing in the driveway.

Getting out of the car, she looked up at the neat outline of the freshly pollarded tree. The tree had been neutered, contained, its clean black lines sharp and defined.

Sean was standing at the foot of the tree, watching Naomi's face as she took in what had been done to the tree. She was looking at it, but all she was seeing was herself: the change that had been done to her. Her eyes took on a peculiar cast, as if she was looking far out to sea.

'Is it OK?' Sean asked, his voice hesitant. 'It was difficult,' he continued, 'but I'm pleased with the results. If you're going to do something this brutal to a living thing, then you need to at least do it with some care.'

Naomi swallowed hard. Her slender throat stretched up as she continued to stare at the cropped tree. The denuded nubs of the tree branches were like clenched, impotent fists. It looked painfully beautiful against the bright blue, late winter sky.

Given that this was something she'd thought she wanted, Naomi wondered why she felt so much like crying.

'Yes,' she managed. 'Yes... What do I owe you?' she added, her voice still soft.

'Two hundred, please.'

'Fine... I'll just get my cheque book.'

Naomi went into the house and returned a few moments later with a cheque. The lines of her signature were thin, pale, indistinct.

'Thank you,' he said. 'If there are any questions or problems, just give me a call.'

Naomi nodded. She was staring up at the tree. Eyes still misty, seeing some other recent devastation.

Stepping back, and with a slight bow of his head, Tree Man walked away.

Naomi shut her eyes and, the cropped lines of the tree still etched on her retina, she went inside.

It was now two days later. Every day was determined by how long it had been since that day. That night. Those one hundred and twenty minutes that had changed everything.

Sitting upstairs and unable to concentrate on work, she willed him to message her. The computer beeped and her stomach flipped over. It was him.

I have to see you again.

And even though all she had thought about for these past two days was this, now she had what she wanted her mind instantly rejected it. Oh, God, she thought, so soon?

She had gone through these last two days on autopilot, trying to seem normal but with her mind playing over and over the scenes it had isolated from their time together. His hand between her legs, sliding his fingers high up inside her. His mouth going slack as he came. Hearing her own voice in her ears, crying out *No* as she too had come.

He had felt so different from Scott: hadn't seemed to fit on her. Sensing the foreign nature of the territory, her arms had flailed, unsure of where to place themselves on a back that was so much broader than the one they had touched and held for nearly two decades. The main difference had been the force and urgency of the experience. He had come at her like an animal. When had she last *wanted* Scott? Or he her? They were no longer hungry for each other and she knew that. Their weekly couplings were fine, had been enough for a long time, but now – now she had had a taste of something else. How much she wanted to have it again terrified her.

I want you. I have to have you again, he repeated now, echoing her thoughts.

The buzz was beginning again: her heart was speeding up. The beats coming faster and faster, her mind a blank except for the words etched in black on the glowing, white screen. Gasping, she was suffocating. She had to try and remember to breathe.

A dash downstairs. A studiedly casual conversation. An even faster dash back up the stairs. A date set, for the Wednesday after next. Naomi knew that, between now and then, it would be all she could or would think of.

Chapter Nine

Monday 4th to Monday 10th March

Matthew

The morning walk to school was a bright, sunny one. Matthew felt the sun on his skin and wished that his own mood were as light. He changed the song he was listening to: he needed something more cheerful to try to chase away the Monday blues. Just because he had begun to care less did not mean that the anxiety about Mondays, about the start of yet another demanding and draining school week, was any less powerful.

Sitting in the classroom, waiting for the day to begin, he knew he should do something, anything, to take his mind off the feeling of dread in the pit of his stomach, but it seemed that the less he did, the less he wanted to do. It wasn't so much a vicious cycle as a steep, slippery slope, a slope that led straight into the pit of the Undead. Was he still one of them if he had passions elsewhere? He wasn't sure. Maybe the fact that he still felt nervous was a good thing? At least he still felt something, even if it was uncomfortable.

The bell rang and he started a little. He stood up and took a deep breath. Form time.

As his form class filed out twenty minutes later, the bell ringing in the background, Matthew heard their enthusiasm and chatter and part of him wished he still felt the same but he didn't. He decided he had to stop fighting that feeling now. Preparing the room for the first lesson, he glanced out of the window and frowned as he saw the clouds thickening low in the blue sky. 'You can't change how you feel any more than you can change the weather,' he recalled Polly saying to him over the half-term break. Thinking of her made him smile.

Some of the same pupils from his form class began to file back into the room. There was a special affection for any of the kids that you had in your form group: knowing them slightly better, you cared about them more.

As David lumbered into the room, though, Matthew struggled to keep his face neutral. The boy provoked mixed feelings. More than most, Matthew understood the issues behind the weight, but he also felt frustrated – frustrated that so little was being done either by the boy or his family.

He caught himself gnawing at his thumb.

And remember, his mind sharply reminded him, David isn't *smoking* to help himself lose weight.

Matthew didn't appreciate the memory. It made him feel simultaneously very guilty, and very much like having a cigarette. Just get through the day, he thought, then you get to see Polly. The bell rang, and he took another deep breath.

David

It was the fourth Monday. Three whole weeks. It had been worse this time than ever before. Tears, arguments and tension. All caused by the hunger in Kerri's belly, the pressures of work and home, the absence of immediate results. David and the girls kept out of the way as much as they could.

'It's like when Dad tried to give up smoking that time...' said Jess, sighing.

'Yeah, you're right,' agreed David.

'Was that when he threw his dinner on the floor?'

'Ha, yes!'

They all laughed at the memory and then there was silence. It had not been funny at the time. Not funny at all.

'And there was the next time when he just went to bed at 7pm every night for a week. Remember that?' David said.

'He would be in bed before us,' laughed Emily. 'I used to go in and kiss him goodnight and sometimes he'd already be asleep!'

'Yeah, well,' said Jess, dismissively. 'This'll be over soon enough. She never manages more than a few weeks.'

'She's trying hard this time,' David said.

'Yeah, she is,' agreed Emily.

'Whatever. It won't last,' Jess repeated from the floor of the living room as she continued to flick through her magazine.

'Maybe it would help if you didn't sit there all night eating Haribo,' added David.

Their eyes met. Jess went to say something and then stopped. David winced. He knew what she had been going to say as much as she did: well, *I'm* not fat.

Scowling, she carried on flicking, unseeing, through her magazine. God, she looks like Kerri when she does that, David thought.

'Dinner's coming!'

They all looked at each other again and rolled their eyes.

The salad was crunchy and curiously watery, the grilled chicken dry. Heavy on artificial sweeteners and light on actual flavour, the low-fat dressing with which they all doused the greenery was of little help. The television was a welcome distraction as they masticated their way slowly through yet another chewy, effortful meal. The girls had a batch of potato wedges to go with theirs. Emily ate all of these first and was now pushing the chicken under the salad.

The usual chatter was replaced by silence as forks scraped against plates. David and Kerri worked through the food with an almost grim determination. Afterwards, they all sat and watched the television, both David and Kerri playing with their phones in lieu of further snacking. Jess and Emily were sent off to bed after a couple of low-fat yoghurts. Kerri got up to put the cartons in the bin, moving quickly in what David recognised was her way of resisting the urge to lick what was left of the dessert out of the little pots.

They were both fidgeting. David was aware that Kerri's left foot was twitching, toes tapping against the leg of the coffee table. David continued to scroll through his news feed whilst half-watching the TV. His feelings were tangled up, his stomach knotted. Part of him wanted Kerri to stay strong, to show him that she could do it – that it could be done – but part of him wanted this to be over. That part wanted to get back to how things had been before. The salad and tasteless food, the fidgeting and the silence were really uncomfortable and he didn't like it, not one bit.

He glanced over at Kerri. She was looking at him. They both looked back at the television. Neither of them would have been able to say what they were watching.

David was *not* going to be the first to crack. He was still hungry, but this diet was Kerri's choice, and she had to be the one to break it.

All of a sudden, an idea came to him. He decided to be crafty.

'Dinner was nice…' he began, still staring, unseeing, at the television. 'I feel nice and full,' he continued. 'Sated. Replete.'

Kerri's lips turned in on themselves to contain the grin that was trying to escape.

'I think it's the magical combination of low-fat protein and leafy greens that has caused me to feel this way,' David continued, voice light, a tremor of laughter beginning to build up in his stomach and chest. 'Very satisfy—'

He burst out laughing and, hearing him, Kerri released the knot on her lips and joined in. They laughed and then, comically slowly, they both hauled themselves up off the sofa and, with a rueful smile, their faces mirror images of each other for that moment, they both dashed to the kitchen.

'Bagsie the last of the Walkers!' cried David, making a bee-line for the cupboard while Kerri bobbed past him and opened the fridge door.

'I've got my eye on the girls' chocolate!' Kerri replied, hand reaching down to the salad crisper, which was stuffed full of mini bags of Buttons and other treat-sized bars of chocolate. These treats had been purchased by way of buying the girls' compliance at the supermarket, as well as a reward for them doing their homework.

They filled their arms up. David took a bottle of lemonade and a few bags of crisps, and Kerri two huge handfuls of tiny bags of chocolate buttons.

As they ate, exchanging bags of crisps for bags of chocolate, they talked. Something about the act of breaking the diet, breaking the rules together, created a moment of camaraderie and openness between mother and son that was usually absent. The talk was inconsequential but it was conversation nevertheless, and while, like the food that was now filling their stomachs, it was ultimately unsatisfying, it felt really good. This was as much a part of the ritual as the clearing-out of the cupboards at the start. It was the sense of breaking free: of running for home and finding it as welcoming as one had always hoped it would be.

The bell rang for the end of the school day. David's headache was worse than usual. It was a pulsing, nausea-inducing pain behind his dry eyes. This, combined with his aching back and his chafing thighs, meant that he felt even more irritable and short-tempered than usual. James bounded over and David tried not to scowl at his friend, tried not to show his envy for the other boy's energy and ease.

'All right?' said James, still bouncing on the spot. 'Gonna get the bus today?'

'Yeah, sure,' replied David, kicking at his bag.

There were throngs of kids all around them. Pupils came to the school from all over the county and so there were many coaches parked outside the school gates as well as the inevitable Range Rovers containing mothers anxious that their precious offspring not be exposed to the other pupils by having to spend time with them on an actual bus.

The playground was noisy and crowded, but David could still see Christianne. At the moment, he seemed to be permanently aware of where she was, ever alert and sensitive to her presence. She stood talking to one of the Three Graces; the short, red-haired one. The girls were out of earshot, but their body language gave away the intensity of their conversation. Perhaps, he thought, a surge of hope rising inside him like sunshine, perhaps she's talking about me?

Christianne's hair was falling in a sheet over her face as she spoke directly into her friend's ear. Simultaneously, they looked up and over. David followed her gaze, followed it past himself and all the way to the bouncing form of James. The girls looked away and continued to whisper to each other, the shorter one now nudging her friend.

David picked up his bag. 'Might walk,' he grunted, his voice low and head down.

'Really? Jeez. OK, then.'

James tossed his own bag over his shoulder and loped alongside as David lumbered towards the gate. The walk would be slow and uncomfortable, but it was still preferable to seeing the expression on Christianne's face as she looked at his best friend.

Walking down the road, they managed to avoid the other pupils and, once they had left the school a few hundred metres behind them, David visibly relaxed, letting his bag fall to the ground. He pulled it along for a bit, then stopped and took out some crisps. He wanted to hate James, but he was too caught up in hating himself to have any energy left over for it.

'Want some?' he said as he popped open the grab bag.

'Sure,' said James, reaching in.

They walked and ate. David taking handfuls then offering the bag again to James.

'Remember what Holmesy said about these bags? The sharing ones?'

'Yeah, that was funny.'

They were recalling the recent form lesson when Mr Holmes had brought in a selection of grab bags and standard crisp packets. There had also been some of the super-size and duo-bars of chocolate alongside the standard single bars.

'Question, then,' he had said, perched as ever on the end of his desk. 'Who here likes to share?'

There had been a few sniggers and a few raised hands.

Matthew had looked at the raised hands and said, 'Really? You like to share?'

The pupils with their hands up (all girls, all eager to be seen to be good, to give the right answer) had flushed and pulled their hands down as they realised that, this time, the right answer was wrong.

'Anyone got younger siblings? Little ones? Aged two, three, four? What do your parents spend most of their time teaching them how to do?'

'Share, sir!'

'Yeah, my little cousin has a meltdown if anyone goes near her fruit chews!'

'My dad still hasn't learnt – you should see his face if you try and take his portion of chips out of the bargain bucket!'

There had been a burst of laughter.

'No one likes to share,' Matthew had said, smiling. 'From an evolutionary perspective this makes complete sense, of course: the human race wouldn't have survived very long if it had gone around giving away its food. Survival of the fittest meant that people who had the edge, those who were the bravest, the most resourceful, got the most food. Again, those early people wouldn't have continued to survive if they had gone: *Oh, no, you take that last portion of buffalo meat, no please... No, really, I insist...*'

More laughter.

Matthew had picked up the grab bags and the larger of the chocolate bars.

'So, what does that tell you about these things?'

'People just eat the whole bag themselves, sir.'

'Yes, they do. They eat the lot. I do it. I'm sure you do it, too. We open them up and our natural instinct is to finish off the lot. One of these plus one of these and you're looking at well over five or six hundred calories as well as your fat intake for the day if you're an adult woman, and around fifteen teaspoons of sugar! So, either fight your natural instincts and do share, or buy small bags when you can, or, better still, don't buy these things at all!'

Yeah, right, David had thought at the time: his mouth had been watering just at the sight of the brightly coloured packets.

David handed the last of the bag over to James.

'You sure, mate? You might not make the evolutionary cut, you know?' James looked at him and smiled.

David smiled back. 'Gonna have an oversized chocolate bar next...' he replied. He nearly made a joke about his weight but then stopped; he couldn't ever quite do it. It really wasn't funny.

'Holmesy's project seems like it might be OK, though. Do you think eating this is like research?'

'Yeah! Definitely!'

They walked, ate and talked. They had plans to catch a film at the weekend, since James's mum had offered to pay for them, and they always enjoyed arguing over which one.

When they got to the end of the main road, it was time to part company. James had a short walk to the bus stop to get a bus back to the village he lived in, and David was a short way up the road, past the petrol station.

'See ya tomorrow!' said James, checking the time on his phone. 'I'd better run for the two minutes past.'

He punched David playfully on the shoulder and then ran off. Hitching his bag up high, his long, thin legs stretching out effortlessly along the grey tarmac, he dodged round the other pedestrians, blond hair swept back. David watched him: the other boy looked as though he was flying.

After another forgettable takeaway dinner (why had he missed those so much?), David went upstairs to get away from the oppressive silence of Kerri's broken-diet remorse. He found himself looking in the smeared mirror that was almost hidden by the film posters which covered the exposed wall to the left of his bed. He rarely examined his own appearance very closely, preferring sideways glances and always averting his eyes when he walked past shop windows or mirrors. He rarely made eye contact with anyone.

Twisting his neck around to ease the tension he always felt there, he pulled his shirt collar down and rubbed at his skin. There was a mark, a dark brown smudge around his neck. Turning on the tap, he wetted his hand in the tepid water and then rubbed at the skin again. Still there. He spat on his shirt sleeve and rubbed hard at the mark, this tideline on his skin. As he rubbed hard, the skin began to redden but the mark was still there: persistent, brown and watery, like an old tea-stain on a Formica table-top.

David twisted round again and looked at the other side of his neck. It was there too. His hands flopped down to his sides and then he lifted them again and looked at his hands. The fat stopped at his wrists, leaving cuffs of fat suspended, like a hardened magma flow, skirting hands that were strangely slim. He turned these slender, almost feminine parts of himself over slowly, staring at them, not really sure what he was looking for. Some sort of answer, perhaps, but there was only one way he could get an answer. Locking the door, he typed 'dirty mark on neck' into Google.

Several minutes later, he threw the tablet down and, reaching into the drawer, took out two bars and ate them both quickly.

He watched a few videos. But the thoughts in his head were not having it today. No amount of funny was going to keep them away.

Because all he could think about was how it wasn't ever going to be enough. That moment, the other week, when he had made her laugh – that was never going to be enough for her to like him.

He glanced up at the TV. There was an advert for a comedy DVD. Was there anyone on TV who was fat who wasn't also funny? It was the ultimate disarmament – laugh with me, not at me – and yet it was still not enough. There was just no future in being fat. The market in you was one that no one wanted to trade in. The futures were flat. When you're fat, he thought, it's hard to be anything else.

Getting up again, feeling restless and knowing full well why, he checked the door was locked, walked away, and then went back and checked it again. Turning the TV volume up to the point where it would drown out any noise but not get him told off, he pulled his school trousers off and lay down on his side on the bed.

He couldn't use his computer for this, as Kerri had put security locks on it, but he didn't need the web anyway. Opening up his phone messages, he brought up the messages from Ryan: he always sent the best photos.

He was already nearly hard. He knew the first time wouldn't take long so it was always best to get it done with so he could properly enjoy the second, longer one. Sighing, he reached round and under the rolls of fat that lay on his stomach and put his hand round himself. Staring at the picture of the woman, her legs splayed wide open to show what was still, to David, a bewildering array of flaps and pinkness, he found himself closing his eyes and thinking of Christianne. Of Christianne and her pale cheeks. The meaty rawness of this open-mouthed woman was nothing in comparison to the sight of the soft roundedness of Christianne's face. As he was about to come, David imagined placing his lips on them, imagined kissing them, imagined seeing her smile at him. A broad, welcoming smile. Acceptance.

With a gasp, he came.

His brain went instantly blank: like the signal being dropped and the digital sharpness of the television's images being replaced by hot black and white interference. With a deep sigh, he enjoyed the sensation of himself throbbing against his wet hand. Feeling the warmth turn cold and clammy, he couldn't quite bring himself to move. Wiping his hand on the bed, he lay back for a moment, his mind blissfully blank; and then, after a little while, he felt himself beginning to get hard again. And, hand gentle round his stiffening self, he began to enjoy the longer, slower experience of the second time.

Twenty minutes later, the pleasure receptors deep in the centre of his brain blinked off and, as he cleaned up using some tissues, his brain flickered back on: normal service had been resumed.

And, for David, normal service meant shame, guilt, anger and fear. It meant wondering if he would ever have sex, not the way other boys wondered about it but with a genuine sense of terror, a deep and real sense that, because of his size, it might be something he *never* got to do.

The emptiness he felt after masturbating was terrifying: it was as if someone had dropped him suddenly into a deep, lightless pit. He had Googled it once. There was some fancy psychological term for it but the name, and the fact that it was common, did not help David deal with the basic fact of it, the sheer hollow bleakness of it. He had realised pretty quickly that the contents of his secret drawer helped. And so that was what he did now: he ate himself to sleep.

Matthew

That evening, making dinner, Matthew mused that mostly it felt good to be useful. To feel as though he was making a difference. The website was nearly done: he could see the evidence of his hard work and that felt good, really good.

Polly had sent him a link this afternoon: they had just reached fifteen thousand followers. She was delighted. With that, and with him. That felt good too.

He was hoping that she would show how delighted she was when she eventually turned up.

That thought made him feel even better.

He stirred the pot of vegetarian chilli and then rinsed the brown rice. It had to go on now or it wouldn't be ready in time. Polly wouldn't eat white rice and so neither did he.

Humming to himself, he glanced at the clock. Hopefully she would be here shortly.

The half-term week and the first week he'd been back at work had gone quickly, despite his not having seen as much of her as he had hoped he would. She had been working and so, during the half-term, he had gone home for a few days to see his parents. He had thought about asking her to come along but had changed his mind.

And, given how the visit had gone, he was glad of that.

The doorbell rang. He grinned and ran to answer it. I really must get her a key cut, he thought. I wonder what she'll say when I suggest that…

'Hey,' he said, pulling the door open.

'Hey,' she said, smiling.

They embraced, him holding her small frame close to him and kissing her hard.

'Oh,' she said, looking up at him, eyes wide. 'What a nice welcome!'

'I missed you,' he said, simply, smiling at her.

She kissed him again. 'Me too,' she said. 'And that smells amazing. What is it?'

'Chilli,' he said, going back into the kitchen. 'Cooked with lots of red wine. And served with lots of red wine…'

'My favourite!' she said. 'And look: I can't wait to show you the latest stats on the site.'

'I can't wait to see them!' he called back from the kitchen.

As they ate, next to each other on the little mustard sofa, she asked him about seeing his parents.

'It was OK,' he said. 'Not great but, you know, I survived…'

'What do you mean by *not great*?'

'Well…' Matthew recalled the awkward silences around the dinner table as he had talked about Polly and the activist work she was involved with. His dad's *grumpy old man* routine had really been perfected in recent years and he had gone on a belligerent rant. It had reminded Matthew of certain ageing TV personalities railing against the way things had had the nerve to move on since 1975. The only people not happy about the reducing influence of privileged white males were privileged white males. Polly had helped him see that. 'It was the usual things… It just feels different now, different because I've changed. I used to find the rants kind of funny, but now…'

'Is he still saying what you told me before?'

'Haha, yes…!' laughed Matthew. He put on his best *grumpy old man* voice: 'Bloody Greens… Think they can save the bloody planet one bloody baked bean tin at a time…'

'That's exactly how we *are* changing the world,' said Polly, laughing. 'One step at a time. How else are we going to do it?'

They shared a smile. In that shared feeling and that look was everything: Matthew felt her acceptance and affection for him and, feeling it, he took it and reflected it right back at her. The energy between them was palpable at that point. And that wasn't the only thing… He shifted awkwardly.

She glanced down and smiled cheekily. 'I think we might have to get something else taken care of before we get to work this evening…'

Matthew blushed.

'I love it when you blush… Makes you look even hotter,' she said, pressing closer to him.

Sometimes savouring a moment was more important than saving the world.

Naomi

Going into the bathroom that evening, Naomi stood in front of the huge mirror and stared at her reflection. A week or so on and she looked the same. How could that be? How could she feel so different and yet still look the same? There was no visible trace of what she had done, of the desire she had given in to.

Running yet another hot bath, she stripped to her underwear. Unable to look herself in the eye, she looked down. There, on her shoulder, she saw the pock marks, the small but deep scars from when, aged seven, she had caught chicken pox.

No siblings and few play dates meant that she had not contracted it as a toddler as many children did and, being older, she had caught it hard. Despite her initial annoyance at having to take time off work, her mother had seemed happy to administer care and attention while Naomi lay, hot and feverish, her temperature soaring to 42°C, on the couch in the playroom. Lynne had bathed her face and read to her as she stumbled down the long path from drowsiness to sleep. She had happily prepared and helped her to eat nourishing soups and creamy milkshakes. But a few days later, when the fever broke and the hectic rash of red spots changed to scabby sores, sores that covered Naomi from head to toe, Lynne had become impatient. 'Don't pick at them!' she had snapped. 'You'll only make them worse!'

Naomi had lain on the sofa, pressing herself into the hard cushions to relieve the itching sensation that crawled across her skin. The urge to pick at, to scratch at the burning, crusted sores had been unbearable. She vividly remembered clenching her little fists, pinning her hands to her side.

One afternoon, her mother had gone out. Left alone with the burning, itching need, Naomi had wriggled on the sofa, whimpering with pain, clenching her fists harder, digging blunt nails into her soft palms.

All of a sudden, it had become too much. Without the fear of immediate reprisal, she had remembered telling herself, even at seven, that she could scratch a little, just a little.

She had begun on her head. Rubbing the sores on her scalp, the sense of relief had been exquisite as she pressed down on the nubbly spots that seethed under her fine blonde hair. The pads of her fingers had traced over and pressed gently and then a little harder.

Slowly, she had moved her hands down to her slim, pale arms, tracing her fingers over the miniature mountain range of her forearm. The spots were huge and raised there: red volcanoes topped with crusted yellow. Her tender skin had tingled as she knocked the crusty peaks from off the tight, heated mounds. A wave of nausea had swept over her as, revulsed but also fascinated, she felt the gaps under her thin nails clogging up. Ignoring it, she had let a fingernail graze over the top of a particularly large spot on her wrist. A roll of pleasure rippled down her spine, and she scratched another. Then another. Having given in to the impulse, the relief was intense and she had revelled in it, her hands clawing all over her skin.

When her mother came back, she had found Naomi on the floor of the sitting room, nails bloody, skin aflame, her eyes rolled back in her sockets, a smile of agonised ecstasy on her face. Lynne had screamed at her, slapped her hands and dragged her, crying and bleeding up the stairs before forcing her to take a cold bath. In spite of the pain, Naomi had realised something then: that you could do what you wanted, even something that you knew was wrong, and that the consequences, while very bad, were still more bearable than the strain and effort of not doing what you wanted.

Lying in the hot bath now, she felt fine. Normal. Then, moments later, an image came to her. Carla's face. Then, worse: Scott's face. It was only imaginary but it felt real: the cold hatred of the betrayed. It had felt so good at the time and, yet, now, she just felt sick and hollow. She looked the same but she knew could never feel the same again. Something had died. An idea of herself, of who she was, had gone.

When was the last time she had lied? Apart from telling white lies to James about Santa and the Easter bunny, she hadn't lied so much in years and yet now, during these last few weeks, it was all she had done. So, she was a liar and a cheat.

Was there anything worse?

She shut her eyes. The sick feeling churned in her stomach.

No. There was nothing worse – except for the idea of never getting to do it again.

Sinking beneath the water, she wondered what it would be like to stay here, to let the water take her. Part of her felt as though she deserved to die. Part of her could not wait to do it again. She resurfaced. Twisting the tap to add more hot water, she wondered if maybe more heat would cleanse her, purify her. But she knew it wasn't as simple as that. There was no washing away what she had done. And the fact that part of her didn't want to ever forget it made it even harder.

Getting out, she wrapped herself up in her robe and went upstairs to dress.

What she needed to do was focus, she told herself: focus on her family, focus on here instead of that room, his mouth, his dick. She had to be here and she had to be here now. Only then could she deserve it: if everyone else was happy, then she was allowed.

I will try, she said to herself. I will try to make it all right. I will try to deserve my treat.

A few days later, at home on Sunday evening, Naomi found a kind of release from being absorbed with mundane tasks. Sorting laundry, compiling lists, shopping online, making plans for next weekend and the months ahead. When she engaged with her life she felt free from her appetite. She would feel hungry for real food, for sitting in the living room chatting to James and Scott, for her actual life. On those nights, she went to sleep and enjoyed a restful six or seven hours but then, something would shift, she would wake up and the words would be there, scrolling in front of her:

I am going to fuck you so hard.

I want to hear you call out my name when you come.

I have to have you now.

Then the rest of her body would disappear, leaving behind only a blistering, burning pussy, a cunt that ached with need. She felt unmanned, the desire to be filled up, sated, taken, so overwhelming that she could barely think straight. His words made her hungry for him, for his wanting, and it would start all over again. Her mind was stuffed full of the words and, feeling pursued, hunted, she would slump, breathless, in front of the computer, exhausted from spending her day trying to outrun her desire.

Well over a week had gone by since they had met at the hotel, and, apart from arranging the next time, she hadn't heard from him. Beginning to hate him for not wanting to talk to her as much as she wanted to talk to him, she asked herself, how could he not be online? How could he not feel the same as her? She wished there were some sort of code, some way that he could let her know he was thinking of her, but she didn't dare ask, didn't dare to let him see how desperately she needed to know it. Her need terrified her. It was dark and endless.

Cursing him, she would want to know what he was doing, who he was with. She would pump Carla for information and be relieved when it was revealed that they had been at a friend's for the evening, or that they had had company at home, because then she could picture him occupied, not just ignoring her. She felt neglected when he wasn't in touch with her. The old messages soon got worn with over-handling; she needed fresh words, fresh fuel for her fire. His words were her new life source; without them she could feel herself fading away, like a vampire who had waited too long in between sweet, bloody bites.

Passing mirrors, she would check her reflection, keeping herself under surveillance so that she could say, *Yes, you are still getting away with it.*

Sitting in the living room in the evenings, she would feel safe – safe and free from it. The nights were the worst, but the desire also hunted her through the day, through the meetings, through her calls, through her commute, through the meal prep and the loading and unloading of the dishwasher. Wherever she built the dams, the waves of desire crashed away, eroding her defences and sending the water rushing on ahead. She had acquired control of so much in her life – food, drink, her love for James – but this, this need had surfaced: wet and insistent, pushing and swelling until it burst out of her carefully constructed boundaries.

Where would these needs take her? Having fought them for so long, she was weak, and now, having acquiesced once, she felt powerless. She was being pulled downwards, down to the dark depths of something that she had never expected and never wanted. Depths that scared her. How had she ended up here? How had she got so lost?

Scott had been busier than ever over the last few weeks and, now, sitting together on the sofa, half-watching the television while James was upstairs, it felt odd. She had no idea what to say to him. Her head was a mess, a stew of sour thoughts and fears, and yet the need to talk, to connect, to actually communicate directly with a person and not a screen, was overwhelming. But what to say? *Oh, by the way, I think I have managed to ruin everything good about my life by doing something I thought I wanted and which now I can't seem to stop even though it's making me feel like shit eighty per cent of the time. I am a lying deceitful bitch...?*

She looked at Scott, sitting next to her. Did she still love him? She had to believe she did. She hated herself but *please*, she pleaded with her soul, *please say I am still capable of loving him? That this hasn't taken it all away for good?*

She was still staring into space, lost in her own thoughts, when Scott turned to her and smiled.

'I'll go and check on James and then make some tea if you'd like some?' he said, getting up.

To Naomi, feeling as she did right now, it seemed like the nicest thing anyone had said to her, ever. She suppressed the urge to cry and instead just nodded, saying, as naturally as she could manage, 'Lovely, thanks!'

Scott came back in. He handed her the mug of tea. Looking up at her husband's gentle smile, Naomi felt her throat contract. How could she have done this to him?

Suddenly she felt really angry, not with herself but Mike. *He* had seduced *her*. He had *pursued* her. It was all *his* fault.

She couldn't do it again. If he wasn't going to stay in touch with her, then he didn't deserve to have her again.

'Scott...' she began. That was it. She was going to tell him. Maybe, if she told him, it would stop? Maybe if she said it out loud it would kill it off for good? 'Scott,' she repeated.

'Mmmh?' he said.

She looked at him as he turned to face her. His eyes were soft, tired but content and full of affection. Affection for her. His cheating, lying wife. If she told him, would he ever look at her like that again?

'Thanks,' she said, 'for the tea. Just what I needed.'

'No problem!' he said, smiling. 'Are you all right? You look a little tired.'

'Yeah,' she said, 'I am pretty tired.'

'Maybe we need an early night?' he said, squeezing her leg.

Internally, she cringed. Then, she thought, *I have to*. Maybe it would help?

And it did. In a way. The rhythm and regularity, the familiarity of it calmed her; and yet, lying there afterwards, warm and comfortable, listening to Scott's slow breathing as he began to fall asleep, she stared at the ceiling and thought, It's not enough, it's not enough. I wish it were but it isn't.

For, lying there, staring up into the blackness, she could feel the tide of dark desire begin to wash back towards her. And with it came a feeling of excitement. It was the anticipation, the thrill of the forbidden, and she knew that the next morning, the moment she was up and in front of the computer, she would be back there, indulging again, binging and gorging on his words, feasting on his need for her, stuffing herself with it until she felt sick. Getting ready for the next time.

Walking into the office the next day, it still seemed completely surreal to her, completely odd that no one could tell what she was up to. She recalled a book from university in which a woman was made to wear a red cloth letter on her clothes, a large A to mark her as an adulteress.

How could no one tell what she was thinking?

She felt her face flush again and then the blood left her face, pulsing down to the new centre of herself. She felt it swelling, her legs scissoring as she strode past the security guards, hips swaying. Her whole body was moving to a different rhythm: the drumbeat of desire.

Simultaneously terrified and elated, she could barely breathe as, whenever she was alone, as she was now, sitting at her desk, scene after scene would run through her mind. She was never where she was: she was always there. There in that hotel room. A room which her imagination had barely bothered to furnish. It was just a bed, a chair and a full-length mirror. A bare room in which she now permanently resided, imagining, conjuring up the drama in her mind. She would come to and would find that she had been sitting for twenty minutes staring into space, her eyes glazed over and her crotch numb with a need that the thinking only aggravated.

With two days to go, the only thing that made the waiting bearable was the fact that she was so behind that she had no choice but to work hard. The next two days were full of meetings and, with the month almost halfway through, that April deadline which had seemed so distant before Christmas was now looming and there were certain things that she could no longer put off.

Looking again at the technical report for the Kale Kooler, she picked up the phone and dialled the number for the lab. There was nothing like talking to some techies to cool herself down. As the number rang off, she glanced at the clock and decided to head to the lab herself.

The tech lab was in another building, separated from the central offices by a parched piece of landscape, all concrete and dusty weeds. Naomi walked through the office, enjoying the noise of the sales floor as she walked past and then passing through the calm of the foyer out into the bright winter sun. It was mild today and she smiled up at the pale sky, enjoying the feel of the sun.

Hearing the click of her heels on the hard concrete path, she straightened her back and took a deep breath. Something

217

about that sound had the power to make Naomi feel efficient, even if she had resorted to shaking her head to stop thoughts of Mike taking hold. Glancing again at the folder she was carrying, she focused her mind on the conversation she needed to have with Alex and his team in the lab.

'Ah!' said a smooth, deep voice, sounding amused. 'The old wandering-about-with-a-folder trick – I'd forgotten about that one!'

Naomi looked up, startled out of her reverie by the voice and the laughter that followed it.

It was Jonathan Winters. She stopped and, shielding her eyes from the sun, looked at him. He had stopped just in front of her; stepping into the shade, he gestured to her to come closer. They stood facing each other on the empty concrete path, in the dead zone between the two buildings. He smiled at her again. Naomi felt surprised at how much friendlier the smile made his eyes look: he had seemed so cold when they had met at the start of the year.

'How are you settling in?' he asked. 'I keep meaning to pop by but I just don't seem to have had a moment this month. Are you enjoying it here at VitSip?'

'Yes, of course,' Naomi replied, returning his smile a little sardonically. As if she was going to say anything other than that to someone who was basically her immediate superior.

'Not that this – ' he gestured around him ' – can match the glamour of a central London location, but hopefully the project is glamour enough…' He paused, looking at her directly with his sharp blue-grey eyes. 'Or do we need to make things more exciting for you? Get you more involved? Get more involved with each other…'

She looked away – always best to give the illusion of consideration, even if all you were doing was hiding your own internal panicky dialogue. What was he getting at? Was he hinting at another role? Or was he *flirting* with her? She had no idea. She decided to be assertive and go for option one. He deserved to be brought to account for basically ignoring her for the past few months.

'Well,' she replied, returning his direct look, her chin tilted up, as if daring him to challenge her, 'I'm disappointed not to be asked more direct questions about the project when we have meetings. And I think, with the potential of this project, it would be more appropriate for me to be reporting directly to Grahame. He did hire me, after all, and I know this project is an important one for him, especially as it might be his last big launch before...' She trailed off, concerned now that she had gone too far. Everyone in the industry knew that Grahame Cox was on his last legs, but it was rarely said out loud.

Jonathan stared at her hard with those unforgiving eyes. Naomi stared hard back.

He looked down and then, looking back at her, he smiled a little.

'I think I know what you're getting at. I can be a little overbearing in meetings and for that I apologise.' His stare seemed to get a fraction more intense. 'You're right, though,' he continued. 'I'll talk to Grahame about it this week. I am sure a one-to-one would put everyone's minds at rest. Help to ensure that we all know where we stand and how the project is coming along as well as to make everyone feel that they are...' he paused again '...very much wanted...'

He stopped and Naomi looked at him, unsure as to why they were now just stood here looking at each other. The sun passed behind a slow-moving grey cloud and a shiver ran down her back.

'Well, I'll see you at the end of the week, Mrs Taylor,' he said, and, walking away, she turned to watch him go towards the building, his dark grey suit blending in with the shadows.

With another shake of her head, she walked quickly into the other building, feeling relieved when she got through the door and into the cool of the air-conditioned lab.

'Oh, and now another one,' Alex said drolly, without even looking up. 'Winters was just here, looking for an update… What's the matter? Management getting jittery?'

Was he now? she thought. Sly bastard. I'll have to watch out for him. 'Yes,' she said, the lie coming quickly and easily, 'I know. I saw him too. He knows we're on top of things.'

She smiled at Alex's raised eyebrow.

'So,' she said, coming in close and nudging him, 'now we've both lied to Winters – how *are* we going to get on top of things?'

'Well, you know what the issue is…'

'The sugar levels,' Naomi said quickly.

No one needed to remind her what the main problem here was. Yes, the drink contained healthy kale (five per cent) and spinach (two per cent), but it also contained sugar (twenty per cent) and glucose syrup (twelve per cent) to counteract the overpowering bitterness of the kale and spinach extracts. The only version of the drink that had been considered remotely palatable by the test groups so far had been the one containing almost fifty per cent sugars. The new version they were working on contained less, but even that was still giving the senior team a headache. The simple fact was that no one would drink it without the sugar but no one wanted to admit how much sugar was in it, neither the people making it, nor the people who would be buying it.

'We have to find some way to overcome the anxiety about the sugar,' Naomi mused. 'Can we get any more stats on the benefits of even a tiny amount of kale?'

'That might help. Or we just do what everyone else does and carry on regardless. Hope that no one notices. Hope that everyone just sees what they want to see: a lovely green, health-giving juice.'

Naomi smiled and looked at Alex with surprise. 'You should be in sales…an enormous degree of cynicism is always needed in *that* particular department.' she said.

'Nah, my problem is that I can't lie.' Alex shrugged. 'That's why I'm safer here, crafting lies rather than telling them. Less involved that way.' He stood up and walked over to the drinks machine. 'Coffee?'

'No, sorry. I'd love to but I'd better get back before I need to go. Thanks, though, Alex, I think you're right: the bold move might be just to go ahead as if there was nothing wrong here at all…'

And as she walked away she couldn't help but compare what she was about to suggest to her boss with what she was about to do with Mike. Both strategies were reckless, dangerous and could possibly cost her everything, but she was going to go ahead anyway.

Chapter Ten

Wednesday 13th March

Naomi

The days had passed. They had had to, she supposed. Not that she had noticed them. She was in a desire bubble, a vacuum where only her thoughts of what they had done and what they might do existed.

Wednesday. Such an innocuous day and yet rapidly becoming her favourite of the seven.

Perhaps Wednesdays could be their day? she pondered as she prepared to leave. It was all very convenient. Scott could get away from work, James had no after-school commitments that required lifts, and she rarely got much done mid-week anyway. She wondered how often they would keep seeing each other. Once a month? Every week?

As she combed her hair through, she grinned at herself in the mirror. He had been messaging her all day yesterday. Finally. Every line of it was etched in her memory. But the last few in particular had stayed with her.

Can I ask you something? he had typed.

Yes, of course.

Do you trust me?

Yes.

Completely?

Yes, completely.

Good girl. Remember that when you get there tomorrow.

And that, that 'good girl', had made her head spin.

Now, as she was getting ready, her stomach felt all fluttery. It was like a second date. All the potential of the first time but fewer nerves. She knew what to expect now. With the room being at the same hotel, elements of the evening could be anticipated. Would he come at her like that again? She hoped so. That was the main thing she recalled from the first time: how he had lunged at her as soon as they were in the room. The hunger in his kisses. He had kissed her so hard, too hard, pressing on her, crushing her lips, a salty, unfamiliar tongue pushing its way into her mouth. She closed her eyes as her stomach fizzed and her pussy began to swell up, blood pulsing into her labia. Up inside of her she could feel the slickening of her vagina, its readiness. Having thought of little else since the date had been arranged, she was so horny now, she wasn't certain she could even get down the stairs.

But no one even noticed her leaving. Scott was working and James was in his room. Would they notice if I never came back? she wondered, as she walked through the door and out into the car. Would they even care?

She dismissed the thought, too excited about what she was about to do to give that idea any more consideration.

Driving in the car, she kept the radio off. Her mind was noisy enough without any additional distractions. Images from the first time flipped through her mind, without pause, like one of those children's books where you flipped the pages quickly to see a story: a series of rapidly shifting images together telling a tale of desire and wanting.

Except this story, she hoped, would have no end, would just be endless pleasure, a fuck flicker-book to treasure. She smiled wickedly at the words in her mind: what was it about this wanting that made her so coarse? So dirty?

Her phone beeped and, ignoring the road, she reached into her handbag which was on the passenger seat next to her and pulled it out. It was him.

Room 26.

Pulling into the hotel car park, she nearly flew out of the car. It was incredible to her how different this felt from two weeks ago. Knowing the layout now, she went in through the side door, past the hotel bar and reception, up the stairs to the second floor. Standing outside the room, she barely even registered the number on the door before tapping at it urgently. She thought about calling out, *Room service!* But didn't. This wasn't funny. She was here to fuck, and that was a serious business.

The door was opened inwards, and she saw him standing in the door frame. Without even a flicker of a smile he stepped forward, pulled her into the room and up against his body. Arms round her, strong and tight, he kissed her hard. She kissed him back even harder.

Suddenly, his hand was around her neck.

She gasped.

He pushed her against the mirror on the wall.

She gasped again, eyes widening, mouth a comical O. Shocked. Stunned. Unbelievably turned on.

Looking straight at her, he said, 'Don't say anything. Do you understand? Just do exactly as I tell you.'

She nodded, stunned. Mute.

Turning her around, he pressed her against the mirror, then slowly ran his hand down the length of her back. His other hand was gently holding her steady as her whole body vibrated.

Stroking her hips and buttocks through the thick cotton of her charcoal pencil skirt, he leant in close. His warm breath made the skin on the back of her neck prickle. Moving her hair to one side, he softly kissed her neck and her cheek.

She sighed.

Then he slapped her backside. Hard. The noise was softened by the cotton, but the impact wasn't.

'Oh!' she cried out again.

'Quiet, slut.'

She shut her eyes as her whole body quivered, a never-before-experienced mixture of fear and pleasure.

Turning her round, face impassive, he said, 'On to your knees.'

She hesitated. Face still burning. Backside tingling.

'On. Your. Knees. Now.' And, after another moment, he grabbed her hair in his fist and pushed her down on to the floor. 'Unzip me.'

And she did so, the command releasing her, blissfully, from thinking.

Knees pressing on the cold hard floor, she could see how hard he was: could see him outlined against his black trousers. A tailored suit on a man was, for her, like lingerie on a woman to most men: irresistible. Hands shaking a little, she unzipped him, gently teasing his dick out of his underwear with careful fingers. Taking him into her mouth, she felt the pressure to perform but also a desire to please that was so intense that she couldn't think, didn't want to think, about anything else. This was all there was now: her mouth, her lips, her tongue and his dick.

He had his hand in her hair. Controlling her head, pushing her, pulling her. She looked up, eyes wide, and was rewarded with the sight of a small, satisfied smile playing on his lips.

'You're good at that…'

'Thank you,' she murmured.

He reached down and, still smiling at her, slapped her face.

'Oh!'

'Did I say you could speak?'

She shook her head. Her breath was catching. She had never felt more turned on.

Just as her knees began to throb and ache, he lifted her up and with a kiss on her cheek carried her over to the bed.

'You are so beautiful,' he said, as he unbuttoned and removed her clothes. Mouth pressed on hers, body pushing down on her, he ran his hand down her torso. Tracing his fingers over her skin, teasing her, he then slid his fingers up and inside her. Naomi sighed, pushing her hips up and against his fingers and palm.

Stroking her breasts with his other hand gently, he then pinched her nipple, plucking till it stung. Crying out, she tried to pull away a little, but he pressed her chest, pinning her down hard. Then, reaching over to the table by the bed for one of the three condoms that were there, he gave one to her. Feeling a pang of anxiety, she opened the packet with her now free hands while he completely undressed in front of her. She so desperately didn't want to fumble...and then it was on and, as she went to cup his balls in her hand and stroke his stomach, his thighs, the hair so soft there, he pulled her hands away and, shoving her back down on to the bed, hard, he slid himself inside her, eyes on hers.

The rhythm and motion of their desire took over and, mouths locked, they fucked. Him looking at her, taking in every whimper and sigh, adjusting the pressure and his own rhythm according to her need. Tuned into her completely, he made her come. And then, turning her over, he said, 'Lie still.'

Lying there, pink backside exposed, she heard a noise, felt something cool and liquid against her ass and, wriggling and feeling panicked, she tried to move away. He pressed her back down. Holding her hands above her head, he leant in close to her and whispered, 'I want all of you. I will have all of you. You are mine.'

And, after a momentary burst of pain, she pressed her mouth into the bed, letting him take what he wanted. And it felt good: really good. Letting go, giving in, clit pressed hard against the bed, she felt herself come and cried out his name.

Afterwards, as they lay next to each other on the bed, the room was silent except for their breathing. Naomi had never experienced a silence like it. Her arm was across his chest, her body turned towards his; she could feel his heart beating. The tiny room smelt of sweat and satisfaction. They began to kiss again. The kissing was so good. They kissed and kissed until he began to stiffen against her again.

Naomi began to shift down his body, kissing his chest, running her hands over the soft, dark hair on his chest, feeling the individual hairs underneath her fingers. Tracing her fingertips over the smooth, soft skin at the top of his pelvis.

Taking him in her hand, she felt the thickness of his penis, the weight of it against her hand and, with a glance up at his face, she bent her head down and placed her mouth over him. Taking him all in, she felt a momentary gag, a pause where she had to adjust herself and then she relaxed. Rotating her tongue round the shaft, she heard a soft sigh. Pleased, she balanced herself with her right hand on the bed and then cupped his balls in her left hand. Massaging them, she placed her hand round the bottom of his dick and began to rhythmically run her hand up and down the length of him, hand gripping firmly. He was wet from her mouth; she flicked her tongue over the tip, and he groaned as she massaged him with her hand. Building up the rhythm, she listened to his breathing quicken, and as his pelvis began to move against her hand and mouth she felt herself excited too, not like she was about to come, but enjoying the sensation of having him so in her control. They moved like that together for a few more moments and then, hearing his breathing quicken again, she sensed that he was close.

'I'm going to come,' he gasped.

She closed her eyes tight as the thin, hot, salty liquid came across her tongue and, with a relish she had never experienced before, she swallowed it down, licking and kissing him afterwards, her mouth as hungry for him as the rest of her was.

Creeping back up to lie by his side, she heard him whisper, 'Fuck...that was amazing...'

They looked at each other and he smiled. Pulling her close, he kissed her. Tenderly this time. And, then, they lay back and listened to the silence together, his hand stroking her back in long gentle sweeps.

Later, much later, a glance at the digital clock by the bed and then at each other. It was time to go. Wordlessly, they got dressed and then, as they stood, facing each other, he kissed her again and then cupped her cheek in his hand.

'I'll see you soon.'

'Yes.'

He opened the door and she walked out, looking up at him. Their eyes met one last time and then the door closed behind her.

Are you back? Are you OK?

Naomi was grateful for these words, grateful for the attention. She had driven home in a state of euphoria, head light, her whole body the same. It was as if someone had pressed the reset button: she felt new. She felt alive.

And now, sitting here, everyone else asleep and the glow from the computer filling the dim room, she was so grateful for him checking on her that she wanted to cry. Happy tears, the kinds of tears that people shed when they hear that someone they had thought was dying has been brought miraculously back to full health.

I'm back, she typed. *And I feel great. Thank you. How are you?*

Amazing, he replied.

Really?

Oh, yes. That was amazing. You are amazing.

Naomi stared at the screen, feeling as if she would burst. The joy seemed to stretch her skin outwards. Grinning, her skin still tender from his kisses and her lips still swollen and tender from his biting them, she typed back, *Honestly? You honestly mean that?*

I honestly do.

There was a pause.

Just makes it even more annoying that I'm away for a bit.

No! she wanted to cry out. No!

Oh? she typed, refusing to let him know how disappointed she felt. *Where are you off to? Somewhere fun?*

It's just work. I need to go out to the West Country – catch up with the guys at the branch office.

I don't want to hear about bloody work! she thought, I want to hear more about what you thought of me!

I'm sure that will be fun! she replied.

I'm not asking how long you're away for, she thought, suddenly angry with him.

I WILL be in touch…as much as I can be, he added.

That would be great.

There was a pause.

What to say? What was there to say to any of this? Naomi had no idea. Staring at the screen, she hoped beyond hope that he would keep the chat going.

I'd better go xx, he said.

She typed, adding an exclamation mark and then another, and sent: *Of course!!*

There was no way she was going to say how she really felt. To admit that what she really wanted was to hear him tell her over and over how much he wanted her, how amazing she was. She wanted to feel the way he had made her feel again and again. And for that feeling to never stop.

Chapter Eleven

Naomi

It was Friday and Naomi was still on a high from her experience with Mike. As she got ready, travelled into work and went about her usual routine, she felt the same but also different: as if she had been transformed in some way. Her mind felt calmer, as if a reset button had been pressed, and physically, now that the aches and soreness had gone, she felt lighter but also stronger. The ease reflected itself in her movements and in how she felt about herself. She felt new. Improved. Better.

She was also busy enough in advance of the Kale Kooler launch to be able to pretend that she didn't care that he was going to be away and that no new date had been agreed. Scott was away too. He had been working late all week so that he could go to see his parents on Thursday night straight from work and stay the night there before coming back Friday afternoon for the weekend. Nothing much had changed since his last visit to them. If anything, that visit had seemed to help settle things down. Elaine had been sounding more like her old self on the phone. Perhaps, she thought, it was a good thing that Mike was away. It would give him a chance to miss her a little…if only she could trust herself not to panic about not hearing from him after a few days.

Hopefully, the fact that I'm busy will help, she thought.

Getting into the office for the usual time, Naomi got a coffee and, grateful that no one else was about just yet, she went to her office and turned on the computer. Looking at the printed-off agenda for today, she checked over her notes and the printouts whilst she waited for the computer to get going.

Checking the site was her habit now, a default the moment she was up and running. Nothing. She huffed.

You're busy, he's busy, it's fine, she told herself.

She left it open though. Just in case.

Today's meeting was a key one. She had to present the last parts of the research and also give an update on the marketing strategy. Carla had been off ill quite a bit recently, so Naomi had been dealing with the rest of the team, which had been slightly easier.

I should see if Carla is about, though, she thought; it would look odd if I stop talking to her completely…

Making a note in her diary to get in touch with Carla, Naomi then checked her emails and, after another coffee, pulled her things together for the meeting.

Going out of her room and into the corridor, she began to walk towards the lifts. All of a sudden, she felt very conscious of herself, very aware of her hips, her hair falling against her shoulders; she could feel eyes burning into the back of her. Stopping, she turned and looked behind her. It was Jonathan.

'Ready for this?' he asked, tone as clipped as it had been that very first time they had met. There was no hint of the flirtation that they had engaged in outside, no hint of the chemistry between them. His eyes were flat and grey, his expression completely neutral, functional even.

'I am,' she replied, equally briskly.

'You'd better be,' he said and, with a nod, he walked past her.

Bastard, she thought. Such a power player. It's so bloody eighties...

Running through the key points in her head for what felt like the hundredth time, Naomi walked slowly down the corridor. Jonathan had turned off and headed towards Grahame's office. They would invariably walk in together.

He's like Grahame's sodding shadow, Naomi thought, sourly. I could do that job. And, after this launch, who knows. Maybe I will...

This thought, and the recollection of the months of preparation she had done, gave her the boost she needed. Feeling confident and ready, she walked into the room, saw that all twelve seats around the large oval wooden table were full bar the three seats for her, Jonathan and Grahame, and smiled.

Simon, the marketing manager, got up as she came in and joined her at the head of the table by the laptop. He was someone she had really enjoyed getting to know as they had worked together on this project.

'We all set?' she asked him, placing her notes down on the table.

'Yes, of course.'

He smiled at her and she grinned back. They had had some fun over the last days as they had agreed the strategy.

The Kale Kooler, with its five per cent kale and two per cent spinach extracts and its now nearly forty per cent sugar, ten per cent glucose and five per cent caffeine, was the sugariest drink they had ever produced. Its launch would only work if it was undertaken with absolute, brazen confidence. Among the staff, the strategy behind this launch even had its own acronym: FIS. *Fuck It and See*.

Naomi poured a coffee from the metal pot on the table as well as two little glasses of water. She even took a biscuit and, eating it, looked around the room. This was it. Today was the day.

The chatter stopped.

Jonathan, looking every inch the detached and superior MD, and the chief executive, Grahame, had entered the room. With two gestures, Jonathan made it clear that everyone should sit and that the youngest member of the team, some wet-behind-the-ears trainee called Daniel something or other, should pour him a coffee.

He then walked to the front of the room.

'Good morning, everyone. Today's meeting is the last step before the launch of our latest product, the Kale Kooler. No one here needs to be told how important this is. Our market share continues to stagnate and, without this product, and what will hopefully be a new line in super-juices, we can't afford to maintain the current scale of our operations. This is a crucial launch for us. Crucial.'

He paused. He was good at pauses. They were a Winters trademark.

'Now, I am going to hand over to Mrs Taylor.'

There was an awkward moment as one of the younger members of the team began to clap. Jonathan silenced him with look.

'Thank you, *Jonathan*,' Naomi said, smiling sweetly. She knew using his first name would annoy him and she took pleasure in the slight darkening of his face as he sat down.

Standing and talking, Naomi felt good, in control. When she was in work mode she could do this: could be completely focused and ruthless. It was this focus that had helped her to get four A-levels even after struggling to pass most of her GCSEs. It was this focus that had helped her to get a place at one of the best universities in the country, on one of the best business courses. It was moments like this, moments when she knew she was, as James would say, *nailing it*, that she felt truly happy.

'Yes, the approach is bold,' she added, as the last image glowed on the flat screen. 'But I think it's time we stopped apologising for selling things that people want. This is not about ignoring our responsibilities but about working with our customers – about a partnership; about uniting their desire for a thirst-quenching drink with their appetite for health; about saying: yes, we *can* all benefit here. Speaking frankly, it is about no longer feeling bad for enjoying what you want, for *having* what you want. The *Take Charge When You Recharge* campaign is one that we can *all* feel good about.'

This time it was Jonathan who started the applause.

Naomi floated back to the office. Smiling, still hearing the words in her ears – 'The confidence and belief in us as a business that Mrs Taylor has shown here today are an example to us all' – she walked into her office.

Still grinning, she went and sat at her desk. By her mouse, there was a folder. A purple folder. One of Carla's folders. Seeing the PC screen lit-up and the message screen open, her grin vanished.

'Oh. Shit.'

In a panic and not knowing what to do, Naomi went to the lab to share the news about the presentation with Alex. She knew he appreciated being kept up to date and she needed to get away from the main building.

Getting in a state will not help, she tried to tell herself.

There was still a steely edge in her at this moment, the edge that had helped her get through that presentation. It was this part of her that thought, If it's discovered, then it's over. Maybe that's for the best. Maybe.

But then the weaker part of her, the hunger, screeched, clawing its grasping fingers into her stomach: *No, no, no, I need it…I need it*. Gollum-esque, the whine of need was ugly, but it was a part of her as much as the edge was.

Hiding away in the lab until after lunchtime, she chatted with Alex and the tech team. There were a few ideas already lined up for the next wave of *Take Charge* drinks and it was fun to talk about these, to feel excited about something as well as to keep her mind off the fact that her whole life could be unravelling while she sat here.

There was a cold sense of fear as she walked back along the path to the main building. As she pushed the door open, she told herself: Right, just *go*. Go to Marketing. See her. Face it. You have to.

She took the lift up the four floors to the marketing department, her stomach tense and tight. Walking out of the lift, she could feel her jaw clench, her shoulders stiffen. Braced for a cat-calling chorus of 'Bitch! Cow! Cheat!', she was slightly surprised when she heard a voice cry out, 'Wow! Naomi! Well done!'

It was Carla. Smiling. Still oblivious.

The relief was like a rush of blood to the head, like the tingling, nauseating rush of that first *Sod it, I'll give up another time* cigarette after having stopped for weeks. Naomi staggered slightly under the sheer weight of the feeling.

'Hey! Are you OK? You're as white as a sheet!' Carla was next to her now, eyes crinkled in concern.

'Oh, yes, yes, I'm fine! Just had a moment there...'

And, having said that out loud, having got away with it this time, Naomi smiled at the younger woman and continued, 'Thanks so much! You look well. How are you? How's Mike?'

As Carla chattered away, Naomi smiled and nodded, thinking, I'm sorry. I truly am, but I can't stop. But I can be more careful. And I promise it will never hurt you; it will never hurt you because you will never know.

It was only when she got home that the enormity of what had nearly happened really hit her. Without even thinking about it, she raced upstairs, read the recent messages over and, in a frenzy, flung herself on to the floor and began to masturbate.

She came hard, over and over, crying out, releasing the frustration, sobbing a little, each wave of pleasure driving her on to do it again and again. It was never enough. Coming loudly, she called out Mike's name, allowing herself the release of it while she imagined him fucking her.

An hour later, she went back downstairs and into the kitchen for a cold drink.

'Oh! James! When did you get home?'

Glancing up at her from where he was sitting at the table in front of a magazine, his face told her everything she needed to know. He had heard her.

It was the same look her father had given her that time she had scratched at the chicken pox scabs. Until now she had forgotten about that look. Naomi could vividly recall the screams and slaps of her mother but it was only now, seeing the look on James's face, that she remembered the much more painful silence from her father. He had said nothing then, as James said nothing now – had just looked at her with such disappointment, such *sadness*.

I expected more of you, the look had said. *I thought you were capable of being better than that.*

But then he had gone and let her down in the most complete way possible, by dying on her, dying just as she began to reach womanhood, just when she needed a father the most.

And was she now doing the same to James: leaving him, lost in her own distractions while he muddled through his teen years? The guilt washed over her in waves.

'I was about to have a Coke – want one?' he asked, avoiding her eyes now as walked over to the fridge.

'Yes. Yes, please.' She replied, quietly.

He offered her a cold can. She took it. James seemed to have got taller, she thought, looking up at him. At this moment, he was the adult.

They sat down at the table together, the silence a promise of a silence of another kind.

And, promising to be better, telling herself that she could no longer do this if she didn't get better at the rest of it, Naomi took a long draught of the cold, fizzy drink. Nothing had ever tasted sweeter.

Later that evening, Naomi was in the kitchen, trying to focus on what James was saying but barely listening. The ups and downs of the day had left her exhausted. There was no one to share this with, not even Mike. She could hardly admit to him that she had nearly let Carla see his messages. Rubbing her forehead, trying to ease the tension there, she poured a glass of water and attempted to concentrate on what she was doing.

Peeling open the pack of pre-prepared chicken breasts, she tucked them into the roasting tray among the thickly sliced vegetables and potato wedges.

Why was she cooking? she thought. She had wanted to be healthy, had wanted to make something nourishing, but now she really wished she hadn't bothered.

'Lay the table please, James, and go and tell Dad it's nearly ready.'

James was texting.

'James! Table!'

'Gnnf,' came the reply.

Naomi scowled and snapped again, 'James – now!'

James piled his books up and placed them on the side, then he slouched over to the drawer. Placing the cutlery on the table, he picked up his phone again and, still texting, went to get Scott.

They ate.

'Can I have some sauce?' asked James, as he took a second helping.

'Yes,' said Naomi, not really listening, mind still elsewhere. She poked the vegetables around her plate.

'Oh, and just to remind you I'm out at golf tomorrow,' Scott said. 'With Peter. He said Susan's taking Sassy out shopping. Girly day out. You are welcome to go along with them if you like...'

'Sure, uh-huh,' said Naomi, who couldn't think of anything she wanted to do less.

'You OK?' he asked.

'Yes, yes, of course.' She looked up and gave a smile.

'You've not eaten much,' Scott added, brow furrowed.

'I'm fine, I had a big lunch,' Naomi lied.

It was effortless now, the lying. Almost everything she said was a lie: *Yes, I am listening. Yes, of course we can spend Easter with your family. Yes, James, that sum looks right. Yes, I am eating enough. Yes, of course, I'm all right. Sorry, I have a really bad headache again. No, sorry, I can't make the book club meeting this month, I need to work.*

And it wasn't just what had nearly happened today. It was the whole thing. Sometimes she felt exhilarated, but mostly she felt anxious and tired. It was exhausting. She also couldn't be without it.

After the dinner things had been cleared away, Naomi remembered the promises she had made mere hours ago, promises to spend more time with James and Scott when they were all at home. Promises to be better, to do better. But all she wanted to do was read Mike's messages, to sit and think about him, to think about their time together and to fantasise about what would happen next. Walking past the living room, she saw James and Scott sitting in there and knew she should join them. She glanced up the stairs.

Just twenty minutes, she said to herself, just twenty minutes, then I'll come back down...

Forcing herself to walk rather than run up the stairs, she reached the door of her room and, using every muscle to contain the haste in her body, she shut it as quietly and carefully as she could. Then, unable to contain it any longer, she ran over to the desk and restarted the computer. It seemed to take for ever. She spent those seconds that seemed like months alternatively cursing and coaxing the machine as if it were a sentient being. It certainly had more control over her life now than any person that she knew.

Back online and seeing no new messages, she tried to tell herself that no news was good news.

Scrolling over their conversations, she thought back. Her memories were like wrapped sweets in a tin, abundant, brightly coloured, shiny and tempting. She unwrapped them one by one, savouring every moment as she relived what they had done and how she had felt during the time they had had together.

And, as with those sweets that her Mum had only ever bought at Christmas, the ones that glittered purple, red, yellow, green and orange, their wrappers catching the sparkling Christmas tree lights, she could never enjoy just one, had to have more, and more still. She had eaten those sweets till she felt sick and she was doing the same now: gorging on the memories until she felt ill, until her stomach was burning.

The weight of what had nearly happened today was still heavy on her. Leaning back in her chair, she closed her eyes. She was scared to tell Mike about it; it was a secret within the secret. A layer of deception that she was not sure she could stomach. When was the last time she had kept a secret? Really kept one? Not since she had been a teenager. Not, she thought, since those years after Daddy died.

Yes. She had kept her secrets then. Had had to. There had been no one to tell, no one to talk to, and so she had kept her mouth shut.

Having been left alone after school as well as at the weekends too while her mother worked and 'got on', Naomi had got on in her own way. An early developer and restless, especially since her mother had caught her and she had promised never to touch herself again, she had begun to attract the attentions of some of the older boys at school. Inevitably, she'd begun to invite them back to the empty house.

The first time she had been in love. Naomi had truly believed the boy when he said that he loved her, and afterwards, when he had moved on to another budding flower, she had cried for weeks, tears that went unnoticed by a mother who was 'getting on'. And after that there were others, many other secret after-school and weekend visitors, and, well, they had not been love and even if they said they were she no longer believed them.

It was only after being taken aside by a well-meaning teacher and warned that, unless her work improved, her mother would have to be called in to the school that Naomi had decided to get on in a different way.

Studying hard, she had eschewed the eager boys with their frantic kisses, forgoing the fast, dry, orgasm-less sex and the swallowing of salty teenage sperm that had been experienced on her pink, ballet-girl bedspread in favour of books and time away, hidden in the library, among the scratched wooden tables and tall towering shelves. The thin, musty cardboard of index cards, the green glow of the beige computer's DOS system had been her refuge until, having got a place at Warwick University, she had met Scott. And then, finally feeling ready, she was able to share some of her secrets. And, entrusted with them, he was, in his final year of an extended postgrad degree, then entrusted with her future happiness.

How simple it had all seemed then, back when finding Scott had seemed to be the answer to all the pain and loneliness of the years since her father had died. Sometimes now she thought she was lucky that there had been no temptations, no desire to stray in the interim, that the last fifteen-plus years had passed with no need for anything or anyone else. But that also seemed to make it harder now. The element of surprise had been so powerful: she had been shocked by it and the shock had made her susceptible – susceptible to Mike and what he had wanted.

The secret she thought she had wished for, the something just for her, well, it seemed now that that had not been the answer after all. What had once seemed valuable, what had once been something that she could carry about with her, a small and precious pearl, had now transformed back into grit, into something irritating, chafing and painful. Staring at the screen, she was getting lost in her secret world, moving further and further away from the real one that was waiting for her downstairs.

Chapter Twelve

Matthew

Polly had been up and out at 8am that morning. Matthew knew it couldn't be helped but he also couldn't help feeling that, sometimes, the causes might wait the hour or so it would take them to have sex again and eat croissants.

'Sorry,' she had said again, just before leaving. The apology was sincerely meant, and he remembered what she had told him when they met: *This is my life. This is all I want to do.* She had been honest with him from the start. It was just that sometimes a lie-in and a latte might have been nice.

With the weekend stretching ahead, he knew he should get on with some work too. There was the site to finally finish as well the research plus school coursework and exam preparation. But, as he lay there, his mind suddenly brought up the image of the card. The mysterious Valentine's card. Getting up, he went to the drawer and, digging about, he had a moment of panic when he couldn't find it. Had she discovered it? Then, feeling the hard edge, he tugged it out from underneath the folded jumpers and looked at it again. All those years of receiving cards from kids and he had never had an actual, real one sent to him at home before. Looking

242

closely at the card, he felt curious. Someone wanted him. But who? He made a coffee and then, staring at all the work he had to do, he decided to go back to bed.

Waking up again a few hours later, he grabbed the phone off the bedside table and checked his messages. Nothing. There was something vaguely depressing about tuning out for a few hours only to see that no one had noticed your absence. He fired off a couple of hellos: to Sol, to Iain, to Jim and, of course, to Polly. He wanted to double-check that he was still seeing her later.

Getting out of the shower, he checked his phone. A message from Polly. He grinned at his phone.

Sorry, something has come up. A meet with another group. I'll text you when it's done. P xxx

The disappointment was solid; it weighed down on his chest. 'That sucks,' he said, hoping that verbalising it would help. It didn't. He sent a cheery message back. There was no point sulking; he would just have to find something else to do.

He stared at the work pile. It stared back.

He looked at his phone. Seeing Jim was online he texted him: *Pub? Please?*

Sorry, mate, no can do. Catch you next week?

Sure thing… Matthew texted back.

A wave of annoyance flooded him and then he remembered that he had pretty much ignored Jim – and Solange – since the start of term. If they didn't want to hang out with him on the one Saturday he was free, whose fault was that?

Sighing, he looked at the pile of marking and, taking the top book off the pile, he got to work.

David

The mornings and evenings were getting brighter. The middle of the day expanded out on either side like a giant stirring from a heavy sleep: arms and fingers stretching out into the mornings and evenings, tickling the dawn and the dusk away. The branches of the few trees that lined David's walk to school were stippled with buds, textured with the promise of spring. These last few weeks had passed easily enough at school: the routines and rhythms of the end of the spring term were less demanding than those at the end of the summer with its exams and presentations.

Having arranged to meet James at the cinema that Saturday afternoon after the other boy's full-on morning of sport, David felt even more pleased than usual to have an excuse to be out of the house. The twins, tired as the end of term approached, were arguing even more than usual. This was something that Kerri had never dealt with well and still didn't, preferring to placate them with TV and sweets rather than address the real issues. Jessica's envy at their mother's poorly concealed preference for the sweeter-natured Emily had, as they had turned from girls to tweens, soured into genuine meanness. The other week, David had caught her about to put water in her sister's bed in attempt to make it look as if she had wet herself. David did his best to play referee but it was their mother's attention they were vying for, not his. As a result, he tried to keep his distance, but he was still always within earshot of the bickering unless he was out of the house or had the volume on his own TV up to masturbation-noise-covering levels. Again, this was something he didn't like to do too often. Though how often was too often was a question not even the internet could answer. As he approached fourteen, his few-times-a-week a habit was increasingly not enough. His appetite for it had grown and he tried to quash the shame and guilt he felt afterwards with a bottle of Coke and a few packs of crisps.

As March drew to a close, the diet magazines had been recycled, that initial sortie in the battle of the bulge having been stalled by the usual combination of apathy and reluctance to change as well as a heavily marketed need to make the most of the cold weather and snuggle up with hot chocolates and marshmallows. Kerri had recently been spending an unusual amount of time online and was increasingly preoccupied. Preoccupied with what exactly, David didn't know, but, in the same way that trees knew a change in season was coming, he could sense something was shifting.

James was already at the cinema when he arrived. David saw him standing in the queue for drinks and popcorn. The boy waved at David with both arms as soon as he saw him, wiggling the tickets in his left hand. David nodded in recognition, keeping his hands in his pockets as he continued to shuffle through the faded foyer of the once glorious multiplex. He remembered this retail park opening several years ago. Remembered Kerri and Gary (still Mummy and Daddy then) bringing him to watch films on rainy afternoons. Even now he occasionally caught the scent of toasted and popped maize in his nostrils on wet and grey afternoons: the association was a strong one. It was something the three of them had done a lot before the twins had been born, but never since. Three tickets to the cinema was expensive, but five was crippling.

Ten years ago this had been a vast, white brick temple to the glory of surround-sound, all bright glass and acres of gently napped blue carpet, but now, as David felt stale popcorn crunch under his feet and saw, under the harsh fluorescents, the faded worn underlay, it looked more like an old lady's badly hoovered front room. And no wonder: with the advent of enormous flatscreen HD TVs in every home, who would choose to pay fifteen quid a head to sit in close proximity to strangers in an ill-heated oversized room and eat mushy hot dogs?

'Popcorn?' James asked as David approached.

'Sure.'

'Sweet?'

'Of course.'

'No one actually ever orders salty, do they?' James grinned.

'No, they do not.' David grinned back.

He tried to ignore the voices behind him. A slim middle-aged couple in the queue weren't even bothering to keep their voices down. People didn't, really. And it was usually the older ones who were the worst: it was as if they believed it to be vital that you hear their opinion on you, and on everything else for that matter, regardless of whether it was actually appropriate or even polite.

'How do people let their kids get *so* big?'

'How will he fit in a seat here? How *do* they manage?'

'And look at his friend! So slim…'

'Make that a large for me, then, please, mate!' yelled James, looking pointedly at the couple, 'And a water for my friend: his CAN-CER treatment causes him to be thirsty as well as gain weight!'

The couple went red and their mouths snapped shut.

David flushed with embarrassment and delight.

James winked at him.

As they sat, waiting for the film to start, they munched through the popcorn and, in between mouthfuls, David pulled two Wispa bars out of his pocket. He had brought them along as he knew they were James's favourite. He handed one to James and they tapped them together. 'Cheers!'

'Y'all right, then?' asked David.

'Yeah, good to be out, Mum's being strange…I think it must be the hormones.'

'What's she doing?'

James shrugged and grabbed another handful of popcorn before looking again at his unchanged phone screen. People used to avert their eyes by looking at the floor but now they just stared at their phones instead.

'Mine's on her tablet like all the time,' David added. 'Don't think I've spoken more than a word or two to her now for about a week.'

'Yeah,' James agreed, 'Mine's the same. She says it's work, but...' He trailed off.

David glanced over.

James looked back at him, a sideways glance, misery shrinking his pupils.

'I heard her laughing,' he said, quietly. 'And then I heard her...you know...in the room where the computer is...'

The room darkened and the curtains began to lift.

'Jeez... Sorry.' David whispered as the peppy trumpet of the Pearl and Dean tune began.

'S'all right,' James said, looking down and beginning to unwrap the chocolate bar. 'Wispa! Love it!'

They shared a smile in the dark and for a moment David felt like reaching out and touching his friend's arm, but he didn't. That would be weird, he said to himself but he suddenly felt very sad for his friend and very sad for himself. Then the loud action of the trailers began. Settling back awkwardly, he let the 15-rated action mayhem white noise wash over him, the relentless graphics numbing his mind.

Stomachs full of sweets and minds stuffed full of crashes and explosions, they erupted out of the dark cinema and into the bright afternoon sunshine like space rockets re-entering the earth's atmosphere. Talking fast, lit up from inside by the action and only a little disorientated, they blazed across the car park. James was spinning about, re-enacting a particularly spectacular scene which had inexplicably contained both giant robots and dinosaurs. There had also been the standard Egyptian setting and the necessary near ending of the world. Fortunately there had also been a couple of teenage boys to put it all right.

David laughed as James wheeled and exploded. The thinner boy had a particularly effective range of explosion noises that he had been perfecting since Reception class.

As they waited for the bus, there was a moment of quiet as they both realised the afternoon was over and they were on their way home.

I don't want to go home, thought David

'I don't want to go home,' muttered James.

But they were not free to stay out. It was Saturday teatime and they were both expected back.

On the bus, the silence darkened like the afternoon sky, shades of blue deepening to violet and black. David stared out of the opaque glass and, seeing his bloated reflection in the fingerprint-smeared window, he shut his eyes for a moment and then turned to his friend.

'Monday, then?'

'Monday.'

'Text ya later?'

'Yeah, later.'

'You all right?'

'Yeah. You?'

'Yeah.'

It was nearly time to get off. The bus jerked to a halt and, with a nod, David got up and began to move to the door. As the bus pulled away, he saw James looking out at him from inside. The dull lights in the bus and the contrasting dimness outside distorted David's vision: was James crying? He squinted, trying to see, but then the bus was gone. Pulling his jacket round him, David walked slowly home.

Naomi

Another solo Saturday. James was out with David at the cinema. Scott had left early to go and enjoy yet another day of golf and night of overpriced merlot with Peter. Naomi had always enjoyed having some time to herself, but today she felt lonely and bored.

Though at least with Scott out she didn't have to listen to him talking about work, or deal with yet another conversation about his parents.

Even though things had settled down, Scott was still anxious about his mum and dad. It was something that, having lost her father so long ago and having never been close to her own mother who had also passed away several years ago, Naomi just didn't really understand. She tolerated her in-laws and struggled to see what was so special about them. On the worst of the days she had had in recent months, she had hated Scott for being so much like his brow-beaten father...that had not felt good. But finding him annoying, feeling let down by him, was partly how she could justify behaving the way she was.

Though if Elaine's forgetfulness gets worse, she thought, then they'll take up even more time.

Images of the care needed by, and efforts needed to look after, Scott's ageing parents filled Naomi's mind rapidly: grey and wearying like the people themselves. It seemed inevitable. It was also terrifying.

Picking up her phone, she tried to distract herself. She scrolled through her recent texts. There weren't many. She wondered to herself, Who did I used to see? Who are my friends?

She clicked on Contacts and scrolled through the list. Having gone back to work full-time once James had started school, she had never made many friends among the other mums. Sure, she had gone to the occasional coffee morning if she could, or the odd evening out, but they had always been awkward affairs for her. She had felt left out. The stay-at-home mums felt entitled to complain, but the working mums weren't really allowed to. Sure, you could say you missed your kids, but work was seen as a break, not as an exhausting and challenging thing you did all day. Some of the women who had worked before would sympathise, but, in reality, they too had forgotten how hard work could be when it was going badly, how draining a challenging day at the office could feel. She got the complaining while they were small but, surely, when the kids were at school full-time, these women at home had it made: time at home and time with the kids. Sounded lovely. Even though she knew she could never not work, she had still resented the assumption that, just because you mostly enjoyed your job, it was all sunshine and rainbows.

Every choice had a price, and it was the quality of the rest of her life that had paid it. They rarely saw anyone outside of family, had no time to arrange social events, to get out for trips to the cinema or theatre or even dinner. Sure, they could do these things with James now that he was older, but it was fun adult company that she lacked. There never seemed to be any time. And, on the occasions she had arranged things, they always needed to be booked two months in advance and it was never quite the same. She missed the spontaneity, she supposed. She missed that element of excitement and of variety.

That's why I'm here, I suppose, she thought, slightly sadly. Waiting to hear from a lover. Craving the excitement of it.

'But, God, it's going to be a long day if I sit here like this,' she muttered to herself out loud.

Walking round the house, she tidied up, picking up magazines, tidying piles of books, arranging DVDs...these were all things that had once been enough of a diversion but they weren't any more. Why not? Why not? Shaking her head, she thought, *Oh, fuck it, I have to get out of here.*

And so she went shopping, buying lots of treats and rubbish that she didn't need, but in that tiny moment, in the moment of seeing it and wanting it and simply getting it, she felt good. Very good. Lots of tiny pleasure-hits seemed to help but, arriving back at the empty house a few hours later, she felt her dark mood returning.

Dumping the shopping, feeling restless, she paced about the house like a caged animal.

By the time it got to 5pm she had exhausted herself. Sitting at the kitchen table, not reading her book club book but scrolling through messages on her phone, she felt calmer, better. It was as if the bad feeling had burned out. Her mood felt lighter, brighter. She texted Scott and asked how he was enjoying golf – wished him a fun evening. Asked if he had any preferences for dinner tomorrow. She was happy to make him whatever he liked. For a moment, as she read and then prepared to send the text, she felt suffused with affection for Scott. Something that felt easier and more possible when he wasn't actually there. She smiled wryly at herself. And, seeing that it was 6pm and soon James would be home, she grabbed a bottle of wine and the takeaway menu and went into the living room.

David

Back at home, David was glad to see the table full of bowls and packets. Saturday night was snack night. How this differed from other nights would be unclear to an external observer but what it meant, what the weekend meant, was that food could be consumed without guilt. It was Saturday and therefore treats and snacks *had* to be consumed, TV *had* to be watched. It was allowed, it was permissible: it was the weekend. The fact that the weekend now seemed to start on Thursday was largely ignored by everyone who used the same logic to justify their own behaviour.

Pizza was a midweek treat, as was fried chicken, curries were always for Fridays or Saturdays and, if they were enjoyed on another day, they always made that day feel like a Friday or a Saturday. Was this something formed by habit, David wondered, or was it a social norm?

Everything always seemed better when he was in here. Here, with the curtains drawn early, the glow from the TV screen lighting the room and the heating on. It was warm, there was plenty of food within reach...he felt safe. His weight, his pains, school: it all seemed a lifetime away on a Saturday night. It was the peak of his week. The sadness that most people experienced on a Sunday evening was crippling for David. The thought of the coming school week was only ever a bleak one.

Kerri shooed the girls up to bed at 9pm and then returned to the sofa with the inevitable tea and biscuits. They sat in the new silence, the TV in the background.

At least, David thought as he glanced over at Kerri who was tapping and scrolling at the iPad, at least I know she's not doing anything stupid.

She looked up and over at him then smiled. He smiled back.

Then she said, 'David. I was going to chat to you now the girls had gone to bed.'

He glanced up at her over his tablet. She put her tablet down. This is serious, he thought, gripping his even tighter.

'I'm going to get a gastric band.'

Chapter Thirteen

Monday 25th to Tuesday 26th March

Naomi

There are rare times, sacred times when the internal and external weather are in happy synchrony.

Standing on the platform at the station, Naomi smiled up at the blue sky. The low sun was a creamy yellow, along the exposed platform a cool breeze blew, but it was mild, balmy even, and, dressed in her navy skirt and jacket, Naomi could feel the warmth of the air through the wool suit.

Monday morning and, having received a few messages on and off across the weekend, today she felt light, as light as air, her mind as fluffy as the cumulus clouds that drifted across the sky. Thoughts of him, of how it had been when they were together, scudded across her mind, and the future seemed sun-dappled. She imagined more meetings, more time. She felt effervescent: inside her there was a honeycomb sensation of bubbles and fizz and light. The warmth spoke of the coming spring and she felt alive, really alive, for the first time in years. Like the energy contained within a bud, she was all potential: as if at any moment she would burst out of her dull skin into full flower.

While there had been no physical evidence of what she had done, she knew that she looked different. Her skin glowed, her eyes danced, a smile often played on her lips. The invisible audience that so many of us imagine had become real. She felt as if he had fully seen her and now, having been seen, it was as if she was emitting a glow, a life force that was irresistible.

On the train looking out of the window, work forgotten, she daydreamed and fantasised, the potential of it all laid out before her like an endless summer. Smiling, she felt almost foolish for noticing the lines of trees, the distant glint of the river as the train made its way out through the countryside. Even the more built-up areas, even the small homes and the concreted yards seemed appealing in this light. Naomi saw the primary colours of toys in the back gardens, saw the light play on the windows of the tower blocks, felt the essence of optimism in the buds that were visible on the trees as they sped past. Walking from the station, she noticed the pale green darts of daffodils, the patches of crocuses scattered along the grey path. Having only worked here in the winter so far, she had not expected there to be flowers. Had only ever seen the functionality of the place and yet here were crocuses: pale yellow and purple, their stalks a luminous green, they seemed to be there only for her, their flowers adding to her joy. Their colours seemed to enhance the fresh green of the surrounding grass, seemed to speak of hope, of the perfection of all that was natural. Impulsively she stopped and, bending down, aware of how her skirt stretched across her thighs, aware of the glances of those striding by, she picked some and carried a small bunch with her.

In her office, she arranged the crocuses in a small glass and, smiling at them again, she drank her coffee, reading over their exchange from last night. Him saying again how much he had enjoyed their evening together, him asking when he could see her again.

The challenges of the day were met effortlessly. The weeks ahead were going to be interesting. The meeting with Grahame and Jonathan scheduled for next week still needed some additional preparation, but she felt increasingly sure that the approach she had planned was the right one. That she could make it work.

And this, she thought, staring again at the messages that she could not quite bear to close, this is going to work too.

Arriving home from work, Naomi got out of the car and glanced up at the pollarded tree. The stark, black-brown branches were outlined against the ribbed, fishbone-like clouds that Daddy had always called a mackerel sky. Naomi wasn't even sure people used that phrase any more but she liked it, always had. The evening was cool, the heat going out of the day as soon as the sun began to go down, but it was still pleasant and, looking up at the sky, she smiled at the variety of colours: the pale blue of the upper reaches, the pinks and yellows and greys as the light faded, and the darker tinges on the horizon. A peaceful palette.

She prepared salad for dinner: it seemed too nice to be thinking about eating casseroles or pies, the usual things that she would pick up at this time of year. Taking the food she needed out of the fridge, she hummed away to herself: a song in her head, a song about life, about love.

James glanced up from his school books and looked at her. Naomi beamed back. Without comment, James continued reading while also glancing across at his phone.

'Can you move your books in a minute, please!'

She took the marinated salmon out of the packet and arranged it on the wooden platter, then she opened the two bags of mixed leaves. Chopping an avocado, she mixed the salad in the large wooden bowl.

'How are you getting on there?' she asked James as she tossed the salad, liberally pouring dressing all over the leaves.

'Fine... Maths and science project stuff.'

James looked at her again and frowned. The slightly manic smiling of the past week was a little unsettling. He texted David.

'Cool,' Naomi said. 'I'd love to have a look after dinner.'

''Kay.' James shrugged. He texted David again: *wtf, she wants to look at my homework now.*

With Mike away, Naomi was making an effort to spend more time downstairs.

James's phone beeped. He checked it.

Maybe the Mum of the Year award is up for renewal?

'Can you go and tell Dad dinner's ready?' Naomi said sweetly, as she took the salad to the table and laid the plates out. The platter of salmon she popped in the centre of the table, along with a bowl of cooked new potatoes in butter. Not that she had noticed but they were out of season: air-freighted from Israel months in advance of the English season.

James walked out of the kitchen, texting.

He came back in, still texting, with Scott behind him. Scott was also staring at his phone.

'Boys! Phones!' scolded Naomi, laughingly.

Both of them looked at her. Scott put his phone on the side by the kettle and James did the same. The phones always went there before family meals. Scott sat down and James ran back and grabbed his phone. 'Just. One. More. Scroll,' he gasped, pretending to be dying. Naomi laughed and, exchanging a smile with Scott, filled their wine glasses.

They all sat down and the sticky smoked salmon, salad and potatoes were served up. As they ate, Naomi chattered away.

'So the weather is lovely, isn't it? Meant to be like this for a while now. Work OK today?' she added, forking salad into her mouth.

'Yes, not easing up any time soon but it's good: the new CV software is still causing us problems but it will be worth it once the bugs are fixed. It should really save time in the long run.'

Naomi uh-huh'ed and then she turned her bright gaze on to James. 'James is working on a science project. He's going to show it to me after supper!' she said, taking a sip of wine.

James refilled his glass with Coke and then helped himself to more salmon.

More questions and chat and then Naomi cleared the plates into the dishwasher and said, 'Oh! I forgot – I bought pudding!'

And she took the box of éclairs out of the fridge. Taking three plates out of the cupboard, she placed the cakes and plates on the table and smiled again as James and Scott both went to grab the box at the same time. They both shared Granny Taylor's sweet tooth.

After chatting to James and then spending some time with Scott in the living room by the fire, Naomi got ready for bed, still feeling happy. There was something about all of this: about having a sweet distraction as well as a lovely family. She spat the last of the toothpaste out and looked at her reflection in the mirror. Smiling, she said to herself: I love my family and I get to have some fun thinking about him too. I'm so lucky!

And that was how she felt: lucky. Lucky to be having it all.

Climbing into bed, she reached over to Scott and pulled him close to her, pressing herself into him. I'm so happy about Mike, she thought, that I want to have sex with Scott...

On Tuesday, Naomi went into London for a meeting. Sitting in a café beforehand, she watched the men and women all around her: on their phones, staring hard at laptops, the screens opaque, entranced expressions on their faces.

How many of these people were doing the same thing as her? Flirting, arranging assignations, charting out their cheating: lying, loving, risking everything? They were just words but they all added up to so much more: a world of passion and pain being created with every tap and click.

It can't just be me? she thought. I can't be the only one.

Logging into the wifi herself, she tried not to show her impatience as the browser loaded – it seemed to take an age. Part of her knew she should stay offline so that she could avoid going on to check her messages or see if he was about, but part of her also thought, Why shouldn't I be online? Why can't I be? Everyone else is.

At last, it connected. She logged into the site and scrolled through the latest updates. Nothing from him. But he was there. Sometimes she could manage a few minutes without looking across at the toolbar to see if he was there, but today she didn't. Today she didn't even try.

Taking a sip of the hot, milky coffee, she finished her *pain au chocolat* and then took one of Carla's purple marketing folders out of her leather bag. Putting the plate to one side, she extracted the papers she needed and started scanning over the relevant pages.

The computer bipped. Her stomach rolled over.

Putting the papers down hastily, she opened up the screen.

Hey, sexy – what you up to?

Smiling she typed back: *In London for work – you?*

Bored. Sitting in my hotel room. In between stuff.

Oh. OK. How is it all going?

Pffft – dull. What are you wearing?

She raised her eyebrows but smiled.

Clothes :P

Smart arse – *tell* me what you're wearing.

A suit – a short skirt and jacket – very fitted – high heels.

Mmm…heels and short skirts. That should be a corporate guideline – no more bloody trouser suits or leggings. Ever.

Not everyone can be as stylish as you ☺

And underneath?

I'm in a café – I can't do that here!

Yes, you can ☺

No!

Spoilsport.

Maybe play later?

Her mind spun ahead at the idea of an evening of playing. They hadn't done that for a while and she missed the buzz, the excitement of having him tell her how much he wanted her, what he wanted to do.

Sorry. No. I'm out later.

Her stomach tensed with disappointment. It was worse to hear from him and have him not want to play, or to be busy, than it was to not hear from him at all. Worse still was when she suggested something and had him knock it back – she felt so foolish, sick to her stomach almost. As if her whole self was being rejected, found wanting in some way.

Naomi glanced at the time. She had work to do: she had to prepare for this meeting – but she couldn't bring herself to end the chat.

When are you back? she asked.

Next week. Actually I was going to ask you something...

Fire away.

Sitting upright, she stared at her screen, excited, anxious. What was he going to say? What was he going to ask her? Another date very soon? Maybe a weekend away! The idea of being able to spend a day and a night together, of waking up next to him, had got into her head recently and now she couldn't stop thinking about it.

One of my team is really underperforming – have you ever had to do any disciplinary stuff? How did you get started?

Naomi smiled, mentally rolled up her sleeves and dug in.

After twenty minutes of chat, he said, *That was really helpful – thank you!*

No problem – happy to help ☺

Better go.

Yeah, me too!

Speak later?

Sure ☺

And with that he was gone. She had five minutes before she had to get going herself. Logging the computer off, she waited for the screen to shut down and, as she did, she sent Scott a text: *I'll be home early today and I'll pick up something from town for dinner. Maybe we can watch a movie later? xxx*

Luckily, the meeting went well, very well.

Picking up wine, crisps and some ready meals at the train station's mini Waitrose, she walked past the large W.H. Smith and, with ten minutes until her train was due, she ran in and grabbed a couple of movie magazines for James as well as a photography one for Scott. He always enjoyed those.

As she sat on the train, eating an apple and sipping some water, the food shopping, bag of magazines and her bag on the seat next to her, she smiled. Looking at the buildings as they shot by, she felt a surge of warmth run through her.

I'm doing it, she thought. I'm being the perfect wife, the perfect mistress, the perfect mother and the perfect employee. I'm doing it and it feels great. Really bloody great.

Chapter Fourteen

Friday 12th April

Matthew

It was lunchtime, and, with no lunch duties, Matthew was sitting at his desk when Solange appeared at the doorway. Her hair was tied back in a high ponytail and her face was flushed pink from the cool air.

'Come outside,' she said.

'Yes, OK,' he said and, grateful for the distraction, he put his phone away in the drawer and got up.

In the courtyard, the sky had cleared and the air was fresh and cool, the sun beginning to shine weakly through the thinning clouds. Solange lit a cigarette. 'So, you are still seeing the girl?' she asked, through a hiss of grey smoke.

'Yeah,' said Matthew. He pulled his hand through his hair and tried not to make it too obvious that he was deliberately breathing in the smoke as Solange breathed it out across the weed-filled courtyard. 'She's great.'

His voice was strangely flat; he sounded as if he was talking about an OFSTED meeting, not a girlfriend.

Solange looked at him sharply. Tucking a strand of long, dark hair behind her ear, she said, 'It does not sound so great. You are so, how do you say, down in the dumps. What is it?'

'I'm all right. She *is* great. She met some new people recently and she's all excited and it's just that, you know, someone being great can be a little bit, well, exhausting. She can be hard to keep up with. I thought I was pretty cool but then you meet someone like that and you realise just how much there is to do, just how much needs fixing and, well, she seems to find it energising but all I want to do sometimes is curl up and have a nap.'

He laughed a little. He knew he sounded absurd but this was how he felt today. Polly had showed him a whole new set of plans this week, some ideas that had come from the guy who headed up the other group she had recently got in touch with. He had felt strangely jealous.

Solange was watching him closely. 'I think maybe it is not meant to be tiring. These first few months are meant to be fun, *non*?'

She lit another cigarette with the tip of the one she had nearly finished.

Dismayed by the feeling, Matthew had been desperately trying to ignore it. Staring at the floor so that he didn't look as Solange lit up another cigarette, he was attempting to focus his mind on how awful it must taste. The first cigarette was always awful. It was best not to think about how much better the second one was.

'It is fun!' he protested, his voice rising a little sharply at the end. 'She is great. Really great. In fact, I'm going to invite her to my parents' house for Easter and then I'm thinking about asking her to move in. She's round at mine so much anyway, it kind of makes sense. Yeah, it makes sense.'

Solange stared at him and nodded. 'Easter. Yes, I am looking forward to going home for a couple of weeks. Sunshine, rather than this.' She shrugged up at the sky. 'Why is it so cold here still?'

'April is like this sometimes,' Matthew said, 'Can be really hot and sunny – remember last year when we were having drinks outside at the end of term? That was this time last year and yet now it is about to snow…'

'That was fun,' said Solange. 'I love it when it is sunny here. It never gets too hot and everyone is happy. The weather lifts in a way that nothing else can! We just have to hope that the winter is over soon.'

She looked at Matthew searchingly. He was still trying to avoid looking at the cigarette she was smoking and was scuffing the concrete with his shoe like one of the kids.

'Time to go in,' she said, glancing at her watch.

'Is it?' he said, and he found himself, for a moment, very much wishing that they could stay out here, talking and watching the wisps of blue grey smoke, for ever.

David

It had been nearly three weeks since Kerri's announcement about the band and David's anger with her still lingered. He remained stuffed with it, had little appetite for anything other than the rage he was now chewing over like a cud, the bitterness of it failing to fade as he went over and over it. His mother was going to have an *operation* – risk an anaesthetic, put herself in danger, maybe take weeks to recover – just because she couldn't stick to a diet. What if something went wrong? He tried to imagine himself living with Gary and his perfect new family – him, Jess and Emily with their bickering, starting at a new school, leaving his only friend in the world; he tried to make it OK, in his imagination, but he really couldn't.

School was only bearable because of the thought of home. It was almost Easter and there would be at least a few days when the girls would be involved in activities and he would be at home on his own. It was the thought of this time that was keeping him going.

But, he thought, there was Christianne. He wouldn't see her for two weeks.

'Right, nearly time to wrap up and then I can talk to you about your Easter course work!'

David started slightly: the volume at which Mrs Williams was speaking had jerked him out of his reverie. Sheets of paper began to get passed from the front of the class to the back. Every day for the last week, he had taken home a bag full of coursework and projects. Every teacher expected you to give their subject the most attention. Every night, David had piled the worksheets up on his crowded, messy desk and sighed. An hour later, waiting for James on the edges of the lunch hall, he kept his head down, scanning the toes of the passers-by for evidence of Christianne. He recognised her non-regulation footwear now and even just thinking about it made him feel odd, as if he had an internal wind blowing through him. It made him feel both hot and cold, excited and scared all at the same time.

'D'oh! What you staring at the floor for?' laughed James.

David flushed and punched him on the arm. He followed James into the lunch hall and braced against himself against the noise as he breathed in the greasy hot smell.

The room was packed. There was rarely any absenteeism on the last day of term. There was always something going on, and everyone was afraid of missing it. Fear of missing out. FOMO. There was nothing like applying an acronym to an emotion to both validate it and encourage its spread.

David had more than that reason for being here today, though. The last day of term was, in his mind, the ideal opportunity to ask Christianne if he could see her over the holidays.

Stalking the playground after lunch, he pretended to listen to James's chatter while he scanned around looking for Christianne. Where was she? The twenty minutes passed with no sign of her or the Three Graces.

Regretting having forgone a snack after lunch, David hung back and ducked into the bathrooms. He had a few swigs of Coke and ate one of the Twix bars he had in his bag. Where there was one there would always be another. Or two. Staring at the back of the toilet door as he chewed, he tried not to feel disheartened. Later, he told himself, later. I will see her later.

And he did.

The rush to leave the school grounds was always delayed on the last day. Though suddenly free to go, there was a seeming reluctance to leave those black gates behind them. For David, having spotted Christianne and the Three Graces over by the gates, there was an important thing to do.

He hadn't told James what he was planning. He had not wanted to, and now, with the other boy occupied saying goodbye to his music and football friends, David stood, taking a moment to give himself one last pep talk.

As he took a deep breath and prepared to walk over, he noticed that she was coming towards him.

She was smiling. He smiled back.

Yes, he thought, *yes*. Here we go.

'Hey, David,' she said.

'Hi,' he replied.

It took all his effort to lift his eyes up from her regulation footwear to her very non-regulation cornflower-blue eyes.

'So pleased term is over!'

'Yeah, me too,' he said.

'You up to much in the holidays?'

Now, his mind shouted, *now!*

He hesitated.

Her eyes were on his. He opened his mouth. Then her eyes moved to the right and a change rippled over her features: the smile widened, the eyes brightened and widened, pupils dilating, her cheeks flushed.

'Hi,' Christianne said, now looking at the ground herself.

265

Out of the corner of his eye, David saw the Three Graces clutching each other, hands and hair fluttering, as James bounced over.

'Easter!' burst out James. David felt like hitting him. 'You up to much?' he asked Christianne.

She glanced up and, still flushing said, 'I was going to catch a film – you fancy coming along?'

James stopped bouncing.

He glanced at David.

'What?' David asked him, shrugging but unable to hide the tremor in his voice. Then, he added, 'You love going to the cinema…'

James still looked uncertain. 'Sure, yeah.'

'I'll text you, then…' said Christianne; the worst over, she seemed to find the confidence to close the deal.

'Yeah, sure,' James said.

'Cool! See ya,' she said, and she turned, unable to hide quite how relieved and pleased she was as she raced at top speed back to her friends.

The Graces made a show of suitably muted pleasure. They were too cool to squeal. David began to walk towards the gates of the school. James grabbed his bags and quickly followed.

'You fucker,' David hissed. 'You know I like her.'

James said, 'Sorry…' but, just for a moment, his eyes were saying something different, and it was those words that David read.

'Why shouldn't she like me? Why shouldn't she?' His face was hot with anger.

James opened his mouth again, the look gone, his pupils now contracted in misery. 'You practically arranged it yourself… I…' He hesitated.

'Fuck you,' David hissed. 'I thought you were my friend but you…' his voice broke with feeling '…you're just like the rest of them. Even you think I'm too fat to have a girlfriend.'

'I didn't say that,' James protested, stood limply, arms hanging by his side.

'You didn't have to.'

David hitched his bag up and stopped still. He glared at James and continued to glare at him while the other boy looked at him pleadingly.

'Go away! Go on – fuck off. You're not my friend…'

James turned and, head down, walked away. Even knowing that the other boy had walked away first because he knew David was too slow to get away couldn't change his overwhelming feelings of hatred and disappointment.

Naomi

Naomi was in a frenzy trying to catch up as well as get ahead of herself before the long Easter weekend.

'Bloody bank holidays…' she sighed, staring resignedly at and flicking through the enormous stack of paperwork in front of her. 'Why do people seem to go into hibernation just when we need them? Right…' Lifting her head up, she focused her attention back on Simon. 'I want all the print media advert proofs finished and with me ready for sign-off right after Easter. And I need you to arrange a final meeting with Winters. Just to let him have his chance to have the last word: you know that keeps him happy.'

They both exchanged a smile. Simon had recently married his long-term boyfriend, but it was a truth silently and fully acknowledged that *everyone* at VitSip thought Jonathan was hot.

'And if the sales team could start fishing around for possible deals… There's no way the local newspapers are going to keep charging us those rates. I know the rates that other companies get and, while I know we won't be able to secure those because of the volumes, we can add maybe twenty per cent to the baseline and use that as a starting point in the negotiations. I'll add that to the list of stuff I send you before I go,' she continued, adding yet another bullet point on to the *Before I go I HAVE to* list.

Her lists were a bit of a laughing stock in a business that had synced calendars and electronic everything, but she liked them: there really was nothing more satisfying than crossing something off a list…

Well, her mind, piped up, almost nothing as satisfying…

And, suddenly, there was an image and along with the image was the intense physical sensation of that last time: of her coming and him slapping her and how she had felt afterwards. The memory suffused her body and mind, forcing her to close her eyes to stop herself from shuddering. How was it possible that one thought could transport her body right back? She had read a book once, in the days when she read a lot of books, a book about childbirth that said the body had no memory. But that's wrong, she thought; all mine does is remember – remember and crave those feelings. Wanting to feel them again.

'Naomi?'

'Yes, sorry. Right.' Naomi smiled and squinted at the papers in front of them. 'What were we talking about?'

'The sales rates?'

'Yes, OK, so I'll get those rates to you and you're going to sort the meeting with Jonathan and now I just have a fortnight's worth of stuff to get done in the next…' she glanced at her watch '…three hours. See you when I get back.'

Back in her office, she worked like crazy until 5pm and then she had to go. With a briefcase stuffed full of folders, she picked up the two purple folders she also needed, brushing away the memory of that time Carla had come in to the office, and ran to catch her train. The last day of spring term meant she and James had their end-of-term McDonald's ritual to enjoy and then an evening to work before the weekend. The plan for the Easter break was to drive over to Scott's parents on Good Friday morning and spend the long weekend there before heading back for home. She still wasn't sure quite how she was going to manage three full days of her in-laws…

With lots of chocolate and wine, she told herself. And, hopefully, a chance to message Mike while she quote-unquote 'checked her emails'.

Smiling, she sat back on the train and stared out of the window, the scenery passing in a blur.

Matthew

Even on the last day of the spring term, going round the supermarket after work was a uniquely depressing experience. The same unnatural silence that he had noticed upon his return from Brazil surrounded him, and he marvelled at how he had never noticed this before, never noticed how no one talked to each other, acknowledged each other or even noticed that anyone else was there while they were shopping. There were occasional huffs or puffs, muttered '*excuse me*'s as people pushed past the cages full of boxes that the staff used to top up the already groaning shelves, but mostly people were oblivious to each other.

After he'd collected the fruit and vegetables he needed, Matthew walked through the aisles towards the bread. This section was the furthest one away from the main entrance. He was tired, hungry and fed up. He was Big Food's ideal shopper. Staring down the twenty-metre-long aisle, he realised that he was now flanked on either side by dozens of varieties of crisps, nuts and crackers. Before he even noticed what he was doing, he had grabbed some salted nuts and some chilli-spiced crisps and then, at the end of the aisle where there was a mountain of cans of Pepsi, he grabbed a pack of six. The next aisle was full of biscuits – buy one, get one free. Without even thinking, he took two of the purple boxes and placed them into the basket.

Walking on, he deliberately avoided the confectionery aisle, but when he got to the bakery section he found himself face to face with a mountain of brownies, flapjacks, mini-doughnuts, mini-muffins and chocolate shortbreads. There was an army of mini-gingerbread men contained in those plastic boxes. Enough sweet biscuits to feed a county.

The cake counter was to his right and, past the standalone biscuit Everest, there was another aisle filled with boxed chocolate rolls, carrot cakes, loaf-cakes and other factory-made confections that contained enough preservatives to withstand a nuclear winter. Out of curiosity, he picked up one of the celebration cakes. Aimed at kids and their harassed parents, there were cakes to suit any taste – there was SpongeBob, Barbie and Spider-Man. There was a caterpillar, a fairy and a train. The one he had picked up was a Batman symbol; the yellow was very yellow and the black very black.

Placing the cake back carefully, he crossed the aisle and, looking for the familiar yellow packaging of his preferred brand of bread, he scanned the varieties – thick, medium, half-loaf and toasting. Grabbing the medium-cut wholemeal loaf, he walked as quickly as he could to the checkout.

It was then that the smell hit him. The fresh produce might not smell, but here, as he walked past the rôtisserie and hot food section, all was aroma. He knew now the extent of the mistake he had made in shopping when he was hungry. His stomach grumbled loudly. The smell of sticky ribs, sausages, spit-roast chickens, damp and hot inside the ovenproof foil bags; the crisp pepperoni slices on the thick-base pizzas. There was salt, fat and sugar in the air and it smelled good. Really good.

A glance at the frigid, scentless greens in his basket was the final straw. He walked over to the counter.

'A large pepperoni pizza, please,' he said, his voice low, as if he were scoring drugs in an unfamiliar part of town.

The man didn't bother to meet his eye as he pushed the box, lid askew, over the counter.

Matthew placed the hot box on top of his basket and then walked quickly to the checkout, anxious to get home and eat.

As he waited in the queue, he glanced over to the right, where a large woman with pretty, long blonde hair was unloading her trolley on to the conveyor belt. Why did he stare? Why was what other people ate so fascinating? He saw two boxes of Krave, one of the crates of Pepsi that had been on offer, a bag of grapes and four pizzas, garlic bread, frozen curries (three for two) as well as two loaves of thick-sliced white bread. And then there were the Creme Eggs: carton after carton of Creme Eggs. Chocolate mousses. Easter cakes. Eight large Easter eggs. And another half-dozen bags of mini-eggs.

She glanced up and saw him staring. Then she looked at his shopping: Pepsi, crisps, peanuts and a pizza. Her pale blue eyes met his again: they were dull but he could see the challenge in them.

Looking away, embarrassed, he kept his eyes fixed firmly on the floor as he went through the checkout. This was why no one looked at each other in these places. Because none of them could control themselves and they were all ashamed.

Naomi

There was no sign of James when she got in. Given how much he enjoyed McDonald's, this was a surprise. Even Naomi had been looking forward to this today: there was something Pavlovian about knowing you were going to be eating a certain thing on a certain occasion. All day she had been thinking about the sticky barbecue sauce, the hot, salty chips, the tang of gherkin against the processed beef patty. As with the inevitably overdone Christmas turkey, ritualised treats like this were tastier in anticipation than in actuality. The parallels with her own cravings and anticipation of seeing Mike were yet to be acknowledged.

Fast food was still relatively rationed here Chez Taylor, though Naomi knew James ate a lot of it when he was out on his own; what she didn't see, she didn't mind. As long as he was eating properly at home, she always told herself.

Taking advantage of the fact that he wasn't here just now, Naomi trotted straight upstairs and decided to get online and start work before he *was* home.

Settling down, she began to sort through her notes and start typing; the draft of the latest report needed to be finished before she went away. Obviously, she logged on first.

As she typed, frowning and concentrating, the words flowing out as she focused on what she needed to do, the PC bipped at her.

A message. Her stomach rolled, but, despite having waited days to hear that sound, she found herself thinking, Oh, no, not now...

Clicking on the site, she saw it:

Hey.

The word seemed to glow. Those three letters contained all her longing of recent days. They spoke of promise, of hope, of a chance to meet again and be lost in pleasure. They promised all this and yet right now she wished they weren't there.

She could leave it. She probably *should* leave it.

Hey, she typed.

Quickly clicking back on her document, she carried on working, hoping to get some more done in the inevitable gap between replies.

What a week. I missed you.

She smiled. *Sorry to hear that – what's up?*

Work's pretty awful and, well, like I say: I missed you.

I missed you too.

She went back to her document. She had to get some more done. She really didn't have time for this. Just tell me, she

272

thought, tell me when I'm seeing you and then we're done. And the next thought was: I don't care about your work, I don't care, I just want to know when I'm seeing you.

But: *What is it with companies and changing shit all the time?* he typed. *Honestly, I thought the last place I worked at was bad but this is even worse.*

What's happened? Maybe we can chat about it when I see you?

She carried on typing and hoped he would write a lengthier reply so she could carry on working.

Ugh, it's just the usual shit, I suppose. Should just forget about it. You OK?

Yes. Busy. We're going away for Easter next week and I have so much to do!

OK. Launch going well, then?

Yes! Thanks! Maybe I can tell you about it when I see you?

It was always worth asking the question again, she thought; she really had no time to mess about.

There was a pause. Typing and reading, Naomi clicked back on and saw the dots that showed he was typing a reply when suddenly she heard a loud crash.

With a look of exasperation at the screen, she got up.

'James!' she called out as she ran down the stairs. 'James! Is that you?'

There was more crashing. What was it? What was he doing?

She ran into the kitchen. James was kicking his school bag round the room. His face was red, his eyes were red, he looked as if he might have been crying, but he hadn't cried since he was about ten so she couldn't quite believe it.

'James! Stop! What is it? What's happened?'

As he kicked and grunted, he was muttering, 'Shit, shit, shit,' under his breath. He seemed oblivious to her even standing there, and she waved her arms ineffectually as she tried to get near him. He was so tall now, seemed so big, even

273

in spite of his thin frame, that she felt wary of getting too close as he kicked and cursed.

'*James!*' She screamed it out this time, with an edge to her voice that she hadn't used in a long time, and he stopped, looking at her again but seeing her for the first time.

He stood there, his breath fast and shallow, a sheen of sweat on his forehead.

Naomi approached him slowly, the way one would approach a horse that had finally stopped after bolting. Hands and arms up, and with as calm an expression as she could manage, she said, 'What is it? What's wrong?'

The words *expulsion*, *teen pregnancy* and *STD* were all crossing her mind in rapid succession. It was always slightly funny and odd that the things her own mother had been worried about when Naomi was fourteen were the same things that Naomi worried about now.

James looked down. His breathing had slowed down and now, still red-faced, he just looked very young and very sad and a bit embarrassed.

'Nothing,' he muttered.

'Don't …' said Naomi, warningly, but then, seeing his face, she stopped herself from repeating her own mother's chidings. 'Look,' she said, 'I can see you're upset. Why don't you go upstairs and clean yourself up. I'll log the PC off and then we'll go and get McDonald's. If you feel like a chat we can do it over our burgers, eh?'

James looked up at her. His eyes spoke of his relief, even though he said nothing.

Naomi smiled back, and then with a nod and a brief touch of his arm she went back upstairs. God, what had all that been about? Well, she would hopefully find out soon enough.

Her own difficult teenage years were still fresh in her mind, vivid, tacky and sour-smelling like fresh paint, and she felt an empathy for James that she had rarely experienced when he had had similar tantrums as a toddler and preschooler.

Those had been so frustrating, the melt-downs over the way the sandwich had been cut or about the colour of the plate. Teenage problems, though, she understood; teenage problems she *got*.

At the computer, she closed the report. That would have to wait till she got back. It's going to be a late one, she thought, with a sigh. But at least, with Scott working too, she could work after the meal out and not feel guilty for ignoring him.

And maybe, the voice in her head piped up, maybe Mike will be there and you can chat?

Yes, she agreed with herself, trying to stay calm.

He had messaged her back but all he had said was, *Sure. What are you up to now?*

And now he was offline and she felt like crying out in frustration. Ugh. Nearly two weeks of endless time to chat and, then, when she had a hundred things to do, he was there; and now, now that she was back and had ten minutes spare, he was gone again. So frustrating.

She typed a reply.

Off out for some supper now… Can we chat later?

Logging off, she went to her room and got changed into some jeans and a long-sleeved top before going to the bathroom.

Back downstairs, James was waiting in the hallway.

'Let's go,' she said.

Sitting down across the mauve-coloured booth, Naomi looked at James. His face looked pale and a little green under the harsh fluorescent lighting. And he was a bit spotty again. Bless him, she thought, must be tired now it's the end of term…

She smiled at him as she began to unload the tray on to the smeared and smudged plastic table. What was it with this place that, no matter how much anti-bacterial spray they used, the tables were always sticky.

The restaurant was busy, a low-level hum of rustling, chatting and eating set against a background of tinny pop music.

Naomi handed James his Big Mac box, the thin cardboard warm and softening under the weight of the steaming bun and meat inside, and, as she began to unwrap her own thin paper packet of cheeseburger and open her box of six nuggets, she watched, smiling at the grin on his face, as he tipped the large fries into the box lid and then peeled back the lid of the barbecue sauce.

'The fries are the best bit,' he said, not looking up.

Naomi reached over and pinched a few.

'Get your own!' he protested.

Laughing, she took a bite of her own burger: the sweet bun, the sticky relish, the sliver of gherkin, the thin beef patty, the bright orange of the perfect square of processed cheese. It was disgusting and delicious at the same time.

Chewing and swallowing, she took a sip of Diet Coke from the cup in front of her, and said, 'I can't believe it's the Easter holidays already. Your last day OK?'

'Gnnnnfff.'

'I know Dad is looking forward to us all being together for a few days. It will be good to see Granny and Grandad Taylor.'

They both ate some more.

James was draining his large Coke. The burger had been dispatched and now he was eating the rest of his fries. He was also glancing at Naomi's remaining nuggets. She'd eaten one, but her mind had drifted on to Mike and her appetite for food was fading.

'Can I have one of those?' he asked, fingers reaching across the table.

'Sure! Here,' she said, pushing the little box towards him. 'Finish them off,' she added. 'I only ordered them for you.'

Glancing round the room, she saw tired-looking families, a mum with three kids under six, a guy in his sixties sitting on his own, reading a newspaper and drinking a paper mug of what was actually more than passable coffee. There were young couples eating before a night out, teenagers, and also middle-aged men and women. All looking to eat quickly and cheaply. No one was ever going to stand up in court and say this food was *good* for you but, at the same time, it served a purpose.

The meal was nearly done. Now for the next stage of the ritual.

'Right, I'll get you a pudding,' she said, getting up. 'What would you like?'

'A Crunchie McFlurry and a doughnut, please.'

'Both?' She raised her eyebrows.

'Please...!' James tried to look deserving.

'Oh, OK...'

Naomi went and stood in the queue. She still remembered Kerri saying to her once, 'There are two types of mum: the ones who let their kids eat McDonald's and admit it, and the ones who let their kids eat McDonald's but will never admit it.'

Smiling at the memory, she approached the counter and ordered James's ice cream. 'And a chocolate doughnut please.'

Taking the dessert back to the table, she smiled as James tucked in. Why was it so pleasurable to watch someone else enjoying food, even if it was crappy food? She had no idea. When he was small it used to be the silence – treats had been her way of buying five minutes of quiet – but now, well, it just felt good to let him be happy – he liked his sweet stuff, and she was happy to let him be happy eating it. It wasn't as if he had weight problems, after all, and life really was hard enough. And on that note, she thought...

'So, do you want to talk about earlier?'

James glanced up from his pot of McFlurry and shrugged. Naomi took that as meaning, *Yes, but right now I am eating my ice cream.*

She sipped the last of her drink. It was warm as well as flat now. Sitting back, she went to take her phone out of her bag and then made herself stop. She needed to focus on what she was doing, not start checking for messages. Fidgeting, the restraint making her uncomfortable for a moment, she tried to sit up straight and then put her hands on the table to stop herself. If they were out of sight, they could not be trusted not to just grab the phone and start checking under the table.

'So…' she prompted as James pushed the empty pot aside and began to eat the doughnut.

'S'just me and D… We fell out.'

'Oh!' Naomi was surprised.

'He texted me after and said never to speak to him again.'

'Oh, I'm sure he doesn't mean it.'

'He does.'

'No, I'm sure it will all be fine. You two are so close.'

'Yeah, well, he was pretty pissed at me.'

'James!'

'Sorry but he was, and, like, it wasn't even my fault, it's not like I even like her, *she* asked *me* and now he thinks I was after her and trying to steal her off him and, well, like, it's such a nightmare as now he won't listen to me even when I'm saying I *won't* see her during the holidays.'

It all came out in a garbled rush, the words falling out of his mouth in a tumble, peppered with *like*s and barely audible at times as his voice dipped in and out of the mumbling tone that he always adopted when he was upset.

'Oh! Right. Who asked you out?'

'Grrffnnn…doesn't matter… God, I don't even like her, so… He's just so stubborn and, well…' He trailed off.

'What…?'

'Nothing.'

'You sure?'

'Mmhh.'

'OK.' Naomi paused.

'I'm sure it will all be OK, James. These things always blow over in the end.'

'Mmmnnfff.'

'Let's go home,' she said.

Scott was there when they got back. He was looking relaxed with his feet up on the table, real ale in one hand and remote in the other. They all needed the weekend.

Tired but also keen to be on her own and online, Naomi left Scott and James in the living room watching TV while she went back upstairs. She wasn't too worried about him if it was just a falling out with David. She was sure this would be all sorted by the end of the weekend.

Logging on, she went straight to the site. A message.

Clicking on it, she sighed and slumped.

Sure – I'm out tonight with Carla but chat soon…?

What the hell, she thought, what is going on?

She went back downstairs and poured herself a huge glass of red wine. Going back up and drinking as she climbed the stairs, she got to the top and the glass was empty. She went back down, picked up the bottle, and headed back up.

Her mind spun with potential options.

The strategy began its life as: *Leave it, you are not going to plead with him to see you.* Two glasses later it had evolved into: *Maybe I should just send a light, funny message?* And then, two more glasses later, she was online and typing:

Hey – when am I seeing you?

No attempt at humour. Just an out-and-out beg.

Staggering slightly, she went to bed.

Matthew

Sitting slumped on the sofa, he knew he had made a mistake. Asking Polly to see his parents over Easter had seemed like an excellent idea beforehand but clearly, he had realised afterwards, it had not been excellent at all. In fact, it had been a dreadful idea.

It had seemed important to move things on, had seemed like a shift was necessary but, now, having *done* something, he wished he hadn't. The conversation he had just had was playing over and over in his head.

Hey.

Hey.

How are you?

Busy! Sam – you know, Sam from the other group – has so many great ideas – we're all together getting some things done! You?

Yeah, I'm good. Missing you…

Mmmhhh.

I was wondering about Easter. I thought you could come and have lunch with me and maybe meet my mum. She's really keen to meet you!

Oh, no, I'm away over Easter. We're going to protest at a factory over in Norfolk.

Oh, well, that sounds good!

Yes, it'll be great! Sam's friend Lauren has organised it all – should be excellent. Really hard-hitting!

When are you back?

I'll be in touch, yeah?

Oh, OK.

I need to go. Sorry! Speak to you soon!

OK… Bye…

Maybe he shouldn't have called her? Maybe he should have texted. Maybe he shouldn't have suggested the visit to his parents? Maybe he could have just suggested a day out?

It seemed to him that if he had just said something different, done something different, then maybe he would have got the answer he wanted. The multiple permutations of behaviour, the variables he felt he should have allowed for, were driving him mad. He was playing it all over and over and yet the reality remained the same: she was away over Easter, and, he realised, he didn't know when he was seeing her next at all. He could feel the anxiety corroding his stomach: it burned and ached. He felt as though he would do anything to stop feeling like this. The uncertainty was unbearable. That, and the fact that he felt he had no control over what was happening; that he could do nothing now except wait to hear from her.

He opened another beer but, in reality, the foggier his thoughts got, the sharper his anxiety became, and the more he felt as though it was his behaviour at fault, as if it was all going wrong because of something *he* had done. He worried that she hated him.

The worry seemed to spiral out of control: to spread out from his stomach and eat away at his bones, his very flesh. It was a horrible feeling.

Staring at the walls, fiddling with his phone, ignoring the pile of marking that sat in the corner, he sat there, unable to move. Part of him knew that working would help, but he didn't feel able to focus. He just kept playing the conversation over. The temptation to search online for *how do I tell if she is about to break up with me* was overwhelming.

He picked up his phone and then put it down again. His generation had grown up using search engines the way people in the Middle Ages had used priests and confession boxes: as a faceless source of comfort and advice. They were used to it always having the right answer, and so it seemed logical to ask it, even if, on another level, he knew it was totally illogical. The need for certainty though, the need to *know* was so intense, so all-consuming, that he had to do it.

Typing into the search box: *is she going*...the autofill began to suggest endings to his sentence as soon as he began to type: *to break up with me*.../*to leave me*... It was both reassuring to see how common these searches were and yet also frustrating. He could not believe that other people felt as intensely as he did.

Scanning over the links the search brought up, he thought about what he really wanted to type, the question he really wanted to ask but which he knew he would never get the answer to. *Does Polly still care for Matthew...?*

And, ignoring the reproachful pile of marking, he clicked on the first link.

Chapter Fifteen

Friday 19th to Monday 22nd April (Easter)

Naomi

It was Good Friday. The drive had been easy enough though James had just stared at his phone or out of the window, his free hand constantly dipping in and out of a giant bag of Haribo. They had stopped on the way and, despite the apples and water she'd packed, James had insisted on sweets and Coke. After yet another late night and yet another three too many glasses of wine, Naomi had not had the energy to say no.

They pulled into the gravel drive of the Taylor family home.

'James!' Naomi hissed as she looked around to the back seat and saw the empty sweet bag on the floor. 'I didn't expect you to eat all of them! Granny will have lunch ready soon!'

'I was hungry,' said James, as he unbuckled his seat belt and got out.

'Well, you'd better still be hungry now…' she said through gritted teeth as she fixed a hard smile to her face and got out too.

Walking behind Scott, to the front door, she tried to wet the inside of her mouth with her own saliva. Her tongue stuck drily to the roof of her mouth and her head hurt. There was an ache in her jaw which she knew was from grinding her teeth while she was sleeping.

'Naomi! You're so thin!' Elaine exclaimed, as she came out of the door. 'And you, James! So pale…' She ushered them in, her sinewy arms bare in the spring sunshine.

'It's good to see you too, Elaine,' said Naomi.

They followed Elaine inside. 'Lunch is nearly ready!' she trilled, heading for the kitchen. 'Put your things in your rooms and then we can eat.'

Scott took the cases upstairs and Naomi followed, carrying the laptop bag up to the bedroom at the back of the house and placing it carefully on to the small wooden writing table in the corner.

Trying to keep her tone light rather than annoyed, she said, 'Your mum is her usual self, I see…'

'Yes,' he said. 'The medication for the cough seems to be helping.'

'Oh, I am pleased,' said Naomi, thinking, Thank goodness, I don't have to worry about that for now, then… But she was also slightly fearful that Elaine being well meant that she would be around for ever. The presence of these old, slowly sickening and ageing people in her life made her feel so uncomfortable. The fact that Elaine had a habit of watching her every move across the open-plan living space of the converted barn meant that Naomi usually spent the whole time she was here craving a small, snug room to curl up in. Elaine made her feel like a mouse, exposed and running in the open, desperately seeking safety from a circling owl.

Going back downstairs, Naomi took a seat in the sitting room and looked about her. She had never liked the house. Most of the similar conversions Naomi had seen were light and airy, but this place was just cold and draughty. Even with the early spring warmth, the place seemed icy: a chill lay on the rooms, like a morning frost. The natural wood fires were attractive but ineffectual.

Hearing activity in the kitchen and feeling as though she should be doing something, even though she knew she was never allowed to help, she went into the other room.

'Sit down! We might as well have lunch…'

One by one, Elaine placed earthenware bowls of soup in front of them. The steam curled and dissipated; the thick orange broth was sprinkled with toasted pumpkin seeds. A breadboard and knife were placed in the middle of the table, along with a plate of thickly buttered granary bloomer slices.

James began to swirl the soup with his spoon, sinking the seeds one by one, as if they were enemy subs descending to the depths of the bowl.

'James!' Naomi hissed again, as she glanced over. 'Stop it!'

He began to spoon the soup into his mouth and then reached over for the bread. 'Do you want some bread, Grandad?' he asked.

'He can do it for himself,' Elaine interjected, sharply. 'We all need to do things for ourselves – can't be getting waited on, can we, Leonard?' She had raised her voice, bellowing down the table.

Scott smiled at James and, saying, 'Thanks,' he let James help himself to another slice of the bread and then took the plate from him. Elaine clicked her teeth, a familiar sign of her easily flaring irritation, and Scott, still smiling mildly, placed the thickly buttered bread on to his father's side plate.

After they had eaten the soup, Elaine brought out an apple cake crusted thickly with brown sugar. Placing it in the middle of the table along with a bowl of whipped cream, she went to get a knife to cut it with.

Naomi glanced over at James's bowl. Despite his attempts to paste the thick soup all over the sides, it was clearly still half full. 'James won't have any dessert, Elaine – he's hardly touched his soup.'

'Nonsense! Boy needs feeding up! He's so thin!' she said, smiling at her only grandson. 'I'll cut you a nice big piece.'

Elaine cut a huge wedge of the cake and handed it to James with a large dollop of cream on the side. He ate it with relish, pausing occasionally to smile sheepishly at his mother. Naomi chose to ignore him as she took small forkfuls of her own slim slice.

After being allowed to help clear the lunch things away, Naomi dried her hands on a damp, slightly sour-smelling tea towel (Elaine didn't believe in dishwashers). James was still at the kitchen table playing on his phone and as oblivious to the activity going on around him as he was when he was at home. Scott and Leonard had gone to sit in the living room.

'I'm going to need to go and do some work for a few hours,' Naomi began as Elaine stacked the clean and dry bowls, one by one, neatly on the dresser.

With a blank expression that was more withering than any put-down, Elaine pointedly balanced the last bowl very carefully and then, in her briskest sergeant-major voice, she sing-songed, 'Shall we go for a walk, James? Shame to be inside on such a glorious spring day!'

'Yes, Granny!'

Naomi smiled gratefully at her son, squeezing his hand as he went by. She walked through to the living room. Glancing around, she saw that Scott and Leonard were in the big, worn blue armchairs nearest the fire. In the open-plan space, the fire was the warmest spot and so, like simple animals, they had gathered round it after lunch and settled down to sleep. She raised both eyebrows in mild exasperation, trying not to think about how similar the two men looked. At least she had an hour or two to herself.

Upstairs, she turned on the laptop.

Nothing from Mike. Growling to herself, in frustration, she decided to actually do some work. There was still some things left over from yesterday's less than productive evening.

But even the demanding final stages of the launch could not quite distract her from the sense of disquiet.

David

It was Buy One, Get One Free on all Easter eggs. There were discounts to be had on all large bags of sweets too. And cakes. And biscuits. And snacks. Every advert featured smiling faces and happy shoppers, all filling their baskets with discounted treats. There was a funny advert for Creme Eggs. Despite the fact that they had been available to buy since Boxing Day, it was now Easter and their shelf-life was coming to an end: no Creme Egg wanted to be left in a discount bin. For David, though, cut-price chocolate was the highlight of any retail season. He still remembered how many Hallowe'en treats he had been able to buy in December, and the volume of chocolate tree decorations he had eaten in January. He had no idea why people couldn't eat snowflake-patterned boxes of crisps and sweets in June. Some people were just *way* too fussy. Every TV advert seemed to be about food or holidays. As he was not likely to be booking a holiday any time soon, David absorbed the food commercials instead. The images of families sitting around tables together either annoyed him or made him feel wistful. They had never really had a table to sit around, just the fold-away thing that Kerri got out when they had guests – which, since Dad had gone, was never; but there was always the thought in the back of his mind that maybe, if they had had a table like in the ads, maybe they would have been a happier family. James's family ate their meals at a table. Those families, the ones sitting together, looked content.

He understood that most people did not live lives like that, but the images were honed for maximum impact, and had an appeal that was hard to resist. Something about the smiles set to soft music, the warm tones of the lighting and the conscious mismatch of the soft furnishings all made him long for that sense of togetherness. After absorbing these images for fifteen years, it would take more than two hour-long sessions on advertising in a PSHE class to rub the gloss away.

The programme came back on. He had seen this episode before. Flicking through the channels, he raised his eyebrows at the sound of Jess and Emily walking down the stairs: or rather, not walking but squabbling. Everything they did at the moment was accompanied by low-level bickering. They squabbled down the stairs, squabbled through their meals. Squabbled: was that an adverb or an adjective? David had no idea. English was always after lunch and so he was usually sated rather than alert.

Still flicking, he felt irritated by the television's inability to distract him. It was only a few days into the Easter break but already he was bored. And he missed James. The James-shaped gap in his life, and his day, was a large and awkward one: there was nothing else that quite did the job, not even extra helpings of TV and chocolate.

David smiled at his sisters as they burst into the room. Inspired by the advert he had just watched, he said, 'Shall we play Monopoly?'

Both girls groaned as they flopped down on to the sofa, and Jess took advantage of the fact that David had momentarily put down the remote to grab it and begin flicking through the on-screen guide.

'Aw, come on, just for a bit…' he said, shifting uncomfortably away as Emily sat next to him. He really did take up a lot of the sofa now. Brushing the thought away, he sighed as the squabbling began again. If he and James hadn't fallen out, he would have been with him all day today, eating burgers and playing computer games.

The girls had found something to watch now and, looking up, he saw yet another advert: a large extended family sitting down and eating a banquet of filo-wrapped prawns, mini minted lamb cutlets, buttery potatoes and melting-middle chocolate puddings. Here was another advert for all the Easter television: a new drama, yet another must-see TV series. Chill. Eat. The exhortations to sit and consume were relentless. Why fight it? thought David, and, tired, uncomfortable and above all, lonely, he checked his silent phone and then stared at the TV.

And, like all families, the Wallaces had their holiday rituals. Kerri came home late on Easter Saturday (she always had a lot to clear on the long weekend) and, as it was Saturday, it was *Feed a Family for under Fifteen!* at the fried chicken shop, so she arrived with, alongside more food shopping ('I hate the idea of running out of anything...'), three big brown paper bags. There were large families, and then there were small families with large appetites.

Kerri had asked David to download some new films for the long weekend. As she unpacked the paper bags on to the coffee table, she asked, 'Want to put a film on? And can one of you girls go put the kettle on for me? And grab the lemonade out of the fridge? I'll put the food away later...'

Emily and Jess both got up and, taking advantage of the fact that she was slightly bigger and faster, Jess pushed Emily back on to the sofa and dashed into the kitchen.

'Which one shall we watch, Em?' David asked, trying to distract her. Emily shrugged. David pulled a face at her and then, selecting a film he thought she would like, he then passed her a soft cardboard box with a chicken burger in. She took it, eyes still downcast. David frowned and glanced over at Kerri, who was now powering up her tablet, preoccupied. Had she even noticed the shoving? It seemed to him that the teasing was getting too much now, that it was beginning to wear Emily down, but what to say? He could barely handle his own bullies, let alone begin to help Emily deal with her sister.

Smiling at Jess as she came in with the lemonade and glasses, Kerri said, 'Thanks, sweetie, that's really helpful!'

Emily seemed to shrink further into the sofa and, placing the half-eaten burger back in its damp box, she picked up a paper parcel of fries and began to eat them listlessly, staring at the screen. Jess watched the screen too, but in contrast she was humming while she ate. David couldn't help observing that, in the increasingly unhealthy dynamic between the two girls, one seemed to suffer and the other seemed to grow stronger. Like the battle of superhero and villain playing out on the flat screen, there seemed to be no escape from that eternal dualism.

As Kerri began to collect the boxes, sachets and half-used bleached white paper napkins and stuffed it all into one of the big brown bags, David grabbed the leftover chips and the spare burger and ate them. The chips were always rubbish from the chicken place (what was it that McDonald's got so right about their fries?) but, even lukewarm, the spiced chicken burger was one of his favourite things. The crunch of the breadcrumbs, the heat of the chilli, the bland, soft chicken, the creaminess of the mayonnaise, the watery crispness of the sliced iceberg lettuce against the sweet, pappy dough with its *faux*-toasted glaze. It seemed to require little or no effort to eat, and that made it even more delicious.

Why wasn't everything in life as good and easy as that sandwich? As the girls began to argue over the last glassful of lemonade, he wished the food could fill his ears in the same way that it filled his stomach.

'But I want some more too...' Emily pleaded, her voice wavering. She sounded as though she was about to cry.

Glancing around to make sure Kerri wasn't watching, which she wasn't, Jess pinched her sister and then, as the other girl squealed, Jess grabbed the lemonade and poured the last of it into her own glass.

'Jess...' David shouted, voice sharp.

She stuck her tongue out at him. He had no authority with her. Never had had. It was only ever Dad she had listened to.

Despairing a little as Emily moaned and rubbed her arm, David thought about getting up to take his rubbish out but, feeling full, decided not to bother. He was about to say something to Emily when Kerri got up and then came back in the room with her hands behind her back.

'Can we pause this?' she asked, 'I have something important for us all to do.'

David rolled his eyes. What was she up to now?

Jess sipped her lemonade and stuck her tongue out again, this time at Emily.

Kerri said, 'Ta da!'

Bringing her arms round, she held out two egg boxes, or rather two purple and yellow egg boxes: a dozen Creme Eggs.

'Eggsterminate! Eggsterminate!' she cried.

They all looked at each other and laughed, the squabbling instantly forgotten. 'The Creme Egg challenge!' cried Jess and Emily in unusual harmony.

David stifled a burp. He was already full, but a challenge was a challenge.

With all four of them holding a peeled chocolate egg in their hand, and with at least half a dozen more on the table in front of them, Kerri said, 'Go!'

And they all popped an egg into their mouths.

With determination in their eyes, they each grabbed another and went to put that in too. There were stifled laughs and splutters as they tried to chew and squash the second egg in at the same time. The girls couldn't quite manage it but David stretched and manoeuvred his mouth to accommodate the second. He fist-pumped the air in triumph.

Emily was contorting her whole face to try and get purchase on the sticky mess in her mouth, and Jessica was holding her cheeks while working her jaw. David and Kerri had the slight advantage of size and experience, but with two eggs each in their mouths they too were struggling to both chew and swallow. David watched Kerri's face twist and her eyes scrunch and then widen as a thin trickle of brown drool ran down her chin. She wiped it away with her hand and then began to unwrap the purple and yellow foil off a third egg. David widened his eyes too, twisting his mouth, and she looked at him, almost defiantly.

He took another one and began to peel it, letting his hands work on the wrapper automatically and unconsciously as he concentrated on not choking.

The girls had managed two at once now. This was usually enough for both of them, but this time Jessica grabbed a third and said, 'Bet you can't eat three?' to Emily in an unpleasant tone.

With his mouth stuffed full, David couldn't speak. Nor could Kerri. Emily looked at them both and David watched on with mute frustration as Kerri waved her on, encouraging her with her eyes and hands.

And then he saw the misery on his sister's face and a light flickered inside his mind. But, just as quickly, it went out again. It was a glimmer, almost imperceptible, a moment of comprehension.

When the game was over the four of them sat together, gasping and breathless around the table. Kerri got up and brought more lemonade in. 'This'll help wash it away,' she said, smiling. They all slumped back on to the sofas, Jess smiling but Emily looking more than a little queasy. Kerri and Jess chattered as David and Emily sat in silence.

Half an hour later, Kerri asked the girls to get ready for bed and, once they were upstairs, she made some tea and sat back down.

'That was fun!' she said to David.

He looked at her. And, without knowing why, he did something he had never consciously done to her before: he lied. 'Yes – yes, it was.'

'I love Easter!' Kerri continued. 'As long off work as Christmas but without all the pressure. We can just all stay in and eat all weekend!'

David nodded and then went in to the kitchen.

'I stocked us right up,' Kerri called out as he stood there. 'Thought we could have a real blow-out before I go and get the band fitted!'

And she meant it. David hadn't noticed earlier but on the counter in the kitchen there were boxes and boxes of food. Or rather, not food, but stuff masquerading as food. Almost everything was in yellow or pastel packaging. There were flowers on everything. It all looked so inviting on the boxes and in the bags.

David picked up one of the boxes of Easter cakes. The list of ingredients ran the whole length of the packaging.

He looked in the fridge. It was stuffed full of pizzas, ready-meal curries, cream cakes, chilled mousses, a trifle. Even full as he was, he felt his mind reacting. His mouth watered. A hot spot in his brain pulsed.

Reaching in, he took out a mousse. He loved these things! As he peeled the thick silver foil back, he wasn't even aware of getting the spoon and was even less aware of eating the mousse…

When he came to, David found himself staring at four empty mousse pots. He felt a wave of nausea roil through his stomach. He burped and a hot, sour backwash of bile came up his throat. Another wave followed that one.

It wasn't as if he hadn't felt like this before. Lying down was usually the thing that helped the most.

Lying in bed, he waited to feel better. It was all about waiting. The nausea always passed eventually. He knew this because he had been here so many times before. And, he knew, he would be here again.

What if it weren't? he wondered. What if it didn't have to be like this?

Something flickered and then went out again: a synapse not quite snapping, its spark arrested by the sugar that was still coursing through him. He felt heavy and yet his blood seemed to fizz. It was a sensation he was very used to. His heart was beating with an irregular rhythm, like an exhausted and overworked clerk who stays later and later, works harder and harder, only to get less and less done.

It would all pass soon enough.

And he knew, even as he lay there, body trembling under the strain of the evening, as close to being nothing as he had ever been, that he would do it all over again tomorrow.

Naomi

Naomi looked out of the window. It was a beautiful Easter Sunday morning. The room they slept in here was at the top and back of the barn. Taking up the full length of the building, it had a large window that looked out on to the garden and beyond on to the gently rolling fields that surrounded the property. The garden looked dewy and fresh. Weeks of mild weather had brought out the flowers in the borders. The garden, on this clear, bright morning, was a riot of yellow, purple, pink and white. A carpet of crocuses filled the gaps, and the daffodils bobbed heavy golden trumpets, poised and perfect like orchestral instruments held delicately between fingers during a pause in the music.

Naomi was rested and Naomi was happy. For Naomi had a plan. It was Easter, wasn't it? And Easter, being an *occasion*, gave her the perfect *excuse* to send a message. As soon as breakfast was over, she intended to get on the computer and send a cheerful, light happy message: *Happy Easter! Has the Easter bunny been generous? Oh, and by the way, I would love to give you your Easter present – me wrapped up in a bow...want to take a bite?*

As soon as they had all finished breakfast, she went upstairs, telling everyone she was taking a bath. While it was running, she logged on and sent the message. Then, getting into the hot, foamy water, she lay back and smiled. Perfect

– the message was perfect. And he had been online when she had sent it. He could not fail to get back to her. She lay in the bath for as long as she could, knowing that a delay was a good thing, knowing that she had to wait at least a small amount of time before replying. As soon as she climbed out, though, she dashed over, half covered in a towel and dripping bubbles all over the floor, clicked on the keypad and brought up the screen.

Carla is pregnant.

Naomi clapped her hands to her mouth. The damp towel dropped to the floor.

I can't do this any more. Sorry. It was amazing and I hope it was for you too. I've been meaning to tell you but it never felt like the right time. Sorry again. Hopefully we can still be friends.

'No, no, no, no!' she cried out. 'NO!'

This was *not* happening. Stamping her feet, she felt a surge of anger and she did it again: stamp, stamp, stamp. One foot on the floor rhythmically thumping. The bed was still unmade. Picking up the pillows, she punched and kicked at them flinging them on the floor and then picking them up and doing it again. Then with a shout of frustration she began to punch the bed. She had to hit something, had to release the anger, let it out before she exploded. Her heart was racing, she was crying, but more than the tears she wanted to scream.

'I have to get out,' she gasped. 'I have to get out of here.'

She felt her hands clawing at her neck, nails blunt but scraping at the thin, fragile flesh. Her face was hot. Tears continued to stream and she could feel snot bubbling out of her nose. Quickly splashing some cold water on her face, she got dressed and then stood in front of the mirror. Seeing the state she was in, she shut her eyes and then, with the flat of her right hand, she slapped herself across the cheek. Hard.

The stinging and the pain took her mind off her thoughts for long enough for her to turn off the computer and go downstairs. It also enabled her to explain, calmly, that she needed to run down to the village for a magazine, and also enabled her to walk out of the door as if she didn't have a care in the world. Only when she was out of sight of the house did she begin to run. The village was two miles down the lane. She ran for a mile without stopping.

And, then, panting, out of breath and agonised, hand on her chest, she looked round. Once she was sure she was completely alone, she began to scream.

Her chest ached, her vision blurred, snot filled her nose. Eyes burning, the tears ran down her face. She knew they would stop, supposed they had to at some point, but the pain ached and throbbed in her chest – not her heart, no, that had frozen over. She felt both chilled and raw, the fire she had been feeling of late put out in an instant. It was as if she would never feel like that again.

How could he take that away, that feeling of warmth? How good it had felt to be wanted like that. She wanted it for ever. 'Give it back!' she screamed. 'I want the feeling back. Give it back. Come back and want me, want me, need me, want me, fuck me.'

It was only when her voice went that she stopped.

The thought of never again running her hand through that soft hair, never feeling his arms around her, never feeling his fingers, slim, long, deft, up inside her…and, then, there, she was sobbing again, the pain caused by the thought as instantaneous as the light when the switch was flipped. The thought carried the feeling, and the image in her mind of her loss, of her grief, was so vivid; the pain it created it was equally vicious. The tears came even harder this time.

She sat down on the verge by the lane, and eventually the tears slowed again. Suddenly worried about being out too long, she began to walk slowly back to the house, trying desperately to think of reasons to be positive. At least I won't have to worry about getting caught any more, she thought; at least I won't have to worry about why I have or haven't heard from him. Maybe I'll sleep better. Maybe I'll eat better.

But not right now, her mind added, not right now.

She sobbed again. Part of her felt ridiculous: why had she pinned so much on to this one thing? Why had it become so important to her so quickly? There were things she couldn't face, things she didn't want to think about or deal with, and the affair had been a useful distraction. Without it, all she was left with was work and the demands and obligations of a young as well as an ageing family, a marriage that seemed to be held together only by habit. She bit her clenched fist to stop herself from screaming again.

Wiping at her face with the scrap of tissue she had found in her pocket, she took some deep breaths.

A memory of how he felt in her arms flooded her mind and body. How it had felt to touch his warm, soft skin. When had she last been that physically *present* with someone? Not since James was a baby perhaps. The pain stabbed into her chest. She felt sick. It was the idea of never having it again. It just hurt so much. Exactly like being dumped had hurt at sixteen. God, it just *hurt*. It was crazy, but it was so fresh and so agonising. A wave of pity came over her: pity for James, for the fact that he had all this ahead of him – rejection and misery and loss. She tried to stop herself from crying again but couldn't. Couldn't quite manage it.

As the barn came into view, she managed to calm down a little. The thought about James had then turned to a thought about Scott and she now felt ashamed and guilty and sad. She deserved to feel this way. Her pain was deserved, for all the potential pain she would have caused Scott and James if she had carried on, if she had been found out.

You deserve to be miserable, her mind told her.

Yes, she agreed, yes, I do.

And, bowed, weighed down by her own secret loss as well as by guilt at the pain that she had not even caused, she acted her way through the rest of the day, the façade as thin as the shells of the Easter eggs they exchanged that afternoon.

David

David had lain, slowly waking, for a little while. Watery sunshine filtered into the room through his curtains. His body ached. The nausea was barely gone. The long weekend stretched ahead of him.

He reached for the handle to his drawer. Then he stopped. Rolling back, he stared up at the ceiling.

What if he *didn't* open the drawer? What if he *didn't* eat something?

The thought was a new one. What would happen?

He lay there, waiting.

Nothing.

A few moments later he leaned over again. And then rolled back. And this time?

Still nothing.

He could hear his breathing.

The thoughts in his mind seemed to pause for a moment. There was a *settling*, like the moment in which the last of the flakes come to rest on the base of a snow globe, the encased scene clearly visible for the first time.

What was he thinking?

It seemed to not matter. The fact was that he had made a change. Resisted an urge. That was one bar of chocolate he would never eat.

What if I never did it again? he thought. What if I could feel bad and not have to eat chocolate? What if I could feel good and not have to eat chocolate?

The thought made him feel suddenly very, very scared. What? Never again?

Perhaps, yes. Never.

But 'never' seems so final, said a pensive voice in his mind. Perhaps you could maybe sometimes? it continued, sounding very calm and sensible, nodding over steepled fingertips. Maybe sometimes? In certain circumstances?

David pushed out his bottom lip, squinted as he thought it over. That was not an unreasonable idea, was it?

But then... He paused again. In his mind he suddenly saw Kerri and remembered the times she had sat and negotiated with herself.

Yes, but you're not Kerri, are you? said the voice, calmly again. Always this voice was very calm.

David sat up, the rationalising suddenly making him feel very cross.

He felt a powerful urge to stop the conscious thinking and put the television on. It was funny: the glimmers of something he had experienced yesterday were expanding outwards, as if someone was slowly opening a door in his dark mind, light beginning to spread and widen.

Having not eaten the chocolate bar, having not turned the television on, he just let the feeling of fear he was experiencing be. What was surprising was how heavy it was. It weighed down on him, right in the middle of his chest, the centre of his breast-bone, bearing down. The weight made it hard to breathe, as if someone was kneeling on his chest, forcing wet concrete into his mouth, down his throat, into his lungs.

He *wanted* to reach into the drawer. The urge was overwhelming. Anything. He wanted to do anything other than feel like this: to feel this anxiety and pain.

He breathed. In. Out.

And, breathing, he felt the pause. The space between the in and out breath.

The urge was still there.

He observed it as he breathed.

And, as he lay there, feeling the pain, a soothing reflex kicked in. Not an immediate soothing in the way that chocolate was immediate, but one that followed the pause and felt nourishing: satisfying in a way that food could never be. The feeling of control.

Suddenly, he began to laugh.

At lunchtime, David felt the same. There was a sense of space and light: as if he was observing himself from a cool vantage point, up in the corner of the living room.

Kerri had folded out the little table that they used at Christmas and on the other rare occasions when people came over. The table chatter and the ever-present sound of the television faded into the background. David saw the plate of food in front of him as if it were in high definition. It looked tempting enough, but the focus sharpened its appearance, helped him to see it for what it was. Food. Not the ultimate answer to life, the universe and everything. Just food.

He smiled to himself, trying not to laugh out loud again, worried that he would sound insane. He did feel slightly mad, though, as if the very simplicity of it had driven him crazy.

'What are you smiling about?' Jessica asked, eyes narrowing suspiciously. She scanned his plate: the equal distribution of the roast potatoes was a crucial issue for Jess and she clearly suspected that David had somehow been shown some special favour.

David grinned back, quite enjoying the expression on her face. He suspected he would see it on a lot of faces from now on.

He ate slowly and carefully. What was the rush? The sliced, processed turkey, the thin, salty gravy, the crusted potatoes, the overdone vegetables. A plate of food. It deserved neither worshipping nor reviling: it just was. He chewed and looked round the table. Emily was poking at the meat and vegetables with the tips of her cutlery: having eaten her potatoes, she was displaying her usual reluctance to consume anything else. Kerri had nearly finished; she always ate as if someone was about to whip the plate away from her. Jess was eating carelessly, mostly focused on watching the television.

David chewed and swallowed. Feeling as if his body was operating in slow motion, he placed the cutlery down in between mouthfuls, looking off into the middle distance, occasionally looking back at his family gathered around the small and ever so slightly wobbly table.

The meal finished, Kerri cleared the plates and brought an enormous plastic bowl of trifle into the room. With the curved side of the huge serving spoon, she etched out four lines, marking out four enormous portions on the ersatz cream.

'Mmmh…' said Jess, rubbing her hands together, still half watching the TV. 'Can I get down to eat it?'

'Let's stay at the table till we're done,' said Kerri. 'And then we can all have a sit. I'll go and get the bowls and spoons.'

Jess stuck her tongue out at Emily and the other girl looked away, eyes downcast and defeated. David frowned.

The trifle was served up, the yellow custard and the bright white cream billowing out of the oversized bowls, a miniature Everest of fat and sugar. David ate a few spoonfuls and then stopped. He stopped and leant back from the bowl and the table. He had had enough. It was time to stop.

Kerri looked up, spoon poised like a pickaxe to help her scale the mountain of dessert.

'You all right, David?' she asked, 'Do you not like it?'

'I've had enough,' he replied and, trying not to smile, he watched himself sit back and breathe.

The others continued to eat; even Emily finished hers. David pretended not to notice the way Kerri was looking at the remains in his bowl.

After the bowls were put in the kitchen, they all sat down and spent the rest of the afternoon sitting, chatting and watching the TV. As the afternoon light faded to evening's darkness, the sensation of being outside himself also began to fade. David felt himself gradually returning to his body, like a slow-motion video of a snail retracting into its shell. Kerri tapped at her tablet, the girls played on their phones; David looked into the middle distance and then, feeling that he was fully returned, took himself up to his bedroom. Lying down on his bed, he smiled a little to himself. It all seemed so easy.

If he had known that when he woke up the feeling would be gone – and that the hard work had not yet even begun – he would never have gone to sleep.

Naomi

After a restless night, Naomi was tired. Getting out of bed, she went over to the window seat and, curling up, she looked out through the slightly parted curtains. The garden was beautiful. The sky was blue. The sun was shining. It was awful.

Naomi smiled thinly and thought, Well, at least it's sunny for the drive home.

Scott was still asleep. Glancing at the clock, Naomi saw that it was only 6am. Grabbing her dressing gown, she went downstairs quietly and put the kettle on. If she was lucky it would be another hour or so before anyone came downstairs. Leonard and Elaine had a teasmaid. It had been the height of sophistication when they had got married and their morning routine was sacrosanct. They always stayed in bed for as long as possible, drinking badly made tea, Elaine with her pile of cookbooks by the bed and Leonard with his newspapers.

Naomi waited for the kettle to boil.

I wonder how they did it, she thought, how they managed to stay so content for so long. They've been married, what? Forty-five years? And to still be here, together, now. You can see how close they still are, even with her constant chivvying.

Pouring the hot water on to the bad instant coffee that Elaine kept in sufferance of pernickety types (i.e. Naomi) who drank coffee instead of her own preferred tea, she went and sat down at the large pine table. Looking out of the window at the garden, the drink hot and warming her hands, she felt oddly content. Maybe I can manage it, she thought. Maybe *we* can. I don't really know how, but I think I would like to try.

The restful quiet of the house and garden, the fact that it was over, truly over, had left her feeling oddly calm.

After a breakfast where she managed to not comment on the amount of sugar James put on his porridge, nor the amount of it that Scott always put in his tea here, they began to take things to the car. Packing the laptop away, she scowled at it and then smiled at herself: it wasn't the computer's fault that she had been dumped.

She laughed to herself as she packed it into her laptop bag.

'What's so funny?' asked Scott as he lifted the suitcase to take it downstairs.

'Oh, nothing.' She looked at him and smiled. 'Looking forward to going home, I suppose.'

'Yes, me too. Curl up on the sofa together…'

'Sure – good idea!' she agreed, wishing she could feel it as genuinely as he had sounded saying it. You gotta fake it to make it, she recalled, old training-course cheesiness coming to mind. She hoped it was true.

They took the bags downstairs and got ready to say their goodbyes. Elaine had her hands in the sink as usual, and continued to wash up as Leonard and Scott had a hug.

'See you, then, Dad. I'll call tomorrow.'

'Ah, no need, no need…'

'I'll call tomorrow, Dad.'

James came over and hugged his grandad tight. All his teenage awkwardness seemed to melt away here. He loved his grandparents and it showed.

Elaine came over, drying her hands on the tea towel. She was still holding it as she let Scott hug her.

Naomi looked down. She knew how much Scott loved his mum and it was hard to see how cool she was with him in return. 'Bye then, love,' she said.

'Bye, Mum – it's been good to see you.' Scott looked into her face.

Elaine hit him gently with the damp towel. 'Well, off you go, then, before the traffic gets bad!'

As she said that, Naomi saw something: the old woman's eye winked, the whole left side of her face spasming, contorting and twisting into a gruesome whorl of skin. Then it was gone, and she looked like Elaine again.

They pulled out over the grass, the frost crunching under the car wheels. It still lay thickly across the garden, a glinting crust over the grass and leaves; and, closing her eyes for a moment, Naomi turned to the brightening sky, trying to avoid looking at the shade.

David

Trapped once again inside his soft leaden body, David felt a wave of despair: where had it gone? Where had the lightness gone? He felt himself panic, a scrabbling sensation in his mind and stomach. Was that it? Was that really it?

Lying there, he forced himself to tune the fear out and to listen to something else. He could hear the birds, their song undaunted by the cold.

There was a long day ahead of him. And an even longer week until he was back at school. He missed James. The loss of his friend ached like a gunshot to the belly.

Moving slowly from the bed to his desk, he stared unseeing at the science homework sheet. The last thing he felt like doing was working, but the faint echo of how he had felt over the weekend was still present. Remembering it, he realised that, for the first time, the only thing he felt less like doing than work was sitting in the living room and watching TV.

David recalled that the work had sounded kind of interesting the day when Mr Holmes had handed it out.

He stared back down at the sheet.

Your project needs to draw on science as well as the social issues we have been covering in PSHE. It is about understanding the role that science can play in our day-to-day lives. Topics you might want to consider are: evolution, sugar, Big Food, advertising. The finished project will need to involve a five-minute presentation which will be delivered at the end-of-year awards and will be rewarded with the highly coveted Science Cup as well as a voucher for £30!

David wanted the prize. That would be cool, he thought. Presenting would suck, but he would do it if he could have the money as well.

Maybe he could start with some online research?

Now that was a good idea.

He idly opened a browser and tapped in 'evolution'.

The next hour was spent in merry amusement reading and watching all the bonkers shit that the Americans and others had to say about Darwin and about the theory of evolution. David laughed till he cried. Even he got this stuff. But, as he continued flicking about, he felt less and less interested in the idea of doing his project on the subject.

He went in to YouTube and watched some music videos.

Then he felt guilty and, without really thinking, he tapped 'sugar' into the search engine.

Staring at the videos, he saw one: a talk by a guy called Lustig. He could watch a talk. That would be like being at school, wouldn't it? Cool.

He clicked on the video and then sat back to watch.

Going downstairs an hour later, David poured a large glass of water, drank it, then poured another and took it upstairs.

Sitting on the edge of his bed, duvet over his legs to keep him warm, he looked out of the small window and sipped at the cool drink, thinking about how he had got here, about how he had got fat.

People always wanted there to be a neat starting point: a single, special Technicolor moment. One that could be shown at the start of the *he-is-getting-fatter* montage. But, knowing what he did now, after watching that talk, he understood that it wasn't as simple as that; he understood that it could not be reduced down to one single moment, one single problem.

Maybe it was the night his dad had walked out and he had gone into the living room holding out a squashed bar of chocolate to his mother who was sitting, weeping, on the sofa? Maybe it was way back when the GP gave him a chocolate star for not crying when he had his injection? Maybe it was when they had got into the habit of eating biscuits at bedtime? Maybe it was his genes? His mother's genes? What she ate in pregnancy? What she ate *before* pregnancy? Maybe it was the fact that there was no greengrocer's on their parade? Maybe it was because his mum worked? Maybe it was because her mum had worked? Maybe it was because her mum's mum *hadn't* worked? Genes? Nature? Nurture? Environment? All of the above?

Sitting on the edge of the bed, feeling the fat cushioned all around him like the duvet on his lap, the weight of it both comforting and weighing down on him, he knew there was no simple reason.

But there was a simple solution.

It was unconscious choices that had got him here, and he would have to undo that with conscious choices from now on.

This is when you have to choose, he thought. This is when you have to choose to change. There are so many different reasons. So many different things and people you could blame. But there is only one person who can do anything about it. And that is you. You have to start choosing for yourself.

Here was the first one: to go downstairs and sit, or to do something else? He checked his phone. He still missed James. The other boy's messages and prompts and company had always helped to structure his time.

I'll just have to do it for myself, he thought.

He looked at the television. He stared out of the bedroom window. He looked back at the television. It seemed to stare back at him, the blank screen mocking him, mocking his intentions.

A surge of anger rose up in him like bile. Fuck you, he thought. I can do it.

The anger provided the momentum he needed and he went back over to his desk.

Chapter Sixteen

Monday 29th April to Thursday 16th May

Matthew

The start of the summer term was always exciting. As the weather began to warm up, so did everyone's mood. The summer holidays could be counted down to in weeks, and, even with the demands of exams and coursework, there was a sense of excitement and anticipation among the students as they began to see how far they had actually come in the last two terms.

Matthew glanced up at the clock on the wall of the classroom and took a deep breath. He was pleased to be back, but the unease that he had felt over the holidays remained.

The air was already warm, and he was glad when he saw Solange's head pop round the door.

'We have half an hour. Come outside,' she said.

Leaning against the wall, she stood in the oblique patch of sunlight that lit up the far left-hand corner of the courtyard; her eyes were closed but her expression was fully open.

'Happy new term,' she said, 'How are you?'

Her arms were bare, and Matthew could see the tiny hairs standing on edge in the breeze. Most of the courtyard was cool and shaded and, standing close to her, Matthew could smell the distinct tang of her cigarettes as well as the light, floral perfume that she always wore. The sun warmed and mixed the scents and he felt a lightness in his head; it reminded him of the chemical rush he used to experience when he smoked.

'Good holidays?' she continued.

'Can I have one of those?' he said.

She raised her eyebrows at him through the grey-blue smoke. 'That bad, *hein*?' she said. 'You are sure?'

'Yes – yes, please.' He hesitated before he admitted, 'I started again over the holidays…' He knew she wouldn't, but added, 'Don't ask…'

She just smiled and handed him the open packet. Pulling a cigarette out, he spent a moment just enjoying the feeling of having the slender paper tube in between his fingers. Habit was a seductive thing, and he had fallen back into this one hard.

'Are you sure you are OK?' she asked, watching him closely.

'I am now,' he said, blowing out smoke and smiling. 'I haven't heard from her all over the holidays. I thought…well, you know, she hasn't said otherwise, she just had a thing to go to, but, well, it's just not going quite as I planned, that's all…'

'You will figure it out,' she said, smoking and looking straight at him. 'Summer is always a good time for that.'

He nodded, and stared at the smoke as it curled up into the pale blue sky.

Matthew was working late three days later when he heard the heavy lab door swing open. Now the summer term had started, it was lighter in the lab, but not too bright, as the sun had moved around the building, leaving the large space cool in the afternoons. A voice called out hesitantly from the crack in the heavy door.

'David,' said Matthew, without looking up. 'What can I do for you?'

'I...' David hesitated. 'I...' he tried to continue.

'Yes?' Matthew tried to sound welcoming. He almost managed it.

'It's just, I was hoping to talk to you about the project and, well, about something...'

'Oh, right. Well, come on in...'

Matthew could hide the fatigue and resignation in his voice but not in his eyes. He didn't notice as the boy looked away, diffident.

'You look like you've lost a couple of pounds,' Matthew said, looking at him properly now and smiling a little. He gestured to the boy to sit next to him.

'Yes – yes, I have.'

'That's great! It's not easy, I know that myself, but it will be worth it.'

'You?'

'Yeah, me. I used to be overweight... Anyway,' Matthew said, unable to avoid glancing at the clock and a little unsure as to how much else to say. His own discomfort at the memories was as bad as seeing the eagerness in the boy's face to discuss them. 'What did you want help with?'

'It was just the project. I had some questions.'

'OK, sure...'

'I...' David fumbled inside his bag.

Matthew sat and waited. He was rigid, sitting very still the way people do when all they want is to get up and move away.

'It was a few things. First, I wanted to check that I had this right. The way the liver metabolises fat? Is this OK?'

He showed Matthew a drawing of the liver with lots of neat captions around it detailing the various toxins that the liver metabolised. Another sheet showed a fatty liver: one that had been swollen and scarred by too much fat and sugar.

'Wow,' said Matthew, genuinely impressed. 'Those look great, and yes, you have that spot-on. Is this for the end-of-term project? My project?'

'Yes, sir, yes it is.'

Matthew felt a pang of guilt. His own lack of interest now felt even more uncomfortable. He pushed the bad feelings away. Unconsciously and with startling ease, his mind looked for someone else to blame for them. It's because you've got so many lazy kids to deal with that you hate teaching so much, said Polly in his head.

'It's looking good.'

'Thanks – I've been working quite hard on it. I also wanted to ask: are you able to tell me some more about leptin? I think I understand it, understand how it works, but I am not sure. Here,' David said, 'I wrote this...'

He handed Matthew a sheaf of crumpled papers.

Matthew frowned at the sheets. He felt his phone vibrate. His mind wandered immediately: Polly?

'And there was something else,' said David, delving back into his bag.

Matthew felt his phone vibrate again. Dismayed at the sight of more sheets being pulled out of David's bag, he glanced at the clock, every nerve in his body straining to take his phone out of his pocket, the desire to see if it was her, to see what she had to say fizzing though him, his mind full of the endless possibilities.

'Sorry,' he said, trying to focus and trying, but failing, to keep the edge of impatience out of his voice. 'What did you say, David?'

Matthew felt his phone go again. It must be her. God, he wanted to talk to her. It had been weeks. He clenched his jaw.

'It's just...well, you mentioned losing weight. I wondered...'

'It was a long time ago,' said Matthew.

'But... I wondered...'

The boy's hesitation and watery eyes all of a sudden began to irritate Matthew.

'This all looks fine, David,' he said. 'Honestly. I really do have to be getting on now.'

311

He stood up and looked away, taking out his phone, and missing the wounded confusion that flashed across David's face.

'Keep up the good work on the project!' he called out.

But the boy had already left the room, the door already shut behind him.

It was Polly. With an overwhelming sense of relief, he opened up her message. Then, reading what she had to say – that she was missing him, really, and that she wished she could see him but she just couldn't right now but she would definitely have some time soon – he kind of wished he hadn't.

David

David had read a lot online and had ordered some books. Kerri never questioned money spent on books, so he had gone crazy and ordered loads.

It was hard. But every time he felt himself struggling with it he went back to the words that changed everything. *Your fat is not your fate, provided you don't surrender.*

Having spent so long feeling both at fault and hopeless, there was nothing that could have helped more.

Reading, he took his time. He wanted to race through, wanted to skip straight to the end, but he tried to take it slow. Writing things down that he did not yet quite understand, he sat there most of the day, and when he was called down for dinner he walked down the stairs still staring at the pages.

'Book down, David, we're about to eat,' Kerri said.

'I'm reading,' he said, not looking at her.

'Put it down,' she repeated, irritably.

He glanced at her. She was pale and tired. They all were. You couldn't eat as much as they had over the last week and not feel more than a little rubbish when the reality of normal life hit.

Acquiescing, he went into the kitchen and poured a glass of water. Drinking it down, he poured another and took it into the living room.

Sitting down heavily, he felt a wave of dismay as he saw the food spread out on the coffee table. What to eat?

He had not got far enough in the book yet to understand how to begin changing, but he knew that this, this meal of potatoes, bread, sweetened chicken and creamy coleslaw, was less than ideal.

He took several pieces of the chicken and, pulling the sticky, sweet skin off, he set that to one side and ate the plain meat underneath. He was relieved when no one commented, though he knew that wouldn't last. He ate a few more pieces and then stopped. He looked at the book again.

'I'm done,' he said. 'Can I go?'

Kerri looked up at hm, surprised. 'Well, yes, of course. If you're sure. You've not eaten very much, though... I got the extra slaw for you.'

'I'm not hungry for that right now,' he said, simply. The formulation seemed odd, but utterly true.

He went back upstairs and continued to devour the book.

Rubbing his eyes an hour later, he yawned. The memory of being snapped at by Mr Holmes came back, unbidden and vivid, and he winced a little. He was used to being found an inconvenience by his fellow pupils, but to experience it from a teacher he liked was hard. Hard, but not as hard as it might have been if he didn't have a lot of other things to focus on. He was trying to understand this more complex level of biology, and words like *michrondites* and *vagus nerve* were confusing him. The absence of help from Mr Holmes was frustrating but it meant he had to do the thinking for himself: to dig deeper, to work harder.

He read over the pages again and then, at his desk, he took a big piece of blank paper and began to draw, in a simplified way, the journey of that mouthful through his body.

It was effortful, but, looking at it when it was done, David felt filled with an emotion he had never felt before about himself: pride. Pride in himself.

And, turning off the light, he went to sleep feeling better than he had in a very long time.

Naomi

Walking into the hallway after a long day at the office, Naomi nearly tripped over something on the floor.

'James! Bag!' she cried out, angrily.

At the moment, she found herself feeling almost constantly irritated. It seemed to be her way of dealing with the fact that everything had changed and yet also nothing had. Scott was still doing long hours. James was still a teenager. Work was still full-on. All of it was the same, and she had to deal with it without any distractions, without anything for herself.

Kicking the bag out of the way with her foot, she sighed and went into the kitchen. James was sitting at the table, books all around him but looking at his phone. He didn't even look up as she came in.

Naomi put the kettle on and took a look in the fridge. Another sigh. The last thing she felt like doing was cooking. Her mind flashed back to the long day she had had and she began to mentally justify a takeaway. It's been a long day. And you had a salad at lunchtime and you can order some stuff tonight for next week. And you deserve it. Deserve a break. James'll like it too... Maybe it'll cheer us both up.

The left brain quickly rationalised the decision that the right brain had already made.

'Shall we get takeaway and watch something crappy?' she said to James as she poured a glass of wine rather than her usual tea. It was Friday so it was the weekend so why not?

'Can we have Thai?'

'Sure, sounds good. I'll get the menu.'

Taking a sip of wine and thinking to herself how this white went perfectly with the idea of Thai, and then wondering whether she should put another bottle in the fridge, Naomi went and got the menu out of the drawer. This was the drawer that existed in every kitchen: the one full of wine stoppers that never got used (left-over wine in a bottle – what a crazy idea), novelty spoons and corkscrews, old phone chargers, dead batteries – and takeaway menus. Lots and lots of takeaway menus.

The Thai menu was near the top, along with the one for the Indian and the pizza place. They only ever really used about three or four of them, but for some reason there were still about fifteen leaflets in here.

It's as if they breed in there, she thought, flipping the menu open to have a look even though she didn't actually need to think about it: she always ordered the same thing.

The thought of breeding triggered an image of her and Mike – him lifting her legs up over her shoulders and fucking her. He had gone at her hard that night, harder than anyone ever had before. How can anything compare to that? she wondered. How do you get over having the best sex you ever had and then not being able to have it again?

She shook her head to try and derail that train of thought. The train's load was frustration, misery and sadness. If it was allowed to pull out of the station, it was guaranteed to become a runaway and then a collision. It was hard enough to cope with everything when she felt good.

Her current strategy was, she thought, as she put two more bottles in the fridge, to take the edge off with wine and then spend way too much time online researching vibrators and extramarital affair sites. She couldn't quite bring herself to do anything about either, but she also couldn't quite bring herself to stop, looking for a possible solution to the loss she was feeling.

'Can I look? I'm starving!' said James, putting his phone down and grabbing the menu from her hand.

'OK, OK,' said Naomi, sitting back and taking a longer draught of wine. Sometimes the alcohol helped; tonight, she suspected, it would not.

'Can I get the toast thingies and some spring rolls and satay and fried noodles... Oh, and crackers!'

'We always get crackers,' she replied absent-mindedly, taking the menu back. She called the order through. Twenty minutes, they said. She turned to James, who was back on his phone. Nodding at the pile of books, she said, 'Right, do you need any help to get finished before we eat?'

'Nah, I'll do it in the morning. Can we watch bad nineties action movies?'

'Sure,' she agreed, hoping it would help improve her mood. 'Let's do that!' It felt good to indulge him. She got out some plates and cutlery – eating out of the boxes crossed the line for Naomi – and twenty-five minutes later, as they sat and ate, she watched James crunching on prawn toast, slathering the sticky peanut sauce all over his chicken satay and fried noodles, and thought, Actually, he is pretty pale at the moment... maybe I need to try a little harder...

As they cleared away, the plates tucked easily in the dishwasher, she glanced at the clock on the wall. It was only eight forty-five. If I had cooked I'd have still been clearing up till well after nine, she thought. You can see why not bothering has such appeal.

Going back into the living room with a refilled glass, she sat with James for half an hour and then, after he sloped off to his room, she picked her tablet up from the table and began surfing. Weather, news, celebrity nonsense. It was about ten minutes before she decided to give in and check the site. She looked at his page. Scanned over the photos. She winced. That not being quite painful enough, she then clicked on Photos and tortured herself for fifteen minutes by looking at him and thinking about him and his body, about how soft his hair was, and about that time, the second time and the silence and the way he had looked at her.

You didn't imagine it, she told herself; you didn't imagine him wanting you.

She went up to bed.

Lying in bed later, radio on because she'd been careful not to make too much noise, her wrist was now aching. Curling in on herself, she began to cry. Why did she do it? It only made her feel worse afterwards. Of course she could make herself come, but she couldn't make him want her any more and she couldn't fake the sensation, the sensation of him inside her, which was what she wanted. It was all about that moment, the way he had looked straight at her as he slid inside her. That look was what she wanted, and, without it, nothing, not even coming five times in a row, was enough.

The following morning, bleary-eyed and bloated from too much wine and salty food, Naomi moved around the house on autopilot. Having got in long after she had gone to bed, Scott was sleeping in. James was out at football. She made coffee and stared blankly at the tablet. She should have deleted all of the old messages but she just couldn't bring herself to get rid of the last evidence she had of what had happened between them.

She stared out of the window and up at the sky. The clouds were oblivious, their greyness only serving to remind her of how all the colour had leached out of her life. What was there for her? What did she have to look forward to now? Even though summer was on the way, it felt instead as if an endless winter lay ahead.

Upstairs, back at the computer, she looked around the room and felt the tears coming. The memories of being in here, messaging and more, flooded back and she cried out, her head stuffed full of painful visions, her nose streaming, her face hot and wet, eyes raw. It was like this all the time. An hour or two would pass but then it would begin all over again. The thought and then the pain and then the tears. The moments of relief were delicious, she felt calm and capable, but they were few and far between. Unaware of the connection between her thinking and how she felt, she would dwell on the thoughts, would think, over and over, *I miss him, I want him; he's gone.*

Gradually, though, the pendulum swing grew longer: there were bigger gaps between the extremes of pain and the relief would last for longer. Without really understanding how or why, she would wake up in a lighter mood, her mind clear, and, thinking she was done, thinking she was free of it for ever, she would set about her day, only to be stunned to find the thoughts arising again; and then, gripping hold of them rather than letting them go, examining them rather than releasing them, she would push the pendulum back and the pain would overwhelm her once more.

And there was no one to tell. Her dreams were full of locked doors and closed cabinets. There was no way to share her burden so she carried it with her; it sat on her chest like a heavy wet toad: ugly, damp and miserable.

Back in the kitchen, she looked at the full laundry basket, the pile of unopened mail, the empty fridge. Her life. That thing she had to pretend to give a toss about without him in it. What was all this? What was this life she had? It was simultaneously too much and not enough. She was full to the brim with responsibilities but still her life seemed to leave her empty. At least when he had been part of if she had sometimes felt satisfied, but now she was both stuffed and starving, her life leaving her as bloated yet unsated as takeaway food.

At work, things were slightly better. With the project coming into the final stages, Naomi was busy, and the days passed in a blur of meetings and more meetings. She had taken to staying longer when she could, to hiding out in the tech lab more and more, enjoying Alex's dry humour and the fact that, here, she was miles away from her computer, miles away from the fact of his existing and still not wanting her.

But there were some things she could not avoid for ever, and Carla was one of them. The first day she had seen the girl had been fine; she'd been braced for it. It was all the other times, the constant unpredictable seeing of her, that was wearing Naomi down.

Like now. Walking back through the marketing department for what was the second time in one afternoon, Naomi was dismayed to see Carla waving a folder at her.

'Hello! How are you?' Naomi asked politely, going over. 'And how is Mike?'

She had to ask. She felt shitty already today; might as well make it worse.

Carla smiled and then frowned. 'He's OK.' Then she added, hesitantly, 'I think... He's been so excited about the baby and he's making a lot of fuss over me, which is great, but I was quite used to having the evenings to myself. It feels odd, him hanging around in the living room all the time.' She laughed a little, still sounding nervous. 'It sounds silly, doesn't it? Moaning about him being around? But he'd been so busy with work until recently that I'd got involved with some local NCT stuff, and now he's complaining that I'm too busy to talk to him!'

Naomi arranged the various planes of her face into what she thought was an expression of concerned and kindly sympathy with a hint of *oh-us-girls-aren't-we-silly-sometimes?* 'Uh-huh,' she managed. The sound was strangled slightly by the anger tightening her entire body, a radius of tension that began in her jaw and spread over her whole frame.

'Yeah,' Carla said, sitting down and then spinning around slightly in her chair to face her. 'He had been so busy recently – was, like, always on the computer in the other room, always working – and I was fed up at first but then you just get used to it, don't you, and now it's like he doesn't seem to understand I have better things to do than just sit around and watch old movies.'

She shrugged and spun back round. 'Anyway,' she continued, 'it would be great to all get together at the pub again soon. When's our next lunch? Be nicer now that we can sit outside, even if I can't have a drink. I can't believe I have another six months to wait before I can get pissed again – so unfair!'

'I'll double-check the dates,' Naomi replied through her clenched teeth, then, clawing up some lightness to put into her voice, she asked, 'When did you say the baby was due?'

'The first week of November.'

'Great, how lovely,' said Naomi, and, with a forced smile, she gave the folder she had taken from Carla a wiggle and, then glancing at her watch and escaped.

Back at her own desk, before she even sat down, she opened up her web browser and typed in 'due date calculator'. It took her a few minutes but she worked back from the date Carla had given her and then did something she knew she shouldn't do. She opened up their messages and scrolled back to that week. 'Fuck you,' she whispered as she read through the messages he had sent her that week.

It wasn't that he had ever said to her that he and Carla were not having sex, and she and he hadn't had sex for the first time yet by then, but when she read things like this...

All I can think about is you, I want to kiss you, want to hold you.

...and this:

I'm not sure how I used to spend my time before we started this; I certainly can't imagine doing anything else now.

...and this:

Every time I see your name on here, my dick starts to get hard.

...she felt stupidly betrayed, which was the supreme irony, wasn't it?

Closing her eyes, she leant her elbows on her desk and pinched the bridge of her nose. She could feel her chest shuddering. Taking a few shaky breaths, she sat back and stared up at the ceiling. I am not going to fucking sit here fucking crying, she thought to herself. It's ridiculous.

But crying was all she wanted to do. She needed to do something, anything to make the pain stop. Looking down, she began digging her nails deep into her palms. Having let her nails grow long again in the hope that it would deter her from masturbating, she had a set of polished talons now, and with all her might she forced them into the soft, fleshy mound beneath her thumb.

'Ow!' she cried out. But it wasn't anywhere near enough.

Looking round her desk, frantic now, she saw the fountain pen that Scott had bought her for her fortieth birthday and didn't hesitate. With a speed and viciousness that shocked even herself, she picked it up with her left hand and drove it straight into the skin between her thumb and forefinger.

With a scream, she dropped the pen. It fell to the desk, she saw the blood well up out of the hole she had made in her flesh. Seeing the pain made visible was a relief. To have how she felt represented physically cleared her mind. Sitting there, staring at the blood, she didn't even hear Simon walk in.

'Jesus! Naomi! Are you OK?'

And, seeing Simon's face pale with shock, she looked down and, as if realising what she had done for the first time, she passed out.

When she came home from work with her hand in a bandage, neither Scott nor James even asked about it.

Struggling to cut her steak at dinner, it was only when James began to laugh as she chased the piece of meat around her plate with her knife and fork that Scott said, 'James! Enough! What happened to your hand, hon?'

'Slipped with a pen at work,' Naomi said, looking down at the steak with a defeated expression.

'Here,' said Scott, and, leaning over, he quickly sliced the steak into strips and then pushed the plate back towards her with a small smile. 'You should take more care...' he added, as he began to eat again.

'Yes,' Naomi muttered to herself. 'Yes, I should.'

Later that week, as she struggled to get the heavy car door open, the pain and the grey sky all seemed to be physical and external echoes of her internal self. For this at least she was grateful. If it had remained sunny and warm, as it had been over Easter, she was not sure she could have borne it.

Her hand was still very sore. She had finally deleted all his messages in a fit of drunken pique and she was no longer checking his profile page every half-hour. The constant updates about the forthcoming baby and Carla's wellbeing seemed deliberate: a conscious effort to present himself as a family man. She understood that only too well, that desire to recreate the self, to erase the past and start over.

Scott was working extra hours but, with the days growing longer, and Naomi on the computer less in the evenings, they sometimes had dinner out at a nice restaurant and made plans for a few weekend days out.

These things were all helping, she realised – all helping to make her feel a little better.

She still felt raw, but the ease of being around Scott, the comfort of the house, were a welcome balm. It had felt so confining before, but now it felt secure: as long as she stayed here, stayed within these bounds, swaddled in and tight, she was safe from the feelings that had caused the trouble in the first place. When she took the bandages off her hand, the bruising had healed but a scar remained. It seemed appropriate. She needed something visual to remind her of the pain she had suffered: the pain that had, ultimately, outweighed any and all of the pleasure.

What had she risked for those few hours? Everything. It seemed appalling to her now that she could have gambled her life for the sake of a few orgasms, for hours that could still be counted on one hand.

The scar was a reminder, a raw, red mark that said, *No. Never do it again.*

Chapter Seventeen

Friday 17th to Sunday 26th May

David

It was the end of the third week back at school. Everything had changed and nothing had changed. Kerri was working late and David had managed to encourage the girls to go up to bed on time by promising them a day out at the shops the following day. Having found some tomato sauce and pasta as well as some salad in the fridge, he had cooked dinner for them all and was feeling OK. Water helped. It always did. Running the tap, he filled the glass and then began to look through the cupboards. There was something comforting about the familiarity of the contents of these shelves. The pale turquoise of the beans, the yellow of the tinned spaghetti. It was food and yet it was dead. He knew that now. It was here, preserved and available, but the one thing it could not do was truly nourish.

This was not food: just a pretence of it, like the fake cardboard boxes in the miniature kitchen that the girls had in their room. He still heard them playing with it occasionally, though they would deny it if you ever asked them.

Then there was the cupboard full of sachets and tins of shakes, the pouches of pre-prepared, calorie-controlled snacks and meals. The powders and the supplements. The costly pills and potions that seemed to accompany any branded dieting technique. It was like a diet version of an archaeological dig. The meal-replacement-shake era, the juice-fast era, the zero-carbs era, the raw-food era. Every attempt had left behind its own special diet detritus. What none of them had ever done was work.

'How not to diet,' muttered David to himself. And then he laughed a little. 'How not to lose weight in ten easy steps and over ten not so easy years!'

He laughed again. Exaggerating the shopping channel tone of his voice, he began, warming up to the subject as he continued, 'Want to remain fat for ever? Want to create the illusion of achieving something but never actually do it? Then here we have the ten glorious steps YOU need to take to achieve your dream of getting fatter and fatter – of being fat for ever after! First, buy lots of pointless supplements, take them for a week then put the pots in the cupboard and leave them there! Then, start replacing real, actual food with powders, bars and chemical shakes which leave you feeling even hungrier than ever! Then, full of guilt if not full of pocket or stomach, you can binge your way through the hundred-calorie snack portions – why eat one full-fat treat when you can eat ten low-fat ones!'

He smiled at the last. He had fallen for that one himself so many times: low-fat, low-calorie. Those straplines only seemed to get you to do one thing: eat more. Which also meant buy more. And that was the crux of it really. It wasn't just people getting fat bottoms from this food: corporate bottom lines were getting fat too. His fourteen-year-old mind grinned internally at the analogy.

Like the sharing bags, food messages were designed to be positive (share! enjoy! have a healthy calorie-controlled treat!) but they only seemed to lead to negative behaviour. The only positive was that more of the stuff was being bought. And that was only positive for one set of people; and they themselves, it seemed from his reading, mostly wouldn't touch the stuff they produced with a bargepole. Like tobacco executives.

David was no longer naïve enough to believe that the food industry was alone in creating the problem. It merely enabled the behaviour. People had always eaten given half a chance: he thought of gouty rich people from the days of Dickens, the bacchanalian feasts of Greek myths. The problem was that the feasting was making some people very rich, and others very fat and very sick. It wasn't any one person's fault, least of all his. He understood that now. Understood enough of the basics of biochemistry to know that the hormones in his body were screwed. That the signals were out of order: the train of his appetite was hurtling ahead with no way to stop itself, not even knowing it was out of control.

But – and this was what it all came down to – there was only one person who could do anything about it.

He closed the diet cupboard and looked in the others. Biscuits, crisps, chocolates, sweets: this one huge cupboard was entirely full of sweets and treats and snacks and nothing else. He remembered that once being just a shelf. Now it was a whole cupboard. He also remembered the small tin his nan, Kerri's mum, had had with sweets in. A tin, a shelf, a cupboard: bigger was not always better.

He looked in the fridge. The salad and vegetables sat there, as they always did, ignored till the end of the week and then thrown away. They ate some, of course. Just not a lot. There was a disconnect between the ideal that the shopping represented and the reality of how they ate. For every home-cooked meal there were three that were out of plastic trays or replaced by takeaways when someone had had a bad day or a good day or even just an indifferent day.

Because the three of them knew how to play her to get what they wanted. If he was honest, he had done it himself so many times. *I'm fed up, can we get pizza? I really fancy a curry, Mum, can we have one? Oooh, look, there's an offer on: can we get Thai? The best one? His favourite? You look tired, Mum – let's sit and have a takeaway and watch a film.* She could never say no to that.

He went back into the living room. He looked at the soft sofa. It was the locus of so many memories. All food-based. Every single one of them.

He knew it was time for that to change. And he was beginning to understand how, but right now all he felt was a massive sense of loss: that something was coming to an end. He felt sad and scared, happy and excited all at the same time. It was overwhelming; his chest tightened. He left the room. He had to get away from the sofa. Its soft embrace had always been so welcoming, but now it only filled him with terror.

Matthew

Matthew was no longer young enough to get away with drinking the amount he had drunk last night. He didn't know how much worse his hangovers would be ten years from now, but he did know that today, mere months from his thirty-second birthday, he felt shocking. His head was so heavy, it was as if it had been encased in concrete. Concrete that was mixed with shards of broken glass and upon which someone was, inexplicably, tapping with a metal spoon. The grey mass shifted uncomfortably, like a very old person trying to get out of a low chair, the gap between it and the inside of his skull full of sharp sand, every inch of the dried-out mass's surface rubbing against the grit, trying to shrink away from itself.

As he shifted under the duvet, the grit inside his brain felt as if it was seeping out of his eye sockets. They felt dry and granular. The sand also seemed to coat his tongue and be banked up inside his throat: a ground-glass desert. Fumbling to the right, his hand knocked into the pint glass of stale tap water he was hoping to find there. Shifting on to his side with a groan, keeping his head mostly under the dove-grey duvet, he took a tentative sip. His entire body protested at the motion. There were aches in his legs and arms (*how long had they played pool for?*) and, whereas his head felt dried-out, his stomach felt greasy and wet, the fatty cheeseburger and chips still sitting there at its base, soaking in the flat lager he had drunk. That was alongside shots of whisky, a quantity of which he had imbibed with very little regard for the health of this, his future self.

He lay back under the duvet, pulling the thick warm wedge of duck-down more tightly over himself, and then he grinned to himself.

Fuck, but it was fun, though.

The smile broadened as he remembered thrashing Iain at the first two games and some of the banter that had gone on. There were very few specifics that he could get a grip on, just that fuzzy, all-over-body sense of having had a really good time.

Stretching out, he filled the bed, his arms and legs enjoying the sensation as the muscles eased out and his back released some of its tension into the firm mattress. Feeling his penis stiffening slightly, the idea of a quick wank crossed his mind, but then, immediately after that, a wave of nausea rolled up from his stomach to his throat and, with a sudden very urgent desire to go for a piss, he lurched up and went to the bathroom.

He fought the urge to climb straight back into bed and instead headed to the kitchen. Filling the kettle, he drank back a pint of ice-cold water. If he could have poured it directly into his skull via his eardrum he would have done so but, filling the pint glass again, he took another long draught, accepting that he would have to hydrate in the old-fashioned way.

'Twelve hours,' he muttered to himself: that was how long it would take for his body to fully recover from the amount he had drunk yesterday. Knowing this had not prevented the drinking, but it did allow for a slightly more relaxed approach to the morning after the night before: he had no expectations about feeling much better before this evening. With that in mind, he wondered how he might enjoy his day.

It was a Saturday, and for the first time since Easter the prospect of a weekend alone, without Polly, did not upset him.

He smiled a little as he made an instant coffee. He felt naughty using the crappy jar of Gold Blend rather than the organic fairtrade stuff that Polly insisted on making in Matthew's knackered cafetière. It was perfect, though. He liked it so much more than the weak, bitter taste of the stuff she made, and it also avoided scalds.

Sitting down on the sofa, he moaned a little as his head throbbed. Digging his phone out of his dressing gown pocket, he began to scroll through the obscene texts that Iain had sent on his way home. He couldn't face opening any of his usual sites till later. Iain was bound to have tagged him in some heinous photos. Luckily he knew how to delete these things, but still, it was yet more post-night-out cleaning-up.

Sniggering as he scrolled and read, he sipped his coffee and then leaned back on the sofa.

God, he thought, the silence is really good.

There was the hum of the road outside but in the flat it was quiet: no TV, no news radio…no chatter about the latest demo or event that Polly was going to. His stomach lurched and he sat up, thinking that he might be sick, but no, it wasn't a lurch: it was a warm, unfamiliar, very light sensation.

Relief?

He stood up, slowly, and went to make another coffee.

After that he got dressed, pulling on last night's soft, worn jeans and his favourite, faded old hooded top. It was branded Coca-Cola (his mum had bought it for him) and he didn't even look himself in the eye as he passed the mirror, knowing that he was only wearing it because Polly wasn't here.

A cursory flick through the television channels revealed the usual dearth of anything remotely entertaining and, beginning to feel hungry, he pulled on his trainers and went out to the shops. It was still cool out and he walked quickly, the cold air making him feel instantly better than he had indoors. The wind was bracing and fresh, like taking a shower with all his clothes on.

His mind went back to the night before. They had been in the pub for hours before hitting the all-night pool place, and the conversation they had had, after the first five pints, had adopted a strangely circular nature.

'She's great!'

'Sure, course she is.'

'No, she really is.'

'Yeah, I know, you said…'

'I really think this is for the long term.'

'Mm-hmm.'

'Because she is great, isn't she? Does so many great things.'

'She does do a lot of things, yes, can't argue with that.'

'Does so many great things, she's great.'

'Yes, you said.'

'So, then, I should definitely ask her to move in.'

'Whatever you like, mate, but it's a big step, isn't it?'

'Big step? Yes. But she's great…'

'Sure, course she is.'

'No, she really is…'

Iain's non-committal comments had eventually worn Matthew down. The fifth pint and the third chaser brought with them the requisite amount of indignation needed to broach a subject that they had both been skirting round for months.

'You don't like her, do you?' he had challenged.

'I never said that, mate!'

Sulkily: 'You don't need to, I can tell.'

'What? You psychic now as well as pissed?'

'No, but come on, you don't, do you?'

'She's great, does a lot of great things, what else do you want me to say?'

'She *is* great.'

'Yes, mate…'

An hour later, Iain was maintaining his increasingly wobbly but still quite dignified silence on the matter. It was only after Matthew had beaten him for the third time and he had drunk three more whiskies in quick succession that the tone and content of the conversation had begun to shift.

'So, she is great,' Matthew had begun again.

'Mate…' Iain said, a hint of warning in his voice

'I knew you didn't like her!'

Iain had slammed his pint glass down and watched with vague dismay as half of the amber liquid slopped over the sides of the glass in a wash of foam and pooled on to the stained table. 'Mate,' he had begun, his voice gentle. 'Mate.'

The word was like a talisman, invoked in the hope that it would ward off any of the potentially negative consequences of what he was about to say.

'We've known each other, what, twelve, thirteen years? When I first saw you in the common room at Sheffield I immediately wrote you off as another pretty-boy-poof primary teacher but, after seeing who you were hanging about with and learning that you were actually planning to teach secondary school *science*, I realised: no, this was no pretty-boy poof. Not at all. I saw that what we had here was a rare species: a pretty boy who was too blind to see how hard he was making life for himself. Secondary science is bad enough, but the girls? Jeez. The girls were always high-maintenance – and not in a *don't chip my nail polish or ruffle my hair I just had it done kind of way,* oh, no, I mean in a *grungy, grimy, I'm too busy preventing the crunching grind of progress to shave under my armpits and if you so much as think that's any of your business then fuck you kind of way.'*

Matthew had stared at him, eyes bleary but full of dawning understanding.

'I've been watching you, mate, watching you for the last thirteen years, and every girl you've ever dated has been the same. It's like you got a taste for chicken madras and pilau rice and decided never to eat anything else ever again, even for breakfast. Well,' he finished, taking a long draught of what was left of his pint, 'maybe it's time to try something else off the menu...'

Iain had looked at Matthew over his pint and Matthew had continued to stare right back at him. Then Iain had stood up without a word and walked to the bar. He had came back with a pair of pints and a new square of blue chalk, and they had played until the early hours of the morning.

All that could be done with today was to manage the hangover. It was like being given a toddler for the afternoon. It needed feeding and it needed distracting and so that was what he would do.

At the corner shop, Matthew bought things he had not bought in a very long time. Things that Polly would never have approved of: cheap bacon, processed white bread, a few bottles of luminous fizzy drink.

And now, sitting here on the sofa, remembering what his friend had said, he realised that he felt different. That, having pretended for the last week or two that he didn't mind that she was beginning to drift away, all of a sudden he actually didn't. The pretence had become the reality. And, sitting back, full of crappy food, mind equally satiated from a rare afternoon binge on bad TV, he felt relieved. Relieved, and even happy.

Sunday morning, and, feeling better for an early night the night before, Matthew was sitting at the small table tucked at the back of the living room, books and papers all around him as he tapped away on the laptop. He was just considering making some fresh coffee when he heard it. He'd given her a key weeks before. He felt a Pavlovian reaction to the sound of it slotting into the lock.

She was talking on her phone as she walked into the narrow hallway of the flat. Going to meet her, he stood awkwardly as she continued talking. 'Yes, oh, yes, I will definitely be there. Tomorrow? Of course. There's so much more to do, I know! So exciting.' Pause. 'Yes. Yes, I am. Oh, he won't mind.'

She glanced at Matthew but her eyes told him that she wasn't really seeing him. He shifted on the spot, his stomach feeling strangely empty. 'Yes... bye, then, bye!'

She tucked the phone into the pocket of her shabby coat. Hair tied back and with no make-up, she looked fresh and plain, hazel eyes alight but still not really looking at him.

'Hey,' he said, stepping towards her. 'You're back.'

'Hey,' she said, shrugging off her coat and dropping it on the floor. 'Sorry! Need the toilet!' and she darted off to the left and went to use the bathroom.

In the kitchen, Matthew put the kettle on and pulled out the herbal teabags that she liked. Coming in, she began to poke about in the fridge. 'I'm so hungry!' she said. 'What is this?' she asked, noticing the white bread.

'Oh, sorry, I just fancied a bacon sandwich, after my night out with Iain.'

Polly didn't even bother commenting as she continued to rummage through the fridge and cupboards. She didn't need to: the disappointment radiated off her in waves. Her shoulders were tense, full eyebrows raised and pink lips white with tension as the corners of her mouth tightened.

'I'll need to go shopping,' she said, voice brisk and unhappy as she stared into the open fridge. 'There is literally nothing that I can eat in here.'

'Oh, I can go,' he said, suddenly feeling desperate to get out of the flat. Her disapproval filled the flat like invisible toxic gas: he felt as if he was slowly suffocating. 'Why don't you sit and enjoy your tea and I'll pick some things up. What would you like?'

'Something fresh that hasn't involved the death and destruction of all that is right on this earth…'

She smiled at him a little, as if trying to lighten what she had said, but there was a hardness in her eyes that even the lilt in her voice couldn't disguise.

As he stepped out into the mild, light afternoon, he wondered at how quickly he had gone from feeling good to feeling lost yet again.

Walking back in to the flat an hour later, he took the canvas bag full of organic groceries into the kitchen.

'Hey,' she said, suddenly standing in the door frame. Coming towards him, arms outstretched, she said, 'I'm awful, aren't I? Of course you can eat what you like, do what you like – but, oh, I have so much to tell you – wait till you hear what Sam and all of us have been talking about! I missed you… Have you missed me?'

'Of course… But…' He hesitated and then continued, 'Why didn't I hear from you? It's been weeks. I didn't know what was going on…'

'Oh, it all got so crazy out there. I can't wait to tell you all about it! And what we have plans for! I'm so excited!'

And, winding her thin arms round his neck, she pressed herself up against him, pulling him close to her. They kissed, mouths wide, tongues twisting round each other, hers probing into his mouth, insistent and urgent.

Staggering out of the kitchen, still kissing, they fell, laughing a little, on to the sofa. She let him pull at her clothes and he felt her soft warm skin under the layers of bright cotton and cheap wool. She rubbed her crotch against him and he felt himself getting hard: he still wanted her so badly.

'I want you,' she said. 'I want you…'

'Me too, me too…' he said, kissing her and burying his face into her chest.

'I need you…' she began.

'Mmmhhh…I need you too…' he said, beginning to pull her skirt up.

Stopping his hand, she said, 'I need you to help with one more thing…'

He stopped, his breath ragged, and looked at her. 'What?'

'Please…' she said, kissing him and placing her hand on him. She unzipped his trousers. She knelt down in front of him.

'Yes,' he said, as she worked her little hand into his underwear, her eyes looking up at him before she took his stiffening penis and put it into her warm, wet mouth. 'Yes, OK… Yes…'

Later, as they ate the steamed greens and spelt noodles he had bought, Matthew listened to her talking about the few weeks she had spent away. He hadn't seen her and had barely heard from her since Easter and yet she acted as if it had been days that had passed, not weeks.

'It was just incredible. In the end it was just me and Lee and Sam, of course, and these guys with rifles facing us down over the land that we're occupying – they were so pissed off that we had been there for a week, and they'd had enough. Sam and I just held hands and faced them down. We were so cool but after, when they were gone, we were just, like, oh, my God, we could have been killed – what was to stop them just shooting us? There and then? And we just collapsed into one another, all the fear that we had held back kicking in.'

Her eyes were wide, her high voice breathy as she recounted the tale. Matthew raised his eyebrows a little and didn't even try to keep the sardonic tone out of his voice.

'It's unlikely that they would have just *shot* you,' he said, 'They're human beings, you know, not complete crazies. They probably just wanted you off their land… This new group you're working with sound like they enjoy causing trouble.'

'Yeah, well, just like the trouble *they* are causing by decimating the mangroves!' she protested hotly. Getting up from the table, she snatched the bowl away from Matthew and took it through to the kitchen without a word.

On the sofa, they occupied far ends of the mustard sofa. A chasm of resentment lay between them, a chasm furnished with badly matched cushions. He stared at her as she curled her legs up beneath herself on the sofa and then, as she sipped her wine, both hands cupped girlishly round the glass, he felt a flash of anger. Instantly, irrevocably, he hated the way she held her glass.

Turning away, he felt his jaw tense. What was happening here? Only a week ago he had longed for her to come back, thought about her being here, right here, and yet now all he wanted was for her to be gone.

'It's incredible what we can do with our database now, you know,' she was saying, her voice still high and fast. 'We can pinpoint people who have been active on green sites as well as those who have a track record of supporting online campaigns for these sorts of issues. We can then trail them through social media and make sure they're seeing lots of anti-sugar messages, make sure they get the real heavy stuff and then, once they have, *then* we can start hitting them with more donation messages…'

'Was that one of yours?' he asked. 'I saw that. It was pretty aggressive…'

'Yes, Sam thinks that's where we've been going wrong. We haven't been aggressive enough. It's time to up our game.'

He glanced at her. 'What do you mean?'

She put her glass down and Matthew knew that he was in for one of her talks. She always needed her hands free for one of those.

'Nothing will change without force. Sam said so and I see that now. People are hopeless. You can't wait for them to figure it out for themselves. They're slow and dumb. Worse than animals...at least animals know better than to destroy their own homes...'

Matthew stared at her.

She carried on, 'Yeah, totally worse than animals. People are stupid and evil and without being shown the way they will never learn. I see it now. Talking, persuading, coaxing – it was a waste of time! Such a waste! It's time to *do* something. To force the change to happen: to do something that will make everyone take notice.'

'Like what?' he asked.

'Well, Sam has some incredible ideas. He's amazing. Totally committed to making a *real* actual difference. I listen to him and I'm just, like, yes, we can do it. He makes me feel like we can achieve anything!'

She trailed off, eyes staring off into the middle distance. Matthew recognised the dreamy look of a converted follower. He had seen it on Lee's face as he looked at Polly on that night in the pub. He had seen it on his own when he had met her for the first time.

Naomi

It had been another good day. There had been a few of them lately. James had spent most of that afternoon and evening in his room and Naomi had enjoyed spending some time with Scott. They had sat, after Sunday lunch, drinking coffee and reading the papers. For a few precious hours, it had almost felt like before. Before Mike. Before all of it. It had felt good.

Scott was flicking through the channels on the TV screen. Sunday night's supper of cheese and crackers had been eaten and cleared away and now, glass of wine in hand, Naomi was feeling warm and settled.

'Do you think James is going to be OK?' she asked Scott as he selected one of the movie channels and sat back, placing the remote on his lap for the inevitable ten minutes until another channel-change.

'Yes, of course,' Scott replied, not really listening.

'I mean about David. Their falling-out seems to have hit him really hard. It's been over a month. I was sure it wouldn't last this long.'

'Mmmmh.'

'Scott!' she said, raising her voice a little. 'Seriously. Aren't you worried about it?'

'Oh, it'll blow over eventually. Boys are as bad as girls sometimes. It'll be all sorted soon enough, you'll see.'

'I'm not so sure...' said Naomi, getting up to fetch another bottle of wine from the kitchen. As she came back in she said, 'Do you think I should call Kerri? Ask her what's going on?'

Scott looked at her. Muting the TV, he replied, 'You're really worried about him, aren't you? Is that why you were so upset at Easter?'

She flushed. 'Yes.'

'Well, if it's bothering you then, yes, give her a call. I'm sure she'd be pleased to hear from you anyway.'

'I'm not so sure...' She remembered her reaction when they had bumped into one another and felt ashamed of herself.

'Hon,' said Scott, putting a reassuring hand on her leg, 'you used to be so close. I'm sure she'll be thrilled you've picked the phone up. So, yes, do it. Give her a call.'

'OK, I guess you're right.'

'I usually am,' he said, lightly.

She laughed. They looked at each other and smiled. The blue of his eyes always came out when he was wearing that shirt. Naomi still remembered buying it for him: she had bought him another as soon as he tried it on, it suited him so well.

He touched her thigh again and their eyes met, the gaze lingering slightly longer this time. She put her glass down and they leaned in towards each other for a kiss. Scott's hands moved up her thighs, over the jogging bottoms she had slung on after lunch, and up, circling her waist. They embraced and continued to kiss, mouths opening wider, her fingers loosening his belt and tugging at his trousers as his hands cupped her breasts.

The phone rang.

'Leave it,' she muttered, her mouth reaching for him as he pulled away a little. 'Just leave it.'

'It might be Mum…'

'She can wait…'

'Sorry,' he said, getting up from the sofa, his erection evident as he walked awkwardly to the phone. 'Hello?'

Naomi sat back on the sofa. She watched as he talked. 'Yes, of course, I'm free to talk…'

Naomi looked down, picked up her wine glass and, as Scott left the room holding the phone and still talking to his mum, she turned the sound of the TV up.

Staring blankly at the TV, Naomi glanced up as James loped into the room and curled his long legs under himself on the armchair. She watched as he checked his phone and then rested it on the arm of the chair next to him.

'Dad's been on the phone for ages. Is Granny OK?' he asked.

'Yes,' Naomi trying to keep her tone neutral. 'Yes, she's fine. Looking forward to seeing us again soon, I'm sure! You know she and your dad like to chat…'

And, as James started flicking though the channels, Naomi picked up her tablet. She scowled at the screen as a wave of disappointment hit her. That moment of intimacy between her and Scott had felt so natural, so right, and then, with one ring of the phone, it had gone.

She glanced up at James. I wouldn't want him spending all his time worrying about me when he's grown up, she thought. It's odd, it's not right… I mean, it's lovely but…

Having not been close to her own mum, and her only memories of her father before he died being from when she was younger than James was now, she had never understood Scott's relationship with his parents. He just loves them so much, she thought. Deep down, that made her feel uncomfortable, resentful. As if there was not enough love left for her...

Scott walked in and returned the phone to its cradle.

'Everything all right?' Naomi asked without looking up.

'Mmm,' said Scott.

She glanced at him. He looked at her with a face that clearly said no but then he turned, smiling, to James. 'Hey, how are you? What are you watching?'

I see, thought Naomi. Joy. I'm going to have to hear about it later...

She topped up her wine glass.

An hour or two later, once James had headed up to bed, Naomi waited tensely for the conversation to begin.

'So... Mum really didn't sound great... she seems so confused. Dad clearly couldn't talk about it with her there but she's definitely getting worse again.'

'What do you mean, worse?'

'Well, remember I said a few months ago that she had forgotten I was meant to be visiting – it's things like that really. She was fine over Easter but earlier this week she went out and then couldn't get back in again because she had forgotten her keys and Dad was out too so she was outside just waiting when he got back. And Dad said she'll go into the kitchen and forget where the kettle is... he's making jokes about it but he sounds worried. I need to talk to her again, I guess. The problem is that she forgets she's been struggling and so, when you try to raise it, she won't even countenance the possibility. And Dad doesn't help by covering up for her. It sounds as if there's been more going on than he's told me, so I don't really know the extent of it...'

'Maybe we need to get her to see a doctor?' suggested Naomi, carefully.

'I mentioned that and she yelled at me! It took me ten minutes to calm her down...' He sat down on the sofa, looking upset.

'Oh.'

With her own mother gone a few years ago from a mercifully fast heart attack after travelling, Naomi had spent the years since watching with growing horror as her older husband's parents went from elderly to old. This was her worst nightmare: ageing parents, teenage son. A grey kaleidoscope of images spun in her mind: wiping elderly backsides, stuck in for weeks at a time, curtains drawn, cooking and pureeing food. It reminded her of the worst parts of the baby years. And it wasn't just the images, it was the smell. It was the idea of the smell that filled her senses now as the memories of those last few months with her father appeared in her mind: the stale stench of sickness and death. It had nearly driven her mad at fourteen and she was terrified that it really would do that now she was forty-four. As the images continued to spin around in her mind, she could feel the panic rising in her chest. A tight knot in her stomach. *I need something, I need something, I need something*... The words spun out from the grey mist that filled her mind.

Draining her third large glass of wine, she felt the alcohol finally beginning to dull her senses. This was what she wanted. She just wanted to be free from thinking about anything for the rest of the night.

David

The weather had truly shifted into summer over the past few weeks. And summer meant only one thing for David: sweat. As May progressed, even taking the shorter route to school left him sweaty. His face was wet and slimy as he approached the buildings, and his obvious discomfort was just another red rag for most of the people he passed on the way.

This new term had seen the start of a new routine for David. Having learnt more about habit and how much of a part that played in what he ate and when, he had realised that the fact that he walked to school was being utterly outweighed by his also visiting convenience stores on the way. So, even though it was difficult, he had begun to take the bus. He had learnt to pack an apple or banana for his bag and, while he was still struggling with them he did it all the same, knowing that those two sugar binges on the way to and from school were doing him no good whatsoever. Having to give up chocolate and then go voluntarily into an environment where he normally could only cope because of the chocolate had been really hard. But he had realised after a few days that it wasn't going to kill him. The same could not be said for what he had been eating.

His choice to brave the bus journey was not an easy one either. As he walked to and from the bus stop every day, it wasn't the builders working on the scaffolding of the latest new apartment block builds he had to worry about, nor the guys digging up the busy main road. It wasn't everyday blokes who mocked the overweight; mostly it was younger people and women. So many women, especially the older, skinnier ones. The pitying stares were the worst, for with those he would imagine what they were saying, and no one could be crueller to David than David himself. Their imagined words joined the mostly self-loathing monologue that ran through his mind on a moment-by-moment basis. He might have been making an effort to alter his diet, but the unappetising repertoire in his mind was proving harder to change. Focusing on the words he'd read in the book helped, but only a little.

Keeping his face down, he walked along the path to the bus stop, trying not to constantly wipe the sweat from his forehead. Dabbing at it with a tissue, he shifted his bag on his shoulder and caught a whiff of his own body odour. He would need to spray again as soon as he got to school.

Standing at the bus stop, keeping away from the other kids, he kicked at the ground. He really wanted to get the book he was reading for his science coursework out, but, because it was about food and fat, he felt too self-conscious to read it anywhere other than at home. He continued to kick at the ground. Imagining the path crumbling, splitting wide open and taking all the other kids and the snotty-faced adults down with them into its granite maw made him smile.

'What you smiling at, you fucking fat bastard?'

Oh, here we go, thought David. So many of his fellow pupils seemed to have a desire to rid themselves of all potential expletives before arriving at school, where they would get you in trouble. He supposed it was a bit like the way he made sure he always did a shit before he went to school. He smirked again, involuntarily, and then the abuse got worse and it carried on all the way from the bus stop to the playground. And then on and off all day long.

They were so unimaginative really, thought David, as he walked back home hours later after a long day. The echoes of *fat bastard* from the bus stop followed him as he passed the frowning, sneering faces of people in the street; there were even stares and finger-pointing from passing cars. He had stopped traffic once. That was often seen to be a desirable thing, but, as experiences went, David had not found it to be a positive one.

As he turned into his road, he was suddenly aware that he had managed to get home without eating – that he had, in fact, not eaten since lunchtime. And in fact he wanted to work on his project more than he wanted to snack before his dinner. This made him feel more than a little hopeful. Another day was nearly done, and he hadn't overeaten. He just had to get up in the morning and do it all over again.

And the irony was that, now, now that he had begun to make changes to how he behaved, he actually preferred being at school to being at home. There at least he was away from food and was less tempted by it; and there was also no one there exhorting him to eat. This was increasingly not the case here.

He hovered outside the living room door, hesitant and anxious. He used to love coming down for dinner, used to love this room – the curtains always drawn, the TV always on, the food supply ample and constant – but now it frightened him. He had developed a deep-seated fear of the sofa. It was as if all his anxieties about food and his body had shifted and, rather than hating himself, he now hated the sofa and what it represented: softness, apathy, comfort, sloth. He knew that it was biochemistry that was to blame for his lethargy and his constant hunger but he also knew, deep down, that the sofa was partly responsible. It wasn't deliberate but it had been too easy to sit in it, too easy to accept its warm and comfortable embrace.

Taking a deep breath, he entered the room.

Jess was hitting Emily on the arm. Punching her hard. This was not unusual. What was unusual was that Emily was just silently taking it.

'Jess!' David cried out sharply. 'Stop it!'

'No! She deserves it!' the other girl hissed.

David went over and took hold of her arm, gripping it in his fingers. He pinched her.

'Ow!' she screamed, deliberately loudly. 'Mum! David's hurting me! Muuuum!'

'Oh, guys, come on! It's dinnertime – can't you just behave…?' came an exasperated voice from the kitchen.

David let go and, giving Jess a sharp look as she stuck her tongue out at him, he turned to Emily and said, 'You OK, Em? Why didn't you call out?'

The girl just shrugged, sitting on the floor now and staring at the TV, her eyes horridly blank. 'Why bother? She doesn't care.'

'Kerri does care,' David insisted.

'No, she doesn't,' Emily repeated, dully.

'She does, she's just…you know, worried about the op, I think.'

'Yeah, we all are,' said Emily, even quieter now.

'You can always talk to me,' he added, bending a little to get closer to her.

'You're always in your room now,' she said coldly.

David felt a pang of guilt. Why did this have to be so hard? 'Well, I have a lot of work to do,' he said, not wanting to apologise but not wanting to push her further away either. 'You can always come and sit with me, you know. I would like that.'

'Really?' she asked, looking up at him.

'Yes, really,' he said, smiling at her.

'Dinner's coming!' Kerri called out.

David squeezed Emily's arm and then went and sat down. As he sank into the soft chair, he braced himself for another meal which he had to eat without really wanting it.

Kerri came, holding two plates by the edges with a tea towel. 'Magazines for laps!' she cried out, 'The plates are hot!'

David saw the girls still staring at the TV and grabbed a few magazines off the coffee table, tossing them along the floor to Emily's feet. The girls took them without looking away from the screen. Jeez, thought David. He felt uneasy. Kerri came in with two more plates and, grateful for the distraction, he let her slide the plate on to the magazine on his lap.

He smiled at Kerri a little and she smiled back, then her eyes went to the screen.

'Oooh, is this a new episode?' she cooed, sitting down on her armchair.

David looked down at his plate. The chop was as expected, but the potatoes looked perfect. Glistening with fat, crispy and golden: was there anything quite as tempting as a roast potato?

Well, perhaps, thought David. The one thing more tempting than a roast potato was a *lot* of roast potatoes.

And Kerri had given him a lot of roast potatoes. About eight, in fact. And when he looked at the plate, actually looked at it rather than just mindlessly forking the food in while staring at the TV screen, he saw just how much food he had in front of him.

He remembered all the times he had asked for more: the times they – his mum and dad, the girls when they were younger, especially Jess before she became very aware of his size – had egged him on to eat another potato, and another. His record stood at fourteen. Fourteen roast potatoes. He wondered what that actually was in weight. Not that it mattered really. He could see now what was too much.

And this was too much. He began to eat. He worked hard to take it slowly. And it was hard because he was hungry but he knew that, if he rushed, he would wolf down this whole plate of food, a plate of food which, with its three chops, eight potatoes and mini-mountain of very buttery and wrinkled peas and very buttery and soggy broccoli, all covered also in a salty, thick gravy with the slightly random frozen Yorkshire pudding on the side (Kerri loved these and seemed to serve them with everything she prepared), was much too much. He had learned what a portion was as part of his research, and it did not look like this. This was for two, if not three, people. Grown, adult people who had active lifestyles, not one teenage boy who could barely manage the walk to the bus stop and who had been excused from games for the last eighteen months.

He sighed a little and cut into the Yorkshire pudding. Salty, soggy and yet also crispy, it tasted of stale fat and flour but it also tasted good, a bland carbohydrate foil to the slight charred and fatty pork, the buttery veg. He ate half of it and then pushed the other half to one side; he would decide later whether he would forgo several of the potatoes or eat the rest of the Yorkshire. He had already checked there was fruit in the fridge and had decided that he would eat most of his dinner and then have some fruit afterwards. These choices, these tiny elements of control did help. And, as he sat, eating and watching the TV, even though he knew he could eat more, he could also feel that his tracksuit was slightly looser – that, even though it was slow going, he was making progress. And that gave him a burst of motivation.

He ate the veg, finished the chops and then decided to leave the Yorkshire pudding in favour of two potatoes. Two would be fine. He ate them slowly, savouring them. Once he was done, he stopped and, rather than putting his plate on the coffee table as usual, he took the plate into the kitchen and hastily tipped the remains of the over-sized meal into the bin.

Putting the plate in the washing-up bowl, he then went back into the living room and sat down. He was hoping no one would comment. He knew his behaviour was changing, but he wasn't sure how he felt about the others noticing yet. Fortunately they were still watching the TV. David watched it too.

The others had all put their plates on the floor and, when the adverts came on, Kerri said, 'Was that OK? I'll get pudding for you now…' and she got up, taking the dirty plates into the kitchen.

She brought two four-packs of chocolate mousses into the living room, with four spoons. The girls took them eagerly, peeling the shiny purple foil back and tucking in.

'I'll have mine later,' David said, avoiding eye contact with Kerri for now and looking at the girls. Jess was eating two mousses at once, dipping her spoon into each one alternately.

'You sure?' Kerri asked, frowning.

'Yeah, sure.'

An hour later, the girls had gone up to bed. Kerri was drinking tea and swiping around on her tablet. She looked up.

'I can get that mousse for you now if you'd like?' she said.

'I'm all right, thanks,' said David, still avoiding her eyes and looking at his phone.

'Really? It's no trouble…I was going to get another one myself…'

She got up and went into the kitchen, When she came back, she had another four-pack of mousses in her hand. And two spoons in the other.

Are we the only family, David wondered, that treats Buy One Get One Free as Buy Two Get Two Free or even going for the treble?

'Here you go,' she said, snapping the four-pack of pots in two.

David hesitated. 'No, really, Mum, I'm fine,' he said.

'Oh, go on. I know you're being good at the minute but you can have a couple of mousses, can't you? Keep me company?'

'Maybe later…' he said, avoiding a confrontation now but knowing, again deep down, that it had to be had eventually.

'I can't believe it's so far into the summer term!' she said, 'Wow. So exciting. How are you finding it?'

He looked at her and smiled. It was nice to be asked, even if she had no idea what she was asking about. 'It's OK.'

'Great! Work is pretty good for me at the minute too. Lots on but not too much. Nothing worse than being too busy. I like to get home on time, see you guys. When I saw Naomi last she looked so frazzled and thin and worn out and that must be her work. It just isn't worth it if it's going to ruin your health like that!'

She put down the first mousse pot and ate the second.

'And,' she said through a mouthful of liquefying chocolate, fat and skimmed milk powder, 'I got the date through for my op so I thought we could have some treats at the weekend. Another few weeks and I won't be able to any more!'

David looked at her again and felt his stomach knot with anxiety. It wasn't just the surgery he was worried about, but how he would cope with the weeks before: the weeks of food free-for-all that would take place as she binged prior to the band being fitted. In the reading he had done online, he had discovered that some people gained another stone or even two in the months leading to the band being fitted. It made him feel cold all over.

'Yes, it'll be great,' she was saying. 'I can do some baking; we can go out to some of our favourite places. Be fun. Like a mini-holiday! I know: we can do a few of our theme days. You know: American brunch with pancakes and crispy bacon and then ribs and coleslaw and popcorn day, and an English day with a full breakfast and then tea with lots of buns and biscuits and sandwiches! You always enjoyed those!'

David noted the lightness and energy in her voice. The enthusiasm with which she discussed these insane plans made him feel even more uncertain.

He let her chatter on. She didn't need his consent to decide these things. It was a *fait accompli*. Always had been, he supposed. At least since Dad had left, anyway. Since then, none of them had been able to say no to her or to each other; they could never bear to see any sadness, but look where that had got them. It had made him obese and it had turned one of his sisters into a bully. He frowned.

'Mmm... These are so good,' Kerri said, scraping her spoon round the inside of the mousse pot. 'Tell you what,' she added. 'There's one pack left? Shall we finish them off? You said you might want one...'

'Sorry, but no,' he replied.

'I'll just go and get them,' she said, getting up.

He stared at her. It was like one of those scenes from a bad nineties teen film.

'I said no.'

She stopped.

'Oh, OK,' she said. She seemed to deflate back down on to her chair, sinking slowly down into it.

And, for a horrifying moment, looking at her, it was as if she and the armchair were one. As if the static, soft chair had begun to talk, or that she had melded with the folds of the chair: was one with it, unable to ever move again, stuffed and doomed to be for ever sitting in this dim room.

'Sorry, no, I really don't. I can't…'

He left the room as fast as he could, straining to take the stairs two at a time in his hurry to get away, but the image of her conjoined with the chair would stay with him for much longer.

The following morning was a Saturday. David went downstairs as soon as he was up and, going into the crepuscular living room, the curtains still drawn from the night before, he went through and into the kitchen. Pouring himself some water, he made tea and then ate a banana while looking in the fridge. It was full, as it always was at the start of the weekend, with sweets and chocolate bars, boxes of ready meals and chilled desserts. There was also a tub of pre-made pancake mix and a tub of chocolate crispy cakes. David could smell the sugar and his mouth watered. He closed the door. He really wished he didn't have to.

He had to get out and get some real food in for the weekend. There was no doubt that he felt nervous about it but, right now, he felt more nervous about spending the whole weekend trapped in the house with all this junk and Kerri on a mission to eat it.

He went back up to get his pocket money and then, as he came out of his room, pulling on his hooded top, he saw Emily.

'Morning,' she said, smiling at him.

Both the girls looked so young, especially when they were relaxed and weren't pulling hard faces at each other and posing; it made his heart ache a little.

'Are you going out already?' she asked.

'Yeah, I need to pick up a few things… I'll get you…' He stopped himself from saying a treat. It was autopilot. Was that because it was what Kerri always said, or because it seemed as if it would be a treat even though he knew it wasn't? He had no idea, but he clamped his mouth shut and, giving her a hug instead, he went downstairs and then out of the house.

The nearest decent-sized supermarket was a good few miles away, so he walked to the end of the road and waited for a bus. It was warm already and, as he stood in the sun, David regretted putting his hoody on, though the last thing he would do now was take it off.

When he got to the shops, he walked into the store, grateful for the cool blast of air that hit him as he passed through the automatic doors.

The display of fresh fruit and vegetables was ahead of him: premium goods displayed like a peacock's tail, arrayed and fanned out in all their Technicolor glory. The seasonal aisles were a multicoloured array of plastic to accompany garden eating and entertaining, and bright signage pointed him towards various multi-buy offers. All this, as well as the enormous mountain of boxed doughnuts and biscuits at the entrance…it was like a mini edible Eiger.

The reading he had been doing recently had not surprised him. The sheer scale of the efforts shops went to to sell you crap did not amaze him. As someone who never had enough money and fantasised about winning the lottery, he knew that the business of making money was a serious one, and hardly any business took that more seriously than the retail sector – even a cursory listen in business studies had taught him that much.

He knew he only had about £15 and he knew he had to get some food to last him until the start of the week. Baked potatoes? Salad? Cheese? Chicken? It all sounded dull but he had to start somewhere. He also knew what *not* to buy. He picked up a couple of lettuces and some other salad stuff: it was salad season and it was all on offer. He collected a lot and calculated it would only cost about £3 or £4. If he bought some baking potatoes and some chicken, could he eat that all weekend?

It seemed so odd: he only needed two aisles, the fresh produce and the fresh meat aisle. But what about the other acre of store? He didn't need to look round to know the answer to that. The temptation to do so was overwhelming, though: almost like a magnetic force that was tugging at him. He knew that if he had needed to buy bread he would have been done for: that was always at the far end of the store and necessitated a walk past all the tempting offers for crap you just didn't need.

He went to pay. He was expecting stares and scowls, so he used the self-checkout and then went to catch the bus.

Waiting, he felt oddly calm. He had just shopped for himself for the first time and he felt really pleased with how he had done. Then he saw the bus and his stomach flipped. Now he just had to go home and explain what he was up to.

As he walked into the hallway, he heard his name being called.

'David!' cried Kerri. 'Great, just in time for lunch!'

He carried the bags into the living room.

'Actually,' he said, looking down, unable to meet her eye, 'I've bought some stuff for my lunch. I...' He hesitated and then, taking a slight inward breath, he continued, 'I really want to keep losing the weight, so I bought some different food to eat his weekend while you, um, while you enjoy yours...' He trailed off, not wanting to upset anyone but also knowing deep down how impossible that was.

'Oh,' said Kerri, looking at the bags. 'Right. What did you buy?'

'Oh, just some salad, a chicken...some potatoes.'

'Right.'

'I thought I'd have some salad now and make a potato and the chicken for later.'

'Did you?'

'The salad was really good, actually…there was loads of it on offer. I suppose because it's nearly summer now…' He trailed off again.

Jess and Emily were just watching them, wide eyes switching between David and Kerri, wondering what was going to happen next. It was like seeing a film that you hadn't Googled first: they had no idea how it was going to end.

'Well. I'm not helping you cook that. I don't have the time to make special food just for you. You're going to have to figure that out for yourself.'

'Yeah, I will. I'll clean up as well, you know – I just really wanted to give it a proper go…' He paused. 'I'm sorry.'

Kerri shrugged as she sat down.

'Well, anyway, *our* lunch is getting spoilt. Go and sort yourself out, then, if that's what you want, and we'll just enjoy this without you.'

David went into the kitchen. He felt sick. Putting the groceries away, he poured a glass of water then opened a bag and set out some salad. He went back into the living room, carrying his plate, and sat down. The table was loaded with Kerri's planned American feast: fried chicken pieces, a bowl of pale and sticky-looking coleslaw…there was a plate full of maple-syrup coated 'ribs' as well as a huge mound of bright yellow potato wedges with various dipping sauces on the side. It was all yellow or pale brown. His own mixed leaves and avocado looked very, very green in comparison.

He ate slowly and carefully, trying to eat as unobtrusively as possible, but the sound of the salad seemed to fill the room. The crisp leaves needed to be chewed and chomped, masticated and crunched until they were crushed and could be swallowed. It was such a different experience from eating the soft yellow food that was spread out on the table, and it made David feel even more self-conscious. It was as if the noise was spilling out of his mouth and into the room: echoing and mocking.

Kerri was working her way through the spread aggressively. Jess was watching the TV, tuning everything else out as usual, and Emily was picking at her food and looking miserable.

'It's whatsit on tonight, isn't it? The special?' David said to her as he took a sip of water.

Emily looked at him and smiled a little.

Kerri continued to eat, and continued to avoid David's eye.

Naomi

A week had passed since the interrupted moment of intimacy. Naomi, frustrated at having reached out and been left dangling in mid-air, had retreated back into her work, James had been mostly home alone after school, and was increasingly moody. Naomi hadn't had time to talk to him again about what had happened with David, but the fight that Scott had said would blow over had become a prolonged and painful stand-off between the two boys.

After the lengthy phone chat, Scott had gone to see his parents the following Friday.

'I'll only be up here for a day or so,' he had said to Naomi, when he called her on Saturday. 'I feel bad not being able to stay longer, but it looks as if Dad hasn't been completely honest about how things are here. She was fine yesterday but then today she seems to be completely lost: it's odd how it comes and goes... Hard to know what to do for the best.'

'I know. It's hard,' Naomi agreed for what felt like the fiftieth time.

What about me? she had wanted to yell. Your son is falling apart and I'm here, working and trying to keep things going, and I've been dumped by someone I thought I was falling in love with and oh, but, no, I have to smile and agree and sympathise down the phone… She had clenched her fists while he continued talking.

Desperately trying to keep her temper in check as she struggled with a sulky James on her own that weekend, the strain of wondering what was going on with Scott's parents felt like an additional punishment for the pleasure she had enjoyed before. Pleasure she felt that she would never have again, ever. Feeling this selfish made her feel even worse, but it was hard not to wallow, and every night over that weekend, sitting alone while James sulked in his room, she poured too many glasses of wine and felt increasingly lonely.

Now it was Sunday night. Scott had said he would head back the following day, Naomi found herself reluctantly logging on. Staring at Mike's profile, at all his chatter about the pregnancy and Carla, she tormented herself with what might or might not have happened: stewing in her own thoughts.

I'm just too ugly. I'm just too old. He must have been doing it for a bet, or a laugh…

The wine seemed to make her thoughts as sour as her stomach but it was also the only thing that seemed able to stop her thinking, to stop her thoughts from spiralling out of control.

Drinking also meant that she had begun to put some weight back on. That, as well as the fact that, with Scott worried and James so unhappy, she had taken to bringing bags full of treats home for supper ever day. They had eaten pizzas and garlic bread (with no salad!) that week; fries and Southern spiced and breaded chicken as well as lasagnes, and flaky pies with mashed potato. The vegetables were all pre-prepared or processed if they bothered with them at all, and they had also eaten chocolate desserts by the dozen as well as family packs of doughnuts and biscuits.

The treats had seemed to work for most of the week, but now, as Sunday evening dragged on, Naomi noticed that she had already finished one bottle of wine on top of the gin and tonics she had been sipping since lunch. She suddenly felt completely and utterly angry with herself.

'You have to fucking stop,' she hissed at herself. 'Just stop.'

Hearing James creeping downstairs and to the kitchen, and the inevitable hiss as he opened yet another can of Coke on his way back upstairs, she thought, Kerri, I need to call Kerri.

Picking up the handset, she went to the address book. Kerri's number was still in here. They had been so close but it had been, what, five years, seven maybe, since they had spent any real time together? What would she say? Her stomach tensed but, taking a deep breath, she pressed the button and listened to the ringing.

'Naomi. Hi.'

Caller ID. At least Kerri had seen it was her and still answered the phone. That was a good start.

'Kerri. Hi. Sorry to bother you...'

'Not at all. It's good to hear from you. How *are* you?'

The question, asked with such genuine warmth and feeling, caused Naomi's eyes to prickle with tears. There was a pause.

Kerri spoke again. 'Remember we used to joke about the long answer and the short answer to that question? Maybe,' she continued, 'we could do the long one over dinner some time? For now, I imagine you've called to talk to me about James and David.'

Naomi felt gratitude and relief flood through her. What was it about being understood? About being heard even when you said nothing? Struggling to remember the last time she had felt like that, she managed to croak out, 'Yes. James is in *such* a state. I can't even get him out of his room today! And it's half-term next week, which will make it worse.'

'It's similar here,' sighed Kerri. 'He's working hard on some project for school but he's so subdued at the same time. I know he misses James. They can't really hide their feelings at this age, can they?'

'Oh, no!' said Naomi, laughing a little, 'It's pretty obvious what's going on… Do you know why they fell out?'

'No. David won't say but I'm guessing there's a girl involved. I've noticed some doodling going on of late.'

Naomi flushed slightly as she recalled her own scribblings: drawing Mike's initials on her notepad at work. Not much really changed between fourteen and forty-four.

'What shall we do?' she asked.

'Why don't you come round? Bring him over and we can have a chat while they make up. I know the girls would love to see you.'

Naomi felt another flush. Of shame this time. How had she let this lovely woman down? How had she managed to walk away at a time when she probably needed friends more than anything? 'Thank you,' she said, her voice a little hushed. 'And, I'm sorry – sorry it has been so long.'

'Pssht. Don't get all Hallmarky on me, Taylor!'

Naomi laughed. 'OK, I won't! Tomorrow, then, if that's OK? I'm not sure I can bear another day of him sulking…'

'Tomorrow is great. Come round any time from seven. We'll have finished tea by then.'

'Great, OK, See you then.'

'Bye, Naomi!'

Naomi ended the call and sat back. Doing something positive felt good. It also highlighted how bloated and tired she felt after a week of eating rubbish. And that made her think of Kerri…remember her shock a few months ago, at seeing how big she had become. I need to be neutral tomorrow, she told herself, keep my face neutral.

And, turning off the muted TV, she went to the kitchen to put her glass in the dishwasher.

James was standing by the kitchen door. Arms rigid by his sides. Naomi was instantly struck by how much he looked like her when she was angry. His spotty face had gone puce with swallowed-down rage.

'I heard you!' he cried. The words exploded out of his mouth in a rush; they tumbled over each other like rocks coming down during a landslide: hard and painful. 'How dare you? How dare you interfere! We're not little kids that have fallen out over who gets to use the swing next! You can't just organise a…a…*play-date* and expect us to make up! This is *serious*!' he burst out, the gravel shower of his anger making him spit.

'I didn't mean…'

'Yeah!' He put his hand up.

This was another gesture that Naomi recognised and, wincing, she stepped back, trying to relax her own body. It was clear how angry he was and she knew that she just had to soak it up, as she had when he was small, let him work his tantrum out and wait till afterwards to try and explain.

'Yeah! Like you mean anything,' he continued, not really caring that this was not in context nor making any sense. 'Like I said, you can't just step in and fix it. We'll sort it out between ourselves. It's up to us!'

'OK, James, OK. I'm sorry. I really am. I didn't…we, Kerri and I, we didn't mean to interfere…'

'Hnnnffhh…' James trumpeted the word out between pursed lips. The worst of the explosion was over: there was now just smoke, in the form of various pre-verbal exhalations of breath.

'Sorry.' Naomi stepped forward, hand outstretched, face and eyes soft. 'We were just worried, that was all…'

'Mmmnnnffhfh… I really can't go round there, Mum…'

'OK, it's OK, of course,' she replied, touching his arm gently with her hand and giving it a light squeeze. She had learnt a while ago – and as with all parenting lessons she had learnt it the hard way – that you approached teenage boys with the same caution and neutral expression with which you approached an unpredictable dog or wild animal.

James shifted slightly so the touch could not become that

most dreaded and feared of all things, an *actual* hug, but he did allow her to squeeze his arm again.

'Gonna have a Coke. Want one?' he muttered, as if he had just walked into the kitchen and opened the fridge door.

'I was going to head up, but if you want to watch something we can?' Naomi offered.

She was tempted by the idea of another glass of wine but, putting the kettle on, she made some camomile tea instead. In the living room, they sat on the sofas and watched some old episodes of *The Simpsons*. Looking at her son from the side as he grinned at the screen, Naomi smiled. James was right. He had to sort out his own friendships and, following his example, she would take responsibility for sorting out hers.

Picking the phone back up, she dialled Kerri's number.

'Hi, yes, it's me again! No. Nothing's wrong, but I'm afraid James isn't up for reconciliation talks just now so we won't be coming round tomorrow. But why don't you and I go for dinner instead? When are you free?'

Chapter Eighteen

Thursday 13th to Friday 14th June

Naomi

As the seasons changed, and the weather shifted to warmer, longer, brighter June days, a similar shift happened in Naomi's moods.

Like clouds, thoughts scudded across her mind. Sometimes they were low and grey, other times bright, but, rather than watching them drift by, her mind latched on to them. Grappling helplessly at the insubstantial haze, she took each one so seriously, examining them and considering them as if they were of weight and importance rather than seeing them for what they truly were: passing moments. Unaware that she should, as with the clouds, pay them little mind, for they would always pass and change, she analysed them, saw in that fleeting fluff a solid world of pain or pleasure, of hope or misery. Scenarios spun out ahead of her, a kaleidoscope of images that translated, in fractions of a moment, into intense physical feelings. She thought sad thoughts: she felt sad. She thought happy, confident thoughts: she felt happy and confident. But the connection was so swift, so instantaneous that she believed the feeling to be real rather than just a reaction to the thought. Like medieval man believing that the weather was cause-and-effect, that the bad rains or the droughts or the good rains or the mild winter were a direct result of things he had or had not done, so Naomi believed her feelings were something separate and real rather than just a reaction to her constant, changeable thinking.

This week, she was waking up to not only blue skies out of the window but clear skies inside her mind. She felt sunny, light: happy. It seemed perverse to be happy when so little was actually going well. James was still sulking, and still not talking to David. Scott was still working long hours while keeping in touch with his parents. Having managed to get Elaine to the doctor during his last visit, he was now spending most weekends there, helping his mum and dad deal with the painful reality of an Alzheimer's diagnosis. It was Leonard who seemed the most affected by it. Now that they knew Elaine was genuinely ill, Leonard was unable to put it down to an off-day or to simply ignore it. He rarely ate or slept well unless Scott was there. Naomi had her head down at work and was busy, but not so busy that she didn't spend a fair bit of time stalking Mike online and clicking on the names of any new female friend or commenter, imaging that she was the new 'her'. There were also the constant pregnancy updates and baby-related links that Carla kept posting. Any one of those could send her spiralling off for a few days if she let it.

But no, this week, despite all that, her mood was light and sunny. She found herself waking early, feeling calm and happy. As in the height of summer we forget what it is like to be in the depths of winter, so she could barely recall how mere weeks ago there had been a hoar frost upon her heart. She felt an internal glow that was a mere result of a chemical shift and yet for which she took full personal responsibility. Events which had seemed onerous and to be avoided were now eagerly anticipated.

'You remember I'm seeing Kerri later and then I'm out again tomorrow?' she said to Scott and James as she prepared to leave. The bag containing her new dress was in her arms and her new shoes were in there too, all ready to be taken into the office in advance of the afternoon departure to the hotel tomorrow.

'Mmm…? Sure…yeah…' said Scott, as he stared at his phone.

James was doing the same as he sat at the kitchen table.

'There's casserole in the fridge, and greens. And pizza and salad for tomorrow…'

'Great, thanks.'

'OK, then…' she said, hovering for a moment, wondering if any member of her family was going to make eye contact with her before she left.

No. No, they weren't.

As Naomi walked along the path from the station to the office, she noticed that the palette around her had changed. Rather than navy and black and grey, the colours of winter overcoats and jackets, she noticed red, blue and white, even pink and yellow: shirts and blouses, soft cotton, as bright and exuberant as the leaves of freshly unfurled flowers. The optimism with which jumpers and jackets had been left off reflected the way the flowers unfurled from their green leaf housing and the leaves spread out on the trees. It was an automatic response to the warmth of soft blue skies and sunny mornings.

Naomi found herself smiling in spite of herself. Her new wardrobe continued to flatter and, as she passed an unfamiliar face, a man, tall, younger than her, with dark-blond hair and blue eyes, there was a moment of extended eye contact. A few seconds as they passed each other and continued to hold each other's gaze. Unable to resist, she glanced back as he passed. He was looking back too. They both smiled a little and then, walking on, both continued on their way, their steps a little lighter.

Dropping her bags into her office, she went to use the bathroom. She looked at herself as she rinsed her hands: the natural light from the windows around the large, pale blue and white room cast her face in a flattering light.

Having put on a few pounds but not too many, and having taken some care over the last few weeks to eat better and drink less, she looked well: very well. Her hair was long and healthy, her skin glowing and eyes clear. Like a sodding show pony, she thought drily, flicking her ponytail in the mirror.

The smile faded. At rest, in this light, she looked almost youthful, but she knew she wasn't. Looking good for her age was the best she could manage now. And she wondered why. Why look good? Who was it for?

You should look good for you, not for boys, her mother piped up in the back of her mind. This was the line that had been trotted out to her as a teenager.

Right, Mother, of course you're right as ever, but, thought Naomi, not quite. Because if nature made the flowers beautiful to attract the bees, and made youth beautiful to help the procreation of the species, then what is the point of this: why flower now?

It wasn't as if she could have another baby even if she wanted to. The way she looked, the way she felt: it had no point, no function.

The door swung open and, surprised out of her reverie, Naomi snapped her brisk manner in place as quickly as one would snap a compact shut.

Back in her office, the business of managing the second phase of the launch kept her busy. Since her meltdown after seeing Carla she had managed to hold it together at work, but she still generally preferred to arrange separate meetings with Simon or communicate via email. It was easy enough to avoid actual contact.

The main topic of non-work-related conversation at the moment was the awards dinner. An annual event, this was the industry's chance to give itself a pat on the back and reward its sales and marketing staff with a lukewarm chicken dinner and several free bars supplying plentiful cheap booze. Naomi had been going to these things since she was a sales rep and, while they no longer seemed quite the glamorous affairs they had back then when she was a wet-behind-the-ears twenty-four-year-old, there was still something fun about seeing everyone else get excited. And it had been a nice excuse to treat herself to a new dress.

Partners were never allowed to attend, and Naomi had already heard that Carla wasn't going – she said couldn't face it 'without at least a bottle in me so I'd rather stay at home and eat ice-cream'. And so Naomi was now actually quite looking forward to it. It had been a while since she had had the chance to dress up and go dancing.

New Year, her mind reminded her as she sat at her desk. It was New Year. Remember. He watched you dancing.

'Fuck off,' she hissed at herself, and, opening up the marketing plan, she got back to work.

Two nights out in one week felt almost decadent to Naomi. As she walked into town, having caught the train all the way into the town centre rather than getting off at her usual station, she felt physically, as well as emotionally, light. She had been looking forward to seeing Kerri. She was in a better place now than she had been a few weeks ago, and she was hopeful that the evening would only add to her already buoyant mood.

They had arranged to meet in one of the many Italian restaurants that seemed to be the only type that flourished in the town. Walking down the high street, she noticed that there were hardly any other people about. It was about 7pm but, as usual, most people were already home or were somewhere other than Rivenoak town centre. Naomi sighed a little. She missed the buzz of London. Walking down the grey, almost empty street, looking at all the darkened shop fronts, she found herself suddenly feeling a little sad. Everything shut at 6pm here and, with only a few pubs still trading, there was hardly any cause to come into town.

As she walked past what was widely known as the bar that served underage kids, Naomi's eye caught the eye of a few twenty-year-olds who were hanging outside smoking. One of them, tall, in a blue and white checked shirt and a fabulously thick quiff of blond hair sticking up off his head, smiled at her as she passed. Naomi smiled back and then, managing to avoid glancing back (*he's WAY too young*) she walked on. That little glance. That moment of visible desire. That was the hit she wanted, needed. The look that said, *You, yes, YOU, the way you look, appeals to me.*

That's what I want, she thought: I want to be wanted. Not loved or even needed but wanted, desired... That's all. That's OK, isn't it?

Kerri was waiting inside when Naomi arrived. She was sipping a lemonade and eating the salted and roasted nuts they always placed on the table. Seeing her move awkwardly to get up, Naomi found herself motioning for her to stay put. 'Hi! It's good to see you! Sorry if you've been waiting...' Her eye caught the already half-empty bread basket and then she quickly looked away, cross with herself already for judging the other woman.

'No! No, only been here five minutes! Wow – you look great!'

Naomi felt pleased but shrugged a little, smiled and said, 'So do you!'

Kerri looked down.

'To be honest, it's nice to be out so I can eat what I like without feeling guilty. David is dieting and, well, he's doing so well, but I can't quite seem to manage it... It's harder as you get older, I think. Metabolism and all that...' She took another large piece of freshly baked white bread and pressed it down hard in the saucer of grassy-green olive oil.

'How are the girls?' Naomi asked as she poured some water from the carafe on the table and tried to catch the eye of the waitress.

And, with that, the desire to connect with the other woman became bound by conventional questions and compromised by restaurant rituals. By only half-listening because you wanted to get the glass of wine ordered instead; by not paying full attention because you were trying to decide between what you wanted to eat and what you thought you should be eating. By noticing that the waiter serving the other tables was kind of hot and thinking that, while you really shouldn't stare as that was so not the cool thing to do, you couldn't help but half notice that he did just look at you and…

Even with Naomi's genuine desire to see Kerri, it was still so much easier to watch her own thoughts, to think about herself, than it was to truly listen to this other woman.

This other woman who was saying, 'And, well, I suppose I just don't understand why he has taken it all so seriously all of a sudden. I know I should be pleased but it just makes me feel even worse about the way we've eaten since he was small – or since Gary left, in particular. I know we should be eating better but I like the food we eat and, you know, I get so tired after work. He keeps telling me a better diet would help with that, but I just don't *want* to eat salad every day, you know? I've had a long day and I just want some biscuits or a cake, and I just think, one is OK but then David is staring at me and…really, it is just so nice to be out and talking to someone else about it all…'

'Mm-hhm,' said Naomi, staring at the menu, trying to make the starter-or-dessert decision.

The waitress came over.

'Can I have the garlic bread with cheese to start with and then the lasagne please…' said Kerri.

'Is that with chips or salad?'

'Oh, chips, please.'

'And for you?'

'The grilled hake please. With salad.'

'Of course.' The waitress smiled and then walked away.

'And you? How are you?' asked Kerri, smiling across at Naomi, her eyes wide in her broad, flushed face.

Naomi sipped her wine. Part of her wanted to say, *I've been having an affair. I think about sex with strangers all the time. My marriage is crumbling under the pressure of dealing with two elderly parents-in-law and a very much more sour than sweet teenager. And, after nearly twenty years, I sometimes think I would rather be alone for ever than have to share my space with anyone else ever again.*

'Things are fine!' she said brightly.

For how did you tell the truth? She thought that perhaps she had forgotten how to – or perhaps she had never been taught? Perhaps she had never once told the truth, for now, here, when asked, by someone who genuinely wanted to know, she just couldn't do it. Could not even begin to say out loud how she really felt. The realisation was both a relief and also completely terrifying. Had she never had an authentic conversation?

Not since her early twenties, she thought. As you got older, the opportunities to be honest, to admit that it was still all pretty crap, that you felt cheated because your life had never really ever made your heart sing as you were promised it would do – those opportunities vanished. People got busier with work, and caught up with their own problems and with, well, just life itself, and so the long chats that you had in your twenties were replaced with cursory texts and life-edited-to-be-perfect status updates. For Naomi knew, more than ever before, just how little those sites that were designed to connect you really did that. All they seemed to do was put more distance between everyone.

'Are they?' asked Kerri, looking straight at her for a moment.

And there it was: the chance to be honest, the chance to tell the truth or even part of the truth. Which bit to choose? Which was the most palatable?

'Well…' Naomi hesitated. 'You know… James isn't easy – lovely, but not easy, especially since he fell out with David, and, well, Scott's mum has recently been diagnosed with Alzheimer's, and…'

'Gosh, really? I'm so sorry!'

Naomi shrugged. 'There's very little we can do… I guess I just worry about it dragging on. But you just have to get on with it, I suppose. We're fine, though, you know, really. How's work for you?'

It was a pre-packaged, individual and unsatisfying serving, but it had been the truth, and about as much of it as Naomi could stomach right now.

'Work's good…'

They chattered about their individual projects, Naomi letting Kerri lead the conversation and then talking about the Kale Kooler launch, while Kerri ate her garlic bread.

'Did you want some?' asked Kerri. 'There's loads!'

'No, no! Thanks, though…' Naomi drank some more wine, unable to stop herself from mentally calculating the amount of fat that was in the garlic bread. 'And Gary…is he still pretty involved with the kids?'

'No, not really,' said Kerri, looking down. 'He remarried within the year, started another family. That's been one of the hardest things, really. He has started over and, well, he clearly makes so much more effort with her and them than he ever did with me… It's – well, it's like we…I…wasn't worth making the effort for…' She stopped.

Naomi looked down too and then reached her hand out and squeezed the other woman's hand. 'You are… You know, I always thought he was hopeless…'

Kerri looked up and smiled a little. 'Him cheating on me…then leaving while the girls were so small…well, it just kind of broke me. I felt so awful and so low. I suppose I still do, really. I'm not sure I've ever really stopped hearing him saying, *I've been sleeping with someone else, I want her, not you...*' She hiccuped a little, stifling a sob.

Naomi squeezed her hand again but could not look her in the eyes. Where were the mains? she wanted to ask, suddenly feeling desperate to eat and go.

And this is why no one wants to see or hear the truth, she thought as the main courses arrived. No one wants to know because it hurts: hurts to hear someone else's pain, to see someone else so lost and lonely. If we see it there, in front of us, we have to acknowledge our own pain, and we can't, or rather we don't want to – will do anything not to.

She understood it; she just didn't know how to not turn away from it.

Her mind began its defence. *We have enough discomfort of our own to tolerate without taking on someone else's... Look at your life, look at all your problems...*

'Let's order a crazy amount of dessert after this!' she said, just wanting to do something to take this woman's sadness away and knowing no other easy way to do it.

They ate puddings and drank milky coffees and, as they stood by the door, they said their goodbyes.

'We must catch up again soon...' said Naomi.

'Yes, yes, I'd like that,' replied Kerri, smiling.

'OK, I'd better go and get a cab!' said Naomi brightly, and, giving Kerri a quick hug, arms loose around the woman's enormous back and shoulders, she dashed out of the door and away.

And, scanning round as she walked, she looked for a set of eyes, any set of eyes that could take her own pain away. A look, that was all she wanted: a glance, a moment. There was someone, older, not even that attractive but yes, he looked, stared at her hungrily, and with a shudder of delight Naomi went towards the waiting taxi.

Matthew

Matthew had claimed to be busy in the few weeks since Polly had been back, but now he had run out of excuses.

She called him that morning before he had even left the flat to go to school.

'The website needs some changes.'

'Sorry?' Matthew coughed, surprised. 'Changes? What changes?'

'It's the next part of the plan! It's Sam's idea and it's incredible! I'll tell you all about it, but to start it all off it just needs a timer. You know, a countdown clock kind of thing, on the home page. Right in the middle. One that dominates the whole screen. Oh, and then I have a new page to add.'

'Countdown?' asked Matthew, picking up his bags and glancing at the wall clock. He had his meeting with Barraclough today and he needed to go.

'Yes! We need a countdown clock!'

'Right... I guess I'll need to know some details. Like, how long do you want it for...'

'Can I give you the info later?'

'Sure...but it might take a while. When do you need it to be up there by?'

'By the weekend?'

'It's already Thursday,' he said, frowning.

'Please...'

'I'll see what I can do,' he said.

'I'll pop over later and see how it's coming along?'

'Wait – what's it for?'

'What's it for?' she said. 'It's a countdown to blowing up that drinks factory!'

Walking to school, Matthew wanted to think about what Polly had said, but surely she was not serious and he was too preoccupied with what lay immediately ahead of him. He had received the email about the meeting a few days ago and had thought about little else since.

Dropping his bags off in his classroom, Matthew sat outside the office and felt a twinge in his stomach. His face was flushed. His scalp itched. Being called to see Barraclough was as terrifying for a teacher as it was for a student. Part of him felt ridiculous, part of him resented Barraclough for making him feel nervous, but mostly he was just resigned. He knew exactly what to expect here. He knew exactly why he was being called in.

The secretary looked up and smiled at him.

'You can go in now, Mr Holmes,' she said.

'Thanks,' he replied, running his hand through his hair.

'Take a seat, Matthew! Take a seat! Be *right* with you!'

Barraclough glanced up from his screen to ensure compliance and then looked back, frowning. From what Matthew had observed, being head seemed to involve a hell of a lot of frowning at a screen.

He sat down and looked round the room while he waited. Among the usual framed certificates and diplomas were photos of Barraclough meeting various local figures, including some celebrated sports people. He was very much involved with the community, and keen that everyone be aware of this.

'So, yes, a quick word was all I needed.'

Barraclough smiled at Matthew, and that was when Matthew felt truly concerned. The head's eyes were as cold and dead as a fish's.

'I am a little bit – I have to say perhaps more than a little bit – concerned about this project you have handed out to the Year 9s. I've been receiving some worrying feedback from the heads of humanities and maths. It seems that among the, ahem, student body there is talk of little else – that effort is being applied where perhaps we do not *require* so much effort to be applied.'

He paused, steepling his fingers and resting his chin and his cool, wide smile upon it.

'It does seem to have captured their imagination,' Matthew began. 'I think the flexibility, the freedom to choose and make some of the decisions themselves about what they produce the work on, and how they deliver it, has really fired them up.'

'Positively inspired, they are,' smiled Barraclough, smile broadening but still leaving the upper half of his face untouched by its brilliance. 'Which is, obviously, wonderful. Truly wonderful! No one loves to hear news of inspired pupils more than I do. But – and yes, there is a but, as I am sure you suspected – I tend to prefer hearing about pupils being inspired by and focusing on *core* subjects. Inspiration has to result in something concrete! It has to be…statistically relevant, as it were…'

'Surely the science results are important too…' Matthew began.

'Of course they are, of course they are. Very important, you won't hear me saying otherwise, but sometimes, just sometimes, it's important to refocus, to ensure that efforts are being directed, like a laser beam,' he said, pointing his steepled fingers ahead of him to imitate a laser, 'on to the key issues, the key issues being the measurable, core ones that I have already touched on.'

'Science is a key issue to me,' said Matthew. 'I thought it was important to you, and the school, too.'

'I know,' said Barraclough, smile fading, lower lip sticking out in an approximation of empathy. 'And I appreciate your passion for your subject, always have, but, well, I think I have made myself as clear as I need to today.'

He leaned back. Chin still poised above his fingers, eyes still deadly cold.

'I—' Matthew began.

'As I say, I think I have made myself clear.' His eyes returned to the screen.

Matthew waited a moment, staring at his own hands, which were curled lifelessly in his lap. Then he got up and left the room.

It was the anger that carried him through the work. It carried him through that evening's conversation with Polly, a conversation he barely listened to, no longer needing to be convinced that people were fundamentally stupid; he just wanted to do something and have it done. The rage he had suppressed throughout the school day poured out of his fingers and made the recoding, the effort required, feel effortless.

And now, having done what she had asked of him and received a very thorough blow job by way of reward, he lay alone in his bed.

It had been satisfying solving the problems of the changes. The clock had been easy enough in the end, but trying to make sensible copy out of the slightly hysterical narrative that had been written by 'Sam' – his name was always set out in derisive inverted commas to Matthew – had proved more difficult. But now, with her gone, he was thinking about what she had said and feeling increasingly concerned.

Having spent most of the early part of the evening reassuring him that no one was going to be hurt, that they had an insider who knew that the lines would be down by then, that the factory would be empty and that the only damage would be to the equipment and to VitSip's profits, Polly had convinced him. But now, lying on his own, all he had were doubts. He knew change was needed, but was this really the best way to go about it?

Her voice piped up in his mind again. *You know it is. You know that nothing changes without force. We need to wake people up! That's why I wanted the countdown to look like an alarm clock: it's a wake-up call, an alarm that has been set to help people wake up from their sugar-induced comas. People won't change on their own, they're so immune now: we have to wake them up with a shock, a blast!*

He wanted to believe her, wanted to believe that it would make the difference that they had both talked about, but he was increasingly unsure. And yet...and yet. Remembering that meeting with Barraclough, and also that lunch break when the kids had all eaten rubbish and drunk even more rubbish, even though they had all spent the morning talking about how you shouldn't, he felt anger pass through him in a wave. Breaking against the shore of what he had just done, it transformed into a warm glow of satisfaction. Rolling over, he went to sleep.

Naomi

Shifting a little in her very new and very uncomfortable shoes, Naomi was about to mentally curse herself for never learning anything. Having wanted to gain the extra few inches of height, she had sacrificed all physical comfort, like a young girl who takes no coat to wear on a winter's night out.

Then she caught sight of herself in the reflective pillar by the bar.

It was totally worth it, she thought. Like those lovely young girls: we all know that no coat looks cold but we also know that it looks much sexier and *that* is why we do it.

The new dress she had bought was floor-length, and the extra height from the shoes gave it the edge. Rich navy satin, it made her look as if she was rising out of the sea, like a nymph. The younger girls had pretty braids in their hair, fleshy bodies tumbling appealingly out of cheap, sparkly high-street dresses. It was the ones in their thirties, the ones still struggling to figure out how to make that transition from being twenty-something to being older but not quite old, who looked the least attractive. Young, but not quite young enough to pull off completely flat, straight hair and cheap little black dresses, thought Naomi, a little unkindly.

Though she had been there once: lumpen and sad in an ill-fitting shift dress in the years after James had been born.

It will get better, she thought, smiling at the uncomfortable-looking women; it gets better, but you have to take some responsibility for making it so.

Sipping her tonic water, she also knew that staying sober was important. No one looked good pissed, but least of all a middle-aged woman. She had had enough nights in the last few months looking at her blotchy face and bloodshot eyes at bedtime, and again in the morning when her skin was grey and tight from dehydration, to know that alcohol was no longer her friend.

After the meal, Naomi saw the speakers coming on to the stage. The awards and speeches were about to start. Feeling bored already – this part of the evening was always interminably dull – Naomi got up and went to find the bathroom.

Walking down the long, empty corridor, she approached the heavy double doors that led through to the bathrooms, or Powder Rooms as they were rather fussily called on the dated, swirly signage. As she reached out, Jonathan came into the corridor from a side door. He didn't see her, and his hand also went straight to the door.

There was a pause. Their hands were locked together on the ornate gold handle and he looked up, eyes widening a little in surprise.

Naomi laughed. Returning his gaze steadily, she smiled.

'Sorry,' he said, quickly moving his hand.

Naomi could still feel the warmth and weight of his hand on hers. A slight flush flared up on her cheekbones as she replied, 'No, *I'm* sorry!'

This time they both smiled.

'Please,' she said, stepping back proudly. 'You first.'

'Thank you,' he said, mock bowing and smiling as she let him pass. He touched her arm lightly as he went by. Their eyes met again. 'I just wanted to say well done. Again,' he said. 'That launch strategy was really something else. Very impressive.'

'Thank you,' she said, shrugging a little, but straightening up too. She glanced towards the doors that led back into the main room. The speeches were audible, the monotone drone of the CFO coming under the double doors like a draught.

'Let's have a drink once the speeches are over?' she said. 'I usually need at least two once they're done.'

They shared a smile and, with a nod, parted.

Returning to the table, Naomi could still feel the featherlight touch of his fingers on her upper arm. Seeing that her glass had been refilled to near the brim with red wine, she took a sip and then put on her listening face.

Later, at the bar, she used that face again as one of the team was talking to her.

'It's just that,' Neill was saying, 'you know…I thought now would be a good chance to ask how I'm doing? I need the feedback. I think I'm doing a good job but, you know, how long do I have to wait till I get a promotion?'

Naomi looked at him. What was it with this batch of grads? They seemed to think that six months was all they needed to do and then they'd be getting the ear of the exec team. Did he not realise that she hadn't even made that team until she was thirty-five? She took another sip of wine and, glancing up, she saw Jonathan smiling at her from the bar. Forcing a smile on to her face, she patted Neill reassuringly on the arm and said, 'Now is not a good time, Neill, sorry. Let's get a date in the diary and we can discuss your career path in the office.'

'You won't forget?' He glanced anxiously at her glass.

She gave him a tolerant look. 'I won't. Now go. Run off and have fun with the other…' She paused, not saying the word *children* but trusting that her meaning was clear.

She turned away and walked over to Jonathan.

'Wine?' he asked.

'Yes, he did.'

They laughed.

'I meant what I said earlier...'

Naomi raised a hand and said, 'Enough! No shop talk. I am *done* with talking about the bloody launch. What's your favourite film?' she asked. 'Or the funniest book you've read recently. Anything! Just not work talk. Please.'

Laughing, he said, 'Sure, whatever you say. You're in charge...'

They chatted for the next hour about everything other than work.

There was a pause and they both looked around. The tiny dance floor was now packed and the bar was busy, people talking loudly, faces flushed, laughter a little too high and forced to be natural. Everyone was drunk.

'We could always go somewhere a little quieter?' she suggested, voice low. 'These things tend to go downhill pretty rapidly from this point, don't they?' And with a hand placed gently on his arm, she added, 'Why don't I meet you upstairs. You're on the third floor, aren't you? Say, five minutes?'

Jonathan nodded.

Without looking back into the room where Jonathan lay, sleeping now, Naomi closed the door quietly behind her. Looking up and down the beige and gold corridor, all she could see was door after door. They were all the same, all blank bar their tarnished yellow-bronze numerals.

Part of her brain registered that the numbers all began with a three, and then another part of her brain picked up that message and, with a snap of a synapse, it started her legs moving automatically towards the lift. She travelled down to the ground floor and walked out of the glass double doors and into the cool night.

The air was full of moisture; the dampness made her dress cling to her skin and she shivered a little as she felt the raindrops on her bare shoulders and back. She got into one of the waiting white and yellow taxis and, as it pulled away from the hotel, she stared out of the window.

She could see James's face from one Christmas a long time ago. It was the year he had been four, nearly five. As soon as he had seen the space suit, he had wanted it – wanted it with a force that had shocked her at the time. Watching the adverts for it on the television, he had been mesmerised by the astronaut boy who seemed to blast into the inky sky, off to explore distant galaxies. Tumbling in zero gravity, making emergency repairs, collecting specimens as well as defeating many tentacled aliens, all while wearing this magical suit.

Now she could see his face when he had caught sight of the big box under the tree, the red and white paper catching the fairy lights. He couldn't contain himself as he tore the paper off, squealing with delight as he saw what was beneath. When he pulled the box apart, the suit, as it was tugged from its cardboard, was revealed to be worth the money: beautifully made out of thick, quality cotton, it was technically accurate. Even the helmet fitted perfectly. Photos were taken, he began to run around downstairs, and then, suddenly, he went to the front door, flinging it open. Bemused, Naomi and Scott had stood behind him, wrapped in their dressing gowns, still bleary-eyed from being woken at 5am. They had watched as James lifted his arms like the boy in the advert and there was a moment, a single moment, as he closed his eyes, his face lit up with anticipation.

And then, nothing.

His eyes had snapped open. Looking down at where he was, still on the step, feet still firmly on the grey ground, he had let out a wail, a low sound that came from deep within. He had turned to them, his eyes clouded over and flat with misery as his lower lip trembled and the tears began.

She remembered how her heart had broken for him, seeing the tears tracking down his cheeks.

Silently, she mouthed the words he had said to her. 'Why doesn't it make me fly? Why?'

Looking at her own rain-spattered reflection in the taxi window, she met her own fallow stare and there, in her eyes, she saw the same anguished disappointment that she had seen on James's face when, at four years old, he had realised that he would never be able to fly to the moon.

Chapter Nineteen

Friday 21st June

David

The reading for his project was mostly done. He was amazed at how many books he had got through. Once he had started reading he had been unable to stop: the subject matter had proven to be more appealing than he had ever believed possible and so, instead of gorging on food, he had been binging on words and ideas instead over these past weeks.

Looking at the books piled all around his small desk, he noticed the gaming console hidden underneath. He hadn't used that for weeks now, too wrapped up in the books and his internet research to care much for games. He still loved them, but he wanted to give this project his all in the same way that he was now giving the weight loss his all. It felt right to focus on it. And the subject matter had made it easy.

Food. How it was made and marketed. The industry behind the things he had been eating as well as the biology side of it: how his body used the food. What it could and could not cope with.

School could only touch on so much and the field he was researching – the science behind food manufacturing and the way the body could or mostly couldn't cope with the sugar and fat in foods – made for such fascinating reading. It was relevant and meaningful in a way that most schoolwork couldn't ever be. He cared about history and the past, he was interested in how the earth was put together and in how to order lunch in a French or Spanish café, but the fact was that food made up so much of his life, and so to spend time actually learning about it only seemed right.

Now he just needed to begin the hard work of pulling it all together, but he was still unsure how he was going to present it. As he began to look through his notes, he found himself thinking, This is going to be the hard bit.

Aware of the thought, he felt the resistance. Felt the urge to stop. Having just moments ago dismissed the console as a waste of time, he now found himself thinking, I could just play a game instead.

He sat back in his chair. Downstairs he could hear the TV. The girls laughing. He missed them. He missed sitting with them and watching. Laughing.

And yet, he thought, and yet... What he wanted and what he needed were not, David realised, the same thing. Anything but, in fact; and if that was true for him it was probably true for most people.

He looked up at the little note he had written for himself. It was naff. It was cheesy. He was so embarrassed by it that he hid it every morning before he left the room so that neither Kerri nor his sisters saw it. Ever. It was just a Post-it note he had stuck to the wall above his desk. On it he had written:

You can do it, David

And while the idea of anyone seeing made him cringe, the reality was that whenever he looked at it he felt better. He was not really conscious of why he had put it there, of the way in which he had put his name on it as if the encouraging sentence were being spoken by someone else, as if he was getting actual and real support, but he was aware that it helped him to think he could, helped him to think that it was possible for him to change.

Looking back down at the pile of paper, he stared at his notes. The material all made perfect sense. It was almost as if he had known it before. So much of his reading time had been spent having eureka moments. Moments where he had thought, So *that* is why that happens and *that* is why I feel like that.

What he didn't know was how to present it. He made some notes. They seemed kind of lame.

He felt a pang of hunger in his stomach and drank some water. He needed to be occupied to take his mind off the hunger. He felt his mind begin to speed up, his thoughts beginning to pick up the pace as if they were in a race to get somewhere.

If I eat I'll never stop… But I'm hungry, I'm empty and I've been good all day. I'm tired. I'm lonely. I want to eat. I need to understand this. I'm not getting anywhere. I'm hungry. I'm too stupid to figure this out. It'll be crap anyway. Everyone will laugh at me. It is rubbish. I'm hungry. I'm rubbish.

He shut his eyes. His mind was spinning. The words going faster and faster until he felt as if he was going to fall off his chair.

He reached up, clutching his hands to his head.

He took a few deep breaths.

When he opened his eyes he saw the games console again.

'That's it!' he said, laughing.

Most people knew what they should be eating but the whole system was set up so they failed. Like one of his games. The game would always win. You had to cheat if you were ever going to get on to the next level. Like every game he had ever played, the system was rigged in the manufacturer's favour. It was designed to fool you, to catch you out, and it was designed to leave you wanting more, created and engineered to be addictive.

And, thinking of it like a game, he decided there was no point in getting angry. No purpose to that at all. Instead, as with his gaming, he had to be creative. What cheats could he work out? How he could share them?

He began to sketch out the presentation.

Naomi

It was Friday evening and Scott was home for the weekend. He'd been at his parents' again, taking a couple of days off work because they had both had doctor's visits. Kicking James's bag out of the way, Naomi went into the kitchen and poured herself a glass of wine before going into the living room.

Taking a long draught, she sat on the sofa and stared into space. It had been a long day. It had been a long week. No wine before today. Lots of healthy food. None of these things had taken away the pain of what had happened, or rather not happened, when she had had sex with Jonathan. She still felt awful but not quite as awful as before. Just hollowed out.

Hearing the living room door open, she felt her shoulders tense up, her back go rigid. With James out till late it could only be Scott. The idea of having to be civil, polite, nice even, after the day, the week (*the year?* her mind added) she had had made her grip the glass, her hand tight and tense enough to crush it if she wanted to. It had been so much easier to come home and chat to James, to play with the tablet or read a magazine. Not having Scott there had meant more leisure time, more staring into space and surfing time, and, now he was home, she resented having to make the effort again.

'Hey,' he said warmly, as he came into the living room. 'It's good to be here, good to see you.'

No, she thought angrily, I will not have sex with you later. Being polite was Scott's idea of foreplay, always had been, and, while she used not to mind, right now it made her want to punch him in the face.

Be nice, she heard her mother say.

All right, all right, she snapped back in her head, in the same irritated tone she had always used when talking to her mum as a teenager. Mother was always right.

'Hey,' she said, forcing her herself to make an effort.

He sat down next to her and she felt a sudden and powerful urge to get up and move away, but forced herself to sit still. He kissed her. She tried to relax into him but it was hard. Having been keeping so much in for so long, it was as if the only thing holding the shattered pieces of herself together was the tension, and she feared that, if she relaxed, her entire self would collapse into a heap of broken shards on the floor.

Scott held her against him, and again she tried to relax into his embrace. She managed to a little, enough for him to pull back and, smiling at her, say, 'James is out – let's go upstairs before I get dinner sorted? I brought your favourite back with me from that fishmonger's near the office: the salmon? *En croûte*? I'll sort it out later but I thought now...'

He smiled at her again and, with what felt like liquid relief, relief at having him take charge and just tell her, Naomi allowed herself to acquiesce. Nodding mutely, she took his hand and he led her upstairs.

Half an hour later, she was back on the sofa. Scott was opening more wine and preparing some vegetables while she sat not watching the TV and trying not to compare the perfectly acceptable sex she had just had with the times she had been with Mike. It was hard, but she did try. Before, she had just let the thoughts take over, but this time at least she tried to shoo them away, flicking at them in her mind as if they were persistent and annoying flies. Be here, she told herself, just for now, just be here.

Scott came back in with wine and a bowl of crisps.

'Everything been OK?' he asked. 'How's work?'

There was the truth: *I seduced the man who is effectively my boss and am now worried that I have jeopardised my only chance of promotion. I have a product that is so sugary even I feel guilty selling it, and every time I walk into marketing I see my ex-lover's pregnant wife grinning at me over her little round belly and I want to gouge my own eyes out with a pen.*

'Fine!' she said, brightly, taking a sip of wine. 'And you? How are things with your mum?'

'When she's bad she's really bad, she can barely remember where she is, but then she has some days where she's just like her old self and then she refuses to get help. Refuses to even discuss it because she can't remember the bad days. I've been doing some research and it has really made me think about how we are eating. Did you know that excess sugar is linked to Alzheimer's? Hold on, I'll get the book I bought...'

He got up and went back into the kitchen.

Naomi drank some more wine and then quickly topped up her glass. God, she thought, sourly. The last thing I need right now is Scott on a crusade about curing Alzheimer's.

Coming back in, he thrust a weighty-looking textbook at her. Naomi arranged her features into an expression that was all interest and engagement.

'It's fascinating,' he said, taking the book back and opening it up to one of the many folded-back pages. 'Look: this page here directly links the increase of sugar intake with the rise in mental health problems in older people. Sugar speeds everything up! It basically ages the brain so that it doesn't function properly. Add to that the fact that people don't eat enough oily fish or greens and other proteins and complex fatty acids and, well, it's kind of easy to see how we're in the position we are in...'

That explains the salmon, Naomi thought.

'It's so terrifying to see her like that and be thinking what if it happens to me? You know Mum and I have always shared a sweet tooth. God, she baked every day when I was growing up! Every *day*…'

Naomi looked at him, seeing his brow crease as he stared at the open book on his lap. Suddenly she felt a wave of compassion for him. It washed through her, sweeping away the ugliness of her previous thoughts. He's as scared as I am of getting old, she thought. We both are, just in different ways. Maybe we all are…

'It'll be fine,' she said, touching his leg gently. 'We can make some changes here if you like. Let's chat about it over the weekend when we have more time. And,' she added, hitting him playfully on the shoulder, '*you* can be the one to explain it to James!'

Chapter Twenty

Naomi

Saturday morning and James was already out of the house, cricket practice having taken over from football now that the summer was under way. The last few weeks of term were busy, with sports days and tests and also the end-of-year presentations.

Scott was at the kitchen table: papers spread out before him, mug of coffee to his right, plate full of toast crumbs to his left. Naomi watched him as he read and drank: he looked content. He looked happy. Naomi wished she could feel the same.

Sipping her own coffee, she glanced at her phone and then back at Scott. Weekends were relaxing for him, a change of routine; they had been the same for her once she had gone back to work full-time. The change of pace was a welcome one. She felt safer here too. Home was the one place where she could be trusted not to make an utter fool of herself.

Pouring the last of the coffee from the cafetiere into her mug, she drank some more, the still hot, bitter liquid a welcome distraction from her own bitter shame. Shame at how she had behaved with Jonathan, who was really just a passing attraction; shame at how much time she had spent upset over Mike. Shame that was slowly turning, after weeks of pretending everything was OK, that she didn't need anything other than her family and her job, into a frustration and a restlessness that was getting increasingly hard to ignore.

'Can I have the paper?' she asked Scott, going to sit at the table.

She had read once that if you acted as if you were happy, if you just smiled, your body and mind would eventually fall for the illusion and the happy feelings would quickly follow. It was worth another try.

Sitting at the table, she began to flick through the magazine. As ever, it was full of images of people just like her only better-dressed and better-looking. She imagined her and Scott as if they were in one of these glossy adverts: sitting together in their beautiful but well-loved kitchen, drinking organic fair-trade coffee, nibbling on pieces of artisanal bread spread with unsalted butter, a companionable silence as the digital radio played faultless classical music in the background.

If it looks like happiness then why doesn't it feel like it? she thought, her skin prickling horribly as she felt unease and restlessness crawling over it like insects. And what do you do if you've got what you wanted but then decide you don't want it any more?

She got up, the knot in her stomach, the itching on her skin only tolerable if she was moving.

Upstairs, she sorted the laundry then had a very hot shower and got dressed. She began to make the bed. Laundry, shopping, food ordering, admin, dinner, calls…I've got to get on, she thought – and then she stopped.

God, I sound like my mother.

Scott had offered to go to the shops and sort lunch out for the day, so she went back down to the kitchen and jotted down a list of the things that, despite editing the food shopping online about five times, she had still managed to forget.

'There's just a few things on there. And can you fill the car up? The light's been on for two days…'

'Sure,' he said, as he folded the list into his pocket. 'This won't take me long.'

'I think James is back at noon so we need to eat before one otherwise he'll just start hoovering things up out of the fridge and the cupboard. You know what he's like…'

The front door burst open noisily and there was a loud scuffle as bags and boots were slung across the hallway floor.

'James! Boots outside!' she called from upstairs.

'Ggrrgrghh… 'K.'

The sound of cupboards being opened and slammed shut filled the background. She and Scott looked at each other. Nothing needed to be said: it was one of those instant moments of telepathy that married couples share.

'James!' they both called out warningly in unison, and then smiled at each other a little. Naomi jerked her head as if to say, *You can go and stop him this time*, and she watched as he left to speak to their son.

Seated at the kitchen table that lunchtime, James leaned back in his chair and then, rocking forward, he scanned over the food on the table, eyes widening in barely concealed horror.

'This isn't what we normally have on Saturdays!'

Naomi silently raised her eyes to the ceiling and then, smiling placidly, she turned her forcedly neutral gaze on to Scott. 'Hon?' she said, smile fixed in place.

Scott spread his arms out over the lunch he had prepared and said, 'We're trying something new today! Quinoa and roasted vegetables with feta cheese. A big green salad with alfalfa and mixed seeds.'

Naomi smiled. It did look delicious, but the look of appalled horror on James's face was a testimony to the extent that they had eaten ham and cheese rolls and crisps or hot dogs almost every Saturday since he was four. She began to serve herself some food. 'It looks great, Scott. Thank you!'

She watched as James poked the spindly pieces of sprout around the plate. 'It looks like grass,' he muttered, eyes dark, shoulders hunched.

'It's full of amino acids,' Scott said, cheerfully.

'Ugh, you sound like one of my teachers. That's all I get at school now.'

'How is David?' Naomi asked, cautiously.

'Dunno. We're still not talking. He's lost loads of weight, though…' And James continued to scowl at the salad.

I really must call Kerri back, Naomi thought, a knot of guilt twisting in her stomach.

James was picking the feta out of the vegetables and pushing the roasted courgettes underneath the salad leaves.

'James…' Scott began.

The phone rang.

'I'll get it!' Naomi sang, keen to get away from the table. Picking up the receiver, she said, 'Hello?'

'It's Leonard…I…'

Naomi didn't even stop to listen. 'I'll get Scott,' she trilled, unthinking.

Back in the kitchen, James and Scott were arguing too hard to notice her.

'But I don't like it!'

'You haven't tried it!'

'Scott… Scott!' Naomi had to raise her voice.

They both looked at her.

'It's your dad… Can you go and talk to him?'

James smirked into his lunch.

'Don't think that means you don't have to try that…' she said warningly, 'Dad is keen for us to eat a bit better.'

'Grrrfffh…'

'Just try it. You can have something else after, but just try it!'

She sat back down and began to eat some more of her own portion. In truth, it was quite delicious, and even James looked surprised once he had actually managed to get some of it down. 'There,' she said, 'Not so bad, eh?'

Scott walked back in.

'Everything OK…? Maybe we should send your mum some quinoa…that would really give her something to complain about…'

Naomi sniggered at her own joke, as did James. Then she looked Scott's face, and the sniggering stopped.

'She's had a stroke,' said Scott. 'She's had a stroke and she's in the hospital.'

'Oh, fuck!' said Naomi, not even noticing James's look of surprise at hearing her swear. Getting up, she went over to Scott and hugged him, holding him tight. 'Are you going to go now? We can all go…'

'Yes,' he said. 'We need to go.'

And, with that, grabbing phones and bags, they all got in the car and left the house, the food left mostly untouched on their plates.

I suppose the one advantage of this is that Scott hasn't got any time to feed us quinoa, thought Naomi as she scraped yet another lot of half-eaten ready meals into the bin.

The kitchen was silent. Moments of quiet and calm had been rare in the past few days. Ever since that interrupted lunch, their world had been sent into a tailspin. Scott's mum had had another stroke while in the hospital and was now in a hospice near to Rivenoak. Leonard was struggling. He had lost weight in recent weeks and was not sleeping properly. Walking, forlorn, around their home, he was pale and shaky, grieving already for the wife he had lost and the shell he had now been left with. 'I just always assumed it would me be that would go first…' he kept saying whenever they sat and talked.

He had been staying with them since it happened. With the end of term approaching, and both Scott and Naomi busy at work, there was no other way this time. And, without needing to say it, they also knew that they might not have long to all be together, so it made sense to have Elaine nearby. James was visiting her almost every day after school. It seemed that seeing her, and spending time with her, was helping make the decline in her condition easier for him to bear.

Having had the luxury of half an hour to herself, even though it had just been while getting the kitchen straight, Naomi sighed, and then went back into the living room.

'Where's your dad?' she asked Scott as she came in.

'He's gone up.'

'Oh, OK. You all right?' she asked, sitting down. 'Have you checked that James has turned his light off?'

'Yes, he has…but…' There was a pause.

'Mmm?' Naomi prompted, as she began to turn her tablet on; she hadn't looked at the news for a few days.

'Well, he seems so tired all the time…'

'Your dad?' she said, not really listening.

'No, James…'

'Ah, it's the end of term, he's always tired then.'

'Seems worse than usual…'

Naomi shrugged, her eyes scanning over the flat surface of the tablet. 'Sure he's fine…' She clicked on a headline and began to read. 'There's a lot going on. We're all tired.'

'OK, if you think so.'

'Mmhhh…'

Naomi read some articles, one on family communication and one on mock exam success, and then she went up to bed. It would all begin again in the morning.

Returning home from work the next day, Naomi found Leonard sitting in exactly the same position as he had been when she had left in the morning. Often, if he wasn't at an after-school activity or visiting Elaine, James would sit beside him on the sofa. He was there now, this Thursday evening, talking to his grandad about his day, trying to engage him in what was going on. The older man was smiling and nodding.

Naomi stood in the doorway.

He gets that from Scott, she thought, that gentleness, that consideration. Not from me. He gets all his better qualities from Scott.

The thought made her feel sad. They hadn't seen her and so she continued to watch and listen, smiling as she heard Leonard laugh for the first time in what must have been weeks.

Going back into the kitchen, she unpacked the bag of food shopping. Having decided on the way home that they really couldn't eat takeaway again, and not having had time to order any food, she had gone to the supermarket and picked up some lamb chops and green beans for dinner. Nothing exciting, but it had to be better than more noodles or pizza.

Scott was working late, after being at the hospice that morning. His bosses seemed to make little allowance for people having family or friends who were waiting to die.

And that's all we're doing now, she thought, as she put the groceries away, just waiting for the inevitable. How long, though? How long will it take?

It had been five days now and, while she was coping, the routine was stifling, and with Leonard here the house was beginning to have a particular smell that brought back unpleasant memories.

Going upstairs to change, she went into her study first and turned on the computer. There was work she had to do later, though it would have to wait till after supper. Leonard needed to eat. Doubtless he had done little more than pick at the sandwich she had left him in the fridge that morning.

She passed the spare room where Leonard was sleeping and stopped. Pushing the door open, she went in. The smell was immediately recognisable: stale urine and sweat; anxiety and sadness. It hit her with such force that she cried out.

Instantly she saw her own father, face grey and desiccated…recalled how his sickness had seemed to permeate everything: her clothes, her hair. It had even seemed to affect her skin, seeping into her very pores. Aged fourteen, her friends had spent hours scrubbing at their faces to keep spots at bay, whereas her hours in the bathroom had been spent trying to rub the smell of death off her skin. It had felt as if she was wearing it: was death itself.

Hand clamped over her mouth, she edged into the room and tried to locate the source of the smell, but it was everywhere: the room was soaked in it. The bed remained unmade and there was a blanket slung over the duvet, as if Leonard had been sleeping on top of the bed rather than in it. Tentatively, Naomi pulled back the thin summer duvet and the smell hit her with intensity: ammonia and shame. Gagging, Naomi opened all the windows and hastily began stripping the bed, trying not to breathe in at the same time. She took the sheets straight downstairs, found some clean ones, and remade the bed. The duvet would need taking to the dry cleaners. Yet another errand, she thought, feeling defeated.

Supper was an almost silent affair. Naomi was too preoccupied, James too tired and Leonard too sad to eat much or talk. This is when we need Scott, thought Naomi; he always seems able to get everyone talking. Her own mind was still too full of her own father for her to even try to start a conversation.

'Thank you, Naomi,' said Leonard, voice stiff.

'There's really no need to thank me, Leonard. We all need to eat,' she added – more shortly than she meant to, but the constant politeness made Naomi feel irrationally irritated. Scott's placid face appeared in her mind, overlaid on Leonard's, and her stomach tensed.

Getting up, she cleared the plates.

'I'm going to head to bed, I think,' said Leonard, standing up stiffly by the table.

'Oh, there's no need to go yet!' Naomi cried, feeling suddenly guilty for snapping.

'No, no, I'm tired. I can read up there, give you your evening…'

Leonard seemed to bow and Naomi wanted to shake him.

'I'm going to go up to my room too,' said James, once they were alone.

'Thank you for spending time with your grandfather earlier,' she said, looking up from the dishwasher.

He looked at her, eyes shadowed and dark. His pupils seemed vast: glittering like ancient stardust. They looked just as they had when she had looked into them when he was born. As if they contained something eternal and all-knowing deep within the black.

'We all need to be listened to,' he replied, echoing her thoughts.

'James!' she called out, but he had already turned and gone.

And now I have to work, she thought. After all that. I still have to work.

And so she did, wading through the marketing reports and the strategy documents until her eyes felt as if they were bleeding.

Logging off finally, she walked out of the room, looking forward to sitting down.

And then she heard crying. Deep, low, sad. Standing on the landing, she realised it wasn't coming from behind the bedroom doors: it was coming from downstairs. It was Scott.

At the top of the stairs, she stood, listening. The sobs were loud but intermittent, like an animal that was wounded but knew it would live; live but always be in pain. Naomi dug her nails into her palms. Her whole body tingled, her eyes prickled; a ripple of misery flowed over her skin.

Her mind whispered: I can't handle this, I can't handle this.

And, stifling a sob of her own, she ran up to the study and logged on. She messaged rapidly and completely unconsciously: *I have to see you. I need to see you.*

She pressed *send* and at that very moment, the moment she had stated her need, she felt ashamed of it, weakened by it. Why? she demanded of herself. Why can't you cope on your own?

Pressing her nails into the skin of her palms again, she felt the need to send him another message to say: *No, don't worry.*

But she logged off. She had to face it. Had to face it.

'This is it,' she whispered to herself. 'Do it now or you're lost for ever.'

She sat and did nothing.

Ten minutes later, still able to hear Scott crying, she went to her room. Staring at herself in the mirror, she wished she could cut her eyes out so she would never have to look at her own cowardice ever again.

Staring at the message she had sent, Naomi could see that he had seen it and read it but he had still not replied. It had been two days now and she had spent all that time wishing she had never sent it. At the same time, she was desperately hoping that he would reply and give her what she wanted.

The computer screen remained unchanged. The way she felt was unchanged too. Elaine was still in the hospice and, while caring for Leonard was hardly onerous – the bed-wetting had stopped – the idea of it was. Sitting up here, things were no different from how they had ever been, but there was a shadow playing across the room: the shadow of her own father's illness, the images of long, grey, dull days when she had been forced to be quiet or to sit and talk or read to him while her mother went out. She had frequently made Naomi do that, and the teenage Naomi had been unable to say no.

That young girl had not known that what her mum was asking was too much, that she was using her daughter as a proxy carer, a role for which she was not remotely emotionally or physically ready.

Naomi rubbed her fingers in small circles against the side of her forehead.

Why was it that even knowing, as she did now, that that was a very difficult, some might say impossible thing for a child to have had to deal with still did not ease her feelings of guilt?

Fidgeting on the hard seat, Naomi looked at the clock. It was 10pm. Not late, and she knew she should go downstairs, but work continued to be a convenient reason not to be in the same room as them: those three men who all needed her but in ways in which she didn't want to be needed. Fear gripped her stomach and shot up to her brain, hitting the base of it: a hot, red pulse of panic, panic and fear radiating out from that thought: the thought of everyone needing her. It felt as if her very self would be torn apart by other people's needs, that there would be nothing left for her; and, threatened, that self began to think of ways to protect itself.

I have to get out, she thought. I have to get out, get out, get away. Somewhere.

What she really wanted to do was log on to a dating site she had heard about, but she truly did not dare to. She had logged on at work once and nearly uploaded a fake profile, but Simon had come in and, as she'd fumbled about trying to close the site down, she had realised how foolish that was. Constantly worried about being caught out, having talked so much about the *many horrors of the internet*, she was utterly convinced of them and of the fact that both Scott and James would be able to see what she had been doing.

No, she thought, I really can't risk it.

She heard her inner voice start up. *Do it the old-fashioned way, then. Go out. Go to a bar.*

Yes, she thought in reply, a warm sensation filling her, the screeching bright red pulse of panic shifting in tone and colour to a richer, deeper sensation of excitement. Yes. *That* I could do...

Chapter Twenty-One

Saturday 29th to Sunday 30 June

David

For every few days that were easy, there was at least one that was hard.

This was where, David thought as he lay in bed, tired and uncomfortable, I could do with a montage.

But there was no editing of the effort. Time passed as it always did: one twenty-four-hour cycle at a time. There were no jump-cuts or fast-forwards. He had to live it, do it.

Kerri had begun to buy in extra fruit and vegetables but she was still filling the fridge and the kitchen cupboards with sweets, crisps and biscuits, and still serving meals that were way beyond what was necessary in terms of portions. She had been ordering fewer takeaways – mostly, he knew, because he was no longer always asking for them – and yet they remained the staple food of the weekends.

It was Saturday morning and it was already hot. The curtains were still drawn but the heat of the sun had filled the room, glowing bright behind the thick, dark cotton, beaming through the tiny gaps in the heavy warp and weft of the cloth.

And today was different because today they were seeing Gary. David got up, opening the curtains to reveal a beautiful blue sky. Feeling a surge of high mood, he tried to damp it down, to keep his emotions in check. It was always best to have low expectations when it came to his dad.

As they all sat in the living room waiting for Gary, Kerri was looking at her tablet, pretending to be absorbed in what she was reading, but David saw how she constantly glanced at the clock, knew that she was as anxious as they were.

Even though it was exactly what they were waiting for, they all started when the doorbell rang.

Kerri went to answer the door.

'Hello,' she said, her voice stiffly polite.

'Hello,' Gary replied, equally stiff and equally polite. 'How are you?'

'I'll get the kids to come out,' she replied.

David winced. Why not pretend to be happy? he wondered. Why did she let him know she was miserable? He hated her for that sometimes, hated her for showing him the emotions that he would never dare to reveal.

'Ready, then, gang?' Gary called out from the doorway. Like a vampire, he needed to be invited to cross the threshold, and he never was invited.

They filed out of the living room, suppressing their excitement for Kerri's sake. This was part of the ritual: the pretence of reluctance, none of them wanting to hurt Kerri's feelings by showing too much enthusiasm for their day out. Gary's car was outside the house and they all climbed in, David at the back where there was more room, and Jess at the front as always.

David smiled at Emily as Gary got in the driving seat.

'Let's go to London, then!' Gary said, as he started the engine.

As soon as the house was out of sight, Emily squeezed David's hand and grinned and Jess called out, 'Whoop!'

Gary laughed and said, 'It's great to see you all. Let's turn it up loud!'

He put the radio on and, with the music blasting out of the open windows, David listened as the girls sang their hearts out, the day ahead full of promise and possibility.

Things began to fall apart in the museum shop. David saw it in Gary's jawline. It had hardened and tensed, the muscle in his left cheek beginning to pulse. Gary rarely looked at him and so he could observe him undetected. The weight of his father's shame at his son's appearance was one that David was aware he would be carrying long after the excess pounds had been shed, and now, after five weeks, they really were starting to go. Even he could see it now. His clothes were looser and his skin clearer. He had even caught himself smiling the other day and had been amazed at the difference that made to his face and how he felt.

He had been waiting for Gary to comment, but he hadn't.

'I said one thing…' Gary exhaled the words wearily, each syllable stretched out with a long sigh.

David saw him glance at his watch. And you've only been around them for a few hours, he thought, watching the girls as they squabbled over whose sparkly ruler was the prettiest.

He felt a wave of love for Kerri at that moment, something he rarely felt when she was actually there in the same room, the same house. Loved her for always being there. Loved her for loving them even though they were like this. Even though *he* was like this.

Gary gave him a brief glance. 'You want to get something?' he asked. 'A book or a DVD?'

'No. No, thank you,' said David.

'Suit yourself.'

Gary went back to the girls. 'Oh, go on,' he said, 'pick one more thing each, then, and we can go for lunch…'

'I want this too!' cried Jess.

'Yes, yes, OK,' he snapped back.

'I'll wait outside,' said David.

He stood outside the shop and checked his phone. Nothing. No James meant no texts. He thought about texting Kerri then changed his mind.

Looking around instead, he noticed how busy and noisy it was. Why did parents take toddlers to museums? David wondered, as he looked at the miserable faces, little bodies straining against pushchair straps or, worse, the forced enjoyment visible on all the faces around him.

He smiled. He knew why. People wanted to pretend life hadn't changed, or wanted to pretend that this was a 'valuable' experience, where playing in the sandpit on a sunny day was not. People were fucking weird sometimes.

'Right,' said Gary as he came out. 'Lunch. I've booked somewhere a bit different...' He walked towards the exit purposefully.

Going into the sushi restaurant, they were greeted by the sight of the open central counter where the fish was being prepared. Emily backed away and into David a little. She looked up at him, her eyes watery with terror at the sight of glistening fish eyes and quivering slabs of purple-pink tuna.

David had learnt to give new experiences a go, but the girls were as unwilling as ever. It was pretty typical of his dad, he now realised, to make things as uncomfortable as possible. He called it *learning*, called it *expanding your comfort zone*, but, in reality, it just made everyone want to retreat to the couch and eat chips.

Jess was more enthusiastic, but then she always was with anything Gary suggested.

'I love the salmon!' she cried. 'And these little plates! Can I have a purple one!'

'Yes, of course!' Gary said, glancing smugly round the room, making sure that sufficient people were witnessing what an exceptional job he had done to raise a child so keen on the concept of raw fish for lunch.

David whispered down to Emily, 'Be all right – ask for the katsu curry with the sauce on the side – it's like fried chicken and rice, you'll like that.'

There were times when having had a best mate with a bigger weekend lunch budget than you paid off, he thought. He and James had gone through a phase of liking the deep-fried dishes in the local branch of a popular Japanese chain when it had first opened up in town. Ignoring the familiar pang of loss at the thought of his friend, he wondered what he himself should eat here. Lots of sashimi and some soup? And maybe some edamame beans?

He smiled internally – he was getting the hang of this now. He offered up his usual silent prayer of thanks to Lustig, his guru in the battle against sugar.

Gary manoeuvred them into a booth; they looked at the menus and Gary said, 'I was going to order lots of the hand rolls, you'll all enjoy those.'

'Oh, yes!' said Jess, still overdoing the enthusiasm.

'A mixed selection of the hand rolls for four, then, please,' said Gary to the waitress who was waiting right by them.

David nudged Emily. Emily stared at the table.

'Can you make that for two, please,' David said clearly, looking at the waitress with a confidence he had never felt before. 'Emily would prefer the katsu curry with the sauce on the side and I would like a large miso soup, some greens and a sashimi platter.'

Gary looked at David, clearly seeing him for the first time that day. He looked pleased but also confused. The waitress scribbled.

'You've lost weight,' Gary said.

'He's done so well,' Emily jumped in. 'He's been amazing!'

And David just nodded. The phrase, one so stuffed with social approval, seemed to have a different texture at this point. It was not just about his having lost physical weight but also about having lost the weight of it *on* himself. His sense of self was no longer dictated by his size: he was beginning to discover his true self beneath it, and also, ironically, because of it.

As the food arrived, Gary looked at David's order. 'That looks delicious,' he said, envy making his voice crack a little.

And it was.

Several hours later, they walked back into the house, subdued. Gary had taken them to a show in the afternoon, which had been amazing, but both girls were now overtired. Emily had grey smudges under her eyes and Jess was yawning as they went into the living room. Fortunately, they were also too tired to bicker.

Kerri was slumped in front of the television. On the table, despite knowing that they had been out and eating all day, she had laid out bowl after bowl of crisps and sweets. A reward for coming home – and for looking less than happy.

'Hi,' she said. 'Come and sit down! How was your day? Was it fun?'

'Was all right…' the girls replied, and Kerri poured lemonade into glasses and passed one to David.

'And you? Did you have fun?' she asked, eyes begging him to say no.

'I'm going to get some water,' he said, getting up, wanting to get away from the need in her eyes. Feeling light from his lunch, he went back into the living room and, seeing Kerri trying desperately to ask and yet not ask for more details about their day, he looked at the bowls, at the evidence of that need, and felt a moment of panic.

'Please,' she said, again, 'please have something…'

And so he ate for her, and, as he did so, he could feel the sofa soft and yielding beneath him. It was comfortable, but it was also death.

Over the rest of the weekend, David's high mood continued in spite of the assault on his system. Kerri, delighted by David's appetite for what she offered and by what she had heard of Gary's extravagant lunch, insisted on taking them out on Sunday to the local barbecue restaurant, where she over-ordered and they all overate.

The afternoon was spent once again on the sofa. Like a bank of approaching fog, Monday rolled slowly and inevitably towards the room, filling the horizon with gloom.

When David came back into the living room after going upstairs to say goodnight to the girls, Kerri was wiping her eyes and blowing her nose. Then she did that thing that all mums did when they were trying to convince you that they hadn't just been crying: she smiled, a strained, watery and red-eyed smile that fooled no one.

David knew she didn't like her job, had always known that she worked locally for convenience rather then preference. He also knew that much of that was down to Gary and the limitations that both his absence and his own preference for the girls to stay at their private school imposed. He still felt a little queasy from lunch but, seeing Kerri's face, he knew she would want company tonight: food company. He felt able to do that, to meet her need, but he also wished he knew how to talk to her about how little it would really help. He knew that now, or rather he knew it most of the time, and, most of the time, knowing was enough to stop the behaviour.

He had been watching less TV of late, preferring to read in his room, but he knew he would have to stay in here tonight. Sitting down, he went to the TV menu and began flicking through it.

'The – the…appointment…it's coming round so fast,' she said, her voice a whisper.

'Oh,' he said. He still couldn't quite believe that she was looking for sympathy about something she had chosen to do. He looked away, trying to keep his feelings hidden.

'I suppose I'm just worried about it,' she said, voice still quiet. 'But I'm sure it will be fine.'

'Why would you even go through with it if you didn't think it would be fine?' he asked, trying to keep the challenge out of his voice but not entirely successful.

'I'm sorry, David,' she said. 'It's the only thing that's going to work for me. I can't do it on my own – I've tried and I can't. You've done well, really well, but I…well, I just can't. If a diet was going to work for me, then it would have worked by now.'

'But it's not about dieting,' he said. 'It's about making bigger changes, and making them for good.'

'I just need to eat less,' she said. 'That's what the band will do: make me eat less.'

'But it's about *what* you eat, too,' he continued. 'You need to change how and what you eat. Not just the amount.'

She looked at him a little blankly.

She was an intelligent woman, he knew that, so why did she not get it? And why was she not curious about it? In fact, why did *no one* want to hear about it?

He hadn't talked about it much, but he knew from the complete lack of questions he had been asked since he had lost the weight how little anyone was really interested. No one wanted to know. Or rather, if it wasn't down to a fad diet or a pill or some other magic wand being waved, they didn't want to know. The idea that what might actually be necessary were slow, gradual and especially *permanent* changes to how one ate and behaved seemed to appeal to no one. He understood that, he totally got it, but, knowing how much better he felt already, he just wanted to grab and shake Kerri, and everyone else at the school, grab them by the shoulders and yell in their faces.

He supposed people just didn't want their own ideas about how things worked to be challenged, and he also suspected that being able to blame an individual's greed and sloth was much simpler than facing up to the complex reality. He knew that himself: the whole thing made his brain hurt sometimes and even after weeks of reading he still felt as if he had so much to learn.

The issue was so tied up in social, cultural and emotional issues that it was impossible to unpick them all. Tangled and complex; if he tugged out one idea it just tightened the knot somewhere else. But he knew enough to have got where he was now and, even with the eating this weekend, he was hopeful that he might go down another notch on his belt this week. That was his measure: those much-hated billowing grey polycotton school trousers. Every time he felt them get that little bit looser, he felt a surge of joy.

He got up to get some water. His stomach sank when he saw the food in the kitchen, the bright cardboard packaging of yet more brown and yellow food. Sunday night was also snack night. He opened the fridge: there was still salad in there, but not much. He couldn't face any more yellow food. He was done. The last day and a half had been a fun respite from his diet, but there was a heaviness in his gut that he had not felt for a while, a greasy weight that came from suddenly eating badly again. He was less used to it now and had seen a fresh crop of spots on his cheek this evening: the first in weeks. His skin was like an early warning system of something going wrong: like the first scattered protestors outside a badly behaved government's building, red placards raised in protest.

He just had to make one last effort for Kerri's sake. The memory that eating the way he had eaten this weekend used to be the norm reminded him of just how far he had come.

Going back into the room and seeing her soft, tearstained face, he thought, *just one more evening*.

Chapter Twenty-Two

Monday 1st to Saturday 6th July

David

Having already been told off in English that Monday morning for not listening, David felt low. The weekend's food binge had left him feeling worse than he could remember.

I used to feel like this all the time, he thought, his head pounding and his stomach knotting.

He just wanted to make it to the end of the day.

He gave a good impression of listening during maths. Taking the homework sheets and putting them in his bag, he felt the weight of his overstuffed bag increase as each class teacher added to the load. They all expected the best of you, all wanted you to give their subject priority, all wanted their pound of flesh.

It began at lunchtime. The standard discomfort in his stomach was replaced with sharp, stabbing cramps. He ate very little. He was sitting with two boys from his form, Ravi and Eduardo. They were chattering away but David wasn't even pretending to listen. The pains he had been ignoring all day, that he had thought he had become used to, were now worse than ever. He could feel the sweat forming on his brow, the individual pores swelling and releasing their beads of moisture. His face felt hot and clammy but his back was cold, slick with damp sweat. His crotch also felt damp. A line of sweat dribbled down the back of his right knee. Twitching his legs and fidgeting on his chair, David tried to make himself more comfortable, but the movement shifted something in his stomach and the cramps intensified.

'You all right?' said Ravi, his mouth full.

David saw the chewed-up chips in the other boy's mouth. As if in high definition, he saw the mushed potato, thick with butter and saliva, being crushed into a bolus by the bright white molars. He could see Ravi's tongue shifting the potato pulp around his mouth, pushing it into the centre and then to the back, masticating and moistening, then he saw him swallow, the ball of food pressed downwards towards the throat by the rippling of the boy's long, thin oesophagus.

David staggered up. His small plastic chair skittered backwards and fell to the floor. Lurching slightly, he stood and walked as fast as he could towards the double doors.

Still sweating, stomach a clenched ball of pain, he stumbled towards the nearest toilets. He would have tried to get to the upper floor if he could, as far away as possible from most of the other kids, but he knew he would never make it.

'David!'

It was James's voice that rang out behind him, full of concern. Waving his right arm at him, David dived into the toilets and fell straight into a cubicle. The toilets were empty but he knew better than to expect them to stay that way. There was no getting away from this now. Nothing else he could do. After what he had eaten over the last two days, he knew what was coming.

Still sweating, his in-breaths sharp and shallow and his out-breaths long and ragged, he fumbled at his trouser button. His fingers were mercifully nimble, though his wrists were slippery with the sweat that now covered his whole body in a damp slick.

Unable to contain the sound, he groaned as he sat down. The cold black plastic felt momentarily cooling but, as he shifted his bulk on the tiny seat, he could feel his thighs slipping. Pressing his palms out on to the sides of the cubicle, he groaned again as his stomach clenched and twisted.

Holding his breath and straining, he began to push. He had often fantasised about shitting the fat away, about having the most enormous shit ever conceived of and ridding his body of itself with it. He wanted to feel emptied, cleaned out, but this was not what was happening here. Crying out as the cramps sharpened, he bent forward and over.

There was noise coming from outside the cubicle now. He could hear the whispers and high chatter as he stared and groaned, bent and struggled.

As he gave another cry, a hot, sticky stream hit the toilet bowl, a sour smell rising up like stagnant steam from a toxic bath. There was no relief, or release, just pain as his stomach and bowels contracted sharply.

Still sweating and bent over, David felt as if he had been sitting here for an eternity. It was as if this shit was his entire life: that there had never been and would never be anything else, just him trapped here, with his own excrement, for ever.

Eventually the cramping began to ease and the stream slowed, spraying the interior of the bowl. Using handful after handful of tissue, David cleaned himself, mopping at his clammy brow and legs. Flushing, he had to wait, as only the third flush even began to be effective.

It was then that he heard the laughter.

Part of him wished he could be that fat person, could be the funny, happy fat person that laughed off something like this, make light of it. But he was not that boy. The smell was disgusting, and the gaggle of teenage boys who had gathered in the toilets made a huge pantomime of fainting and gagging and flailing at the smell as if it were visible, the way farts were visible in comics.

Head bowed, David walked out of the toilets. The relief he felt was immense, but the humiliation that replaced it hurt just as much, and he headed for the main doors, desperate for some air.

James was standing outside, holding the bag he had left behind in his rush to leave the dining hall. Breathing in deeply, David could feel his face being cooled by the crisp air and he squinted slightly at the sharpening sun. James reached out and touched his arm. Flinching, David snatched at his bag and ran towards the school gates, the cries of 'Shitter! Shitter!' echoing behind him as he ran outside and off through the gates.

That evening he hid in his room. Texting Kerri to say he felt ill and not to disturb him, he lay on his bed, feeling more alone than he ever had felt before. And, before he knew it, he had reached for the drawer...

When he woke up the next morning, the cramps and the sweating were back. Having binged again before sleeping, the shame all too much, he had slept badly, and the sense of failure, of having let himself down, was immense. Lying in bed, unable to even think about getting up, he stared at the ceiling. How to cope with today? He couldn't. He just couldn't.

Then his phone made a sound it had not made for a very long time. That special message tone. James's message tone.

David looked at his phone. The text read: *I'm here.*

On the path outside the house, the two boys looked at each other. David didn't think he had ever been more pleased to see anyone ever.

'All right?' said James, eyes looking directly at his friend.

'All right,' said David, looking straight back at him.

'Brace, brace?'

'Hell, yeah...'

They smiled at each other and then, side by side, they walked up the road together.

Maybe, thought David, maybe it won't be so bad after all.

There was a moment of silence and then James began to talk – to talk about everything other than the reason why he was there that morning, and for that David loved him.

'So, yeah, Mum has been having a wobbly about something and my nan is really sick and my grandad is living with us and I couldn't, you know, talk to you, and so yeah, it's all been kind of...' He went to say *shitty* and then changed it to, 'Rubbish, really.'

'Same. Mum's gone mental and decided to get a gastric band. The girls argue constantly and I'm trying to lose weight and seem to have turned myself into even more of a school laughing stock as a result.'

'SSDD?'

'SSDD indeedy.'

They smiled at each other. Early Stephen King books were practically free to download and they had read most of them. *Same shit, different day.*

Though to be fair, thought David, there had been rather more shit yesterday than most days. He flushed at the memory and James glanced at his friend, concern creasing his spotty forehead. 'It'll be all right,' he said, punching his friend lightly on the arm.

'Yeah,' said David, unconvinced.

They got on the bus. It started the moment they boarded.

'Look! Here comes Shitter!' cried one boy, from the year above them.

'Shitter! Shitter! Shitter!'

David bowed his head. Best to look down and ignore it. He had expected this but that didn't make it any easier. Like any sort of bullying, it just needed to be taken. There was nothing to be gained from rehearsing quips or comebacks, from learning martial arts to defeat the leader of the baddies. No, there were no Hollywood moments to be had here, not among the stained seats and stale smell of the bus.

It wasn't that he thought he deserved it, he knew he didn't, but he knew that the mob needed to vent. He was trying to learn to take it all less personally, and so in a way this was good practice, but again, and as always, that did not make it any easier.

He coped with the shouts and yells as he got off the bus. He coped with the mutters and comments in the corridor. He coped with the sniggers and the glances. All of it washed over him more easily than he was expecting and, glancing at James, who was by his side on the walk to form class, he knew that having his friend back was mostly responsible for that. He punched him on the arm. James grinned back, and David knew that he completely understood.

Naomi

Going into the bathroom at work, Naomi saw a few of the younger girls from the office in front of the mirrors, putting on make-up and straightening their hair with tongs. Smiling at them, she slipped into a cubicle with her bag and proceeded to get changed. Organising tonight had been effortless.

'I'm out with work on Friday night. Won't be back till late.'

'Oh, sure, OK.'

At the time, she had felt annoyed that Scott hadn't even bothered to ask her where she was going or who with, but now she didn't care. No questions meant no need to lie. And even just saying she was going out had given her a delicious buzz. She had realised then how much she had missed it: missed deceiving him. It wasn't a nice feeling but then, right now Naomi didn't *feel* very nice. She felt frustrated, bored and angry. And also, as she pulled the slim-fitting summer shift dress on to her frame, she felt excited: very, very excited.

Coming out of the toilet, wedges making her legs look lean and the dress fitting her slim frame perfectly, its cobalt-blue background and large print very flattering against her slightly tanned skin and blonde hair, she began to reapply some of her make-up.

At the station, it felt oddly thrilling to walk to the opposite platform: to be going out rather than home. Her hopes were as high as the shoes she was wearing. And as the train pulled out of the platform, the air-conditioning welcome after the sun-baked platform, Naomi felt her excitement increase. She visualised herself standing outside a busy bar, a cold beer bottle in her hand, or perhaps sipping a fruity cocktail, legs looking good as she surveyed the people standing around her, everyone cheerful in the evening sunshine.

Shoulders hunching in with glee, Naomi stared out of the window and willed the train on to its destination.

Sunshine and smiles and cold beer she had expected; the reaction of people around her, she had not. Having been to a few bars where she had stood in a corner quietly, catching a few people's eyes and getting a few warm smiles and nods but feeling unsure and more nervous than she had anticipated, she had come into a bar near the mainline station (and the late-night taxi rank – she was nothing if not organised) which had a small dance floor and, as the fourth beer kicked in, she found herself swaying along rhythmically to the music.

There was something special about being alone, about not having to make small talk, about just taking in what was around her and seeing everyone so happy. She remembered this from summer nights out when she had been younger: the sense of optimism and excitement. The air seemed to hum with potential.

It was eleven now. Too late to be outside unless you were a smoker and so the bar was busy, the sound of conversations all around her making her feel both included and yet gloriously free. Swaying further into the dance floor, not drunk but high on freedom and all the potential, she heard a song she recognised from the radio, and with a tiny whoop of excitement she began to dance. Feet and arms moving to the music, feeling her hair swing, the long blonde strands brushing against her bare shoulders, she felt alive in a way that she hadn't since...

Mike.

Dancing harder, she pushed the thought away, absorbing herself in the music.

There were other people dancing too, and as the song shifted into a different, harder beat, she opened her eyes and looked around, getting her bearings and deciding that she needed another drink.

Smiling as she shifted through the swaying throng, she pushed her way through to the bar. Looking around, she suddenly remembered why she was here. Half laughing to herself, she wondered if she still needed or wanted to meet anyone. Just being here, just being herself, felt like enough.

Then, as she stood sipping the water she had ordered, she saw a young man on the dance floor: broad shoulders and thick hair, his eyes bright as he bounced along with his friend, his smooth skin shining under the spotlights. Naomi felt a thrill of pleasure run through her.

If it happens it happens, she thought; no chasing. That is just...well, undignified.

She smiled to herself again, mouth turning up in a wry curve that made her eyes dance in as lively a way as her body on the dance floor.

'I would love to know what you're smiling about,' said a voice.

Naomi looked up. It was him. The smooth skin, thick hair and broad shoulders she had caught a glimpse of on the dance floor were now right in front of her.

'Hello,' she said, smiling even more. 'I was just thinking how much fun this place is.'

'Yes,' he replied, not bothering to conceal his glance as he looked her up and down. 'I saw you earlier; you looked as if you were enjoying yourself.' He glanced around her. 'Where are your friends?'

'Oh, I'm here on my own,' Naomi replied, looking down, suddenly feeling silly.

'Oh!' he said, surprised. 'That is so cool! I wish I was brave enough do that. I'm here with my mates and one of them is so drunk he's spent the last hour in the loo. I keep losing the other one. It's so fucking annoying.'

Naomi laughed. 'Yes,' she said, revelling in his directness. 'I bet it fucking is.'

He grinned. 'Jesus, hearing you swear is hot...'

'Really?' She laughed, hitting his arm gently in mock protest. She felt a jolt as she moved her fist away, self-conscious, and also hyper-aware of the firm muscular skin she had touched.

'Haha,' he laughed. 'I deserved that! It was hot, though. *You* are hot.'

Naomi looked at him, eyes a little wide. She had got used to Mike's messages, but being spoken to this way, this directly, in person, was intense.

He smiled at her again, his eyes suddenly serious. 'I was going to smoke,' he said. 'Want to come outside?'

'Yes,' she replied. 'OK.'

He took her hand and, with another cheeky smile, led her to the door. As they stepped out of the stuffy bar into the cool street, Naomi saw the harsh lighting and immediately worried that she would look old under them.

'Wow,' he said. 'Look at you. You look great.'

He lit up, and took a long pull on the hand-rolled cigarette. She stared at the concrete, wishing she felt less self-conscious. She had seen, in the brighter street lights, that he was no more than twenty-five.

'I've got such a thing for older women,' he went on. 'How old are you?'

'Forty-four,' she said, wishing that what he had just said made her feel annoyed rather than aroused. 'And you?' she asked, voice a little firmer now that he had verbalised his desire for her.

'I'm twenty-three...' he said. 'Are you married?' He dropped the cigarette and lit another.

'Divorced,' she replied, with the speed and ease of a pre-planned response.

'Sexy,' he said, looking directly at her.

'Is it?' she asked, genuinely curious.

'Oh, yes... Very.'

He watched her as he smoked. She felt *seen*: his eyes took her in and looked at her with such naked desire and wanting that she could feel herself responding just to his gaze. It had been so long since anyone had looked at her like that: she had seen it on Mike's face that second time, but not before, and certainly not since. Jonathan hadn't looked at her like that – that was why, she realized, she had felt low rather than high after their encounter.

'What do you do?' she asked politely, feeling the need to enquire.

'I work in sales,' he said. 'It sucks, but I'm good at it. I'm saving up to go travelling. I want to hike the Himalayas. And then coast it round to the hot, beachy part of India to get laid...'

She smiled at him. Why did they all want to go travelling? She heard it at work all the time. So unimaginative.

And, as they talked, she knew she didn't really like him. Full of himself, direct bordering on rude and with little to say for himself other than small talk, he was hardly engaging. But then she glanced at his neck, shoulders and arms. She took in the thick, wavy hair, the smooth cheeks, and she knew exactly what she hoped would happen next.

He dropped the second cigarette, crushing it casually under his shoe. His dark brown eyes were on hers as he pulled her closer. Feeling his arms slip around her waist, she felt him run them over the soft fabric of her dress. Pulling her into his chest, he buried his smooth cheek into her long hair. Her skin tingled as he breathed in deeply.

'God, you smell good. I bet you taste even better.'

She pulled back to look at him. 'Want to kiss me and find out?'

'I didn't mean your mouth,' he said, eyes darker now. 'But that'll do for a start.'

And, his hand passing smoothly up her back and over her neck into her hair, he tugged her head back and gave her a hard, dry kiss.

Feeling a moment of panic that someone she knew might see her, Naomi felt herself start to pull away, to resist – but she really didn't want to. She had done this before and no one had noticed. No one really cared what she did.

So, this time, she thought, feeling arms around her, feeling the cool air and the glances of disinterested, drunk strangers, this time I'm going to do it and I'm going to enjoy every bloody minute. Because I also know it won't last...

Waking up late and alone in bed at home the following morning, Naomi stretched out under the warm duvet, enjoying the delicious ache in her feet and calves from wearing high-heeled shoes for too long, and also enjoying the tingling of her lips from too much kissing. She brought her fingers to her face; her cool fingertips felt soothing against the tender soreness of her mouth.

Squeezing her shoulders together and grinding her bottom into the mattress with delight, she stretched out under the duvet one more time and then kicked it off with one leg and got up. Stretching again, she felt lighter than she had in months. The weeks of heaviness, of lying there in the bright sunshine of the early summer wondering what the point of getting up was, had been happily replaced with a sense of optimism and excitement. Ed. Ed. Ed. Her mind was full of his touches, of his breath hot in her ear, his hand tugging her hair, his mouth hard on hers. Knowing what was awaiting her downstairs (Leonard, Scott, James. Demands, misery, sadness), she quickly sat back on the bed and decided to check her phone. Having left her at 2am, Ed had texted her all the way home. Teasing her, suggesting dates when they could meet again. Waiting for her phone to come to life, Naomi remembered having hidden it in her dressing gown pocket so that she could look at it under the covers, look at it before having to face everyone else in the house.

The phone buzzed reassuringly. Suppressing a squeal of delight, she kicked her feet a little against the base of the bed. Opening up his messages, Naomi grinned with delight. I need this, she said to herself. I won't apologise for it any longer. And as long as I'm careful, really careful, who needs to know? No one. No one will know and no one will get hurt.

Reading over what he had said, she grinned. *I can't believe I met someone as hot as you* and *When can I see you again? I'm free most of the next week…*

Naomi looked around the curtained but still bright bedroom, at all the evidence of her married life, and thought, I can have Ed. I can have him and there are so many more, so many others and maybe I can have them too. The sense of abundance, of potential, felt dizzying, and she grinned again. And then, seeing when he had sent the last of the messages, she resolved to ignore them until at least this evening. He wanted a cool, detached yet hot older woman, and she felt confident enough in herself now to play that role.

Slipping on some cool summer clothes, Naomi tripped down the stairs, legs bare and heart and head light as the day that she finally felt able to look forward to.

Everyone was in the living room when she came downstairs. They were always in the living room. Leonard was sitting in the armchair; James was on the sofa staring at his phone, Scott was staring blankly at the TV. So much of their weekend time was spent waiting for it to be time to visit Elaine and, while that time dragged on, it also never seemed long enough to do anything useful with.

They had got into the habit of eating on the way, breaking up the day with what was always a lacklustre meal out but at least one that Naomi did not have to think about, prepare or clean up after.

As she entered the silent room, Naomi consciously dimmed the lightness that last night had given her, switching the internal blaze down to a more appropriate, subdued glow.

'Morning, everyone,' she said softly. 'Can I get anyone some fresh coffee?'

Scott smiled at her, welcoming and gentle as always. 'Thanks, hon, I'll help.' He got up and they went into the sun-bright kitchen together.

'We should all sit in here,' said Naomi, 'It's so dark in the living room.'

She stifled a yawn, the brightness stinging her tired eyes a little.

'Oh, you know that Dad likes to be comfortable. Anyway, sleepy,' Scott continued, as he poured some coffee from the jug on the side, 'enjoy your night out with your friends?'

'Oh, yes,' she said. 'Thank you so much for letting me get out, I needed the break. We should make sure you do it too some time...'

'I like to come home,' he said. 'To you and James.'

Naomi smiled into her coffee and nodded. She could handle being at home if she could be out too; it seemed to her like the perfect balance. She shifted on her tired feet; the aches would be a wonderful reminder all day of the hours she had spent swaying and kissing in the noise-filled dark.

She heard her phone buzz on the side where she had placed it to charge. The promise of that sound filled her with delight.

'I'll do a few things round the house and then we can go out to eat and visit your mum. I might need to stop and pick up some things for supper. We need to stop eating takeaways so much – who knows how long your mum might be sick for. We need to make sure we're all looking after ourselves.'

'Yes, I agree,' Scott said smiling at her. 'Thanks so much for everything you've done, for Mum and Dad; I know it's not been easy.'

Naomi kissed him on the cheek and said, 'Thank you, but I haven't exactly been great. You've been amazing… It must be so hard for you.' And for once she wasn't saying it out of guilt, or obligation, or with an undertone of resentment. Knowing that she was able to get what she wanted really made her feel more compassionate.

Later, after a long, slow lunch and the long, slow hours of sitting in the bright yet uniquely depressing hospice, Naomi hid in the bathroom back at home, reading over the messages. He had been texting her all afternoon. Apparently it was important to let her know how much thinking of her made his dick hard.

Sitting there, before the task of sorting laundry and then preparing food and then clearing up and settling in for a long, quiet, dull evening, she texted back.

I do love hearing that. How are you?

The reply came back instantly.

Great! Where have you been all day? I missed you.

I know, she thought – why do you think I ignored you? I have learnt something in the last few months…

Just busy, she texted back. *Not busy now, though…maybe you can tell me what's going to happen next time I see you…*

You going to book a hotel?

I am, she replied back, *next week. Wednesday, I think you said.*

Oh, fuck…well, then I am going to want you to be lying on the bed in your best underwear waiting for me…

Really? Something silky? she teased.

Oh, yes, he said. *Something silky and classy. And then I'm going to fuck you like an animal.*

Naomi's skin tingled and, grinning at the phone, she went out of the bathroom and into her room to start sorting laundry.

As she began to ball socks and fold Scott's underwear, she texted back: *Filthy boy, tell me more...*

Chapter Twenty-Three

Sunday 7th to Tuesday 9th July

David

It's good to have some company again, thought David, as he sat alone in his room on Sunday night. James was on Messenger and so he had him there while he did his homework. Having eaten the roast chicken that Kerri had served, but avoided the garlic bread, coleslaw and wedges, and the ice cream that followed, he didn't feel full, but he didn't feel hungry either.

He had always thought that he *needed* to be full, to be stuffed, but he was increasingly seeing that not being full meant he could concentrate better and also that he slept better.

As he squinted at the work, he sat back, yawning, and rubbed at his eyes. There seemed to be several paths that were open to him. He could see the choices others had made and wondered at their passion, their commitment. But he didn't want to start a food cult, he didn't want to be a chef, he didn't want to be a crusader for health or an activist against Big Food. All he wanted was for food to be back in its rightful place: in the background of his life, a side dish, not the main course. For it to be something he enjoyed but not the *only* thing that he enjoyed. Something he thought about but not *all* he thought about.

Mostly, he just wanted to be David. A David without a layer of fat hiding him from the world. A David who just was, who could get on with just growing up and doing the important work of figuring out who he was and what he was here for.

Whatever the hell that means, he thought to himself wryly. I might give myself a break before I start trying to figure out the ultimate answer to life, the universe and everything. This phrase from one of his favourite books made him smile again.

His phone beeped. He winced as he read the message: an image of a backed-up toilet. *Shitter. The toilets at school are terrified of your fat arse now…*

He had had many like this all last week. Kids got other kids to pass on phone numbers and, while David could limit who he was friends with online, it was harder to control who had access to his mobile number. He deleted the text. The trick was to not take it personally. He was not naïve enough to panic, to see this for anything other than the pettiness that it was. He longed to grow up, to be free of this – and yet he had seen and heard Kerri in tears after unkind comments had been made to her, or after people whom she'd thought were friends had let her down. It never stops, he thought; you just have to not let it grind you down.

Of course it did sometimes, and that was OK too; it was OK, he realised, to feel shit. Feeling shit didn't kill you but the shit you did to stop feeling shit…well, that definitely could.

He grinned at the profanities, and the idea. 'Ideal cat poster material,' he said out loud, still half laughing. And he opened up the presentation and began to wonder how he could fit that phrase into it, ideally without the swearing.

Or perhaps, he grinned to himself, with it…

David had asked for some of his teacher's time at the end of the school day, but he was regretting it now. Walking down the stuffy corridor, the lingering smells of sweat and deodorant and burnt matches were almost solid in the air. The smell of students, like their noise, filled and echoed in every open space in the school. David shuddered despite the heat: it was nerves rather than a chill. He knew he had to do this, but he really didn't want to.

God, was there anything that wasn't like that?

No, actually, he told himself, I don't think there is.

And he was increasingly getting used to the fact. Getting used to the mental resistance and learning to ignore it.

With a small smile he walked into the room. Seeing Mr Holmes's welcoming smile back made him feel better.

'I have the presentation on this,' David said, holding out a memory stick.

'Great,' said his teacher, taking it from him. 'Well, let's pop it into the laptop and then you can take it from there. It'll be like the real thing then. I'll sit back here or to the side, whatever you prefer...'

'To the side, I guess,' said David, face flushing. 'I've not read it out loud before.'

'It's OK, that's why I'm here...'

David watched as Mr Holmes got the presentation up on to the screen. Part of him wished it would take until the end of time for him to do that so that he would never, ever have to read the presentation out loud. Ever.

It took about thirty seconds.

The front page of the presentation appeared on the screen.

'OK, David, when you're ready...'

David shifted from side to side on his feet, coughed nervously, and began.

'Why am I fat? I know why you *think* I'm fat. I know why I thought I was fat. I thought it was because I ate too much and I didn't get enough exercise. Put a calorie in, take a calorie out, then shake it all about... *That*, we are told, is what it's all about...'

He hesitated and looked at Mr Holmes. Seeing the teacher's encouraging eyes, he looked back down and carried on.

'But what if it was a bit more complicated than that?'

'Ben Goldacre?' interjected the older man.

'Yes,' replied David.

'Perfect!' he said, smiling.

David grinned back, took a deep breath, and continued…

Ten minutes later he came to the end and stopped, out of breath now but also flushed with excitement.

Matthew stood up and took the boy by the shoulders, smiling broadly.

'Wow!' he said, 'that was fantastic!'

'Really?'

'Really.'

They sat down together on the nearest bench.

'I realised,' David said to Matthew, 'that the worse I felt, the more I ate; but then I just realised that I always still felt rubbish afterwards.'

Matthew paused and then looked at him closely. 'Feeling shitty won't kill you, but the stuff you do to stop feeling shitty just might.'

David's eyes widened a little. He and Matthew grinned at each other.

'Yes,' he replied, 'that's it exactly.'

'You've done a great job there, David. Really. Some serious work has gone into that and it shows. I'm so proud of you. And just look at you. The fact that you look the way you do now shows that what you say is true: you are living proof of it.'

David looked down. Hardly anyone had commented on the weight he had lost. He felt both delighted and embarrassed.

'I know how hard it is – I had to lose a few stone as a teenager and so I really know,' Matthew added, 'But what you've told me today blows me away. You've taken the science and the way we live and made it human. It's perfect. You might just need to take the word *wank* out of it, though… Cloughie will have a heart attack!'

They both laughed. Hearing a teacher use the headmaster's nickname was funny, thought David.

Matthew shut the laptop down and handed David back the memory stick. 'I take it you've got that backed up?'

'Oh, yes, of course!'

There was a pause.

'I know all that stuff,' said Matthew, beginning to tidy his desk. 'but somehow you made it more real, more relevant. And it's you,' he added. 'That is the key to this: *you*. You are the visuals to this. Look at you, you're looking great,' he repeated. 'The knowledge is already making a difference!'

'Well, it was your lessons that got me started,' said David, looking down still.

Matthew looked up at the boy in surprise. 'Really?'

David looked back at him and smiled. 'Really.'

There was silence as the two looked at each other. A moment of communion, a moment of being heard.

And, in that silence and space, David felt the need to share the deeper understanding he had gained. But how to say it? How to admit that he talked back to the voices in his head? How to admit that they were there at all? He breathed out unsteadily.

'The other day,' he said, quietly, 'I was lying in bed and I could hear a voice in my head. You know the one I mean? The one that never seems to shut up?'

Matthew looked closely and steadily at the boy. He nodded, listening.

David paused again and then took another slow breath.

'So, it was saying what it always says: *You're lazy, you're fat, you're stupid, you're rubbish*. And, for the first time, I didn't believe it… I thought about what I knew, what I had learnt, and I knew the words weren't true…'

Matthew stepped forward and, taking the boy in his arms, he held him.

After a few moments, they parted. Nothing else needed to be said. They both understood.

Matthew

Matthew sat in the classroom long after David had gone. His phone buzzed and he ignored it. Then, knowing what he needed to do, he went home.

He called out Polly's name as he entered the hallway. Nothing.

Good, he thought to himself.

Walking into the box room, his senses seemed heightened. Through the hazy cloud of dust motes in the air he could tell that she had only recently left, and she had, he could see now, been very busy. It was on afternoons like this, bright summer days, that the old sash windows in this converted town house helped make up for the constant cold that their size caused. Flooding the little room with light, they also gave Matthew a clear view of the bright, cloudless sky.

As he watched the dust settle, he also took a clear look at his flat for what seemed like the first time in months.

In every corner of the room there were piles of leaflets, boxes stuffed full of sheets, sheafs of paper. And it wasn't just one pile, it was all over the room. Rolled-up posters, folders stuffed full of research and notes. She must have been busy – pulling it all together, into a pile in the crazily tiny box room that justified his landlord charging him a small fortune for what he insisted was a two-bed flat.

Matthew began to look through the boxes, quickly in case she came back, but also feeling calm.

Right at the bottom, he found the one he was looking for. Taking it to the sofa, he sat down and opened it up.

It was the work he had done for the coursework he had set. Flicking though the pages, he smiled. Reading the words and hearing his own voice, he could remember the enthusiasm with which he had designed that piece of work. At the back he saw some handwritten notes on a printed-off sheet. Block capitals. Blue pen.

DON'T FORGET, it read, THAT THIS IS WHAT IT IS ALL ABOUT.

He stared at the words. He had forgotten. But his old self had known that that would happen: that we all forget what is important, that we all forget who we are and what we need. Suddenly, he felt flooded with the sensation that had driven him to put that on paper. He *had* cared; he *had* believed he could make a difference. And he felt, all at once, that he could do that again.

And then he thought about David, about the courage of that presentation, the courage of the boy: that child.

He recalled the response to the presentation brief, the things Barraclough had said, the kids' appetite for what he had done, their desire for something to really get their teeth into, and he suddenly thought, What have I been doing?

As he read through the notes he felt that original passion blaze into life. He wondered how many people lost sight of their own desires and appetites, how many people ended up feeding someone else's hunger rather than their own. It had all happened so fast for him, he was still surprised at how easily, how readily, he had been distracted. Now, he could see that a lot of that was down to the fact that his own passions had needed work, had required effort and discipline rather than just enthusiasm and a ready attitude.

Had it really been the work he was scared of? Had it really been as simple as that, in the end?

It was a surprise to him, a genuine shock that he had been able to walk away so completely, that he had been able to stop, that he had not seen what he was doing. Deep down he knew it could happen again, but there was also an awareness now, an awareness that would, he hoped, prevent him from ever again wandering so far away from what was right for him.

And he knew what he needed to do next.

Going to the other room, he picked up his phone and dialled 999.

Naomi

The office was Naomi's refuge, just as much as the texts and the distractions that Ed offered. She stayed as long as she could. She couldn't be on her phone all day long, but somehow she was texting him on and off all day.

She was doing it now. Staring at the last of the messages. She had booked the hotel. He had told her what he would do to her once they were there. The anticipation was giddying. He was much dirtier and coarser than Mike had ever been. She was appalled by how much she liked it.

The office phone rang and, deep in a texting reverie, it made her jump.

'Yes?' she asked, voice high and querulous. Who used the phone network in the office these days? Everyone used email or the internal messaging system, even though there had recently been talk of getting rid of that: so much time was spent on it, according to the data logs, and apparently hardly any of the actual dialogue was work-related. No shit, Sherlock, she had thought when she heard that. As she found herself glancing at her mobile phone even while holding the office handset, she wondered how anything ever got done.

'Are you online?' said a voice in her ear.

It was Simon.

'Of course… What is it?'

'Search for the Snap Out Of It environmental activist group. They've posted something you need to see.'

Naomi did the search. Simon had first shown her the website a few weeks ago – it had come up via a Google alert on the VitSip name – and they had both laughed about it. But this looked different. The purple background had changed to black. The site looked slicker, more professional. Why hadn't Simon noticed the change? Why hadn't he informed her? It had gone, in the space of a few months, from looking like something a hippy had drawn in crayon to a credible, smart website.

The latest post was a picture of an old-fashioned alarm clock, the kind with the big round bells on the top and a huge round face. The time read four o'clock and, underneath, there was a date: WEDNESDAY JULY 10TH. Tomorrow's date.

'What the hell is this?' she said.

'I don't really know. But look at their last post. About the wake-up call? They're obviously planning something.'

'Well, obviously,' Naomi said, trying to keep the sarcasm out of her voice. 'I can't believe you missed this! Who else has seen it now?'

'As soon I saw it I called you... I need to keep looking around but...well, what do you think we should do?'

Fuck knows, thought Naomi, staring at the round white face of the clock. What she said was, 'Keep looking. Spend the next hour looking and pull together all the stuff we have on it. I'll call Jonathan. We'll need a senior management meeting straight away.'

'You think so?'

'Yes, I bloody think so. I'll buzz you back as soon as I've called Jonathan.'

Pushing the other paperwork aside, she pressed the button for Jonathan's extension. As it rang, she could feel the buzz of adrenalin crawling under her skin, fizzing through her veins, making her skin prickle with a charge of excitement. A quote – something she had read years ago, she had no idea where – popped into her mind: *Anyone can handle a crisis; it's the day-to-day that kills you...*

Yes, she thought, whoever you are that said that, you have no idea how right you are.

Jonathan told her and Simon to meet him upstairs in Grahame's office. Naomi called Simon back and then called Scott while she did some more searching online herself.

'Yes, I know. It's mad, but we have to take it seriously.'

Somehow it was easier to be nice when there was something dramatic going on. She wondered why that was.

'Yes, sorry again. OK. Right. See you later. Love you.'

And she did. At the moment, she really did.

It was 6.15. The room they were in smelt of coffee and Grahame's cigarettes. He always smoked in here; it was his private office and, even though it was against regulations, no one had ever been able to make him stop. He refused to touch the drinks that VitSip made, but he would happily get through twenty cigarettes a day. Naomi had often found herself wondering, as he lit up, whether, if they made cigarettes here, would he not smoke but instead drink sugary drinks?

They were all drinking coffee now, though, as Simon continued to run through all the information he had collected.

'Is this a credible threat?' Jonathan asked, leaning back in his chair as he riffled through the printouts of the website. 'If they can barely format a blog, how much of a threat do they really pose to us?'

Simon went to say something.

'What you're looking at there are *old* printouts!' said Simon, his voice a little shaky. He rarely got face-to-face time with Jonathan, let alone Grahame, and his nerves were showing. There was a sheen of sweat on his forehead. 'What was once a very childish-looking site has changed recently,' he continued. 'Something has shifted. They've upped their game. Been actively recruiting. In the dark web, there are rumours and reports of minor sabotages that have been indirectly linked to them. The group are well known to the local police. I'm still waiting for my contact to call me back.'

Simon picked up his phone, checked the screen and then put it down again. Jonathan and Naomi exchanged a glance and Naomi took a sip of her coffee to help hide her smile. She hated to admit how much she was secretly enjoying this. The change from the routine was quite exciting, and it was also a novel reason for being at the office late.

Maybe, she thought, I could use all this drama as my excuse tomorrow? When I go to meet Ed?

The other phone rang.

'Good lord, I didn't even know these things were still connected in here?' said Jonathan, getting up to answer it. 'Yes, yes, of course, bring them straight up. We're in Grahame's office,' he said into the receiver.

He put it down. 'It's the police,' he said, 'They're downstairs. Robin is sending them up now.'

Three police officers entered the room: two younger men, and a woman about Naomi's age.

'Good evening, I'm Detective Sergeant Marie Edwards,' said the woman. 'We received a call earlier today informing us of a potential threat to the factory. There's a van outside, and we need to check the premises.'

'Really?' said Jonathan archly. 'Are we *really* taking this seriously?'

'Of course, sir.' The policewoman's face was completely neutral.

Jonathan snorted. 'But we have production running tonight. We're working on the pre-launch run...'

'That will have to stop, then, sir. We need to evacuate and search the building now.'

'Impossible.' It was Grahame. He puffed out his cigarette smoke.

Naomi looked up, surprised: when had she last heard him speak? She couldn't remember.

'It's got to be a joke,' Jonathan continued. He waved the sheaf of bright purple web pages.

DS Edwards continued to look po-faced. 'We have spoken to someone connected to the group. We have to check, sir.'

'No. It really is impossible,' Jonathan echoed Grahame. 'It will have to wait. I can't believe for a second that this is remotely credible. I mean, look, they can't even spell—'

And, as he cast the papers down on the table, the whole room shook with the force of an explosion.

Seeing the look of total and utter surprise on Jonathan's face, Naomi couldn't help but burst out laughing.

Then, falling, she caught her head on the side of the table and everything went black.

Sitting in the back of the police car, there had been a moment when she had thought of texting Mike, thought of sharing her story, the news, the excitement, with him – but it had passed. I want to tell my family, she realised. I want to be with my family.

Coming in the door, she heard James shout, 'Mum! Are you OK? What happened?'

He hugged her. Just the threat of harm was enough. It jolted them out of their familiar patterns. She hugged him hard back. Even at fourteen, nearly fifteen, he still gripped her round the waist as he had when he was a boy. He was nearly as tall as her now, arms folded round her, his head tilted over her shoulder like a young giraffe bending awkwardly at a water hole. Scott was standing in the doorway to the kitchen. He came over and embraced them both.

'God. I'm so glad you're OK. Wine?'

'Yes, please!' she replied, and, taking James's hand, she followed Scott into the kitchen. Sitting down at the table, she felt Scott squeeze her shoulder as he put the glass of red wine in front of her.

'What *has* been going on?' he asked.

For a moment, unable to see his face, Naomi felt her stomach contract and a chill pass over her body. Fearing that he had discovered some evidence of her affair, of the messages, she felt more terrified at that moment than she had at any point in the last few hours.

It was only as he sat opposite her, face creased with concern, that she felt a rush of relief. He meant today, just today. And with that, feeling suddenly and overwhelmingly happy, she burst into tears.

Scott and James got up and rushed round the table to comfort her. Calmer now, she began to tell them what happened.

Chapter Twenty-Four

Wednesday 10th to Saturday 13th July

David

'Is Taylor's mum dead, then? I heard they blew the stupid cow up.'

'Yeah,' said David, laconically, not even bothering to look at the boy who was speaking, his eyes bright with tiredness. 'That's right. Dead. Blown to smithereens.'

He rolled his eyes and then checked his phone again. He had spent all night responding to James's messages. They were both shattered, but James at least had the rest of the week off. There was also a degree of relief for David: relief that there was something else for the kids at school to talk about.

'The best version I saw online,' said James when they met after school and they were sitting up in his room, 'was the one where everyone died: like, hundreds of people. You'd have to be insane to have got that idea from any of the news reports, but it seems it is possible.'

'And did you see that headline in the paper: *Killjoy Greens in Kale Juice Killing*...'

'Mum said it'll probably end up being their best quarter ever. It has provided so much free publicity: sales will go through the roof when they finally launch the stuff.'

'And the guys that died?'

'Well, everyone is so busy talking about the people they *imagined* died that they aren't focusing too much on the ones who did. Mum has been, though. She's totally blaming herself. The funerals are next week. She's pretty shaken up, to be honest.' He hesitated, the usually ready smile failing to appear. His face looked wan with tiredness. 'It was all pretty scary really.'

'I know,' said David, touching his friend's arm. 'I know.'

'There's a counsellor booked. Try and stop us going mental, I suppose.'

'Bit late for that...'

'Yeah, bit late...'

They smiled and then carried on playing the computer game. The silence was more satisfying than the humour, but both were necessary.

Matthew

The next day the school was full of the news. He had had to be careful about his own reaction. No one could know he had been involved – but when he saw Solange in the doorway he knew that he would have to tell her the truth.

He beckoned her outside.

'How could you?' she demanded, after he'd run through the basic facts.

'I thought I could stop her,' he said. 'I told the police, but she'd lied and it was too late.'

'Lied? How?'

'Well, she told me the wrong date. I had helped, yes, but only to set up the timer, not to *do* anything. It was all an online diversion. This guy she had met – Sam – he knew exactly what he was doing. He wanted to make a statement. I don't even know if she knew that they were going to do it with people there. I haven't been able to talk to her...'

'How have they not arrested you?' she demanded, her face red with appalled fury.

'Polly told them I wasn't involved. I got cautioned. I'm so lucky, but I didn't know. I really didn't. And I was so angry at the time, so fed-up and...' He hesitated, knowing it just sounded like excuses but it had all seemed so real and important at the time. 'And I just got so caught up in it all.'

Solange stared at the ground, not even smoking now, just looking sad. And angry. Really angry.

Matthew looked directly at her. The way she wouldn't return his gaze made him feel sick and ashamed. An unbidden and surprising thought popped into his head as he looked at her: *God, she's even more beautiful when she's angry.* Then he felt a wave of fury at himself. Could he not see how much she hated him right now?

'You are not the person I thought you were,' said Solange, dropping her unsmoked cigarette and crushing it hard with her foot. 'I have to go...'

She left Matthew standing alone in the sun-baked courtyard.

Naomi

'I really don't need it,' Naomi protested down the phone. 'I'm fine! Honestly. Absolutely fine.'

She listened to the calm but insistent voice of Lisa, the ever so slightly scary head of Human Resources.

'OK,' she conceded. 'OK. I understand. Yes. Yes, of course. Tomorrow? Yes. Fine.'

Putting down the phone, Naomi sipped her coffee and stared back out of the window. Leonard was asleep, as he was most afternoons after lunch, and the house was silent. Scott was at work and would be late back after visiting Elaine. James would be with him. They had made plans to all eat separately. Scott had made sure there was food in the fridge for her. She had done nothing but eat for the two days since the bomb. Eating was a welcome distraction. It felt as though whenever she wasn't eating, or wondering what to eat next, she was thinking about the dead bodies: the men killed in the blast, the blast that, moments before it had happened, she and Jonathan had been sniggering about.

Toying with the phone, she thought about what Lisa had said. That counselling would help. That the numbness and the nightmares would pass but they would pass more effectively if she – Naomi, and the others – were able to talk to someone neutral about it. And yet Naomi felt as though all she had done was talk about it. Talk talk talk. She was done with talking. She just wanted to get back to normal. But she didn't even know what normal was any more.

Having cancelled her date with Ed (he had heard what had happened at the factory on the national news), she had not yet heard back from him. She knew that she could pick that up if she wanted to, but right now she couldn't face seeing anyone, let alone him.

And the idea of a counselling session worried her. She worried about what she would say: about *how* much she would say. For she knew already that it would all come tumbling out. The affairs, the lying, the plans she had made to fuck a twenty-three-year-old in a hotel room. It all sounded so naff. She felt like such a cliché. That was the worst of it. The worrying that the therapist would inwardly roll their eyes and think: here we go again, yet another middle-aged woman falling to pieces and thinking that fucking hot young boys is the answer.

But it *had* felt like the answer with Mike, Naomi's mind piped up, it really had, for those few weeks, those weeks when they had become close and then been together. It had felt like the answer to everything.

And the lying? Well, sure, she had lied. But that had been necessary to protect Scott.

No, she thought, I can't do it. I can't talk. I don't want to tell.

The weather was painfully cheerful. Scott had suggested getting out for a walk but, while she knew that was a good idea, it was also the last thing she felt like doing. Hot and tired, she just wanted to eat ice cream and stare out of the window.

Leonard came in. 'Sorry,' he mumbled, apologetic as always, still not used to her being around during the day and still unsure how to talk to her.

'You don't have to apologise,' Naomi snapped, feeling irritated and then annoyed at herself for showing it. She should be dealing with this better, she thought.

She stared at the table as, silently, Leonard put the kettle on. And then he went out again, taking his mug, and his own sadness, out of the room.

Even when this was over, she thought, even when she was back at work and no longer a victim of a bomb blast, she would still have to deal with her crumbling marriage, would still have to deal with the fact that she had her elderly father-in-law living in the house and the fact that Elaine could limp along for months like this, months of being half alive.

And yet there were *dead* people, Naomi's mind reminded her. People who had actually died, killed while she and Jonathan had been sniggering and giggling like spoilt kids. Families left without fathers, without husbands, and she was sitting here feeling sorry because her own family was here, alive, annoyingly alive and present.

I am so crap, she whispered. I am an awful, awful person.

And the feelings fed on themselves, circled around, getting hungrier with each turn.

The only thing that Naomi didn't tell the woman sitting across from her in that calm, quiet room was what she had had for breakfast that day. The rest of it all came flooding out within moments of her conscious mind registering that there was someone sitting opposite her whom she never had to see again, who was being paid to listen and not judge, and who could not tell anyone what she, Naomi, had done.

And now, wiping away the tears from her face, she then discreetly blew her nose into another tissue from the box which the woman, Ellen, had silently handed to her when she had begun to cry.

'I think it would be a good idea to make an appointment for another session very soon,' said Ellen, as Naomi put the box of tissues on the floor by her own feet. 'I think there are various areas we need to work on, and that weekly or bi-weekly sessions would benefit you.'

'Really?' said Naomi. 'But I feel better already. Lighter. Just talking about it really has helped.'

'That's my advice,' said Ellen, smoothly, her face neutral yet warm.

How did she look like that? So calm? So normal? thought Naomi. How? Probably heard it all before, she thought, nothing new happening here. Middle-aged woman feels unloved, ignored, and has affair. Middle-aged woman gets blown up, sees colleagues die and still finds time to feel sorry for herself even though she has sick and ageing parents-in-law and a teenage son to think about.

'Seeking help not only helps you but those around you,' Ellen continued, quietly. 'It is not the recourse of the weak but of the strong. You will find your feet quicker and more readily with a guiding hand.'

'Yes, I understand,' said Naomi.

'Shall we book another appointment in now? For next Friday?'

'Yes, let's do that.'

And she did understand, but there was a part of her that was panicking, that was thinking, What if she says I have to change? What if she says I have to do things differently?

Standing up and shaking the other woman's hand, Naomi left the room.

The phone in her pocket buzzed. She might have texted Ed before she arrived here today. It might have seemed like a good idea. Being anywhere other than home felt like a good idea. She might have suggested meeting up very soon. Taking the phone out of her pocket, she saw it was a reply from Ed and she grinned.

Walking out of the therapist's office, she texted right back: *Yes, I'm free tomorrow. Shall I book it?*

The next evening, it took all of Naomi's willpower not to scream for joy and run out of the door. Like a lifer who had just seen that the prison gate had been left ajar, she forced herself to control her steps, walking with an exaggerated air of indifference and cool towards the freedom that lay just in reach.

'Heading off now?' asked Scott casually as he came out of the kitchen into the hallway while she was pulling on her boots. She was glad she had put her bag of clothes in the car already. She didn't want him to ask what the backpack was for.

'Yeah,' she said, doing a good job of feigning reluctance. 'I can't be bothered really. But, you know, I promised I would go along…'

'Book club, is it?'

'Yes, yes, it is…'

'Have fun!'

'Will do!' she said. 'I hope you're OK on your own…'

'I'll be fine.'

'Bye!'

'Bye…'

Naomi closed the door behind her and got in the car; she put the key in the ignition and then couldn't resist just checking her phone and reading his last message to her again.

Pulling it out of her bag, she opened up the screen. *I want you on the bed, lying there like the fucking adulterous whore that you are...waiting for me and my big cock...*

It had made her shudder the first time she had read it, and it still had that effect now. Her whole body was tingling with anticipation.

There was a tap on the window. It was Scott.

Hastily throwing the phone down on the seat next to her, she couldn't hide her shock. She wound down the window.

'Oh,' she snapped, 'you frightened me! What is it?'

'Your book!' he said, looking confused at her reaction. 'You forgot your book!'

'Book?' she said, equally confused.

'For book club?' he said, giving her a hard look.

'Oh, yes, yes, of course!' She beamed at him now, the façade fully back in place. 'Silly me! Thanks so much! I always get told off for forgetting it... Love you!' she added, and, kissed him on the cheek. She took the book and, smiling and waving, she pulled out.

As soon as she was out of sight she cried out, 'Fuck! Fuck fuck!'

And then she laughed.

What if he had said something? she wondered. What if he had actually challenged me?

I would have gone anyway, she thought angrily. I need this. I need it and I WILL have it. No one is going to fucking stop me. And, face set, her desire now heightened by anger, she drove fast all the way towards town, and the anonymous hotel she had booked.

Waiting had been fun for the first hour. Naomi had freshened up, got into her negligee, done her make-up and hair. She had felt attractive, sexy and excited. Now, having been in the room for an hour and a half, having turned the TV on and then off

443

again, she was now sitting on the bed staring at her phone and feeling restless. She was also starting to worry.

No need, she told herself, scrolling back over his messages. He wants you. He told you he did.

She read the messages again. Her face flushed at some of them even now. *God, but he's filthy…*

She thought about playing with herself then decided that she would send him a message instead…

On your way…? I think I might start without you. ☺

Perfect, she thought, as she sent it. Perfect.

Twenty minutes later she was staring at her phone again. He had got the message but not opened it.

'Aargh!' she cried out in frustration.

They had agreed 7pm and now it was nearly 8.45… Sitting on the edge of the bed, beginning to feel chilly in her underwear, her feet cold and her make-up feeling sticky as she got more agitated, she worried about how she would look. She took a deep breath, trying to calm herself down.

Call him, her mind said.

'I can't call him,' she said to herself.

So, you can have sex with him but you can't call him? It was her mother's voice in her head this time. *What on earth is all that about?*

Another moment passed.

Then she saw he was online and there. He had seen the message. She stared at the handset, willing a reply into being.

As she stared, all of a sudden the photo she had been looking at almost every hour in the days since they had met – of Ed, grinning, at a festival from last summer, all boy-hair and mischievous brown eyes – was gone. Gone, and replaced by a grey circle with a blank white face.

'Oh,' she cried. 'No, no, no, what's happened? What's happened?'

She shook her phone as if that would do something to bring him back, and felt a shot of nausea rise up inside her.

Getting up, she paced about, staring at the handset, unable to be still.

She typed into Google: 'message face greyed out'... The search results told what she already knew: he had blocked her number.

'No!' she cried. 'No, no, *noooo*.'

And, throwing the phone on to the bed, she flung herself down too.

But there were no tears this time. Just anger and frustration. She kicked her feet against the duvet and wanted to scream. Better just to go, she thought, go and eat or do something. Anything but sit in here.

Go out again? her mind whispered. God, no, no, no, can't do it, I can't do it...

And, broken, she got changed. As she sorted out her bags, she found the book. The book club book.

And then, finally, it was all too much, and she slumped down on to the floor and cried.

Chapter Twenty-Five

Monday 15th July

Matthew

The staff meeting had been awkward. Solange still wasn't talking to him and, even though he didn't understand the reason for the falling out, Jim had taken her side. Matthew knew he deserved it but it didn't make it any easier to deal with.

The meeting had gone on for half an hour, the stuffy room even warmer now that Barraclough had filled it with hot air about SATS and parental feedback.

As they began to shift in their seats, getting ready to leave, Matthew half stood up. *Now*, he thought, *I have to say it now.*

He cleared his throat.

'Actually... Actually there is something I was going to say...'

Everyone stopped. They all looked at Barraclough, who stood at the end of the table.

'Mr Holmes...' His voice was disturbingly pleasant and smooth.

'Please,' he said. 'I just have something I wanted to say.'

Matthew felt Solange's eyes on him. She was looking hard at him, her face set. And then she sat down. Jim followed suit and then so did everyone else.

Barraclough remained standing.

Matthew stood up and pulled himself up straight.

'I just wanted to say that I care about what the stats say, about what the school delivers. I care about what the parents say. But, above all that, I care about the students and their futures. I care about all these things and I know that you do too. I know you care because I see you all here, working long hours, every day; I see you here taking care and taking time, giving and giving even when so little is given back.' He paused. 'And it's because I care that I have to stop. Stop pretending that the gap between how things are and how they could be, and should be, cannot be bridged.'

Barraclough glowered at the end of the table. Matthew felt his face flush and ran his hand through his hair.

'It's not *enough* to say we care. We need to help these students to help themselves. We need to help them make decisions, to understand consequences. We need to help them to understand themselves and the world they live in. In that way they can go out into that world, knowing it and its limitations better, and knowing that the difference starts with *them*, the choices *they* make. I know that the test results matter, I know we need to make sure that certain things are done, but I also think there is space and time within that to help them to *be* better, not just *do* better.'

He paused.

Barraclough said, quietly. 'Thank you, Mr Holmes, thank you for that very pretty speech. Perhaps when you have finished re-reading whatever sentimental self-help book that that has been culled from, you can go back to doing your *job* and allow your colleagues and me to do the same.'

'We can do both!' Matthew insisted. 'We can. There are simple changes we can make, changes that will make all the difference. There's a school in Leeds that is—'

'Enough,' said Barraclough. 'That is enough. Mr Holmes, please go to your classroom. I will talk to you later.'

And he left the room.

Everyone stared at Matthew as he sat back down. Looking down at the table, face still flushed, he began to gather up his notebook and papers.

'Christ, mate,' said Jim. 'What was that? I mean, good on you, but wow…'

Solange came over and hugged him. 'I am so proud of you,' she said. 'Come on, let's go.'

And, ignoring the clamour of his colleagues, he followed Solange out of the room.

David

The assembly hall was filled with the scent of summer. Or rather, it was filled with the tang of sweat, Lynx and optimism. Over one hundred fidgeting teenagers and the same number of anxious adults were seated on tiny red plastic chairs, waiting for the end-of-year presentations.

David's presentation was towards the end of the session. That was OK, he told himself. It was all OK.

'And now, we have David Wallace. Come up to the front, please, David.'

Stepping forward, David looked behind him to make sure the presentation was up on the screen. It was. He began.

'I'm fat. Why am I fat? I know why you *think* I'm fat. I know why I thought I was fat. I thought it was because I ate too much and I didn't get enough exercise. Put a calorie in, take a calorie out, shake it all about… *That*, we are told, is what it's all about…'

David glanced up, face hot, and saw Matthew, sitting in the front row, grinning at him and giving him a discreet thumbs-up. He looked back at his notes.

'What if my behaviour, what you see me do, what we *all* do, was being driven mostly by our biochemistry? And what if that biochemistry was being adversely affected by our environment?

'But first I need you to meet the stars of the biological show... First we have your liver: say hi to your liver, everyone.'

'Eugh!' cried the audience in unison.

David smiled at the reaction. It did look gross that close up. 'And next we have your pancreas, and then, last but not least, your brain...'

Mr Holmes had told him to make some pauses; to take his time. He let the images register and then carried on.

'Your brain is like a dog: it likes treats. It's called the reward system, or the hedonic pathway, and without it you wouldn't even get out of bed in the morning. They did tests on an obesity drug that cut short this pathway and people killed themselves. It's *that* important. So, we eat food: we need to do that, remember, to stay alive – that's something to remember for later – that, unlike alcohol and cigarettes, we *need* food – but for now, back to the body and its lovely organs...

'We eat and this is what happens: the food hits the stomach. The small intestine processes it and sends it on to the liver. From here the rising sugars and acids from the food hit the pancreas and then *that* signals insulin. Insulin is the key here: it's also known as the *energy storage hormone*. It usually regulates itself quite happily, but if you eat a lot of fatty and sugary food, or drink a lot of soft drinks, then it increases the amount of insulin that is produced because the levels of sugar in the body are higher than the body wants to have. Sugar is energy, and the body's most important function is to maintain an *energy balance*. It's the first law of thermodynamics: the total energy of an isolated system is constant... Now I can see some of you thinking, Eh? What the hell is he on about? Thermodynamics? I thought we were talking about why he's such a fat bastard...'

There was a loud burst of surprised laughter from around the room. David smiled a little to himself.

'Insulin decides whether you burn the energy or store it, and we have a friendly hormone, called leptin, which is released by the fat cells to let the brain know you've got enough energy stored... But if there's too much insulin, the brain cannot *see* that the cells are full; it can't see the leptin, so even more fat gets stored. On top of all this, just for added biological lolz, the hormones are also telling the rest of your body: *HEY, SLOOOW DOWN, man, you need to rest up, take it easy, you're tired, you have no energy, RELAX...* So you are storing more fat, but you also feel like doing less.

'It's not just girls that are hormonal, you know – we all are... We aren't all about the bass – we're all about the hormones. The things that you think are *my* fault, the things that I used to think were my fault – the laziness, the greed, the two most hated of the seven deadly sins – they are actually created and driven by the *hormones* that keep you alive...

'So, now we know how the body works. But the body doesn't work in isolation: there is you, the person, too; and the average you is stressed. You are used to having busy parents, clubs, stuff to do, fun to be enjoyed. Food is not a priority for most of us: we want to eat and move on...

'And the body doesn't function independently of its environment. I counted the adverts on the way into school – it takes me thirty minutes to get here on foot...'

There was a snigger.

'Yeah, yeah, I'm fat so I walk sloooooow,' said David, not missing a beat. 'But I pass two shops, four takeaway places and twenty advertising boards: over half of them are for food and soft drinks... Because what makes money? Apples or soda? Greens or beefburgers?

'The body likes sweet stuff, fatty stuff. It's programmed to. We wouldn't be here if we didn't. But that programming was set a long time ago, when Man didn't get to pop to the corner shop every time he felt peckish. Now we have Big Food, and Big Food wants to make money: *has* to make money.

'And so what has happened is that Big Food has hijacked our bodies: used science to understand what we like and why we like it, and then used that to sell us stuff. And what we like is *sugar*, and the more the better.

'But, as we've seen, sugar can't be processed: it's a toxin to the body, especially when it isn't packaged up with fibre which in nature it always is. It floods the fragile system, floods it with energy that it has no idea what to do with. So your system just freaks out, like your mum freaks out when she catches you doing something you shouldn't be... And, while the liver and the pancreas are freaking out, your taste buds and your brain are lit up like it's Christmas which is why you keep eating... And the more you eat, the more the hormones get out of whack...so the cycle continues and you get fatter and fatter... Most of us that are overweight are sick. And we're just getting sicker.

'Because we like sugar. But our bodies don't, they really don't. A little, sure...but who can eat just one biscuit? It's like asking a teenager to only have one w— one a week...'

There was more shocked laughter as they all filled in the blank. David saw Barraclough fidgeting in his seat.

'Our bodies are being hijacked by what we eat, and we are being hijacked by advertising and habit – it seems like a vicious circle – that there's no way out. So, what to do? We could give up hope, or we could look back to science for the answer. Or, more specially, we could look to our backsides... Because that's where the answer lies! The answer is to stop eating sugar, to stop blindly eating whatever looks good right now, and to start eating real food – but mostly to eat more fibre. It's as simple as that: fart or get fat...and you do need to do some exercise, but mostly it's about the food: getting back to real, unprocessed food. It's about saying no to the companies that are making money out of making you sick – about saying no to them and taking back control of your own body, and making your own choices.'

As the applause filled the room, David saw Kerri smiling and waving and then looked across and saw James on the end of the row of chairs doing the same. Then he saw Gary. Something was shining from his father's face. It was something that David had never seen before: it was pride.

The sound of applause filled him up. Everywhere he looked he saw smiling faces. He could see how pop stars got hooked on this. He didn't want to make this a mission, but to be able to share these thoughts, to be able to get some understanding across felt important, felt necessary. He felt, all of a sudden, as if he was being understood, as if how he was, and what he was trying to undo, were being fully appreciated.

It was easy to get fat – almost everything conspired to make you so – and yet, to not be fat or to lose the weight was not as simple as not eating. It was about changing everything: how you saw the world, how you saw yourself, how you behaved. It was about taking that pause, about seeing the enormous difference between what you wanted and what you needed.

As the applause continued, as the smiles grew broader, David looked around the room again, grinning himself.

Suddenly, there was a clatter, chairs tumbling over, people crying out and the soft sound of a uniformed thud. And then, on seeing who had fallen, David's voice, high with shock and fear, called out, 'James!' Running to the edge of the stage, he jumped down. Slipping, he stumbled and then ran over.

Naomi was crouched down at James's side and several teachers were pushing people back, moving chairs. Mr Holmes took David's arm. 'David! Please! Stay back! It's better if you stay back. Better for James. The first-aider is already here, look.'

David stood, disbelieving, as his friend was gently moved into the recovery position by Solange. Her hands were moving him carefully; his face was pale and shiny, his breathing shallow and fast, Naomi was being held back too, her face twisted with concern, nostrils flared and eyes wide.

'What's wrong?' she kept saying. 'What's wrong with him?'

David stood, feeling utterly helpless as he watched James lying still on the hard, polished wood floor. The other students were being slowly ushered out of the huge room. Matthew held on to David's shoulders and said, over and over, 'He'll be fine, he'll be fine...'

But David could feel his father's heart racing as he held him, and the sound of his own thumping, panicking pulse filled his head and his ears. James still wasn't moving. David breathed in and out a few times and watched as Naomi began to cry.

'Why isn't he moving?'

The doors clattered open and two ambulance men came in carrying large square bags of equipment, followed by two more bearing a stretcher. The teachers, Naomi and David all stood up as the ambulance team came forward. They turned James on to his back and began CPR.

'James!' screamed Naomi as the ambulance crew counted time and calmly called orders to each other.

'David, David,' said Matthew, voice low and urgent. 'We need to go...'

'I can't leave him...'

'We really must.'

David looked at Matthew. He had stopped saying that James was going to be all right and, suddenly feeling sick, David allowed the teacher to walk him out of the hall, the sounds of the resuscitation attempt filling his ears.

Chapter Twenty-Six

Tuesday 16th to Wednesday 17th July

David

The door was in front of him. Blank and grey, it had a tiny window through which he could see the end of the bed inside. There was pale light coming in through the windows. He closed his eyes. Was he ready for this?

He walked through the door, into the small, cool room.

'Fucker,' he said, voice hoarse. 'You just couldn't stand me getting the applause could you?'

There was silence. What had he expected? On the bed James lay still: pale, eyes shut.

'Nope,' said James, eyes suddenly opening and face breaking out into a familiar wide grin.

'Shame you didn't die, really…' said David, smiling back and beginning to poke about through the pile of magazines and books on the bedside table. 'I would have quite liked to inherit your Xbox games…'

'They are so yours, mate…'

'I should hope so!'

They smiled at each other again. Then, as their relief at seeing each other changed to awkwardness at the depth of their emotions, David punched James on the arm and then began to pull some grapes from the bunch in the fruit bowl.

'Help yourself,' said James. 'Sodding fruit, sodding sick of it already... Did your mum bring you?'

'Yeah, she's waiting outside.'

'You all right?'

'Me?' asked David, surprised. 'What about you? Are you all right? Mum spoke to your mum so I heard what it was.'

'Yeah, looks like I'm diabetic. Type 2. Mum's in bits about it...blames herself, of course, and nothing I say can seem to change that.'

David frowned. 'Mum says you were really ill.'

James frowned too. 'Yeah, I guess I was. Obviously I didn't realise at the time... Suppose it was lucky I collapsed, really, otherwise they might never have found out till it was too late...'

'What does it mean?'

'Well, apparently it's not a good idea to eat Haribo for breakfast,' said James, grinning again.

'No shit, Sherlock...'

'Yeah, I know...'

'But really? What does it mean?

'Well, it means Mum gets even more stressed than usual and makes me eat more broccoli.'

David smiled.

'That's it really. I have to eat better. I have to take some medication for a bit and then, well, they say it might get better but that I may...'

'What?'

'Well, it can make you infertile.'

David raised his eyebrows. 'Fuck, really?'

'Yeah...should make it easier for me with the girls later, eh?' said James trying to laugh but failing.

They were silent for a moment. David had no idea what to say.

'And, luckily, my dick is sooo huge that no one will notice I'm firing blanks,' rallied James. The line had the forced quality of something that had been polished and prepared. 'What did everyone at school say?' he continued.

'About you? Ah, nothing really... No one really noticed, I don't think...'

James lay back and groaned.

'Haha,' said David, 'Well, half of the Year 8s think you're dead and the other half think you're in a coma but other than that... You know, SSDD.'

'SSDD indeedy.'

'Yep.'

'Except, well...' David hesitated.

James looked at him, pale blue eyes suddenly serious. 'What is it?'

'Well, it's pretty amazing really, isn't it? Today?'

'Today? What, now?' said James, looking around him, wondering what was amazing about it.

'Yeah, now, right now...'

James squinted at him. 'You feeling all right?' he asked, his tone dubious and sounding exactly like Naomi.

'Never better,' said David, and with a smile he picked up James's iPad and said, 'Right, now I'm going to surf the web and totally ignore you...'

'Like everyone else has been...' said James.

'Yep, it's the least I can do, seeing as you didn't have the decency to die...'

'Fair.'

Twenty minutes later, seeing that James had fallen asleep, David closed the door gently behind him and walked down the corridor to find Kerri. The corridor was busy, people walking by, occupied and preoccupied. David didn't mind hospitals but he could understand why people did. The smell, and the reminder of death and illness, were overwhelming. To him, though, it seemed quite bracing: he understood their fear but did not feel it himself. He felt only revitalised, as if the presence of death was a positive reminder not to waste too much time.

David saw Kerri sitting on the grey-blue plastic chairs in the waiting area. She was talking to Naomi.

'Hello, David,' said Naomi as he approached. 'Thanks for coming, I know James has been looking forward to seeing you.'

She gave him a hug. He felt her thin arms around him and her tiny shoulders: what had happened to her? Then he remembered some of the things James had said and he flushed a little.

'How are you?' asked Kerri, sounding concerned.

'Mmmh... I'll just get some water...'

'OK.'

Kerri turned back to Naomi. 'How much longer will you be here today?'

'Oh, hours. We have an appointment with the dietician and the consultant today and then, hopefully, by tomorrow we can think about getting him home.'

'Can we come and visit once he's home?'

'Of course... Just give us a few days...'

'Yes, of course.'

Kerri smiled.

'I am sorry,' said Naomi, looking down at the ground.

'Why?' asked Kerri, frowning.

'Oh, you know, I've been such a crap friend...'

'No,' said Kerri. 'No, you haven't. I'll give you another ring later, OK? I'd better get David back to school now.'

'Yes, yes, of course.'

The two women embraced awkwardly, Kerri's frame swamping Naomi's slender form. As they hugged, Naomi began to cry again.

'It's just... I blame myself. How can I have not noticed he was ill? How? I thought it was just end-of-term tiredness, hormones, whatever. But this...'

She sobbed into Kerri's shoulder. The other woman held her, smiling apologetically at David, who was walking back sipping from a bottle of water. He smiled back and took a seat a little distance away.

Kerri held the other woman and let her cry.

David watched discreetly. They had known each other for a long time. But Naomi was also one of the people who had let his mother down after the divorce, one of the many that hadn't returned calls, who had begun to make excuses and stopped visiting, so he had mixed feelings about her. He wanted them to be friends again, but he was also cross with Naomi for not being there when Kerri had needed her. Then he remembered what James had said about his grandmother being sick, about the hours his dad worked, and he felt a surge of compassion for this thin, sad-looking woman. A wave of compassion for all of the people here. A hospital was nothing if not a reminder that sickness and death affected everyone.

After ten minutes or so, Naomi seemed to have calmed down and Kerri said her goodbyes before walking over to David.

'Thank you,' she said. 'I appreciate you waiting so patiently.'

David shrugged. Standing up, he walked alongside her as they followed the complex and multiple signs back to the main entrance.

'Are you OK?' she asked him as they stepped out of the cool building into the warm afternoon sun.

'Yeah. I feel better now I've seen him.'

'I bet. It was all very worrying. If you want to talk to me, you can, you know.'

'I know,' said David. 'And the same goes for you...'

'What?' said Kerri.

'You can talk to me if you need to.'

'Oh... When,' she said, looking at him closely, forehead creasing a little, 'did you get to be so grown-up?'

David shrugged again and then grunted a little, feeling embarrassed now.

458

'That's more like it,' said Kerri, laughing. 'The grunts are back – excellent!'

And, getting back in the car, they drove home.

David got up next day and began to get dressed for school. It was only two days till the end of term now and, as he pulled his trousers on, he looked at the cheap black leather belt: it was worn thin in places from containing his bulk over the last year and yet, now, he was down to the last hole. He pulled it in tight and tucked in his shirt. Looking down at himself, he was aware, not for the first time, that it was all beginning to make a difference. He had been sleeping better for a little while now and he had also noticed that, as he felt less tired, the desire to eat sweet and salty things had dropped off.

In the bathroom, he also noticed that his skin was looking clearer. They could sell you as much spot cream and face wash as they liked but it looked as though eating better made more difference than anything else. He combed his hair and then, after another shy glance at himself in the mirror, he went downstairs.

Kerri was crying in the living room.

'What is it?' he asked, standing there, a little awkward in the face of the tears, but concerned.

'It's just…well, I was so scared by being in the hospital. It just made see the reality of what I'm planning to do and then I think, oh you know, I'm just being silly, so I went online to chat to some of my band buddies about it all and oh, some of the – some of the people on the site… I thought they were my friends but some of the things they're saying…'

She gestured towards the iPad that had been cast to the floor.

David looked at her. Did she not know that the people who frequented public forums were all morons?

'What have they said?' he asked, picking up the tablet.

'That I don't deserve to have the band, that I'm going to die. That I *deserve* to die...'

'Fucking hell...'

'David!'

'Well, seriously! What are you even doing talking to people on something like that for?'

'They have been so supportive! It's been great but just recently, well, some of them have been getting really nasty...'

'I imagine they are scared too,' he said, sitting down next to her. 'Scared of making the change themselves. That's why most people are mean, isn't it? Because they're scared. And you should really only ever talk on moderated forums. This,' he said, glancing at the web page, 'looks pretty dodgy.'

She looked at him, eyes wide.

'Online bullying coaching – we get it at school now,' he said, shrugging.

She looked down. The tears had stopped falling, but had left her cheeks streaky and shiny. David wiped them away with his hand and smiled at her gently.

'I'm scared too,' she said.

'Then don't do it,' he said, quietly.

'I...'

'Don't. Please don't.'

'But what else can I do? I need it! I've...' She laughed, the sound bitter and harsh. 'I've gained another stone in the last month. It's crazy but I can't seem to stop... The band was going to stop me, stop me from just eating and eating and eating.' She looked at him again, eyes red and puffy, her face swollen with fat and the misery the fat was causing her.

'We can help each other,' he said. 'What I'm doing is working but it's hard. It's really hard doing it on my own. If you were helping me...if we did it together...'

He looked down now, embarrassed, aware that he too now felt close to tears. He hadn't cried in front of his mum since – well, since before Dad had left.

'Yes,' she said. 'Yes. OK. I'll cancel the appointment. I'll cancel it and we'll do this…'

'Together,' he said.

'Yes,' she said. 'Together.'

Chapter Twenty-Seven

Sunday 18th August

David

They were working in the garden. Since beginning the diet with David a month ago, Kerri had lost twelve pounds and gained a love for gardening. It was Sunday afternoon and the air was warm but the sky grey, thick with the promise of late summer rain; it was the type of afternoon which two months ago would have seen them all holed up inside watching movies, but which now saw Kerri eager to get jobs completed prior to the now welcome rain.

'Anything that saves me watering is a good thing,' she had said as they had headed outdoors. 'Let's try and get these new bedding plants in, and then the rain can help them settle in.'

The girls enjoyed pulling up weeds and David enjoyed digging and raking as well as planting and so, between them, the work was done easily enough. Kerri began to loosen the bright yellow primroses and the pale purple violas from their plastic trays and look at them carefully, placing them on the brown soil, considering the best layout.

David helped Jess bring a garden sack out of the shed and then began to work with her and Emily to clear the patch of soil.

They all worked together and chatted. The girls had, like the garden, begun to blossom with extra attention. Kerri had cut her hours back a little over the holidays and they were all getting on better as a result of having less pressure on their time. It was not perfect. Emily and Jess were still squabbling and they were still competing endlessly for Kerri's attention. There had also been some resistance from Jess about the changes to how they were eating; mostly it was fine, but she was missing her daily treats, and Kerri had had to spend some time dealing with that.

The first few fat drops of rain began to fall. The girls squealed and then, laughing, began to chase each other round the garden. David tickled them as they ran by and, as the rain got heavier, Kerri began to clear the tools away, taking them back into the shed.

The sky darkened and the rain began to fall, heavy and warm, drenching them. A sudden storm.

Laughing, Kerri looked up at the sky and let the rain fall on her face, washing away the sweat from the work she had been doing. David smiled and then carried on tickling the girls, chasing them indoors. He helped Kerri put the last of the tools away and said, 'I heard you on the phone to Dad earlier.'

'Yeah, he had some news.'

She glanced towards the door to make sure the girls were not within earshot. 'It's Lauren. She's pregnant again.'

'Oh. Right,' said David, looking down at the now wet grass.

'Yeah, and he didn't sound too happy about it, to be honest. I think he thought they were done, but apparently she's desperate for a little girl, so...'

'How are you feeling?' he asked.

'I should be asking you that.'

'We should ask each other,' he countered.

They smiled at each other. They didn't always agree, and things had not all been easy over the summer. But they were better than they had been for a long time.

'It doesn't ever really get any easier,' she said. 'Especially when he sounds sad.'

'It was his choice,' said David.

'I know, but…'

'It was his choice.'

David's voice was firm. He too had had gains and losses over the summer. He had acquired a girlfriend, one of the other of the Three Graces, and had continued to lose more weight. He had lost some of his previous patience with Gary. He had been following James's sessions with his clinical nutritionist with interest – he hadn't known that was a job one could do. And he had gained some respect for his mother, who was working so hard to make positive changes to how they ate. He had learnt to see things differently, to see Kerri's behaviour in the context of her own private hurts and dashed expectations, and, while he still loved his dad, he was more fully aware of the damage he had done, and that made it harder to like him.

David looked at Kerri. They were both drenched. Faces wet with the warm rain, they laughed at the sight of each other's dripping hair and then ran inside.

Matthew

There was not long left until the new term began. Matthew had been coming into school every day for the last two weeks, planning his lessons but also preparing for his new role. Head of science meant more work, but also more opportunity: opportunity to influence the school, opportunity to make a difference.

Sitting at his desk, he went to log on and check the stats on the latest blog post that he, David and the small team they had formed had published. Seeing the stats, a big leap up since last week, he felt a thrill of pleasure, and then an image of him and Polly looking at the background to the site he'd helped build for her filled his mind. She and Sam had been sentenced for the roles they'd played in the bombing and the deaths of the three workers, and, while he remained grateful to her for keeping him out of it in the end, for not telling him the truth about the timings, he couldn't help but feel sad, thinking of their time together.

It led to this, though, his mind whispered, the voice soothing and familiar.

'Indeed it did,' he muttered to himself.

Inspired by David and with the help of a few other students, including James, he had spent some time over the summer developing a site that took the issues David had raised about environment and self and eating and taken them on even further. The website he had spent the summer building was growing steadily, and he was confident that now, having spent the time on that, he would be able to manage it as well as keep on top of what he needed to do here. In fact, having seen what he was doing, having looked at the feedback on the site, and having attended one of the trial sessions that Matthew had organised over the holidays, Barraclough had agreed that the whole subject was one that could form part of the extra classes and seminars that Matthew had proposed.

Pulling the drawer to get something out, Matthew's hand met resistance: the drawer was stuck. He tugged a little harder. Still stuck. Pulling harder still, he got down on his knees, smiling a little at the effort needed.

Kneeling and tensing his back, he pulled and pulled and then, all of a sudden, the drawer came free and he fell backwards, rolling back on to his behind and bursting out into laughter.

The drawer hung half out and half in, hanging awkwardly on its castors.

Getting back up, Matthew reached in and felt around the drawer for what was causing the blockage. His fingers touched something thick and, feeling it wedged into the top of the drawer, he put both hands in and gently tugged it out.

The Brazil brochure.

The days when this had been his touchstone, when this had been important, were days he could think of fondly now. Flicking through, smiling, he brought it up to his nose: the scent was gone. The stains that had evoked instant memories were now just that: stains, flat and brown, evoking nothing.

Not that they ever evoked anything of themselves, he thought. I created that; I created the intensity of it all.

And now, rather than imagining it, he had been doing something based on science and based on facts, something more practical that engaged people and got them involved. They had a website, they had a plan, and they were making small but crucial changes to each other and, hopefully, soon to the wider community. A meeting had been set up with the Council for the autumn to discuss the advertising boards around the school: limiting the constant messages to eat and drink rubbish was only a small step but it was an important one. All the efforts and the work were beginning to pay off. You had to be there doing the work and let people come to you, having found it for themselves. That was the only way: to give people the space and the time to be inspired. It wasn't easy but it was the only way. It all seemed like a world away from being yelled at in his hallway, a world away from Polly and the mistakes they had made together.

He looked back at the brochure and, smile broadening, he threw it into the bin.

A voice came from the doorway. 'What was that?' asked Solange as she came into the room.

'Nothing,' he replied. And this time it was the truth.

Standing up, he walked up to her and, feeling as excited as he had the first time he had done it, he circled his hands round her waist and kissed her.

Naomi

Naomi got out of the air-conditioned car and, checking her bag, she walked across the car park and on to the busy high street. Lifting her hair off her neck for a moment, she sighed. Her skin felt sticky already, even though she had only been out of the car for a few moments. It was a cloudless, sunny day and, with little or no breeze, her cotton dress was clinging to her skin the way her hair clung to her neck.

Cold drink, she thought, I need a cold drink and then I will do what I need to do.

She saw the dim interior of the café and frowned. Glancing at her watch, she saw that it was just after 11am and, knowing that she shouldn't but feeling that she wanted to, she wrinkled her nose in hesitation, face screwed up comically as she allowed the two thoughts to have a quick tussle. When, as suspected, the one that justified her going to a bar for a Pimms won, she smiled and went over the road.

Sitting in the shade of a courtyard beer garden just visible from the high street, Naomi sipped her drink and knew she had made the right choice. Checking her shopping list, she sat back against the wooden chair, relaxing into it and enjoying the chill on her skin as the shade and the drink cooled her. The summer had been glorious so far, even if the circumstances had not. It had been mere weeks since Elaine had passed away and, with Leonard now back in his own home, Naomi was enjoying having some sense of normality; but she was also very aware that what was normal now was not what had passed for normal before. She had changed. Scott had changed. She didn't think he knew what had happened that night when she'd told him she was at the book club meeting, but she also knew he wasn't stupid. She had left too many clues, really, been too careless and, now that there were fewer distractions, he had begun to look at her differently, as if seeing or sensing something about her that he hadn't before.

For herself, she felt done with it all. Nothing had happened since that night. She had gone out again, desperate to get rid of the bad taste that had been left behind with something else sweeter, but it had just been exhausting. A long, uncomfortable evening which had left her, she felt, looking even more tired and older than ever. So, she had settled into being at home and, with James recovering yet still unwell, she had made their eating and a healthy routine her priority.

It seemed successful. James was getting better by the week and Scott had stopped watching her quite so closely. He and James were at home today, neither of them keen to leave the garden on a day like this, and she had offered to go into town and buy the things they needed for a barbecue. She felt glad of the break, of the time alone, even if it was stickier in town.

Sipping her drink, she checked her phone again and then stared into the middle distance.

'Naomi? Is that you? Hi, there!'

Hearing her name, she looked up.

It was Carla. And Mike.

'Oh, hello!' she said, feeling genuinely pleased to see the young couple.

Carla came round to Naomi who, standing up, gave the other woman a warm embrace. Her arms went easily around the woman's shoulders and she kept back from the bump, not wanting to feel it.

Mike stood still, arms by his side, staring at her, waiting. Naomi looked at him and smiled.

'Hey,' she said, a conscious echo of their online conversations.

'Hey,' he replied.

Carla's hands settled around her stomach.

'How are you?' she asked. 'It's been so odd not having you around at work – the marketing department misses you!'

'I'm fine, thanks. Been a tough couple of months but, you know, what doesn't kill you and all that…'

Carla looked at her, eyes wide and mouth sad, and added, 'I heard about your son. Is he OK now?'

'He's much better, thanks. We're just spending lots of time as a family, enjoying the summer, enjoying being together. They never stop worrying you,' she added, looking, for the first time, at Carla's now rounded belly. 'Anyway,' she said, 'how are you? You can't have long to go now!'

'Oh, I have ages!' The younger woman sighed. 'I'm so tired already! And I think Mike is getting fed up with being stuck in with me but I just can't face going out: the heat is too much. I just lie about like a sweaty whale...'

'A beautiful sweaty whale...' said Mike, smiling at her.

'Indeed!' added Naomi, almost sounding as if she meant it and choosing that exact moment to smooth down her slim-fitting cotton dress. 'It's so nice to see you both – what an exciting time for you! You have *so* much to look forward to...'

'We do,' said Mike. 'We're so looking forward to being a family.'

'Well, I'd better get going,' Naomi said, swallowing a little. She looked at Carla. Suddenly she felt as if it was taking every ounce of her strength to keep the pain in her heart hidden away and not to let it show in her eyes. 'It's been so good to see you.'

'Oh, yes! You too!'

'Take care,' said Mike, looking at her.

'Yes...' said Naomi, deliberately not looking back at him.

They exchanged a kiss on the cheek.

Everything had changed between them, but the smell of him had not. Deep, salty, masculine. That room, that evening, filled her mind, flooded her body with sensation. She caught her breath. It was as if she could feel his fingers around her throat, his mouth on hers, the tingling sharpness as he slapped her bottom. Feeling the pressure of his hands on her body, she wanted to believe that he was thinking about that too. A glance at his face as she pulled back showed her that he wasn't. His eyes were on Carla. There was nothing there for her.

'Bye!' she called as she walked away, refusing to turn round and look at them, at him.

How was it that just that, that simple scent, could bring the whole experience flooding back? She was that person again, that version of herself which wanted nothing else other than him.

Just don't think about it, she told herself, don't think about it.

But it was all she could think about. She ran her errands in a daze, angry at and confused by her feelings, her whole self having been thrown back in time to when all she wanted was him.

An hour later, as she walked past the pub and the courtyard again, she caught sight of a group of young lads. All sat round the large wooden table, enjoying the first sips of their cold beer. Naomi stared at them: their freedom poured out of them like sunshine. One of them looked back at her. Naomi felt her face flush. He smiled at her. She smiled back. And then, even though she knew they would be waiting for her at home, she walked back into the courtyard.

Sources and Reading List

Dr Robert Lustig, *Fat Chance: The Hidden Truth about Sugar, Obesity and Disease* (Fourth Estate, 2014)

John Yudkin, *Pure, White and Deadly* (Penguin, 1988 and 2012)

Gary Taubes, *The Case Against Sugar* (Portobello Books, 2016)

Michael Moss, *Salt, Sugar, Fat: How the Food Giants Hooked Us* (W.H. Allen, 2014)

Greg Critser, *Fat Land* (Penguin, 2004)

Daniel Kahneman, *Thinking, Fast and Slow* (Penguin, 2012)

Nassim Nicholas Taleb, *The Black Swan: The Impact of the Highly Improbable* (Penguin, 2008)

Philippa Perry, *How to Stay Sane* (The School of Life, Macmillan, 2012)

Alain de Botton, *How to Think More About Sex* (The School of Life, Macmillan, 2012)

Ben Goldacre, *Bad Science* (Harper Perennial, 2009)

Acknowledgements

Who knew that a writer was not a writer without an editor? I certainly didn't until I was lucky enough to meet Linda McQueen. I really could not have done it without your support, skills and friendship. Thank you. And thank you also to the great team at RedDoor, Anna, Clare and Heather, for their enthusiasm about and commitment to *Appetite*. It has been such a pleasure to work with you all.

A big thank you and hugs to Paul for being there every Monday in Caffè Nero Sevenoaks and at write-ins over the last few years. You are a constant and wonderful source of support and advice.

Thank you to NaNoWriMo, which got me writing; big thanks go in particular to the Kent group, a wonderful community of people who are unbelievably supportive and enthusiastic. Thanks in particular to Elizabeth Haynes, Vikki Thompson, Margo Benson and Tony Benson, as well as all the others who supported my writing in the very early days of *Appetite*.

Thank you and love to my mum, Lesley, and brother, Ian, and my lovely friends Chris, Claire, Craig, Karen B, Karen G, Karen M, Lauren, Seans Scoltock and Smith, Stephy (*kisses*) and all those who have all supported me in my writing over the past few years. I feel very lucky that I have so many new friends to thank for the next book (*waves to Bill, Diana, Kit, Laura*).

Love to my dad, Frank, who always believed I would do it but who is sadly not here to see the book published.

Thank you to Alexander and Kate for their understanding and love as I took time to write.

Thank you and love to Marc, for whom this book is written, and last, but definitely not least, to Andrea, for whom my next book is being written. We are rewriting the rules of love one word at a time.

About the Author

Having enjoyed a ten-year career in London working within regional press as a sales manager and trainer, Anita Cassidy started writing in November 2012 while raising her family. Inspired by National Novel Writing Month, she wrote two short books before starting *Appetite* in 2014. She has two young children, Alexander and Kate, and splits her time between London and Kent. Anita is writing a new book about work and life, alternative relationships and kink.

www.anitacassidy.uk